PRAISE FOR SAVANNAH COMES UNDONE

"Savannah is a new kind of spirited Southern belle. And Hildreth's smart, quirky wit is positively addicting. I'm hooked!"

— Colleen Coble,
author of *Distant Echoes*

"Reading *Savannah Comes Undone* is like taking a virtual vacation. It's a quirky, fun foray into life in the South. And if you loved exploring the colorful eccentricities of Savannah, Georgia, in *The Midnight of Good and Evil,* you must check out *Savannah Comes Undone!* You won't be disappointed."

— Kathy L. Patrick,
founder of The Pulpwood
Queens Book Club

"*Savannah Comes Undone* is funny and impulsive! Savannah draws us in with her adolescent steps to independence and her whimsical life emergencies!"

— Lynnette Cole,
Miss USA 2000

"Hildreth has approached a topic containing as much controversy as you'll find today with grace and wit. A reminder that at the heart of any issue, is the heart itself."

— Michael Reagan,
author of *Twice Adopted*

"Fans of *Savannah from Savannah* will rejoice to see this hilarious heroine back in another laugh-out-loud romantic adventure."

— christianbook.com

"Hildreth uses quirky characters and snappy dialogue to deliver a fresh look at the wit and wisdom of Southern women and their graceful but stelly determination to stand up for what's right while in Kate Spade flip flops."

— Susanna Flory,
graphic designer from
Castro Valley, California

"*Savannah Comes Undone* will make you laugh aloud, skip meals, and stay up past your bedtime. It will make you evaluate your relationships, conscience, and goals in life. You will find yourself reminiscing about your own past and possibly change the way you see your own future. The next time you see a rose, you might even stop to smell it."

— Kathy Greco,
bank teller from
Charleston, South Carolina

"*Savannah Comes Undone* is a hilariously funny, thought-provoking story that will leave you wanting more."

— Jacqueline Wilfong,
recruiting supervisor from
Baton Rouge, Louisiana

"*Savannah Comes Undone* made me laugh out loud. Savannah reminds me of several of my girlfriends wrapped up in one loveable, fumbling young woman trying to set her path in life."

— Cindy Carter,
homemaker from Euless, Texas

"Denise's southern wit and charm carry you through this heartfelt book."

— Dwayne Wellborn,
director of hospitality
from Gainsville, Georgia

SAVANNAH
COMES UNDONE

DENISE HILDRETH

WestBow
P R E S S

A Division of Thomas Nelson Publishers
Since 1798

visit us at www.westbowpress.com

Published in Nashville, Tennessee, by WestBow Press, a division of Thomas
Nelson, Inc.

WestBow Press books may be purchased in bulk for educational, business,
fund-raising, or sales promotional use. For information, please e-mail
SpecialMarkets@ThomasNelson.com.

Publisher's Note: This novel is a work of fiction. Names, characters, places,
and incidents are either products of the author's imagination or used fictitiously.
All characters are fictional, and any similarity to people living or dead is purely
coincidental.

Library of Congress Cataloging-in-Publication Data

Hildreth, Denise, 1969–
    Savannah comes undone / Denise Hildreth.
        p. cm.
    ISBN 0-8499-4456-2 (pbk.)
    1. Women—Georgia—Fiction. 2. Savannah (Ga.)—Fiction. 3. Young women—
Fiction. I. Title.
PS3608.I424S28 2005
813'.6—dc22   2005004093

Printed in the United States of America
05 06 07 08 09 RRD 5 4 3 2 1

CHAPTER ONE

My mother is in chains. Chained to what or for what I have no idea. Thomas only said, "Mother is chained to it."

I didn't ask.

I looked down at the denim bow that tied up my wrap dress. It was slightly tilted, so I straightened it. Now, the bow is an amazing accessory, the way it holds things together. Tying a bow is one of the first achievements of childhood. How unfair: a child, learning how to hold things together. I traced the perfectly symmetrical loops with my index fingers. I thought of childhood and sanity.

The phone rang. Again. I jumped. I snatched up my ringing satchel off the hood of Old Betsy and found my phone conveniently resting on the bottom.

"What?"

"Where are you?" my younger brother, Thomas, asked.

"I'm on my way."

"You said that five minutes ago."

I plopped into the driver's seat. "Are you the clock police?"

"Get down here now. Are you a human-interest writer or not?"

"I am and I'm coming. Just take a breather. I'll be there in a minute."

Welcome to my world. The world of Savannah, where a mother in chains for any reason is no great cause for my alarm.

I pointed my declining Saab away from the newspaper office and toward the courthouse. Something off-kilter hovered in the muggy Savannah humidity. Today I suspected something other than the steamy afternoon sun lured people outside their stores, cooling themselves with makeshift fans. I was certain it had to do with "the woman in chains."

A plump, elderly, floral blur almost attached herself to my front bumper. "Watch where you're going!" I hollered at the closed window. She scampered on up the street, oblivious to the fact that she had narrowly escaped a lovebug's fate.

As I tried to pull up to Wright Square—where both Dad's coffee shop and the U.S. Courthouse stand—I encountered an impassable bottleneck of cars, SUVs, trolleys, and a few unhappy horses toting gawking spectators. This jam was a phenomenon not even experienced on parade day, because cars aren't allowed into the historical district on parade day. But today Savannah had apparently plunged into the depths of downright delirium.

I pulled into the covered parking place at the back of Jake's. My little brother (or rather, *younger* brother; the child stands six feet tall and towers over my five-foot-four-inch frame like a bamboo stalk over a tulip) snatched open the car door.

"Vanni, get out of the car! You've got to get to the courthouse."

"How did you even see me?"

"I've been looking for you for fifteen minutes."

"You only called five minutes ago."

"I called you twice." He grabbed my arm and slammed the door behind me. Thomas, the only one in the world allowed to call me Vanni, dragged me out of the alley and onto the sidewalk in the direction of the courthouse. "What were you doing anyway?"

"I have a job, Thomas. An important job. I have things to finish up before I can just run from my office and jump to the streets."

"Give me a break. You were probably checking your hair."

I would die a thousand deaths before admitting how close he was to the truth.

"Just come on, because you are not going to believe what Mom has done!"

I tried to keep pace with him and actually talk at the same time. "Trust me, I'll believe it. And slow down, I don't run well in heels."

"You shouldn't be wearing heels. The combination is dangerous to society. And trust me, sweet child, you would never have guessed what you're about to see."

We turned the corner and met a scene not witnessed since Tom Hanks sat on a bench and ate a box of chocolates. I could hardly even catch a glimpse of the marble courthouse for the mass of people gathered around something—or dare I say someone—in front of it. ABC and NBC news trucks had arrived. People milled and jabbered like schoolchildren at recess.

We took refuge from the blazing sun with fifteen other shameless gawkers under a live oak near the edge of the square.

"She's in the middle of that, isn't she?"

"You bet your sweet britches she's in the middle of that."

"Does Dad know?"

"Oh yeah, he knows."

"Where is he?"

"He's out there with her."

"Is he angry?"

"Doesn't seem to be."

"Am I going to have to move out of town?"

"Move? Are you kidding? We haven't had this much excitement, since . . . well, since Mom tried to pass that law to neuter all golden retrievers."

"I believe the opposition defined her actions as 'discriminatory.'"

"You should know"—he gave me a beautiful white smile and winked a green eye at me—"Ms. Opposition."

"Just because Duke isn't a lapdog doesn't mean she can ruin his existence." I said, looking around for the golden retriever that had been my mother's nemesis since the day Dad brought him home. "Where is Duke anyway?"

"Tucked away inside Dad's shop."

"Lucky boy. What did he do? Go potty on her Persian again?"

"No, he just can't endure both this squelching heat *and* Mom. A dog can only take so much in one afternoon." Odd but true: Duke had no idea he was actually a dog.

We moved along the sidewalk that passes in front of the court-house, and a few people parted enough for me to make out the lovely vision I left less than an hour ago after a perfectly normal lunch at The Lady & Sons. Her blue capri slacks and floral Kate Spade mules came into view before her face did.

"Does she have a chain wrapped around her?"

Thomas laughed and folded his arms across his chest. "Yes, that would be a chain."

"What's that big stone thing that she's attached to?" I asked, not certain I wanted to know.

"That, my friend, is a six-thousand-pound stone monument of the Ten Commandments."

"You are not serious."

"Dead serious. Judge Hoddicks brought it in yesterday after-noon. Had it delivered right here."

"Who's he trying to be, Roy Moore?"

"Judge Moore called him earlier actually. Right before I left Judge Hoddicks's office." Thomas wiped the beading sweat off of his forehead and pushed it up through his short, sun-kissed brown hair. "Judge Hoddicks says the case belongs to the people, not the courts. So he wants to keep it in the limelight."

"Is there a reason he's not chained to it instead of Mother?" I watched Mother's beaming smile shine over all. She flitted her head from side to side as if she were ringmaster of this circus.

"Well, a suit was filed against the monument and Judge Hoddicks first thing this morning by some attorneys from Athens and by the ACLU. Judge countersued. Mother suggested the judge take care of the legal matters, and she would take care of the monument."

"You mean public relations."

"No, I mean the monument."

I looked down at my own pretty shoes, trying to avoid the eyes of the very woman who had purchased them. "And Jake said?"

"Haven't heard yet. You can ask him yourself." He pointed to Dad, who was standing on the right set of stairs that entered the courthouse. He was talking to Judge Hoddicks and smiling.

Dad caught Thomas's delighted smile and my mortified stare and winked. My gaze followed his secure gait as he walked over to my mother, whispered in her ear, gave her a kiss on the cheek, and brought his striking six-foot-one frame our way.

Dad patted me on my shoulder and was about to walk past me. "Where are you going?"

He stopped to smile at me. "Back to work."

"Back to work! You've got to be kidding me!" I chuckled. He matched my chuckle with his own.

"No. I'm not kidding."

"You mean you're going to leave her here, strapped to a piece of stone, to be aired on the nightly news? Our reputation will be left here on the sidewalk to be feasted on by water bugs!" I added extra effect to my statement by crushing the water bug that had bravely, yet stupidly, made its way to my area of the sidewalk.

He kissed me on my cheek then brushed his hands through his slightly graying brown hair. "Yes, that's exactly what I'm going to do."

I stared at the disappearing image of my father as he casually sauntered back to his world of coffee and calm, khakis and polo shirts.

My father, at the age of fifty-four, had indisputably gone insane. "But . . . how . . . why?" I turned my face upward. "Why me, Lord?"

"Take it easy, Vanni. You've got a story and we've got drama," Thomas said, patting me on the back and heading over to our mother like an overgrown adolescent enjoying the spotlight.

"But I don't need drama." I called out, gesturing to no one in particular. "Really, I can create my own. Who needs extra?"

But then extra arrived. Amber Topaz Childers, the reigning Miss Savannah United States of America, came up from behind and goosed me. I screeched. She giggled. And her aqua-colored eyes, a combination of natural brown irises and artificially colored contact lenses, made taking her serious very difficult.

"Is this not the most exciting thing ever?" she squealed.

"Right up there with an enema," I muttered.

"Right up there with a what?" She crinkled her perfect nose.

"Right up there with an evening at the cinema."

"Oh my word. Are you telling me you, Savannah Phillips"—as if my name were lost on me—"have had more exciting times than this?"

"In abundance."

"All with your mother?"

"Right at the center of it."

"Are you the luckiest girl alive or what?"

"Or what." I looked at this beauty in her little pink pantsuit with matching lipstick and earrings. She could have been mistaken for a flamingo had her hair not been quite so . . . shall we say, lively. But even it was held back with a matching pink grosgrain ribbon.

And with nothing more to say, she flounced along to meet the other present reigning royalty. The former Miss Georgia United States of America. Mrs. Victoria Phillips. Vicky. My mother.

Every other eye was glued to the vision in blue gracefully chained to a monument in the middle of my city. And in one moment of horror, the vision saw me and waved. A few people turned to see who had her attention. I turned with them, hoping it was clear that I didn't know the fettered beauty in front of me. But then she called my name.

"Savannah, darling. Savannah! Yoo-hoo!" She waved like a maniacal Barbie. Amber tried to help her get my attention. It was painful for all involved.

I hoped these people would think the woman just wanted to say hello to her city, Savannah, while the cameras were rolling. I didn't lift my eyes to check on their potential gullibility. But I did notice my bow had come undone. And my dress flap had flown open and exposed my slip. I jerked it closed and held it together in my fist.

"This day had better be no reflection of my week to come," I warned the heat. It laughed. Yes, I'm certain it laughed.

CHAPTER TWO

It's no great feat for a television crew to distract my mother. But when distraction is accompanied by airtime, well, it technically isn't a distraction anymore, now, is it? At least not in her world. Call it what you will. In my book, it was my chance to escape.

As I returned to Jake's, I turned around for one more glimpse of the square. Wright Square was the second square laid in Savannah. It was originally named for Lord Viscount Percival. But in 1763, it was renamed for Savannah's royal governor, James Wright. Of course, now he's buried in Westminster Abbey, and Tomochichi, the Yamacraw chief who helped Oglethorpe establish Savannah, is buried here in Wright Square. And the large rock from Stone Mountain that sits atop his grave—something I avoid at all costs—was given by the Colonial Dames on the sixtieth anniversary of his death. Of course General Oglethorpe, a poor man who came here to deliver us from craziness, has his statue in one square and his name on another. Go figure.

So, maybe today isn't the first day Savannah has done something ridiculous.

"Mr. Phillips, you can trust me. I'll have you a new dishwasher in here first thing tomorrow morning." The young man in a blue uniform picked up his tools on the other side of the kitchen door.

"That will be great, Ron. I'll be here around seven thirty, so if we could get it earlier that would really help us out. Tomorrow's liable to be a crazy day." Dad peered out the window toward the spectacular spectacle across the square.

"I know. I'm going to spend the night out there with everyone else tonight. Need to make sure these people trying to steal our rights know what we stand for, you know, Mr. Phillips."

"Yeah, well, thanks, Ron. Do I need to pay you anything today?"

"Oh, if you could pay for half today, you can give me the rest when I get it installed in the morning." He bent over to pick up the pen he had just dropped. Poor child showed more of his exposed behind to Dad's staff than anyone should be forced to endure. Louise let out a groan. Her twin sister, Mervine, a snicker. Richard cleared his throat and slid his ebony hand over his eyes. Duke whined as if in pain.

Ron stood and hiked up his britches. I couldn't have been more thankful than a seventy-five-year-old Southern woman on beauty-shop day. Because after all, this city has enough attractions.

Dad wrote a check for Mr. Ron, who left a receipt on the counter. Dad proceeded to help himself to the coffeepot, which brewed underneath the blackboard that featured "Jake's Thought for the Day."

"Watch your words and hold your tongue; you'll save yourself a lot of grief."

I didn't really care what it said today. This man calmly pouring himself some java, as if the entire world hadn't turned upside down on his front lawn, wasn't going to quiet me with his renowned blackboard wit. "Surely you are not going to stand here pouring coffee while *your wife* is chained to a monument large enough to crush a small village?"

He kept pouring. I picked up Ron's receipt on the counter. An emblem of a fish was embossed across the entire piece of paper.

I set it down and then followed my question in case it was lost on him in some form or fashion. "Have you noticed that no one is even here?" I said, motioning to the empty tables and coffee bar. "Every other creature within a thirty-mile radius and probably other states is over there, watching her. Why aren't you?"

"Savannah, your mother doesn't need watching."

"Obviously you are mistaken. The woman is chained to a monument, for crying out loud. I think she has needed watching for years!"

He walked to a window table and sat so he could view the spectacle from his chair. Duke followed close behind. Duke has been a virtual "store prisoner" since the incident last summer when mother caught him coming home carrying a bag of empty beer bottles and pork & beans. She wasn't the only one that saw him, however, and the whole episode had the city abuzz with rumors of Victoria Phillips's dog, "the tootin' alcoholic." That, accompanied by last week's dip in her pool, has pretty much kept him staring out the window too. He looked up at my father as if ready for an explanation of this crazy afternoon as well.

"Your mother is using her free will to express herself, well . . . freely." He laughed at his own amused self.

Duke came over and nuzzled his head up under my hand. I obliged and rubbed his ears. "You laugh. Well, I hate to be the one to break it to you, but I don't need this right now. I just started my job at the paper. Shoot, half of them don't even think I should be writing human-interest stories, and the other half look at me as Victoria Phillips's daughter, *the* human-interest story. So, however you want to break this debacle down, she should be restrained."

I stared into those green smirking eyes that had produced both Thomas's and my own.

"She is, actually."

"Ever the comedian, aren't we?" I looked out the window myself only to see two other television trucks make their way to our newly adorned square. "Great, now every network's covered. CBS and FOX have arrived."

"Savannah, the world doesn't revolve around you, in case you haven't noticed." I heard the twins and Richard make their way to the back room. "And this has nothing to do with you, personally." He turned his attention back to the window.

I walked to the front door and opened it, trying to hide what was boiling inside me. "Well, that is where you're wrong, brother. It has everything to do with me. And you. And my mother. And the fact that we are already talked about in the paper more than your average criminal, and in this city, more than the mayor himself."

"That's not true." He took a casual sip of his coffee.

"It is true. And it is about me. And whether you like it or not, it's about you too. Because half of you is across the street in mules and pastels and will have your name and my name on every nightly news network before our heads hit our pillows."

"Don't you need to get back to work, Savannah?"

"Actually what I need is a Valium."

His head jerked around to scold me. "What did you say?"

"If you would have let me finish, I was trying to say, 'Actually, what we need is to go tell 'em to stop this madness.' But I guess no help is going to come from this side of the square." With that inane salvage I walked out the door.

The Ten Commandments of our Lord were being defended by the same woman who came with me to basketball tryouts and spent the entire time yelling, "Good shot, darling!" while I was dribbling. She sat in the stands on a towel, holding her hands out to her side, not touching anything. I don't know who they found more amusing: me, or Vicky and her antibacterial gel. By the time she started hollering "You go, girl!" and all I was doing was sitting on the bench, I decided to cut myself from the team.

I decided to take up a quieter sport. A sport where the people in the stands weren't allowed to say anything. I became a tennis player. I told her it was uncouth to talk at all while people were playing tennis. I didn't even let her think she could cheer between points. So, for four solid years, at every match, Victoria sat on the stands, on a cushion, and never said a word. It was heaven.

And now here she is, fighting for a piece of it.

I looked across the street, and mother was nowhere to be found in the madness. Camera lights were beaming everywhere and microphones were waving in the air, and my life offered more excitement than a recovering beauty queen. Or maybe not. Because the former Miss Georgia United States of America, nestled across the street in chains, was evidently having a pretty exciting afternoon herself.

I walked to the back of Dad's coffee shop and climbed into Old Betsy. The parking space belonged to the apartment above Jake's, an apartment only a paycheck away from being mine. I, Ms. Savannah Phillips, or "Savannah from Savannah" as my mother calls me, was getting her own apartment. Granted, it was above my father's business, but it was out of my mother's house. Liberation, no matter how you defined it. Even though I had only been out of graduate school and back home for just a little more than two weeks, the walls had closed in and were strangling the life from my vibrant, young soul.

My next-door cubicle buddy and self-appointed affliction greeted me in the narrow passageway before I had a chance to enter my redecorated haven of cardboard. I had attempted to make it more homey with the addition of a few books and one Paige Long "original" oil painting. A gift from the painter herself, who happens to be my best friend.

"Have you heard what's going on at the courthouse?" Joshua's annoyingly overconfident, perfectly white smile gleamed down at me, and a loose black curl hung in front of his left eye. I didn't much like men anymore. Since Paige informed me last week that the only man I had ever really dated—or even loved for that matter—is marrying some chick from an all-girls' school, I have sworn off men in general. So, men in general have moved to my *tolerable* category of relationships.

"Could I at least get through the door and sit down?" I pushed him aside.

"You don't have a door. You have a cubicle." He let me pass.

"Is this comedy hour?" I tossed my satchel on the floor next to my chair. I dropped into it and it squealed.

"My, my, my. To have had such a good morning, you sure deteriorate fast."

I stared at my blank computer screen. Now was not the time to discuss the last hour with The Man among men who irritated me so. Turning to look over at his tanned face, piercing dark eyes, and frantic curls, I said, "You know, I really don't need your analysis of my moods, or my days. We both have jobs to do, and that should keep us busy enough to stay out of each other's way. Don't you have a deadline or something?"

"Or something. Okay, well, if you don't want to tell me, I'm sure I'll find out in the morning with the rest of the city."

"I'm sure you will."

"But I could tell you my news if you told me your news." He invited himself in and pulled up the lone chair that rested underneath Paige's painting.

I didn't even look at him.

"So you don't want to know who's coming on Friday?"

I picked up the phone to dial anyone who would rescue me, even though there was no one I knew well enough that would. My only friends here so far were the receptionist, Marla, the sweet little pixie who got her job because she befriended my mother on a trolley car, and this man next to me. Other than these two, few people around here desired my presence at all.

"I guess that means you don't want to know. Okay. Well"—he

stood, performing a pitiful attempt at dejection—"I guess you don't care that the president is headed this way Friday for a visit before he heads off to Sea Island for a meeting with world leaders. Word has it the mayor was going to invite your mother to attend the president's luncheon."

My head swiveled in time to see his right hand grab the corner of my cubicle, showing off the well-defined muscle that ran from his hand to his elbow and disappeared underneath his shirtsleeve.

He knew exactly what was going on in this city. He knew that my mother was at the center of it all. And he wanted me to be the one to tell him all about it. Well. He could read it in the paper. But no matter how perfectly toned his bicep was, he wasn't getting it from me.

CHAPTER THREE

On the drive home, I avoided Wright Square and the dead man's tomb. But I could not avoid the fact that Savannah had officially turned upside down. And this time it had nothing to do with a best-selling book about a murder, or a University of Georgia win.

The behavior that rippled through Savannah today was so unorthodox. I mean, there is only one time a year that the people of Savannah attach a scurry to their step, and that is in preparation for the annual St. Patrick's Day parade. Other than that, this town's pace is set apart by its ability to accomplish even the most pressing tasks in slow motion. Stores actually close for months at a time with nothing more than a note in their window: "Got an itch and will return when the fall clothes arrive or the beach gets too cold."

Truly, there is nothing electric about this place, except what you might see during a thunderstorm. Or during any activity related to my mother. And occasionally during a well-publicized murder. But today, I could practically see the electricity buzzing along the very sidewalks and alleyways.

Pulling on to Abercorn Street, I glanced at Clary's restaurant across the street from my parents' home. The absence of a dinnertime rush offered more proof that something was amiss in the South.

I walked through the second-floor doors of our rather substantial home. Some would consider it a mansion. Vicky considered it a compromise. She had wanted to live in (I kid you not) the Victorian district. But my dad, wanting as uneventful a life as possible with a woman who calls her daughter "Savannah from Savannah" refused to spend the next twenty-some-odd years listening to his wife introduce herself as "Victoria from the Victorian district." So, she settled on this lovely house, a house on the Historical Register large enough to accommodate a small village. Don't tell her I said that. She would think I was making some snide reference to Hillary Clinton's first book.

Home has a smell. Well, it used to. It used to smell like beef roast with potatoes and carrots and gravy with a side of butter beans and macaroni and cheese. But not today. No pungent aromas accosted my senses when I opened the front door. No flurry of activity in the kitchen, no loud conversations. It was then, for the first time, my mental faculties registered the fact that no Victoria meant . . . no dinner. No one else in this entire family knew how to do much more than pour a bowl of cereal.

We discovered this absence of talent the night my father had the brilliant idea of informing my mother that "the only thing someone inherits who stirs up undue trouble in their own house is the wind." In essence, he informed my mother she was a bag of hot air. All because he wouldn't eat the crumbs at the bottom of the potato-chip bag before he opened a new one.

And I do believe he capped it all off by calling her Vicky. My mother hates nothing more than being called Vicky. But when it came from my father's mouth, well, let's just say, "Hold on, Hannah!"

My mother had paused briefly at this comment. She attempted to regather and reload. But nothing came out. She tried. She tried hard. Even stamped her foot a couple times like a horse about to charge. But the poor woman didn't have a comeback. A verbal comeback, that is. She came back all right. She didn't cook for a week. And after he tried to make us a dinner of canned tomato soup by mixing it with water, well, let's just say I didn't even like him much myself at that point. So we ate cereal. Three times a day. I suggested that next time he should make only those observations that would result in his sole punishment.

I walked up the stairs to the sound of my own feet. No patter of paws followed. No, "Dinner's ready!" No smart comment about the fact that my body was actually encased in a dress. I would have welcomed the persecution. But none came.

As I entered my bedroom and proceeded to my bathroom to wash my face, the stress of my mother's antics finally captured me. Toothpaste from the morning brushing had not completely made its way down the sink, and a blob of blue Crest lay on the oil-rubbed bronze drain.

I couldn't help it. I grabbed the Comet, a toothbrush, and a few extra-strength Tylenol and busted up in that bathroom like it hadn't seen in a good two days. I scrubbed faucets. I scrubbed shower tiles. I scrubbed floor tiles. I scrubbed things you wouldn't even know existed unless you got down on all fours and examined the plumbing. By the time I was through, that placed shined as if Mr. Clean on steroids had come through.

The chime from the door alarm declared someone's entrance. I figured I should greet the intruder. My twenty-four-year-old frame felt the two hours of squatting and cleaning, and I required extra care in removing the kneepads and rubber gloves. But you can rest assured, there was not a microscopic remnant of any germs, fungus, or hardened toothpaste to be found.

Thomas, Duke, and Dad came up through the downstairs door from Thomas's floor of the house, otherwise known as a basement.

The child inherited it after I refused it. He'll be there 'til Vicky buys him a house or Dad kicks him out. The former will only happen because of the latter.

I met them in the kitchen. No Vicky. No hope for normalcy inside these four walls this evening.

"Where have you three been?"

Thomas went straight to the refrigerator and pulled out a Dr Pepper. "We've been talking to Mom. She is so into this thing!" He was acting as if this was the greatest thing he had been a part of since he shaved his head for his "knob" year at The Citadel military college. I couldn't hide my disgust.

"When is she coming home?"

Dad looked at me with undisguised disbelief. "Savannah, your mother is staying there until they remove her or the monument."

"You've got to be kidding me."

"I think it's great," Thomas quipped.

"Ever the juvenile, aren't we, Thomas?"

"Ever the girl with the stick up her—"

"Thomas," Dad interrupted. "That's enough."

I nodded. "I think you need to get out more." I turned my attention back to the once-sane leader of this questionable family. "Seriously, Dad, she can't stay there. What's she going to do, sleep outside all night?"

"It looks that way."

His calm demeanor dismayed me. "You mean, you are going to let her sleep out there all night?"

"Savannah, I'll take care of your mother. You don't worry about her. Now, I'm going to get her and me something to eat." He began to make his way to the stairs to perform his usual after-work ritual of a shower and change of clothes. "You want to come have dinner with us?"

"What? And risk a picnic caught on tape? I don't think so."

He continued upstairs. "Have it your way."

"What are Thomas and I going to eat?"

My brother headed downstairs only to call back, "I'm going with Dad."

I looked down at the golden four-legged creature next to me. "I guess we're on our own." Duke remained for one brief second, and then became a golden blur as his flapping furry tail followed Thomas downstairs. Even Duke knew who would really eat dinner tonight.

The kitchen was empty. "Like I said, I guess I'm on my own."

I sat down at the edge of the bar and rested my elbows on the black soapstone countertop. Putting my face in my hands, I let out an extended sigh. But I wasn't totally alone. I was joined by the presence of official Phillips-family collapse. I stared at the empty dinner table where someone always sat. I stared at the empty oven that always had something baking in it by this time of the evening. I stared at the empty pathway between island and counter that always had a woman flittering up and down it. Tonight, my mother was outside on a Friday evening, and not for a dinner engagement.

Well, come to think of it, it was going to end up a dinner engagement.

I stood. Wiped away my cares and declared to the empty room, "Well, this will just get me in practice for living on my own. No one will be there to cook me dinner. So I'm just going to seize the moment."

I called Paige to see what she was eating.

"Do you have any food?" I asked, flopping myself onto one of her two new chocolate-brown leather sofas with stainless-steel legs that flanked her fireplace.

"Child, when have you known me not to have food?"

I let the soft leather cradle my head. "I mean real food. Not Doritos, dip, and Diet Coke."

"Savannah has had a bad day?" She came over and sat on the edge of the sofa beside me and patted my head. "Poor baby needs real food. Real food it is."

With that she called out for pizza delivery and bounced back down on her brown and Tiffany blue velvet-covered ottoman that served as her coffee table. Her perfectly messy short blond hair bounced with her. Not that it's her natural color. But it does look natural on her.

She has had the same great short cut since I met her in sixth grade. Except for our eighth-grade year, when we both had failed attempts at perms. I tried short once. But only once. I looked like a boy and spent the next year suffering through insufferable grow out. No more haircuts above the shoulders since.

"Okay, tell me all your troubles."

I looked up at her in total shock. "You mean you don't know?!" I asked as I reached down to scratch my itching foot.

"What are you doing?"

"I'm scratching my foot. Do you know what that means?"

"It itches?"

"No, it means you're going to walk on new ground."

"You got all of that out of an itching foot?"

"It's just something my mother has always said. She got it from her mother, I think."

"Okay, well, whatever. Just take me with you. Now, back to what I know. Of course I know. My mother's been out there with your mother all day. But you just need to get it off your chest. That's the only way you will heal."

"The only way I will heal is to leave town and change my name to Villamina Venzinhoffer."

"Oh, that wouldn't attract any attention, now, would it? So, your mother's getting a little attention . . ."

"A little? Have you been down there?"

"Actually, I couldn't get through the crowd, but she'll be home by evening. I mean, do you honestly think Miss One-Thousand-Dollar-Suit, Never-Let-Them-See-You-Without-Your-Makeup Woman is going to spend the night outside?"

"Well, Dad said he was taking her dinner. What do you think she's going to do?"

"I think he'll take her dinner and she'll give the evening shift to some poor soul from the Savannah College of Art and Design, along with a crisp hundred-dollar bill and the promise of a great job upon graduation."

"You're absolutely right." I sat up straight on the sofa. This revelation gave me the desire to pace and talk. "Victoria Phillips would never spend the night outside. That lady's idea of camping is a two-star hotel. Shoot, I remember—well, you know, how she takes her own sheets to hotels, Miss Has-Sheets-Will-Travel."

Paige rolled her eyes. "Yes, because of the *20/20* episode on hotels and gyms. I totally know."

"Well, a couple of weeks ago, she went out of state to judge a pageant, and apparently the hotel was more like, well, like a *motel*."

She crinkled her nose. "Oh, don't tell me. The doors were on the outside."

"Yes, sweet sister. The only door on the inside led to the toilet."

"You mean she didn't pack her bags and pay for her own hotel somewhere else?"

"The only other place in town was where the contestants were. So she had no option but to leave. And we are talking beauty pageant here."

"Oh, how silly of me. Please continue. But sit down. I can't stand it when you pace or clean."

I sat back down on the sofa and used my hands to continue my story. "Well, apparently she put her sheets on the bed."

"The five-hundred-dollar set?"

"Are there others? And she slept with a light on all night. In case of bugs."

"Bugs?"

"Yeah, didn't you hear about her friend Cyndi?"

"Cyndi who?"

"You know, Cyndi who found that tick in her ear."

"No way! That is sick!" She shivered as if she had the chills. "Do not tell me any more about that. Just get back to your mother."

"Well, Vicky is petrified something's going to crawl in her ear at night."

"Stop!" She made a gagging sound.

"Yeah, isn't it? Anyway, she puts her sheets on the bed, only to hardly sleep because of the tick thing." I snicker now. "Then, for three straight days she doesn't even let the cleaning ladies in. But, on the fourth day—"

"Oh, Lord, what happened on the fourth day?"

"She forgot to put the 'Do Not Disturb' hanger on the door."

"I'm taking it she got disturbed."

"Honey, when she got back they had made her bed and thrown her sheets in a wadded up pile on the sofa."

"Ew, the sofa."

"Yep, where behinds have sat for centuries."

"Did she wash them?"

"Honey, she threw them away and made them take her to a store so she could buy new ones. She said they were totally unsalvageable."

"And you think this woman would spend the night, outside, on hard concrete, where any kind of bug imaginable could crawl in her ear? Well, you aren't thinking clearly."

The doorbell rang and Paige retrieved our pizza. I followed her to her galley kitchen to prepare our feast. "You're right. What was I thinking?"

"Obviously not much. Here, eat." With that, we devoured our pizza and chattered about endless nothings. She told me all about her new coffee table, who made it, how it was made, and we created a fabulous layout for my nonexistent furniture, for my yet-to-be-mine apartment.

Then she talked about the cute boy who moved in down the hall. She didn't know his name but she had deciphered his cologne. Even though we were supposed to have sworn off men, she had never been very good at resisting tan legs and white smiles.

I walked home enjoying the still warmth of a spring evening. After pizza and Coke, life seemed . . . well, just plain okay.

CHAPTER FOUR

Pulling the covers from my head and hugging my pillow, I looked out the window to see what action Abercorn held this morning. Not much. A few joggers passed, tugging at me to join them. As I washed my face, the silence caught my attention. Eight a.m. on a Saturday in the Phillips's house usually boasted far more activity than seemed to be developing this morning.

My sneakered feet walked out of my bedroom and stopped on the landing. The bed was made in Mom and Dad's bedroom. Nothing new. Vicky never left her bed unmade. She blames the habit on one unforgettable experience before she married when she left her apartment messy and the maintenance guy saw her underwear on the floor.

"So, Savannah, whatever you do, always pick up your panties, always make your bed, and don't call strangers to come fix your toilet."

I can honestly say, in all my life adventures, those three occurrences have never run in tandem.

No lingering smell of chocolate gravy and homemade biscuits lured me to the kitchen. For a moment that fear of ages past gripped me. It first captured me around eight years of age, the fear that the Rapture has taken place and I alone inhabit the world. I had searched the house and yard desperately but found no one. My recent dip into the *Left Behind* series only increased that fear. This morning, I stifled the desire to scream loudly or run up and down the street, knocking on the doors of the most holy people I knew.

Somehow my heart steadied itself and made its way out the front door for a jog and some tilling time. My iPod played my CeCe Winans library. About halfway up Bull Street toward Forsythe Park, Granny Daniels, one of the godliest ladies I know, came walking out of her house right into my path. I stopped right in front of her. Grabbed her with both arms and gave her a big ol' bear hug.

"So good to see you this morning, Granny Daniels."

Trying to catch her breath from my assault, she grabbed her chest. "Well, Savannah, my Lord, child, you look like the Rapture's come and you're the only one left."

"Oh, that's funny!" I said through my nervous laughter of relief. "Wouldn't that be awful?"

She extricated herself from my hold and started walking up the street. "Tell your parents hello for me."

"I will. See ya tomorrow." The heaviness of my trepidation lifted, and I increased my pace. The smell of mothballs stayed with me long after Granny Daniels left. I've never been certain why she smells like them so, though rumor has it she heard they kept snakes away. As far as I know, not many snakes make their way up to the homes of Savannah. Mothballs would be my weapon of choice, however, if I knew they would keep water bugs away. I stared at the ones on the sidewalk, struck down by morning joggers.

The smell of mothballs makes its way into just about everything that comes out of Granny Daniels's house. She once fixed us a big ol' pot of fresh garden-picked butter beans, and Vicky threw them out, because they, too, smelled like mothballs.

And like her odor, her authenticity is just as impossible to miss. You can hear it in the prayers she prays when you sit in front of her at church. Or see it in the weathered Bible that rests on the table by her weathered recliner. But it shows most vibrantly in her letters, which go out at graduations and weddings.

Mine arrived on a Sunday. She slipped it into my palm with a "piece of money," as she liked to call it. She let me know her prayers had followed my mother and father "everywhere they have ever been" and that me and Thomas were in her prayers too. Then she reminded me that there was a "work" for me to do, and that I needed to "live humble and never let pride have no place in your heart."

Then she apologized for her handwriting and asked me to pray for her. So today, I remembered and did some tilling time for Granny Daniels too.

Tilling time is my time to pray, reflect, and listen. I set aside the first moments of the day to get my mind (or soil, as Pastor Brice defined it) focused on an eternal perspective in a temporary world. Duke and I usually till together. Well, to be honest, God alone knows what Duke thinks about while we jog, except I can say he's a hard one to hold when any four-legged female passes by. But Dad must have taken him this morning.

So, between my conversation with Paige and my run-in with Granny Daniels, my steps seemed lighter. Today was bound to be a lovely May day.

I paused a moment on a park bench to enjoy the stillness of the dissipating spring. A ball flew through the air and caught my attention. Joshua. But he wasn't alone. He was accompanied by a beautiful golden retriever.

He never told me he had a dog.

Come to think of it, he's never told me much of anything.

I watched as the boy and his dog played catch. Joshua hardly stopped laughing as he called out to "Shelby," who was clearly a girl. It's not hard to tell these things. They played. They tumbled. I spied. It was weird. I felt like an intruder. But I couldn't turn my gaze. Then I watched in amazement as he held up his finger at that dog and yelled "Bang!" and she fell right to the ground like she was dead. Then she high-fived him. But the be-all and end-all was when he turned his back and that dog grabbed his leg with her paw and tripped that grown man.

Unbelievable.

Well, Duke ain't worth much compared to that. All he does is chase a ball and lie around waiting for food to fall from the counter or ice to fall from the ice maker.

I didn't know he had a dog. He knew my dog. Then, he and Shelby packed up and headed home. I watched. Shameless, I know, but I did it anyway.

I love to walk the streets of Savannah, and the day was too flawless to drive for my morning fix. After a shower I grabbed a book and headed for Dad's shop, which harbored my McDonald's Coke machine. Dad had it installed for me shortly after the cheerless discovery that no McDonald's existed in the Historical District.

The enjoyable route to Jake's runs up Abercorn Street past Lafayette Square (which holds the Hamilton Turner Inn), then past the Colonial Park Cemetery (which holds a few Hamiltons and Turners itself, I'm sure). I don't hang out there much; sister don't do dead people. So usually I hang a left at West Harris and then a right on Bull, which deposits me at Wright Square with York Street and State Street completing the four corners.

It's amazing how a place you know so well feels so excitingly new some mornings. Even though I've passed the same antique stores, women's clothing stores, restaurants, and corner cafés probably a million times through the years, some days the city just feels different. New, fresh . . . dare I say inspiring? Today felt that way. At least it did until I passed Bull and realized things were, new, fresh, and definitely inspiring to someone. Wright Square was as active this morning as it was yesterday.

Crossing York Street, I couldn't see Mother, even though I was certain she was there. She probably started her day off with coffee at Dad's and then wandered back to relieve the pitiable creature who endured the elements of the evening. I crossed to the opposite side of the square in front of the Chatham County Legislative Offices because it kept me away from the fray.

I gazed up at the two iron banisters flanking the French doors to my apartment above Dad's store and assured her it wouldn't be long 'til Mama was home. One more paycheck, one simple conversation with Vicky, and it would be mine. I entered Jake's through the back door so I could get straight to the Coke machine.

Louise and Mervine, the two twins who had worked with Dad since the day he opened eleven years ago, had their backs to me as I entered. They came out of retirement "because your dad was so sweet and cute," they confessed. In fact, all of Dad's employees have worked with him since he opened. Never lost a one.

Oh, well, there was *that* one.

When Dad first opened Jake's, Mother decided she would be the hostess. Dad assured her a coffee shop didn't need a hostess. She assured him it did. She lasted four and a half days. She was fired with these words: "Lady Wisdom builds a lovely home; Lady Fool comes along and tears it down brick by brick."

I think it was the fool part that got her. She grabbed her Louis Vuitton satchel, because we all know you need one to be the hostess at a coffee shop, and the entire place held their breath until the clicking of her Stuart Weitzman heels could no longer be heard from the other side of the square. Remarkably, the place didn't fall apart.

"What are you two doing?"

"That crazy man hasn't gotten here with the dishwasher yet," Louise said, swinging her head around and wiping her face with a suds-covered hand.

I fixed a cup of ice and poured a Coke. Duke ran to my side, chomping at the pieces of ice that fell. "I'll deal with you later." I wagged a finger at him then turned my attention to the Madge wannabes up to their elbows in Palmolive. "I thought Mr. Ron was bringing the dishwasher this morning."

"So did we. But all we've got is a hole." She pointed to the space where the machine used to be. "So, you're looking at the dishwashers." Mervine just looked up and smiled.

"Well, maybe he'll be here shortly."

"I'm sure he will, or I'll hunt him down and strap *his* behind to this sink."

I gave them each a kiss and headed to the front. Richard greeted me with a wink as his black eyes did their customary dance. His dark hand extended a refill to the customer who sat at the window.

Duke returned to me affectionately with his wet mouth. "Give me a high-five, Duke." I grabbed his paw and lifted it to touch my palm. He jerked his leg from my grip.

Dad laughed. "You can't teach an old dog new tricks. Don't you know that?"

"Well, I'm going to. Duke can't do jack." I patted his cute but uneducated head. "You should have taught him how to do more than just retrieve people's trash and chase a ball."

"What else does he need to know?"

"Something more than he does, that's all I know. And you could have left him with me this morning. I would have brought him in."

"Oh, well, we've been here all night." Dad poured some coffee for a kid on the other side of the counter who looked too young to be drinking coffee.

I walked over and set my latest reading material down on top of the granite. It would take a good afternoon to be finished with Peggy Noonan's book on Ronald Reagan, *When Character Was King*. Duke followed me to the counter, walking more slowly than usual, as if his night might have been better spent with me.

"What do you mean *we've* been here all night?"

Dad returned the coffeepot to its warmer. "I mean, I wasn't going to let your mother sleep outside by herself."

I started laughing and slapped the counter. "Oh, you're good. You had me going there for a minute. But you weren't thinking when you added the mother-slept-outside part."

"Think what you will Savannah, but she did. And so did I. And so did Duke. Didn't you, Duke?"

Duke looked up at him, tucking his tail between his legs and scrunching closer to my chair. Maybe he wasn't completely stupid after all. I mean, the poor creature was forced to spend the night outside with a woman who loathes him because he's not a lapdog named Magnolia.

"Wished you'd stayed with me, huh?" His tail wagged as he looked up in acknowledgment of his great error. I turned my attention back to my Dad. "And what did you sleep on, may I ask?"

He headed back into the back room. "You may, and I brought sleeping bags."

"You are too much. So, Victoria Phillips, *the* Victoria Phillips, former Miss Georgia United States of America, head of the Chamber of Commerce turned City of Savannah Diva, spent the night, outside, in a sleeping bag, with no way to take a bath, redo her makeup, or change her clothes. And you think I'm going to believe that?"

"Go see for yourself."

"I will. I'll just go see for myself. Come on, Duke." We headed outside to peer across the square. He was reluctant but came when he realized my arms were free of sleeping paraphernalia. It was necessary to move in closer because my petite mother was easily swallowed whole by the crowd, which was definitely larger than yesterday's. People sat around talking; reporters stood in front of cameras. We stopped to watch a kid too young to drink coffee take his place in front of a news camera to deliver the latest information.

"Standing here in front of the United States Courthouse on Wright Square, in the heart of Savannah, we are waiting on the latest order to be issued from the federal courts on whether this monument, like many before, and I'm certain many after, will get to stay or have to go. At the center of this case is a federal judge by the name of Judge Hoddicks. He brought in the structure late Thursday afternoon, after most courts were closed and people were headed home from work. He is fighting this on the legal end, and Victoria Phillips, the head of the Savannah Chamber of Commerce, is fighting this on the human-rights end along with hundreds of other crusaders. She has been here all night. Many others have gone home to shower and return to work, but she remains, looking exceptionally fresh, I might add. And totally capable of staying until this battle goes one way or the other. Now back to you, Sarah, in the studio."

The camera quit rolling and he plopped down in the grass and took a long swig of his coffee. "Why do I always get the gigs where you have to stay outside?" he asked his cameraman.

About that time the people parted enough for me to catch a glimpse of my mother. She sat on a rolled-up sleeping bag in the same blue suit she had had on yesterday.

At no time in my twenty-four years had I ever, until that exact moment, seen Vicky in the same outfit two days in a row.

Trying to stand back among the others, not wanting her to see me, I observed that she did look exceptionally well for having spent the evening outside. I managed to spot a small stain on the bottom left-hand side of her jacket, and her makeup looked a little tired, but her hair was perfectly fixed. But if she stayed here much longer her hair would probably start to look more like her outfit. I wouldn't put it past her to change her hair to match her outfit, even though she'd become a tad more cautious since the hair-breakage-on-the-pillow incident.

She was talking to Sergeant Millings. And he didn't look really happy. Nothing new. He always looked rather constipated. Of course, he was afraid of my mother. Weird, as she was always exceptionally nice to him, in spite of his customary ability to annoy. Maybe the oddity of niceness was enough to freak out the former Sears security guard.

He stood there, legs spread, one hand on gun, free hand on hip. That stance shouldn't be allowed in public. He was letting her know something clearly and adamantly, until a rather looming federal agent who stepped out of the courthouse tapped him on the shoulder.

"You have no jurisdiction here." The federal agent's booming voice carried all the way to my ears.

"This sidewalk is my responsibility, young fella." I was glad Sergeant Millings hadn't called the six-foot-six man "little fella."

"No sir. We're in front of a federal building, which makes this my jurisdiction."

Mr. Looloo would not give up. "I'll have you know that this sidewalk has been a part of my jurisdiction since before you could spell 'bubba.' So, either you go back inside that courthouse or I'll be seeing you in court."

"I think you should remember that the courthouse is my jurisdiction too."

"Are you threatening me?" Sergeant Millings asked, hand shifting on his gun. A few gawkers stepped back.

"You need to take your hand off your gun, sir. Now."

He shifted his hand casually to his belt buckle, as if it were all his idea. "I'll have you know I've already issued Mrs. Phillips here an Order to Disperse."

"You have not!" Mother protested.

Millings pulled out a notepad. Scribbled on it. Ripped it out and handed it to my mother. "I have now." She refused to take it. "Not taking it, Mrs. Phillips, doesn't change the fact that it's an order."

"Wanna bet?"

The federal agent reentered the conversation. "Sergeant Millings, why don't you and I go have a talk with Judge Hoddicks and see what we can come up with."

"We'll go talk to whoever we need to, sonny, to get you off my sidewalk." He turned his attention back to my mother. "You have until Friday, Mrs. Phillips. If you're not out of here by Friday at five p.m., I will cart you off to jail."

Mother stared a hole into him, causing him to back into the federal agent, who pushed him back toward my mother. I just prayed she wasn't within reach of his gun.

CHAPTER FIVE

ome on, Duke. Let's get out of here." Duke turned himself around, appreciating that he wasn't going to have to spend the afternoon sleeping on sun-soaked concrete too. As I turned around in a bit of a hurry, an exotic-looking beauty careened into my shoulder, spinning me around.

"Oh, excuse me," she said, turning around to make sure I was okay.

"Sorry, I didn't see you." She wasn't from around here. Her accent was Southern, but her look was metropolitan, classy, almost L.A.-like. I tried not to stare, but her long black hair, pulled back into a sleek ponytail, made her striking features and light brown eyes stand out even more. Her flawless olive skin had probably never needed a bottle of "Tan Perfect," the new tanning regimen for the scaredy-cats of Savannah.

She just nodded and continued up the steps of the courthouse, perfection slipping through the glass-and-gold antiqued doors. Her all-black attire was exceptionally odd for a Southern spring. But there wasn't much room in my closet for criticism. Until two weeks ago, about the only color I possessed came from the lone red blouse my mother bought me six years earlier for one of her memorable Christmas parties. I might have done red, but this lovely blouse was adorned by enough layers of ruffles around the neck to cover my face to my hairline. Red has never since adorned my body.

The heat of the afternoon encroached on the countless souls forced to take cover under umbrellas or live oak trees with their Spanish moss. Mother, however, was exposed to the elements. The grand hall of justice would not shield her from the sun until late afternoon. She raised her umbrella, which matched her Kate Spade handbag and shoes.

"Duke, we need another Coke. And I'm going to teach you how to get your own ice." He agreed and led the way to safety.

Richard was cleaning off the two front tables when I entered. "Those people are crazy out there. That's a three-ring circus," I declared.

"Now, Savannah, those are people doing somethin' they believe in. You ought not be callin' them crazy." His gray hairs glistened in the sun that streamed through the front window.

I continued my walk to the back and the fountain of sanity. "Whatever you say. But it looks like craziness to me."

Duke and I took a moment to gather ourselves. I grabbed his paw and used it to slap the ice dispenser attached to my Coke machine. Ice cubes fell to the ground and he ran off with them. I sighed. So easily sidetracked. We would work on his focus later.

A rather loud, Southern female voice distracted me from Duke. I peered through the slats in the swinging door to see who had entered Jake's. Duke, who put away the ice in one swallow, resumed residence beside me.

"I'll have a double espresso, please." She offered my father a smile. The corners of her mouth barely moved. And her eyebrows may as well have been paralyzed. She was a BOTOX butcher block.

"Sorry, young lady, but we just serve regular old coffee."

"Just coffee?" She snickered. Her snicker seemed rather contrived, not to mention unnecessary. "Are you serious?"

"Yes, ma'am, I am. We just keep it simple around here. But I promise you whether you like decaf or the real stuff, you won't get any better anywhere else."

"Well, I don't have time to go anywhere else. So just give me a large of the regular."

Jake turned around to pour the stranger a cup of his magic. "It will be my pleasure."

About that time Duke let out a growl. I had not heard Duke growl since Vicky made him get out of one of the chairs at the dining-room table. "Duke, chill. We'll go out there in a minute."

BOTOX lady carried on for ten more minutes, sipping and drinking and talking and putting her hand up against her bosom like some dainty Southerner. And touching my father no fewer than *ten* annoying times. He tried to be polite. He always was.

She revealed she worked for one of the national affiliates and was there to report the events at the courthouse. On her way to the door she turned around to flash Dad a *vavoom* smile half a dozen times—and with all that collagen, those lips took up half her face. But Duke and I had a moment of satisfaction when she ran smack-dab into the half-open door as my raven-haired stranger entered.

"May I have a decaf, please? Black, no sugar." A lady who appreciated the simple things in life. I liked that. She stood there so elegant and ladylike. It's not that we don't have ladies or elegance in Savannah. It's just most of the time they're adorned with linen and heavy perfume. But she was different, understated, Southern, and by all appearances important. I looked at the bracelet on her right wrist and noticed it was just like the David Yurman bracelet I had been given for graduation. She also had a matching ring on her right ring finger. Nothing on her left hand.

The board above Dad's head caught her attention as she sat her monogrammed leather satchel on the counter to retrieve her money. "What is that?"

He placed her coffee on the counter. "Oh, that's just a little board where I post a thought for the day. Gives everybody a little something to reflect on before they get started."

"Sounds like a religious saying. 'Keep mercy and truth with you always. Wear them as a necklace, write them on your heart. They will keep you respected by both God and man.' Lot of *that* going on around here, huh?"

"Where are you from?'

"Atlanta."

"Oh, I used to live in Atlanta."

I looked down at Duke, whose expression was still sour, for a golden retriever. "What is your problem, Duke?" He answered with another rather nasty growl.

"You lived in Atlanta?"

"Yeah, owned a company there but got tired of the pace. Moved here to slow down and learn how to enjoy living." He leaned on the counter. "What brings you here to Savannah?"

"Oh, I'm here to represent the voice of the people over this monument issue. I represented the last controversy in Jackson, Mississippi, and was asked to handle this one."

"I knew she was important," I said, slapping Duke on the head. I think he might have snarled at me. "Lighten up, old boy. How old do you think she is? Early thirties? Wonder what the *A* stands for on her bag?" Duke crouched as if ready to pounce.

"What voice do you represent exactly?" Dad asked.

"I work for the ACLU. But I won't be here long. The courts will have that thing out of here by the first of the week." She took a drink of her coffee. I caught a glimpse of her expression as the first swallow went down. Sheer satisfaction.

"Well, I hope you find what you're looking for." Dad pushed off the counter and gave her change.

She put it in her pocket and headed for the door. "Just looking for justice."

"Just find you a little truth in your justice," he said about the time her hand caught the handle of the door. I could see her turn around and stare at this new stranger. Then she walked out.

Duke and I came around the corner after the sounds of the bell announcing entrances and exits ceased. I took a stool at the counter, and Duke managed to pull himself up and balance precariously on the one next to me. "Neat lady, huh?"

"Yeah, I'm sure she is. Probably a lot like you. A young woman trying to do her job and figure out what she believes."

"Seems like she knows what she believes. Looks like she has a pretty good job too. Those bags aren't cheap."

"Well, after you work at your job for a while, you can afford nice bags too." He wiped off the counter.

"She liked your coffee."

He laughed. "You noticed that, huh?"

"It was written all over her face. That was the best-tasting stuff she's ever had."

"I know. I could tell."

"Now for the other character. You should lock your doors next time."

"She won't be back. She likes espressos."

"No way, champ. She'll be back. She likes Jake. Plus, she's so processed, the shock of something unprocessed will send her into a tailspin."

"You need to quit the name-calling. And your mother wants to know why you haven't been out there to see her." He prepared more coffee, for tired, hot people who were too addicted to realize that they should be drinking cold drinks in the eclipsing spring.

I turned my stool around to gaze out the front window and watch the action across the street. "Dad, I don't want to go out there. No one needs me in the middle of that."

"No one has asked you to get in the middle of anything. But you could at least go tell your mother hello."

"You and I both know if I go over there to tell her hello, I'm going to end up on the front page somehow as the cause of this entire episode."

"No, she already made the front page of today's paper."

I raised my right eyebrow and turned to stare at him. "Why would I have doubted?"

"Anyway, this is about more than a person, Savannah. One day you'll realize that. So get over yourself and learn from the book you're reading and go tell your mother hello. And that is coming from your father. Now, go."

"Wouldn't you like us to go look at my apartment first? You know, just kind of get an idea about what kind of furniture I might need."

"You don't have any money to get any furniture."

"Yes I do. I got paid yesterday."

"Well, I see your new apartment every day when I come to work, and I doubt one paycheck is going to get you moved in. But you haven't talked to your mother since yesterday. Now, get, and don't come back until you've seen her."

"I'm way too old to be scolded."

His right eyebrow mirrored mine. "You're way too old to need to be scolded."

"Well, huh! Let's go, Duke." Picking my book up off the counter, I pointed my dejected soul for the door, and the second soul wagged his tail the entire way.

"Duke, you're staying here," Dad called out to his loyal companion. So my dejected soul headed to the door alone, and the second dejected soul flung himself to the cold, hard concrete of his coffee-covered world.

CHAPTER SIX

Sheila Long, Paige's mother, stopped by Vicky's latest residence. Dropped in to say hello, I suppose. I stared across the square and watched as my mother pulled a tissue out of her purse and wiped off an area of the sidewalk for Sheila to sit down.

I knew perfectly well that this tissue had been wadded in her purse, probably since last Sunday at church. It's what she always does. And she always says, "It's clean."

How a wadded-up tissue in the bottom of a woman's purse can be considered clean is beyond me. But apparently Sheila fell for it, because she sat down beside Vicky.

Since Mother had a visitor and it was way too early in this beautiful day to throw myself into her world of chaos, I decided to eat. Dad wouldn't be home until evening, if then, so it seemed the perfect opportunity to delay obedience. I would obey eventually. Now just didn't feel like the right time. It felt more like teatime.

Saturdays are perfect days for tea. Even though afternoon tea in Savannah is left mostly to tourists and dainty Southern women,

I continue to enjoy it. A yearning for hot tea accompanied by crab cakes led me to the Gryphon Tea Room by way of Paige's. And no, hot tea and coffee are not the same.

I walked into Paige's small studio behind her parents' antique store across from St. John's Cathedral on Abercorn Street. She was wrapping up a painting for a miserably attired elderly couple. One vintage tourist had bejeweled herself with enough baubles for a family of four, and her companion had inadvertently, or maybe not, forgotten the no-white-knee-socks-with-walking-shorts-and-Florsheim-shoes rule. He smelled of an Old Spice train wreck and she looked as if she'd allowed a three-year-old to apply her blue eye shadow.

Paige slipped the sweet-looking gentleman his receipt, and he tried to insert it into his stitched-shut back pocket. He gave up after several attempts and stuffed it into his front pocket. His wife had similar struggles with her white vinyl bag, whose screw-in clasp didn't want to screw. By the time they were both through, I do believe they were winded.

Yet the wind continued to blow. They talked loud and long, and Paige loved every minute of it. Truth be known, she just liked old people. If all else failed for her, she would start a chain of nursing homes. She would teach the art classes. But she was totally perfect for this setting. She was lively enough to attract all kinds, down-to-earth enough to make them comfortable, and talkative enough to keep them entertained. The colorful duo left totally thrilled with their new purchase.

"Do you smell that?"

She sniffed the air. "Smell what?"

"That. Old-people perfume."

"You are weird. There is no such thing as old-people perfume."

"Oh yes there is. Every old lady that sits down in front of me on Sundays at church wears the same old-lady perfume. Just like old men do."

She moved over to her stool that sat in the corner and picked up a paintbrush to start back on a modern abstract landscape she was working on. "Why are you here? To dissect my clientele?"

"Okay, you made a sale; let's go eat!"

She ran her left hand through the front of her hair the way she always does, as if straightening it. Yet the very essence of her hairstyle is to look as if it's always messed up. "I can't."

"Why? You're the owner. You can do whatever you want to."

"Yes, you're right. Well, no, technically you're wrong. My mother is the owner and continues to inform me of such, and my father informed me, just a few moments ago actually, that if I am going to run a business, they would require some things of me."

"Things?"

"Yes, Savannah, things. Business-owner things. Like punctuality, reliability, those kind of things."

"Ooh, there's a cute guy about to come in here, huh?"

She turned her back to me and walked over to a half-finished canvas and picked up a paintbrush. "I don't know what you're talking about."

"Liar!" I laughed.

She turned back with a grin. "Yes I am. Their son is on his way."

"Excuse me, did you see her and smell him?"

"Yes I did, smarty-pants. But I saw him too." she said with a giggle. "He passed by with them a little while ago, and I saw him through the window." She paused for extra effect. "And he is, shall we say, extremely eligible and extremely fine."

"So you're choosing 'fine' over me and crab cakes?"

She laid down her brush, walked over to me, placed her hand on my back, and pushed me toward the door. "I know it's hard to believe, but it's true. I am about to forgo food to meet this handsome stranger."

"So fickle we are. Well, I hope the boy isn't crazy about the color blue."

"I saw flip-flops."

"Okay. He'll do. So, is that your final answer?"

"Yes. Now, take that little book you have tucked up under your arm and go have you a lovely lunch. By the way, what did your mother say last night about her little adventure?"

"Well, so much for you and your predictions, but my mother slept outside all night."

"I know. Mine slept out there with her. Came home walking like she was ninety. Holding her back and fighting tears."

"Are you serious?"

"Yes, our prissy-wissy mothers—and I say that totally respect-fully—slept outside, all alone . . ."

"Oh, no, they weren't alone."

Paige's face contorted. "What?"

"I mean, my father slept outside too."

"Oh? Oh . . . oh . . . isn't that the sweetest thing you have ever heard?"

"Sweet? Ridiculous maybe, but sweet, give me a break. Grown adults, one strapped to a slab of stone, sleeping in sleeping bags on a sidewalk. Not to mention I hear it made the front page. There is nothing sweet about that."

"Ooh. Like you aren't in the paper enough," she said, making shameless reference to the number of times my mother chooses to publicize my performances in print. My cell phone rang. It was my mother. I sent her to voice mail.

"Your mother?"

"Yes."

"She'll call again."

"She always does. But back to you . . . this isn't about me, this, oh yes, this is totally about my parents." I waved my cell phone at her chest. "And yours too, apparently. Because your mother is with her again today." I made for the door and turned back around. "Anyway, I'm changing my last name first thing Monday morning."

"There's not a soul that would blame you, honey."

"I know."

"Eat a crab cake for me."

"I'm eating two."

"He should keep his religious convictions to himself," one storeowner quipped to another. The streets of Savannah were still busy with murmurs.

"Why? So you can be comfortable? That's part of the problem, isn't it, that everyone's so comfortable the truth that used to make us uncomfortable doesn't anymore?"

"Who are you? God?"

I walked past, losing them somewhere between yelling and cursing. It was evident not much work besides eating, exercising, and engaging were getting done today.

At the Gryphon Tea Room I took a seat in the raised area that looks out the grand picture window at the front of the store. It's an old apothecary, which still reflects the practice of an era gone by with its deep, rich, wood-encased window seats and chairs. Small drawers line the back wall. Today it is known more for its crab cakes and desserts than its medicine. Of course, their cheesecake can cure anything that ails as far as I'm concerned.

After placing my order, I took up my book and ignored the blinking message light on my phone. But a rapid movement drew my eye off the page and out the large window. Had I realized before I turned who it was, I simply would not have looked. My book would have become as interesting as a McDonald's Coke after a twelve-week fast. But no, inquisitive me, Miss Can't-Let-a-Maniac-Pass-by-a-Window-Without-Looking, looked.

There she stood, dressed like she was going to a parade. The reigning Miss Savannah United States of America, my newfound friend, beamed at me. I call her "friend" because I told her only a couple days ago at lunch that is what I'd be, her friend. She looked pitiful that day. She suckered me in. And now, seeing her out there waving like a hummingbird on speed, I knew with certainty that friends were an evaporating commodity in her world.

I smiled as best I could, hoping she would be appeased and prance on by. No such luck. She pranced herself right up to my table and plopped her prance right down beside me.

"I can't believe you're here! Sitting right where we did only a couple weeks ago, when our paths crossed for the first time. I just can't believe it. This is like fate or something. It's like our two-week anniversary!"

Eyes darted in our direction, causing my own to grow large. In this day and age, that wasn't a remark I wanted misconstrued. "Please don't say that so loud." I smiled at the gawking patrons. "Anyway, you look mighty nice for a Saturday."

"Oh well honey, with all the television cameras happening around here, it's best to look your best." She giggled, beside herself with the possibility of celebrity. Sun-streaked tresses teased her bare arm, and her flirty brown fifties-style sundress with a pink ribbon waistband spread pretty as a picture on the padded pew. "You know I heard Julia Roberts was discovered on the streets of Smyrna, Georgia, just for her smile."

"You don't say? Well, I didn't know that." I noticed a tourist across the room taking in the beauty next to me.

"No, I'm joking. But she should have been. She really moved to New York after she graduated from Campbell High School in 1985 and got her first role in the Western *Blood Red* in 1986. Anyway, people say I have that same fabulous smile." She grinned from ear to ear, just in case such information was lost on me. "Okay! Enough about me. Can you believe what your mother is doing? I just think it's awesome. Miss Victoria is such the heroine. Such a woman of power and confidence. I just think she's amazing. You should be so proud of her, out there strapped to that monument like a beauty queen strapped to a rhinestone." She slapped me rather forcefully on the arm.

I rubbed the spot. Didn't we have this conversation yesterday? This caused me to wrinkle my forehead and tilt my head. A move

I learned from Duke. Maybe he did know tricks. My food came at that moment, so I didn't have to worry about pretending to respond to her tribute to my mother, even though none of it warranted a response.

She wrinkled her nose at my beautiful crab cakes, but looked a tad more receptive to the salad. She picked up my unfortunately closed book and studied the cover. "Well, what are you reading? Ooh, Ronald Reagan. I just loved him."

I stared at her, knowing that the only thing she read was *People* magazine. "Oh, you did, did you?"

"Oh, yeah. His life was so interesting."

"And what exactly do you know about his life?" I took a big ol' bite of my delicious lunch, all covered in a mayonnaise-based dressing.

"Ooh, that's disgusting," she said, staring at my mouth as I chewed, but losing interest quickly. "Okay, what do I know about Reagan?" She clasped her hands together and sat more erectly. "Well, he was born on February 6, 1911, as Ronald Wilson Reagan. His mother was Nelle and his father was John, and they had him in Tampico, Illinois."

I stopped chewing and looked behind me to make sure no one was feeding her this information. I comforted myself with the fact that anyone who knew much about history could know this information. Not that I had remembered it, and I was actually reading a book about him, but that didn't matter. However, I felt confident that there was no way Miss Amber Topaz herself could know all of this. She was a beauty queen, for crying out loud.

"Well, that's nice." At least I could act appreciative of her knowledge.

"Yes, I know that's nice, but I know tons more from his days at Eureka College, where he played football and starred in their theater program. After he graduated, he married Jane Wyman and had two beautiful children, Maureen and Michael." I stopped eating and sat back in my chair, crossed my arms, and stared in amazement at this MAC-covered walking encyclopedia.

"So in '52 he married Nancy, and the rest of their life was lived in front of us."

She paused to breathe and I was about to congratulate her, when she started again. Now, I thought her pageant stories were bad. I mean, try to sit with this woman through her tales of beauty queens who tape their boobies, wear dresses backward, and spray "sticky tack" on their behinds to keep their bathing suits from riding up, and you just want to cross on over. But I didn't like history in school, and I really didn't care to hear the book I was reading recited to me by a beauty-queen bombshell. No matter how long I lived, I would always believe she was fed this information through some earpiece connected to a lunatic outside in a black van.

"He turned to politics eventually and became governor of California in 1966, and then he became the fortieth president in 1980. He had 489 electoral votes to Jimmy Carter's 49. How is that for kicking some bu—. Ooh, I almost said the *b* word. How unseemly for a lady."

Other than that she didn't miss a beat. "But nothing can compare to that moment when Reagan stood behind that podium"—and with those words the queen herself rose, put her hand over her heart, and hollered loud enough for the people outside to hear—"MR. GORBACHEV, TEAR DOWN THIS WALL." However, when Reagan said the word *wall*, I'm sure it didn't have two syllables.

The entire restaurant seemed to contemplate whether they needed to rise as well. I'm certain a myriad of thoughts such as saluting, standing, or slapping ran through more minds than my own, because by the time she said *Gorbachawf,* everyone had whiplash. She sniffled and wiped her eyes of either real or artificial tears. Who could be sure?

She leaned into me. I withdrew. "That very speech, Savannah Phillips, set those people free. Set me free too." She giggled. "It helped me win the title of Miss Catfish Stomp Festival Queen when I ended my interview competition with it. Those poor judges were ready to enlist by the time I got through."

If I doubted it before, I now knew for sure that another Victoria actually existed in this world. Amber reached down to pick up my book and studied the cover again.

"Ooh, Peggy Noonan wrote this. I love her too. This is her fifth book, you know?" I can honestly say, I had no idea. "Yes, it is. Her first book was *What I Saw at the Revolution* followed by *Life, Liberty, and the Pursuit of Happiness*, then *Simply Speaking*." She set the book down. "Oh! And my favorite, *The Case Against Hillary Clinton*, and now the one you're reading."

Finally it seemed that she was finished. My mouth hung somewhere around my chest.

She reached down to pick my book up one more time. I swept in and snatched that puppy away and pulled it to my chest.

"How?" was all I could come up with.

"I know you don't think I read, Savannah. But to graduate with a 4.0 you have to read sometimes."

Had I been eating, I would have choked.

She noticed my expression. She had a response. She always has a response. "And if you ever compete in a pageant interview"—she couldn't be that bright to even conjure up such a scenario—"you'll know, that one shall not tread those waters ill-prepared. Well, gotta run. So great to talk with you on our two-week anniversary. Your stories always intrigue me." She leaned over me in a whisper. "Kisses, kisses." And with that, the personification of Trivial Pursuit for Beauty Pageants made her exit before an audience no less flabbergasted than yours truly.

I hadn't even graduated with a 4.0.

Truth be told, my writing scores were high, but most other grades proved how inept I was at anything other than telling a tale.

I eyed my cold crab cakes, which didn't look as appetizing as before. Then the same voice that had filled the restaurant with a Southern-belle rendition of Reagan let loose with a shriek.

"Stop him! Stop him! He stole my purse!"

CHAPTER SEVEN

'm going to stomp you into the pavement, you little sucker!" screamed the woman who was too ladylike to say *butt* only moments before.

I took off after Amber in a full-speed run, which wasn't so easy in flip-flops. But the long-legged maniac in heels was so close to the little fella, I was certain he could smell her Altoid. Obviously, she could run as furiously as she could wave. Her sundress flowed behind her as if created for such activity. And her head was back, Forrest Gump–style. I declare I heard the *Chariots of Fire* sound track playing in my head.

The thief rounded a corner, and a couple men from the store across the street got into the chase. But no one could keep up with Wonder Woman. As if in slow motion, I saw her hand reach out and grab his ponytail, a rebellion he would live to regret for the rest of his adult life. That and the fact that the crotch of his jeans flopped around his knees, preventing a long stride. He clung to his waistband and her purse with equal measures of desperation.

She yanked him to the ground in one tug, hiked up her skirt, and sat on top of his chest like she was The Rock in a cage match.

The three of us in pursuit reached them and doubled over trying to catch our breath, while Amber barely panted. The top of the rather unintelligent youth's wide-eyed head stuck out from one side of her flowing sundress, and his tennis shoes pointed out the other. He wriggled in vain. Her knees pinned his arms, and she perched her hands atop her rather wee waist.

"Who's your mama, young man?" None of us were quite sure what information she sought from this kid who would just as soon whip out a gun as look at you.

He screamed a response anyway. "You are!"

"I'm not your mama!" She slapped him upside the head with her hand.

"Ow!" I said, before he could let out a holler. But his holler followed shortly thereafter. He squirmed some more.

"You may as well forget about getting away from me!" She snatched her pretty little brown and pink bag from his hands. "I could give you a karate chop right in your throat and maim you for the rest of your existence, you little creep. Think you're going to steal my purse?" She finally tried to rise. The two out-of-breath gentlemen quickly found their composure and swooped over to help the damsel, who obviously didn't need it but accepted theirs with her Julia Roberts smile and rapidly returning manners. "Oh, thank you. How sweet."

The bewildered youth tried to stand, but before the two men could grab him, the crazed queen grabbed him by his ponytail and pulled him to her side. "No sirree, little fella." Her six-foot frame towered over his prepubescent self. "You are going with me, and we are going to find your mama!"

So she really *did* mean, "Who's your mama?" She brushed off her skirt, flung her bag back over her shoulder, and thanked us for our assistance, albeit nothing more than emotional.

"How . . . did you . . . run like that?" I asked, still leaning and panting, as she dragged this weary roamer back up the side street.

"Oh, number-one sprinter in track and field. If he'd have gone for distance I'd have never made it." She flashed that smile and winked.

Really. She was probably number-one in the Boston Marathon as well.

She tugged at the boy's ponytail, and I knew no one would ever be so glad to see his mama compared to the Mary Poppins that had a hold of him right now. Amber Topaz, Director of Tourism, was about to give him a tour of Savannah, in a way he had never experienced.

"I know you think I'm impotent," she said underneath her breath to the poor thief. The gentlemen fidgeted and darted their eyes downward at the sound of those words. "But you're about to see how potent I am, little boy."

"She meant *incompetent*," I assured the gentlemen.

They still looked scared.

"And she got a 4.0," I told them. "Go figure." I followed the perfectly coiffed and statuesque beauty who had a death grip on a ponytail and tried not to laugh. No doubt these two wouldn't be running to another woman's rescue anytime soon.

And every person on this street now staring out of windows and gawking from street corners knew for certain they would never try to steal the handbag of one Miss Amber Topaz Childers, the reigning Miss Savannah United States of America.

I myself kept my eyes out for a black van.

The crab cakes had lost their cakiness, the salad its crispness, and the hot tea . . . well, it wasn't so hot anymore. The message light on my cell phone still blinked. In the commotion I had left all of my possessions at the table.

"Darling," came the voice on the message, "I'm so sorry we didn't talk yesterday. The events here just went so quickly I didn't even have time to grab my floss. But you're never going to guess who's having me on their show tonight. I'm going to be on Rita Cosby from FOX News. I would love for you to come watch. She's

just the cutest little thing. Anyway, I missed you last night for dinner. And I want to see you today. I love you. Make sure you eat,
darling. Call me if you get time. Or just stop on by. I'm not going
anywhere." She concluded with an annoying giggle.

Lord have mercy. If she starts getting interviewed, she might
just run the rest of our lives from the sidewalk.

I picked up my book. Maybe if I could actually finish reading
it, I could find some solace from a quiet, confident man. He didn't
say much. But he meant what he said. Maybe I would try that. Not
speak often, just speak wisely.

I took back to the streets of Savannah. The United States
Courthouse and its activities drew onlookers to the square as mag-
netically as Frodo's ring drew others to darkness. As I approached
the square, I noticed that a small lectern with microphones perched
all over it stood nearby.

What a grand scene. The backdrop is truly one of the most
majestic settings in Savannah. The stately building is made of
Georgia marble and is only three stories, but it takes up an entire city
block. The front reads "United States Post Office and Courthouse"
and was built in 1898, but the post office was closed years ago.
Remnants of it exist in the prestigious foyer, however, where empty,
aged boxes line the front wall, their secrets locked up forever.

The sidewalk that spreads out in front of the courthouse is
lined at the street with fresh flowers and tall evergreen trees. Black
iron poles are evenly distributed from one end of the block to the
other, as if they were hitching posts for horses in an era that whispers down back alleys and lives on in women's conversations.

The building can be entered from huge arched doorways at
the far left and right of the building. Under each arch, two large
swinging glass doors with aged brass trim and handles usher
people into the world of security guards and metal detectors, as
it has been since the building was turned over to the Federal
Courthouse.

Six large windows line up between the two brilliant arches.

Above each arch, on both the second and third floors, architecturally timeless balconies indicate the judges' chambers. In front of the building, part of the sidewalk expands into a half moon, where the monument of the moment and my mother made their stand.

Judge Hoddicks came out of the imposing right front doors and descended the marble stairs.

Every journalist, even those who had been catnapping only moments before, rushed the podium, yelling questions and waving microphones in total pandemonium as the judge prepared to speak.

He raised his sixty-eight-year-old hand to quiet the crowd. It worked. I searched for a glimpse of my mother, but the crowd from this morning had probably grown by fifty or so. Judge Hoddicks tapped the microphone. I could hear just fine even at this part of the square. He spoke.

"Ladies and gentlemen. Thank you for being here. We just received word from a federal judge who says this monument, like the ones before it, violates the Constitution's ban on government promotion of religion."

The crowd went crazy. Some were cheering, others were booing, and the reporters started screaming questions as if Judge Hoddicks might actually start answering them. He raised his hands again. His piercing blue eyes scanned the swarm of reporters and flock of pilgrims.

"Please, ladies and gentlemen, I am not through. The order informed us that we have exactly six days to remove this monument, or it will be removed for us."

The onslaught started all over. Standing back in amazement, I found myself interested to watch this moment in history unfold around me. Even little children too young to have convictions of their own beyond food and TV preferences were out here yelling the convictions of their parents.

"I know, I know." Judge Hoddicks started again. "This is a very emotional topic for us all. But please know that I will be petitioning the Supreme Court to stop this order from being enforced. As details become available, I will keep you informed. All I ask is that each party in this extremely passionate issue respect each other. Thank you."

Judge Hoddicks walked over to the vicinity of the monument and my mother. The reporters followed him until he returned to the steps of the courthouse and vanished inside.

The journalists turned their attention to my mother. Sergeant Millings stood in the background, slapping his nightstick against his leg.

"Mrs. Phillips, Mrs. Phillips! How long will you be out here?'

"As long as it takes." She grinned from ear to ear.

I can't wait to see that.

"Why are you doing this?" another hollered above the rest.

"Because this is our heritage. And I want it for my children, for my daughter—"

Please don't . . .

"—Savannah, or Savannah from Savannah as she is known here, and for my son, Thomas, who works with our wonderful Judge Hoddicks."

I am certifiably ruined.

I prayed for a quick end. Lightening. Earthquake. Sergeant Millings's bullet. I would have even settled for a dart through the chest. But the woman had found a television camera willing to record and a crowd willing to listen. It was a full fifteen minutes before the reporters returned to their trucks or their naps.

And me? Well, my next human-interest story had found me. Right on Wright Square.

CHAPTER EIGHT

The reporter couldn't hide his admiration for the raven-haired, expensive-handbag stranger. I, too, watched her closely. Her gestures were few but graceful. Her laugh was feminine and seemingly genuine. And her rapport with the journalist made them seem lifelong friends. Before he could ask his final question, she patted his arm and departed into the courthouse.

I turned to leave when the sight of two young lovers heading my way distracted me once again. Since I found out my longtime-love, Grant, was getting married, and not to me, something inside me had begun to notice the expressions of love. And these two were virtual CliffsNotes. Looking closer, one face seemed awfully familiar. Grant. I ducked behind one of the trees but kept an eye wrapped around the trunk of the live oak. I knew our paths would cross now and then. In 2.2 square miles of history, it's inevitable. But why did it have to be today?

Seeing him walking up the street in khaki shorts and a T-shirt, brown leather flip-flops generating Savannah's only breeze, the overwhelming feeling of loss rushed through me again. To lose one of your best friends, who also happens to have the name you hope to share for the rest of your life, is hard for any young woman.

Of course our relationship dissolved over years of drifting apart. But I had been so self-absorbed that the drifting was lost on me until I found myself clinging to a piece of driftwood and watching the *Titanic* go down. But here was proof. We had drifted so far apart that this flaming redhead had easily docked her little long-legged self right between us. This was the first time my eyes had seen her. The child had hair as auburn as a Southern sunset. It was strikingly beautiful, in a ratty sort of way. A tad poofy. I pulled the ends of my stick-straight mane around to inspect it. I noticed a split end and stuck it in my mouth to try to chew it off. It was that or the fingernails.

She was so tall, and leggy and anorexic. Poor child probably didn't even eat. Couldn't hardly keep her pants up. She had an ample bosom. I was certain they were fake, and instinctively crossed my arms in front of my chest. Paige and I had already determined before we even saw her that she had to be fake. Any girl who goes to an all-girl college could have nothing better to do than sit around and inject things into herself.

I called her a prepackaged Barbie who would probably be a "four-foot-eleven, forty-five-year-old mother of two," if relieved of all her processed beauty.

Paige declared I was talking about my own mother.

I told her not to compare my mother to this woman. That the only thing not real on Vicky was her hair color. Of course we knew that was a lie.

I tried to reach Paige on her cell. She didn't answer. As they came down the street, I gradually scooted around the tree to keep myself hidden.

"Who you hiding from, Savannah?" The voice ran down my spine like ice. Turning around wasn't necessary to know Mr. Curly Locks himself had entered the square.

"Shh. I don't want Grant to see me."

"Who's Grant?"

"None of your business. Now would you please go away and leave me alone?"

"Oh, an old boyfriend." His eyes scanned the square, stopped. "Well, old boyfriend looks like he has a new girlfriend."

"Fiancée, actually. Now get!" I said holding on to the trunk.

He kicked out the kickstand on his blue bike and made it evident he wasn't going anywhere. "Do you know what you look like?"

"A woman annoyed? Because that's what I am."

"No, a girl who's seen one too many bad *Charlie's Angels* flicks."

"What do you know about love?"

"I know it doesn't usually involve hiding behind a tree, chewing on your hair."

I spit my hair out of my mouth. Then I noticed Grant and little Merry Sunshine were walking into the vicinity of my mother. "It was!" I turned to glare at him. "Yes it was love! But not anymore."

"Looks like the new lady's getting to meet your mother," he said, nodding in their direction.

I turned and watched in horror as the love of my life introduced his flaming redheaded future squaw to the woman who, by all intents, purposes, and DNA, was my mother. Vicky leaned over and hugged Grant and then—ugh!—hugged the woman next to him.

"Ooh, looks like they might get invited to dinner."

I turned back to my thorn. "Do you take pleasure in my pain?"

"Pain?! You've got to be kidding."

"No. I'm not kidding. Now would you *please* take your little bike and your little mind and your little self and go away?"

"You are going to have to see them eventually."

"I'm going to have to do a lot of things eventually, but I would prefer not to have to do all of them in one afternoon. Now *get!*"

He placed his perfectly tanned hands on his handlebars, using the most beautiful part of any man—his arms—to lift his body onto his bicycle. His khaki shorts revealed nice legs, but I refused to look.

"Well, I'll see you Monday."

"Yeah, yeah, Monday! And if you want to know, Mr. Smarty Pants, my dog can get ice out of the ice maker all by himself."

He crinkled his brow, contemplating the sheer looniness of my statement. "What are you talking about?"

"Are you still here?" I asked, lifting my hands and bobbing my head.

"You are so odd." I could hear him riding away and turned to notice that he was looking back at me as well. Before I knew it I had stuck my tongue out at him. I was walking in the land of the mature today, for sure. So much for becoming a woman of few words and great wisdom. He threw his head back in laughter, almost running right into a ninety-year-old woman walking her dog. I threw my head back in mimicked disgust.

My mother was now alone. She had even ditched the umbrella, as the towering building now shielded the great summertime aggressor. But there were two who weren't alone. I watched the hand-in-hand lovebirds as they walked up Bull Street. How fitting. He slipped his arm around her waist to pull her toward him, the same arm that had pulled me to him a thousand times. Sickening. My eyes wanted to turn away, to escape from the memories. But they couldn't. They were held captive by recollection, the recollection of a love let go. That flew away, and unlike that stupid saying, never flew back home. Of course my bird feeder was empty and rather nasty, so who would blame the poor bird for finding someone more willing to feed it.

Action near the lovely slab of marble resumed, seizing my attention and relieving it of pathetic metaphors and poor misguided notions.

"You are wasting the taxpayers' money and the people's time, and on top of that you are alienating people who don't share your beliefs, virtually attacking them in their own city."

The voice that responded belonged to the woman of high-heeled mules and now-rumpled blue suit. "Honey, if anyone knows the people of this city, I do."

"Do you really?" I watched as the alluring raven-haired woman walked over to my mother in some rather sharp-looking black open-toed sling-backs.

"Yes, I do really." Mother tugged a tad at her chains.

Her adversary inched closer. "If there ever was a time that cities across this nation needed to operate in unity, it is now."

"Are you calling me divisive?" Mother asked, getting as close as her leash would allow.

"Misguided maybe." The beauty stopped within striking distance of my mother. And by the look on my mother's face, that might not have been such a wise move.

Red flashing lights atop television cameras helped Mother regain her composure. "Well, honey, I'm sorry you feel that way, but your litigation could be considered just as misguided and divisive, depending on whom you ask."

I wondered if intervention might be necessary. I searched the crowd for a suitable arbiter. Sergeant Millings leaned against the side of the courthouse, picking his nose. No option existed but one. Me. So I marched my flip-flop-clad feet into the combat zone.

Now, the last thing I wanted was to be on the evening news for a situation that I honestly cared nothing about. So, I tried to stay calm. I laughed a half laugh as I approached, trying to make mother cool down and back off. But then, she had to speak.

"Oh, Savannah darling. I was wondering when you were going to come see your mother." She squealed, reaching out to me. I stayed beyond her reach, preventing her from stroking my head.

Why do mothers stroke their children's heads? Is it a reflex? Is it a vitamin deficiency? Is it a superiority complex? It's the same way a man greets his golden retriever: "Look at my baby; isn't he a good boy?" So I just left her there. Arms extended and hands moving in a pitiful stroking motion through the air.

The stranger tried to place my face. The craziness of her line of work probably had her encountering a thousand unknown faces.

"Hey, Mother. Why don't you calm down?" I said this under my breath while trying to grin at both the cameras and the striking stranger. "She's just trying to do her job, like you're trying to do, well, whatever it is you're trying to do."

"I'm making a statement, Savannah." Mother dropped her hands, most definitely using her outside voice.

I continued to whisper, hoping it would be infectious. "Yes, ma'am, I see that you are."

The whispering didn't catch on. And Mother turned her attention toward the stranger instead of me. "A statement that apparently this young lady needs to hear!"

The other young lady spoke just as loud. "It's one I've heard, ma'am, a thousand times by a thousand different people and in a thousand different ways."

"Well, you obviously didn't get it!"

I looked at the dark-haired lady. "Sorry, she takes everything that happens in this city very personally."

"Savannah, don't you dare apologize for me to this woman. She has an agenda just like I do, just wrapped in a different package." Mom's voice turned snide for a lady in expensive shoes and a designer suit. "She chooses subtlety. She sneaks up on you. I choose a forward march." Well, it would have to be a forward march in place, apparently. The chain only extended so far. I expected Amber to appear any moment and inform our new tourist of her need to "Tear down this wall!"

"Yes, Mother, you do." I agreed. "Anyway, this will be fought in the courts. We don't have to fight on the sidewalk." I gestured to the sidewalk I desperately desired to melt into.

"Savannah, think what you will, but this is where battles are won—not in courtrooms, but in the daily lives of sacrificial, everyday, ordinary people."

In twenty-four years I had never heard my mother describe

herself as ordinary. Replaying the speech in my mind, I wasn't certain if she intended the adjective for herself or the situation in general. But it was a milestone nonetheless.

Raven spoke again. "You're right, ma'am. This is an issue people are willing to fight for. And it is an issue people have died for. And I am here to fight for the people who need a representative. We are going to fight civil-liberties violations any time and any place we see them occurring. The Bill of Rights will be protected as long as we have a voice. We are here doing the noble thing. You are here trying to take people captive once again to the prison of narrow-mindedness."

"Young lady," Vicky said, tugging at her chains like Duke on a leash, spotting FooFoo the cat, "we are not violating anyone's civil liberties. We are simply trying to make it clear that we have a voice. That there is a right and wrong. That this nation was built upon laws that were intentional and clear, and we are going to stand up for them, whether that interferes with the *agendas* of others or not."

I wasn't sure why I was still there. If I had it my way, I would be sitting in a park, reading a book, looking forward to going home and eating roast and potatoes or pork tenderloin and wild rice. Instead I was standing in the Savannah heat, surrounded by reporters (my least favorite of all people, though I was one myself), a mediator between my temporarily insane mother and this interesting visitor. Trust me, this was not my idea of how to spend a Saturday.

About the time Vicky was to go at it again, raven-lady's cell phone rang. "Ms. Austin," she answered with undue calm. "Yes. Okay. Hold on one moment." She turned her attention back to us. "If you ladies will excuse me, I've got to take this call. I'm sure we'll see each other again soon." And with that she left us alone. Well, as alone as one can be with television cameras, photographers, sojourners, a crazy white woman, and a gigantic slab of marble.

CHAPTER NINE

My reunion with my mother could have been spent debating why it had taken twenty-four hours for me to actually come see her. But that didn't appeal to me, so I chose another option.

"Well, Mother, if this doesn't work, you can take your case to the president."

Her eyes glazed over and the biggest smile swept across her face. To see a grown, married woman with a crush, well, it border-lined on just plain sad. "Oh, I just love him, don't you?"

"Well, I have some amazing news for you," I said shamelessly.

Her brown eyes danced, as she clasped her bound hands together. "Bigger than Rita Cosby?"

I let my eyes get as big as her own and spoke as if to a five-year-old. "Yes, ma'am, bigger than Rita Cosby. You, my sweet lady, are going to get to see the president on Friday. He's coming here."

My mother screamed in sheer delight. "Bushie is going to be here on Friday?" She started to run her hands through her hair and over her wrinkled pants. It was a woeful attempt to fix herself up.

"No," I responded. "The president of the United States of

America is going to be here on Friday. *Bushie* is the pet name of a wife for her husband."

Then she grabbed her chest. "Savannah, don't play with me. If you're playing a joke, I'll whip you from here to South Carolina."

"I'm not." I laughed, though the thought of her whipping me was not attractive. This woman used a flyswatter, the most disgusting thing imaginable to discipline a child with. You wouldn't think this antibacterial champion would want children with fly innards attached to their tails going around town. Thomas was still scarred from his last encounter with it. He was thirteen and in the shower and showing a bad attitude, banging his fists on the wall, and the petite little fireball snatched open the shower door and unloaded on his pubescent body with reckless abandon.

But that was a distant memory. The woman was downright full of glee, clapping her hands together like a three-year-old being exonerated of bath time. "Bushie is coming? You have got to be kidding me." She slapped me on the arm. I had moved too close. "I can't believe this! This is unbelievable!" She reached up, threw her arms around my neck, and cameras could be heard clicking all around.

I whispered into her well-adorned ear. "If this is on the front page of any paper, I will not be happy."

"Oh, get a grip, Savannah." She pushed me away. The woman might be bipolar. "The president's coming. Oh Lord, what will I wear?"

I looked at her in astonishment. "It won't matter what you wear if you're still in the middle of this square, chained to a monument, now, will it? You won't even get to see him."

"Oh, yes I will. I'll see him. We'll just make sure he has to come by here if this matter isn't resolved before then." Of course "we" would. The woman ran this city. Who was I to think she wouldn't dictate the president of the United States' very itinerary?

But I needed to bring her back to more critical matters. "I know you are not staying out here an entire week."

She retained a significantly steady resolve in her eyes. "I'll stay out here as long as it is necessary, Savannah. You do those kind of things when you believe in something."

She couldn't be well. We needed a doctor that made house— I mean, sidewalk—calls. She needed to be medicated. Or maybe she was medicated. Maybe this was like the time we flew to L.A. and hit severe turbulence, and she took enough Xanax for a three-hundred-pound man. They were drugs her friend Theresa gave her when Mother mentioned she had panic attacks when she flew. Not that drug-swapping is a crime or anything.

By the time we landed, she was so out of it she needed Dad to carry her to the car. But he refused. Well, it wasn't his fault. He had warned her clearly as she popped three of the things into her perfectly painted mouth. "If you take those things and don't wake up, I will leave you right here on this plane."

And he did. But when faced with the choice of leaving her on the plane and letting her fly to Kalamazoo, or planting her behind on top of a luggage cart, Thomas and I saw a delightful opportunity. We just smiled at the flight attendant as we carried her off the plane. Thomas had her upper body and I toted her feet. Had she not just recently cut her hair all flippy, then it could have covered her face and salvaged a minute amount of her reputation. But those red lips were in clear view.

We threw her dead weight over the basket of a luggage cart and pushed her right through the terminal, arms and feet dangling like a Charlie McCarthy doll. I made Thomas take pictures so we could blackmail her later. We took pictures of her in the men's bathroom. We took pictures of her picking her nose. We took pictures of her sitting in the race-car machine in the arcade. We took pictures of her sprawled out on a terminal bench with a *GQ* magazine spread across her chest. We didn't stop until Dad called us from his cell phone in the car, where he was waiting at the curb.

By the time she woke up, about three days later, the pictures had been printed in duplicate, one set strewn across her bed. She never told us where she put them. We never asked. We both just always knew that there were duplicates at our immediate disposal.

"Are you doing drugs?" I asked.

"Savannah Grace Phillips, I should just as soon slap you as look at you for that comment."

"You didn't answer my question."

"I'm fixing to answer your question with my hand upside your head."

"Why is it you can ask me if I do drugs, but I can't ask you?"

"Because I'm your mother. I can ask you anything I pretty well please."

"Well, whatever you're on, I hope you come off of it soon and come home, where you should be."

"Where are you going?"

"I said I would come by and say hey. So hey. Love ya. Talk to you soon. I've got to figure out what we're going to have for dinner for the *next week*." And with that I left Vicky to figure out what to do with her "matter." But she wouldn't miss me now. Bushie was coming. Who was I compared to him?

"I need a lawyer."

My new friend Gregory's voice came on over the other end, calm as always. Gregory is a law clerk from Jackson, Mississippi, who helped me out on my last article about rigged beauty pageants. "You have one. Bought and paid for with a buck, remember?"

"Do you have craziness in Jackson?"

"Not until you came here and brought your craziness with you over a rigged beauty pageant."

"I think you just called me crazy."

"Maybe. Judge Tucker has talked to Judge Hoddicks. I hear what's going on over there," he said, sounding as if he was chewing something.

"What are you eating?"

"Lunch."

"Oh, that was clever. Anyway, why don't you come down here and do some lawyering stuff, get my mother unchained from this granite, and make my life less eventful before Monday."

I was certain his chocolate legs were propped up on a desk or sofa or ottoman somewhere as he snacked on whatever it was he was snacking and a beautiful white grin emerged across his face.

"Girl, you couldn't find less eventful if you were a contestant on *The Amazing Race* and searched the world over. You don't know anything but eventful."

I continued walking up Bull toward Forsythe Park with my book tucked safely under my arm. "I do. And I love that show, by the way. Actually tried to be a contestant. Me and Thomas sent in a video. Didn't even get a call back."

"Did you speak on the video?"

"Of course."

"Then that might be why you didn't get a callback."

"Do you hate me?"

He laughed. "No, silly, I don't hate you. But say what you will, you're weird. And you talk too much. But I will tell you that, knowing the law and the previous cases and their decisions, this monument case will probably be remedied sooner than later."

"By Monday?"

He laughed.

"Don't laugh. I'm serious."

"No, Sherlock, this won't be finished by Monday."

"Why? Why do you judicial types take so long to do anything? Just so you can bill people?"

"Honey, if I billed you for all the needless energy you drain from me, you wouldn't see your own apartment until you had private quarters six feet under."

"Aren't you full of yourself today. But I need you. My mother is chained to a monument, harassing a sophisticated lady from Atlanta. Really, this needs to come to a close quickly."

"Well, I might see you this week. Judge Tucker is thinking about coming down to help Judge Hoddicks."

"Oh good. So, be thinking then."

"About what?"

"About how to speed this thing up."

"Okay, Savannah, I'll be doing just that."

"Call me if you think of something good."

"You just wait by your little phone."

"I will, smarty butt. I will." With that I hung up, thankful that I had been able to say *butt* without it being recorded for the evening news.

"Oh, I'm so sorry," I said to the blur that careened into my shoulder as I turned the corner onto Drayton Street.

The blur didn't respond. But it looked vaguely familiar. *It can't be. She doesn't have food hanging from her shirt. There's no way. You think? Maybe it is.* It was. Emma Riley. She and I had experienced another run-in of sorts last week. Actually, I had taken it upon myself to tell her wretched story to the entire city without bothering to care whether she wanted it told. She cared. Oh, did she ever care. The extent of her care reminded me now that it would not be in my best interests to reintroduce myself. No need to make an otherwise miserable day more miserable. She continued up the street, and I headed in the direction of the park, thinking maybe a pinch would prove whether I was just having a nightmare of a day.

"Ow!" I hollered. Yep. Sure enough. I was *wide* awake.

CHAPTER TEN

Saturday and parks go hand in hand for most of us in Savannah. Not so much today. Maybe it was the growing stickiness and encroaching summer temperatures. Walks would be done in the relative cool of the morning or the doable steaminess of the evening. But the action up the street played a greater role in keeping people away today, I was certain.

An empty bench on the front pathway of the park gave me a perfect view of the fountain in the middle, as well as the Oglethorpe Club on Bull Street and the Armstrong Building, which houses the law offices of Bouham, Williams, & Levy, directly across the street from it.

The Oglethorpe Club is the oldest gentleman's club in Georgia. They have two prohibitions. One: No female members. Two: A woman can come with her husband, but she has to wear a dress. And an unwritten law: Your money must be old. Old money looks down on new money. For some reason, if you weren't born with it, it's not legitimate. Never quite made sense to me, because somewhere down the line it was new to somebody. Famed Savannian Jim Williams couldn't get into the club, so he just bought the monstrous Armstrong Building right across the street.

This city and its money have always intrigued me. Most complain about what they don't have while the minority can't seem to get enough. Either way, everybody's trying to get more, causing one to wonder if there ever really is such thing as *enough*.

The lady who sat down on the park bench beside me forced me back into the present. "Beautiful day, isn't it?" she said, wiping her black brow with a yellowed hanky. She hummed softly. A familiar melody, but one I couldn't place.

"Yes, yes it is."

She reached into her well-worn straw bag and pulled out an apple. "Would you like a bite?" she asked, extending her snack.

I giggled, wondering if she would want it back after I had taken a bite. "No, thank you. I just ate actually." Well, had attempted to anyway.

"Okay."

I watched as she stared off into the blue sky that could be seen through the row of houses that lined Drayton Street. She looked intently at the large house on the corner of Drayton and East Gaston, which Charlize Theron used as her residence in *The Legend of Bagger Vance*. The newcomer took up a large portion of the bench. Her worn dress, with a large floral print pattern and faded yellow background, had seen happier days. While perusing her petals, I realized that this was the lady that I had almost hit yesterday in the street. Her straw bag looked as if it had carried apples to park benches for years, but I had never seen her before yesterday.

She took her plump hand with its dirty fingernails and tried to smooth the wiry gray hair poking out from her strained attempt at a ponytail. Her haunting dark eyes seemed older, mysterious, and strange. But friendly. And peaceful.

"Ever wonder what goes on inside these houses?" She gave a

nod to the million-dollar homes. Her enunciation was precise and her dialect truly Southern.

I studied her dark face and watched the movement of her lips as she took a huge chunk out of the front side of her apple. I turned back to my book, hoping to make it clear I really didn't want conversation.

"No, ma'am. I really haven't."

"It's a shame. I would bet you, if I were a betting lady, that is, and not a churchgoing woman"—she gave a determined nod—"that most of the people inside of these homes are in need of something."

I wasn't sure what she meant by that. Her eyes stared so intently down the street that I might have believed she could see straight through the walls.

"Yes ma'am, people in need of something, I'm certain."

She didn't care that I was reading. She hadn't even noticed I was reading. And I was so overcome by curiosity, I had about forgotten I was reading too. I closed the book on my lap.

"Why do you think that?"

"Oh, sweet child, you can see it on their faces." Her ebony hand brought the apple to her lips again. A small dirt smudge on the top of her right cheek marred her otherwise flawless complexion. "They're tired. Just look around their eyes. You can see it. Exhaustion is everywhere. They even walk around like they're tired. And they drive like maniacs trying to get nowhere fast." I felt the sudden urge to cough.

"You all right, child?"

I nodded.

She continued. "This generation is either in a whirlwind rush or a state of utter fatigue. Most of them with sad stories to tell."

I couldn't recall seeing too many whirlwinds in Savannah since moving here years ago. "Hmm . . . hadn't really seen all that." My slight laugh caused her to look at me.

"Even you, little one. You're so young and cute, yet you're tired too. You try too hard. You think too much. You need to enjoy an apple, smell a flower, read a book." She pointed down to the book I would have been reading had we not been having this conversation. "I loved that Mr. Reagan. See what you can learn from him." She stood up to leave. "I'll see you again. Hope you're wearing a bigger smile next time."

Her plump cheeks rose with a smile, causing them to look like the apple she had just finished off. Yet her dark eyes pierced me one more time, causing me to stop and pause. But her smile was infectious. I returned it. Then I watched as she walked up the street and took another apple out of her bag, humming once again.

A tiny little man came rushing past her with his briefcase in his hand and cell phone plastered to his ear. I watched him as he approached my bench, jabbering as if the world was surely collapsing today, right here, in the middle of Forsythe Park around us both.

"What do you mean, you might lose this deal?!" he screamed into the phone. "You lose a sixty-million-dollar deal and you may as well close down the office!"

He sat down on my park bench, totally ignoring me and my book. He flung open his briefcase to find some piece of paper that was either clinging for dear life to another or was wadded up somewhere in the bottomless pit.

"You don't lose deals. You only make deals, Ken. You aren't playing with the little boys anymore; you're playing with the big dogs."

The voice on the other end made futile attempts to secure vindication. "I don't want to hear it. Do you want to keep your nice car and your private jet? Do you want to keep your fancy suits and your big house? Huh? Well, then don't screw up. Jesus, man, don't think for a minute there aren't a thousand men and women ready to take you down and get their name on your office. You better get it together and fast."

His hand finally pulled out a paper, and just about everything in his briefcase came with it. In frustration he threw the mess across the park bench, causing some of it to hit my leg. I pushed it back, which was the first time he even noticed me. He gave me an angry look as if somehow I had invaded his space. My raised right eyebrow made it clear who arrived first.

He grabbed all of the scattered papers and crammed them back into the abyss. It could be years before he ever found what he was actually looking for. He marched onward, still yelling at some lamentable creature all the way. He ascended the stairs of the Oglethorpe Club and disappeared.

I spent the walk home peeking in windows and looking down alleys expecting some precious Allen Funt wannabe to scream at me, "Smile! You're on *Candid Camera!*"

I smiled bigger than I had in years. Looked over every corner of that park, even stood up and held out my arms in case they didn't know I was ready to hear the truth. But no one came. No Allen Funt appeared. No nothing. Reaching the top step of home, I looked back one more time just in case. The only thing that appeared was my shadow.

Either I'm losing my mind, or either . . . well, I'm losing my mind. There really was no other option.

CHAPTER ELEVEN

A mirror can be a cruel thing. It can mock you. Even laugh at you. Today the thing was plumb near hysterical. I scowled at it in return. Looking back was a stranger. My tired, worn, twenty-four-year-old face mocked me. The lines on my forehead must have crept into place in an afternoon. Because they certainly weren't there this morning.

Who did this to me? Who stole my youth? I crinkled my brow up and down. Pulled the side of my eyes back only to discover I would make a woeful-looking Asian. And the process did nothing to remove the deeply embedded crow's-feet. My green eyes drooped and the corners of my lips turned downward. *I need BOTOX. I might need a facelift before I'm thirty. I need to find out who Mother's miracle worker is and stop this madness.*

As I let the corners of my eyes fall back to their basset-hound positions, the apple lady's words echoed in my mind. I was old and tired, ragged and worn, and it took a stranger to let me know. Even my golden brown hair didn't seem to shine. It, too, scoffed at me. My eye caught a sight in the far corner of my shower. It looked like mildew. My right eyebrow raised and the perils of "cleanliness is next to godliness" set in. Retrieving my rubber galoshes, knee pads, and rubber gloves from under the sink, I tore into that bathroom and scrubbed as if I were an exfoliant attacking a buildup of over-obsessing mothers and apathetic fathers.

Hours later I heard a sniffing noise near my behind, which was protruding from the commode, where my efforts were finishing off the pipes that connect the water to the toilet.

"Duke, if you're remotely dirty, you better get off my tile!" He laid himself down and rested his head flat against the tile, eyes looking up at me. "How was your day?"

He raised his right eyebrow.

"Long one, huh?"

He looked down.

I turned around to face him and removed my weapons of war. "Me too! Come on, let's go eat."

We trotted down the stairs, where Dad was putting some dishes in the dishwasher. "What are we going to do for dinner tonight?" I asked.

"I'm doing the same thing I did last night, Savannah." He turned around and leaned against the counter.

I sat down at a stool on the other side of the island. "How long is this charade going to continue? Pretty soon we're going to need clean underwear. What are we going to do then? I say we hire someone to clean the house, fix us dinner, and wash our clothes."

He laughed and crossed his arms. "Savannah, your mother has never let anyone clean her house in her life, and you know it."

"Oh yes, she did. Once."

"Key word in that phrase is *once.*"

No one likes to reminiscence about the day we had a housekeeper. It was the longest day of all of our lives. Victoria is a neat freak. I mean you can move a chair and before you've gotten up from it, she'll put it back to where it "should" be. Everything has its place. Everything has its order. And everything must match, coordinate, or complement. And everything must be clean. We were stupid to even think for a moment that she would appreciate someone's aid.

Shortly after mother went to work at the chamber of commerce, Dad lovingly convinced her that she needed a housekeeper. "I wouldn't dream of having her cook," he assured Vicky, "but at least let someone take some of the load. You can't do it all." He really had her best interests at heart.

Well, she assured him she could do it all and all of us would have been better off for believing her. Because for eleven years, mother has never ceased to resurrect the memory of Mrs. Gonzalez on cleaning days. As for Mrs. Gonzalez, every time she sees mother coming, she hightails it quicker than a cat caught in a tree facing a fire hose. Mrs. Gonzalez is the best in the business. Mother heard about her from Sheila, Paige's mother. In fact, Sheila still uses her to this day.

Mrs. Gonzalez hadn't been in Savannah long and at that time her English was still, shall we say, expanding. She arrived promptly at eight thirty. Mother felt it necessary to take the day off to show her how *she* cleaned the house. By noon Mrs. Gonzalez had done nothing but observe mother clean the house herself. They were doing sign language to communicate. Somewhere around three, Mother made it clear to Mrs. Gonzalez that she didn't think she was going to work out.

"You're . . . just . . . too . . . slow . . ." mother said loudly and slowly, as if volume would remedy Mrs. Gonzalez's inability to understand. Mother added to the insult by showing her the book *The Tortoise and the Hare.* When Mother pointed to the turtle and then to Mrs. Gonzalez, well, let's just say I wish I knew Spanish. But her sign language was interpretation enough.

For kicks, Paige and I will sometimes hug Mrs. Gonzalez and then just whisper Vicky's name in her ear so we can hear the beauty of the range of the Spanish language. Our combined ten years of Spanish study does us no good, but our imaginations fill in.

My dad's continued evaluation brought me back to the kitchen. "Besides, you, Thomas, and I are more than capable of cleaning this house and washing our own clothes."

"You left out meals."

"That is why God made take-out."

"Well, you are missing a wonderful opportunity here. And because mother is totally obsessive-compulsive and thinks no one can clean as well as she can, we could use this opportunity to relieve her of the stress. And on the days that she doesn't feel like cooking, like today, we would have someone here to help us."

"Savannah, I thought you were about to move out."

"I am, but not this week, and tonight I need food."

"I would say for someone so close to moving out, it's high time you wash your own clothes and fix your own meals. What did you do in college?"

"I took everything to the cleaners and ordered takeout or ate in the cafeteria."

"No kidding?"

"Does this look like a face of jest?"

"Girl, it is time you grew up." He walked past me and picked his car keys up off the table.

I turned my legs around in my stool to face him. "Well, I'm sure I can fix something."

"I'm sure you will. Your mother said she saw you briefly today. I expect that to be an everyday occurrence."

He walked over and kissed me and left me there sitting on the stool. Duke followed him, because it was evident who would be eating well tonight, and dogs have their priorities. He would endure stone for steak. He apparently would even endure Vicky. See, he wasn't real bright.

In the refrigerator, the only things that looked familiar were the condiments and the drinks. There was some dip in there that goes great with Doritos, and some sour cream that would be good on a baked potato. *You can do this, Savannah. You're about to be out on your own. Just give it a shot.*

Lady & Son's Cookbook rested on the bar by the telephone. Page 30 offered a lovely looking dish. Some kind of pasta bake. Remembering that most things start with boiling water, I pulled that off without much fanfare or pain. Mother had frozen some homemade ziti noodles and had homemade spaghetti sauce canned and in the pantry. An hour and a half later I pulled a pan full of pasta bake out of the oven.

Except there wasn't much more than a bowlful in the center of the baking dish. It looked nothing like the picture. Something was missing. Scanning the kitchen, trying desperately to figure out why my creation didn't resemble the picture, the tubular noodles resting in the colander in the sink caught my attention. I had a pan of simply "bake."

"Hello, is this Mr. Wong's Chinese Palace?" I asked as soon as I heard the connection. "Do you deliver?"

CHAPTER TWELVE

The biggest problem with Chinese food is that you're hungry two hours after eating it. So by eleven o'clock, I was back to square one. The other problem was that the news wasn't about to help me fall asleep. By the time a person made it to the weather, they were usually too afraid to fall asleep. That's why Leno and Letterman had such high ratings; they catered to all the paranoids too scared to sleep.

Tonight, however, hunger and not fear would keep me awake. That and the picture of my mug that had shown up on the local reports. It appeared shortly after the glib little overprocessed Katie Couric wannabe introduced me as an "episode."

Now, Vicky's name has been attached to the word "episode" on numerous occasions. And her face can find a way to plaster itself across the television screen at any opportunity. Shoot, she could create an occasion. Which is basically what she did here. In fact, she created enough "episodes" in the past two days to sustain her own network. Sit inside any room within the Savannah cable district and turn on your television to public access and you will find Victoria giving a tour of this city through her heavily shaded brown eyes.

She came up with that idea when she decided tourists needed an easy way to get quick information about the sights to see and things to do while in the city. And since it was her idea, well, could there be anyone else to host? You have to ask such a silly question. I mean, she is the head of the Savannah Chamber of Commerce.

So she stands in front of the Andrew Low House in a peach ensemble, and next she's in front of a square in something from the cranberry family, and then she's in front of Lady & Sons wearing floral, and before you know it she's giving a tour of her own office in the Savannah Chamber of Commerce, having donned her favorite color, cream. If cream is even a color. Each ensemble is accessorized and immaculately kept. And for a tour of the city squares themselves, the lady dons a hat bigger than the state of Texas.

So to have to sit here in my own room, in my own home, and view the two of us on camera together, me looking lost and her looking smudged, and labeled together as an "episode," well, it made me downright angry. And the fact that I was sleeping in an empty house on a Saturday night, starving, and that my future husband had walked away with a redhead whom my mother actually embraced, and that I was forced in front of a camera only because my mother had no common sense . . . it was all more than I could bear.

Then came the coup de grâce. An interview with my mother in which she referred to—who? Could a turnip truck carrying turnips be more certain? She referenced me, her Savannah from Savannah. In fact she mentioned just about every accolade I had achieved since potty training. I think she even mentioned that one. *Well, I guess advertisements in the newspaper will never again compare to what she has just accomplished here this evening. Thank God this was only local news.*

I pulled out a pair of jogging shorts and a white T-shirt, and then slipped on my tennis shoes. I would deal with this insanity once and for all. The Phillipses were not going to be the headline news and bathroom folly any longer. Not on my watch.

Grabbing a peanut-butter-and-jelly sandwich, I headed out to stop the madness. The jaunt took a little longer because there was no way sister was walking past the cemetery at the hour of the dead. Yet, even at eleven, the streets of Savannah were still alive. People enjoyed the nightlife here, the restaurants and lounges and music. There was that other coffee shop, which stayed open until past the "godly hour," and parties going on in houses with open doors. You could almost just walk on in. Most people didn't know each other anyway, so what was one more stranger?

Savannah has its own clock. Its own reality. Its own rules. Some hate them, some love them, and others just tolerate them. The people now spread across the square and the small grassy-knoll area in front of the courthouse apparently comprised a few of all three types.

The camera trucks hadn't moved and a few bright lights still glared. But most media members had gone to bed with the eleven o'clock news. A few lonely feeds for the West Coast remained. And Rita Cosby from FOX News. She was chatting with my father. Then I remembered. My demise was confirmed. I, Savannah, had certainly transcended the realm of "local" personality this evening and been thrust into the world of "national." All by the descriptive powers of my mother.

Ms. Austin was standing at the corner with one of our local merchants having a cup of that other shop's coffee. They behaved as if they had known each other for years, until she was interrupted by her cell phone. I continued scanning and noticed Dad was wrapping it up with Rita. He gave her a pat on the shoulder. The man never met a stranger. Then he made his steady but slow stride over to my mother.

Vicky was unpacking her evening gear, silken-clad neck pillow, eye mask, ear plugs, and cream taffeta sleeping bag. I wanted to walk up and shake her out of her obvious delirium. But truth be known, I was too tired to fight.

The rest of the square looked surprisingly clean, considering all the activity. I expected it to be blanketed with paper cups, dinner trash, and empty bottles. But it was just blanketed with people and, well, their blankets. The moon made its way over the square, and its full brilliance spotlighted the stone monument, as if making a statement. Some of the sojourners were ready to rest. Others prayed quietly in groups. And others were talking quietly, holding candles.

Crossing to the sidewalk in front of the courthouse, I stopped when I saw Mother rest her head against the back of the monument. She adjusted her silk eye mask atop her rather smashed tresses. Only a moment later, Dad's head rested next to hers. There, encased in moonlight and looking up with a teenage smile, Dad nestled his arm behind mother's head. They both continued to look into the face of the moon.

The dog and young man lying next to them were in peaceful dreamland and obvious rapture. Duke had even scored his own pillow. Thomas had scored two sleeping bags.

"This is what it was like when we were teenagers." Mother's voice broke the silence.

"Yes, it was. Except I wasn't actually a teenager."

They both laughed. He was eight years older and a "cradle robber" as my grandmother called him.

Vicky nodded at the moon. "It's a shame it takes an event like this to get us to stop long enough to appreciate something so beautiful."

He pulled her toward him. "Yeah, we've been too busy, haven't we?"

"I know I have. You're better. You stop when you need to. I keep going like the Energizer Bunny." She giggled.

"Maybe it's time to make first things first."

"We do, on the whole. We always have dinner together. We take Sundays off, and our children have grown up to be givers instead of takers."

"Yes, but you've still got to let go of some of your responsibilities. You can't do it all."

"I don't try to do it all."

"Oh yes, you do. And I think you do it because you're afraid."

"I'm not afraid." She straightened to make her point. "What would I have to be afraid of?"

"Afraid life might not work if you're not in charge of it. Afraid this city will crumble if you're not there to hold it up. But you don't hold Savannah up now, Victoria. You just think you do."

"I do not." She crossed her arms.

"You most certainly do." Dad nudged her stiffening arms. "You can't hold on so tight. Because at the end of the day, all you can control is you. And Savannah isn't yours. You live here. But it's not yours. And you need to quit making it the most important thing in your life."

"Jake Phillips, how dare you say this is the most important thing in my life. You know you and my children are the most important thing to me."

"Victoria, I know we're important, but you won't even take a vacation because you're afraid this place will fall apart when you leave."

Score one for Jake. I used to will myself to believe that Vicky wanted to direct the chamber of commerce so she could create an atmosphere of true Southern hospitality for visitors to our fair city. Part of me still believes that's true. However, the other part of me thinks that she thinks the city can't make it without her. And I do believe she has convinced most of the city of the same.

Maybe her powers of persuasion are in the perfectly coiffed hair or pristinely applied Mary Kay. They might even be in the way she puts her hand on your arm and laughs that small feminine laugh and stretches one-syllable words into two, like *light* into *lie-it*. Who knows what it is that makes people crumble so, but she is the queen of her domain. And she works in the grandest structure on Bay Street as well.

"I am not afraid of any such thing. This city would be just fine without me. I just . . . I just . . . well, I just don't like turbulent situations. I want the city to know I'm here for them." She pouted and apparently forgot about the moon.

"Turbulent situations? Give me a break. You believe Savannah will slip into the ocean if you leave it for a moment. I mean, think about it: Who is chained to this monument and plans to run her office from here the entire week if necessary? Who makes sure everything runs right around here? Who thinks she has to be at every meeting, make every decision, and be the head of every event?"

"Is this a trick question?"

Dad laughed at her naiveté. "No, this is an adequate assessment. I'm just saying you need to ask yourself some questions, Victoria. And I can't think of any better place to do it than here, outside, looking at that amazing moon." He lifted her chin to the brilliant light that was making its way to the other side of the square.

"I think you're off-base and out of line, Jake Phillips." *Ooh, both names. That's never good.* "Why are you here?"

"To protect you. To keep you warm. To cover you," he said, pulling her close.

"I'm not a child."

"No, you're not."

"Then don't treat me like one."

He pulled her in closer, placing his mouth at her ear. It was a whisper, but I could still hear him. "I love you more than you could ever know."

"I know," she responded, trying to resist his effect on her. It didn't work.

He kissed her softly on the lips and nestled her back under his arm, and fingered her unusually carefree hair. "You could never truly know," he whispered.

Those words hovered in the air like familiar love lingers over the words of a song. They rested there like the knowledge of their love rested in each other. For a child watching such interaction between her parents, it was, well, disgusting. But for a woman to watch such a loving exchange between two people, it was defining.

Their gazes lifted to the moon, and mine fell to the sidewalk. I journeyed to my bed with a new definition of love, commitment, and character. These were the people I had come from. Their love had made me. Their character had defined me. And their choices would affect me.

But my choices would determine where this new revelation would take me.

CHAPTER THIRTEEN

V anni, if you're riding with me you better hurry up."
I wet my hand to press back the golden brown lock that was protruding from an otherwise pristine ponytail. It was Sunday and I could drive myself, but it was about the only time Thomas and I even got to talk anymore. I peered in the mirror one more time and made sure my white suit jacket laid neatly across the matching white skirt, and appreciated the way the delicate black pinstripes elongated my five-foot-six frame.

This suit accomplished in an instant what Pilates could only do in four years. My rather pitiful legs stuck out, but the strappy white sandals (with a heel rather high for my taste) made them look a little better. Usually by this time in May I had a golden tan. But after my smoky run-in with Tan Beautiful last week, and now the revelation that I looked old and tired, well, I would have to rethink the whole tanning ritual. I could only wish for the olive complexion of Ms. Austin.

Thomas was waiting at the bottom of the stairs, and Duke waited by his side. We walked out the front door to his Jeep. "What do you think Duke does on Sundays when we are all gone?" I asked.

Thomas opened my door and shut it behind me. He crawled in the other side. "Oh, after his last two nights, he'll probably sleep."

"I've always pictured him sitting at the table, drinking coffee, reading the paper, then going for a dip in the pool and blow-drying himself off in Mom's bathroom."

"You are weird."

"Weird, but it's still possible. He's that smart, don't you think?"

"No dog is that smart."

"But Duke isn't stupid, is he?"

"No, he's one of the smartest dogs I know. Why? Are you try-ing to get him on a stupid-pet-tricks show?"

"No, I just think he does amazing things when we're not looking."

"Make sure you get prayer for that this morning."

Thomas's Jeep jerked as he took off from the stop sign and headed toward Tybee Island and our interdenominational church.

Thomas got his Jeep—which he has named Leroy, no one knows why—for high-school graduation. Mother had visions of a four-door LTD, but Dad would have nothing to do with it. She was stirring up enough trouble over Thomas's choosing of The Citadel. Believing Charleston to be the illegitimate child of the South, she warned him she wouldn't even visit.

Don't let her fool you. He's going into his senior year and she's already made over the bookstore, brought in a new line of Citadel dishware, and was even asked to represent The Citadel in trying to dissuade the first female applicant from attending.

Vicky herself went to the girl's hometown, took her to lunch, bought her a dress, and did her best to get the young woman to go to a school that would make her appreciate "being a lady."

"They are forming men there, honey. Surely you don't want to spend your life with people thinking you're a she-boy." To this day I am not quite certain what a she-boy is, was, or will be. But Vicky was sure that would work.

Two weeks later Shannon became the first woman in the corps. Vicky was mortified and still to this day calls it an "all-male" academy.

In her quarterly column in The Citadel's *Pass In Review*, entitled "The Making of an All-American Man," Vicky wrote, "If those girls want to be treated like men then I'll just call them men." And so she does.

Anytime she passes a girl on campus, she simply smiles and says, "Well, hello, young man." Hasn't phased them a bit. Downright near sent Mother to the halls of Washington. Fortunately for Washington, she's afraid to fly.

The church was already bustling. It had grown so much over the past year that Pastor Brice decided we needed to go to three services. As I watched the people enter, I was amazed by how many young people there were. Dad greeted us at the door and handed us a bulletin. The usual big hat and red lipstick and happy greeting from the other side of the door was conspicuously absent.

"Savannah, you look beautiful," Dad said, kissing me on the cheek. "Your mother wouldn't have wanted to miss this." That creeped me out. It was as if we were talking about someone who had passed through the eternal gates of glory.

I gave him a raised right eyebrow, and Thomas and I entered the sanctuary. "Where did all these college students come from?" I asked.

"A lot are from the Savannah College of Art and Design. Pastor Brice said the other day that he gave his heart to Jesus over twenty years ago, and he wasn't going anywhere. So, if the music was too loud or the service needed to be a little different to reach his kids and their friends, he was okay with that."

"That's a rather different perspective," I mused. "What's Granny Daniels think?"

"I heard she attends their Sunday-night youth services and keeps up with the best of them."

I laughed, certain he had accurate information. "I wouldn't doubt it. Seems weird today, huh?"

Thomas sat down beside me on a pew in the middle of the left-hand side. "What, with Mom not at the door?"

"No, with her not telling us to take our seats and sit quietly or spitting in her hand to wet your cowlicks down." We both laughed.

The music began, and the very essence of it seemed to lift me. It started with an up-tempo song about faith. The multi-racial choir swayed from one side to the other. By the time they were through, the volume had been brought down to a powerful yet reverent conclusion. Our associate pastor, Tom Jackson, was speaking this morning. The former Washington Redskin, with whom my father liked to chat football, rose to take the platform. His forty-year-old physique oozed professional athlete. And his African American heritage gave him beautiful skin and a magnetic smile.

He towered behind the Plexiglas podium, where he sat his Bible down and took in the thousand pairs of eyes staring back. He moved to the right of the podium and leaned against it. And I looked forward to some inspiring moments away from Vicky and the events of the last two days.

I was not to have them. For the next forty-five minutes, Pastor Jackson delivered a message entitled "Declaration of Dependence," offering insight and reflection on the events transpiring in our city. No one could get away from it. Yet no one else's mother was keeping quite the vigil mine was. I wouldn't be getting away from Vicky until this madness was over.

Thomas started the Jeep. "What are you doing for lunch?"

The question brought revelation. There would be no Sunday roast today. No country-style steak. No rice. No gravy. No home-made biscuits. No nothing. Just take-out.

"I'm going to go find a housekeeper that cooks."

"Dad got a big dinner from Lady & Sons last night and put it in the refrigerator so we could have it today. We're taking it to the square and having lunch with Mom." He noticed my disgust. "Just think of it as a Sunday dinner on the grounds."

"When have you ever been to a Sunday dinner on the grounds?"

"We used to when we would go to Granny's country church."

"They had ants."

"Are you ever positive?"

"Yes, smarty butt, I'm positive you will have a wonderful time. Don't worry about me. I'll get something."

As he pulled up in front of the house, he turned to look back at me. "You really need to get over this pride issue you have. If you are proud of anything, it should be over our mother standing up for something she believes in, no matter how she may look to others." He didn't wait for a reply. He just left me there sitting in the Jeep staring at his backside.

Thomas had been mean in the past. We didn't even like each other much until I left for college. I think we even had a few knock-down, drag-outs that ended with the words "moron!" and "Well, what do you know? You were an accident anyway." Both of which hurt my feelings and left me screaming for my father.

But Thomas had never said anything that stung like those words just did. "Pride? I'm not the one with the pride issue. The one with the pride issue is the silly woman sitting in the middle of a square, holding the city hostage. That's who has a pride issue. You're telling me what to do? I'll do what I want to do. I'm a grown woman who's about to have her own apartment. You're a little bald Citadel boy. Haven't even finished school yet. Need to teach you some manners."

Two fanny-pack-toting tourists on the street watched me quizzically as I ascended the stairs to the front door.

The Sunday newspaper was lying atop the breakfast-room table, where Dad had obviously read it with a morning cup of coffee. Or possibly where Duke had left it. I needed to see if Joshua's dog could do that. By it rested a note and a take-out dinner. *Enjoy your lunch. We'd like to see you today.*

The cover of the paper only caused the anger of last night to return. There I was, betrayed by my own employer. My backside was on the front of the paper, with the beaming face of my mother peering over my shoulder. It would resonate with the world that I agreed with her. I would never wear that outfit again and would do whatever I could to prevent the world from knowing it was me.

Then I noticed the caption underneath. "*Victoria Phillips, head of the chamber of commerce, embraces daughter, Savannah Phillips, in front of Ten Commandments Monument.*"

My cell phone rang. I sent her to voice mail once again. *Does US Air fly to Tanzania?*

CHAPTER FOURTEEN

I wasn't hungry for anything but vengeance. I had two plans of attack. And they were vicious, but well deserved. One: Get a housekeeper. Two: Get a housekeeper that cooks. To sort through strategies, I had always walked. So I walked straight up West Jones Street instead of going near the courthouse. That was nowhere on my agenda today. Con me with food or not, I wasn't biting.

Mr. Fisher was outside his house, trimming the ivy that had overtaken the iron-gate entrance to his spectacular garden. Mr. Fisher's house, a beautiful aged, burnt brick with rich tones and streaks of black, had a side-porch entrance more common to Charleston, South Carolina, architecture. The black shutters and ebony-stained wood door that led to the porch, complemented by a brass lion's-head door-knocker, had all been maintained with extreme care.

Charleston homes were originally taxed based on how many windows they had in the front of their house. So the Southerners got frugal as well as savvy and built all of their homes with side-porches, which served as the main entrance. By building the houses sideways, the "fronts" had as few windows as any other part of the house.

But Vicky's issues are deeply rooted in her competitive spirit with the other "Sister of the South." Stepsister, if you ask her. The fact that any house in Savannah resembled a Charleston residence is a fact Vicky fought tooth and nail, and well, I do mean literally tooth and nail.

It happened one beautiful fall day a couple of years after our arrival here from Atlanta, and only months after I decided to picket in front of our house because there was no McDonald's near our home. About the time Mr. Fisher and his wife were having their furniture unloaded, Mother pranced herself up the street and threw herself on top of their baby grand piano as the movers were trying to carry it into the house.

"What in the tar hill are you doing, young lady?" Mr. Fisher screamed. The young lady part almost caused mother to completely forget why she was there. But the jolt of the piano brought her back to reality.

"I'm saving you!" she replied with great animation.

"You're violating my piano! Now get yourself down!"

The mover provided extra incentive. "You might want to do what he says, lady, because we're about to have to turn this baby on her side, and then you won't be on the top any longer."

"Well, wait just a minute!" she said, still atop her perch. "You don't want to buy this house."

"I already bought it, lady!"

"Well, you don't want to move in."

"And why wouldn't I want to do that? Are you going to tell me it's haunted or something?"

"Lord have mercy, no. I don't like ghosts, and I pray them out of town any chance I get. Even walked a street or two getting them out of here."

"Lady, you're crazy. Now get off of my piano!"

About that time, the dainty Mrs. Fisher walked out with her pretty bobbed gray hair, and pants that looked like jeans but weren't. "Oh my Lord, what is she doing on our piano?"

"She's preparing to get off!" her husband assured her.

"Lady, I'm warning you," the mover said, straining beneath the added one hundred and ten pounds of peculiar. "We are tipping this puppy on three. One, two, three." And with that, three grown men turned the top of the antique baby grand piano on its side, and one Victoria Phillips on her bum. They didn't stop to check on her or survey the damage; they just continued straight in the house.

Mr. Fisher just stared at my mother, but Mrs. Fisher ran over to help her up. "Young lady, what is all this about?"

Mother tried to salvage as much grace as she possibly could after being dumped off a piano. "You live in Savannah. Why in the world would you want to buy a home that looks like Charleston?"

Mrs. Fisher let out a chuckle. "Is that what this nonsense is about? What is your name anyway?"

For one minute, or so the story goes, Mother hesitated. After all, to say that she was the head of the chamber of commerce might make for rather embarrassing dinner conversation. But then again, that revelation wasn't enough to forgo her great pride in her position. "I am Mrs. Victoria Phillips, head of the Savannah Chamber of Commerce."

Mr. Fisher let out a humph. "You have got to be kidding me. Is this how you welcome everyone to the city? If it is, tourism will be destroyed in six months." With that he and Mrs. Fisher left her there with a bruised ego and a bruised bum.

Vicky walked back to our house. Rumor has it there were a couple more similar episodes involving dressers and a dining room table, but the episodes ceased after the washing-machine incident made it on the front page.

Mr. Fisher's voice threw my recollection. "Savannah Phillips, how do you like my garden? Not bad for a Charleston house, huh?" A pretty good memory for his seventy-five years.

I peeked inside the gate and admired how beautifully landscaped and sculpted it was. "Oh, it's beautiful. You've been working hard, haven't you?"

"Oh yeah. Takes up most of my time. But with me still work-ing, it gets away from me and I have to attack it whenever I have free time. Where you off to? Trying to get away from the picture in the paper?" He smiled knowingly.

I picked invisible lint off my khaki capris and made my way up to my white T-shirt. "Just taking a walk before I eat lunch."

"Lunch?" he asked, putting down his trimmers. "Why on earth are you not eating at—oh, that's right, your mother's down at the courthouse. Is she lying on the monument or just sitting beside it?"

That made us both roar with laughter. "She's actually gone to sitting these days," I finally managed.

He took out his hanky and wiped the sweat from his gray bushy eyebrows. His blue eyes were crystal clear and shimmered of a stolen youth, but also of a life still flourishing inside. "Why don't you come eat with me and the Mrs.? She has enough food for us to eat off all week. We're having fish."

"No, that's okay really. I appreciate it. But I've got to do some work this afternoon for my next column, so I'm just going to grab a quick bite at home."

"You sure?" He picked up his clippers.

I patted him on his damp white T-shirt. "Yes, sir, I'm sure. Thanks anyway."

"Will do."

"Uh, Mr. Fisher?"

"Yes?"

"Does Mrs. Fisher ever rent out her cooking services?"

He laughed. "You're asking for trouble, Miss Savannah."

"You think?"

"I've gone a round with your mama. I know."

"Well, tell Mrs. Fisher I said hello."

"You tell your family the same." Fortunately for Victoria, Mr. Fisher was able to let go. Too bad the letter to the editor he wrote about her welcoming party took them four years for the letting go to begin.

I would eat on the stoop. If I sat in the garden, sequestered by ivy, I couldn't really see what was happening on the streets. So, I went out to the stoop and sat on the steps. This is virtually the only way I am like my mother. I do like to see what is going on around me.

Come to think of it, Dad does too. He likes to plant himself at the table by the window in the hopes that some weary straggler will need to bare his soul. He'll act all casual, sitting there petting Duke. Someone will walk in for a quick hello or cup of coffee, but before you know it Jake's helping with marital problems (which he denies having), adolescent terrors (of which he declares he's had many), or financial difficulties (which he overcame). By the time they leave smiling, Dad's sitting back at the window, smiling too.

About two bites into my first piece of catfish, my park-bench friend arrived. I heard her before I saw her. She was humming that same melody she had departed with yesterday. She wore the same dress as yesterday too, carried the same bag, and didn't look much different than she had twenty-four (or forty-eight!) hours earlier. This week anyway, she and Vicky had a thing or two in common.

"Well, well, young lady. Where's your book?"

I laughed, finding it hard to believe she remembered me. "Inside." I motioned to my house. "I didn't bring it for this journey."

But she didn't really care about my book. She didn't care about the house either. Didn't care about Victoria's lovely iron balconies, or stately wooden, black-painted doors. Couldn't have given a rat's rear end for the pristine ivy growing over our own brick wall that surrounded our fortress. No, her eyes were on my plate. She was like Duke eying a tenderloin. I wanted her to pull out her apple and get to eating her own food. She walked up a few steps and planted herself next to me, still fixated on my food. "Ooh, you got a nice Sunday dinner there, don't ya?"

"Yeah, you can get some at Lady & Son's. It's just up the street." I was even gracious enough to point her in the direction.

She wasn't paying a lick of attention to my lead. "Yeah, well maybe I'll try to get over there." But she didn't move. How could she when she never even looked away from my plate?

Well, it was Sunday. "Would you like some?"

She turned away, embarrassed. "Oh no, baby. I don't want to eat your food. You need your food. You can tell I get all the food I need." She patted her stomach. I wasn't going to argue with her. Then she turned quickly back around. "Well, if you really want me to have some, I don't want to hurt your feelings."

I laughed at her sweet expression. "Here. Take two. Who wants to eat Sunday dinner alone anyway?" I laid a napkin out for her. Gave her some catfish and a homemade biscuit. By the time she was through, Garfield couldn't have accomplished cleaner bones. "What's your name?"

"Oh, my name is . . ." She looked off into the distance as if trying to find something to jog her memory or offer her a name. "My name is Joy. Yes, it's Joy." She finally answered as more of a declaration.

"Oh, that's a beautiful name. Here, take a drink." I handed her the tea I had yet to enjoy and offered her the opportunity to wash down what she had virtually inhaled.

"What's your name, precious girl?"

"Savannah," I said, scratching my nose.

"Nose itch?"

"Like crazy. My mother says that means somebody's coming to see you." I raised a right eyebrow at my dinner guest. "Guess she got that one right, huh?"

She looked at me inquisitively. "Well, I think Savannah is a beautiful name for a beautiful girl."

"You don't want to crack a joke about it? Everyone else does."

"Now, who would crack a joke about a beautiful name?"

I wiped my mouth and gave her the rest of my plate. It seemed she needed it more than me. "You'd be surprised."

"I'm surprised by a lot of things, Savannah. I'm surprised by how people rush to and fro. Hardly stop to breathe. Or give thanks for the ability to breathe. So busy working and doing and never simply resting or enjoying. I see the lights on in their windows until late in the night. They type on computers and rummage through papers. All the time doing and never living. And then the one moment, the one day the world is told to rest, it just keeps on moving. We all need rest, Savannah."

"You're telling me."

She looked back at me, not seeming to remember. "You look kind of that way. Like you need some rest."

"You said the same thing yesterday. I didn't realize how bad I was looking until you informed me."

She chuckled, causing her belly to move with her. "Ooh, I'm sorry, baby. I didn't mean that you look bad like you were ugly or something. It's a furrowed brow. It's a heaviness of the eyes. It's seeing the weight someone carries by the mere look in their eyes. But it doesn't have to be that way."

"You aren't going to try to sell me some Anthony Robbins tape series are you?"

"Who's Anthony Robbins?"

"Good."

"No, I don't have anything to sell. Life isn't about selling and buying. It's about knowing and doing. And I'm not talking about the twenty-four-hour-a-day, seven-day-a-week doing. I'm talking about the heart knowing and the life doing."

I leaned my elbows on the step behind me. My mind was so tired. And all of this was just making me more tired. "I'm tired of doing."

"I see you've had all you can take, my sweet Savannah." She rose from her side of the stoop and laid my empty plate neatly beside me. Then she rose and picked up the half glass of tea to take it with her. I couldn't help but smile at her mature innocence.

She seemed so wise, yet her eyes looked so young and vulnerable. "I'm sure I'll see you soon," I assured us both.

She turned and headed to the corner of the house. She stopped and turned back around. "Being, Savannah! That's the word. Not doing, but just being, baby."

I watched her as her skirt shifted tightly across her backside with the movement of her round legs. And I wondered who this stranger was and where she had come from. The thought of a strange elderly woman walking up some street, drinking my tea and singing, caused me to laugh at the absurdity of the last couple days. I would have asked her if she would like a job, but the way she was always hungry, it was evident cooking wasn't her forte. And the blur that passed by me forced my attention elsewhere.

You don't see a lot of lawn mowers in downtown Savannah. Few people actually have yards to be mowed. Most people's yards aren't lawns; they're gardens. And gardens need maintaining, mulching, even manicuring, but nowhere do they need mowing. And if they do, the areas are so small that they pretty much only require a weed eater.

But the city does mow the town. Savannah takes great pride in the preservation of the squares for the enjoyment of the tourists, and the homeowners that claim them as front yards.

The young man driving the mower that zoomed by my house didn't look too happy about his afternoon assignment. I followed him in sheer wonder of this most ordinary activity. He was probably a young college kid desperate for summer money. On a beautiful day like today, a kid his age had a thousand other things he should have been enjoying.

But this one kid now arriving at Lafayette Square, he was commissioned to mow. I sat down on a bench to observe. I don't know why. Wasn't much else to observe, well, nothing that I wanted to get in the middle of now. The grass flew up on the pavement in front of me, making a scattered green hedge along the edge of the sidewalk. The new design would have to be removed by the young worker after completing the first stage of his duty.

I bore easily. As I got up to work my way down the street, the edge of my flip-flop scraped some of the freshly laid hedge back onto the lawn. At least, on the edge of one square of one of the four sidewalks, this small section would not require his attention. It might not save much time, but it may save him a moment.

The two women in front of me didn't quit talking, nor move from my path the entire way to the courthouse. Their hands were loaded down with shopping bags, and they rambled on incessantly for three blocks.

"What are you doing the rest of the day?" the stately, elderly woman said to the medium-built, stout younger one.

"Working. I've got final exams to finish grading before tomorrow. What about you?"

"The same. And next year will only be worse. We are going to have to submit weekly lesson plans."

"Every week? I'm doing good to get mine submitted once a month."

"It's just gotten absurd."

And on and on they went for three straight blocks. They waxed eloquent on everything from how the last week of school would run to who had lunch duty. By the time they were through, I needed a nap. Their incessant rambling made me decide not to think about work until tomorrow. After all, my story wasn't going anywhere. It rested right down the street on that square alive with activity. And all I had to do was sit and observe. By Tuesday, Mr. Hicks would have an article on his desk.

I had no idea yet what I was going to tell people about the upheaval of our city, but I knew that story would consist of a thousand strangers, a large piece of granite, and a woman who claimed to be responsible for my physical birth. She would probably be the one responsible for my occupational death.

CHAPTER FIFTEEN

When the courthouse came into view, I was shocked at what I saw. In a part of the nation known as the Bible Belt, Savannah's church- or cathedral- or synagogue-going population is probably right up there with the likes of Nashville. The name of God is mentioned in most conversations and everyone knows of Him, believes in Him, or knew of Him at one time or another, or at the very least attaches His name to their profanities.

But today, in Savannah, Georgia, church had come to the square. As I scanned the mass of people, most were stretched out, lying with their faces touching cement or the very dust of the earth. And a sound was rising from every corner. Wright Square was enveloped in prayer. The sound of it was overwhelming and amazing. And as if on cue, every prostrate pilgrim rose and began to sing the anthem of ages past, of saints and sinners alike, "Amazing Grace."

I caught sight of Thomas and Dad, apparently headed to the same place I was.

"Brought church to the square today, huh?"

Dad smiled and responded. "Sounds like it, doesn't it?"

We met up on the corner. As the final chorus ended I caught Dad's eye. We each paused. Moments like this weren't textbook, even for the South. None of us rushed it. Who would want to? For or against, some moments in life required everyone's respect. This was one.

"Are y'all going inside the store?"

Dad wrapped his arm around me. "Yeah, I wanted a cup of coffee and it's free at my place. But let's go in the back. I don't want anyone to think I'm open."

Dad opened the back door. The aroma of coffee was so ingrained into the very wood that even on days when it wasn't being brewed, Jake's smelled like coffee. Even the hole where the dishwasher was supposed to be smelled of coffee.

"Did your dishwasher man take off with your cash?" I asked.

Dad shook his head, unable to hide his slight frustration. "Who knows? I've tried to call him three or four times, but he still hasn't responded."

"Didn't you see him on your outing last night?"

"No. He didn't show up there either."

"Mervine and Louise will want a raise."

"And you can bet they'll let me know about it too." He laughed. He put on a pot of coffee and Thomas sat on top of the stainless steel worktable that rested in the center of the room. Duke tried to join him, but lost his footing, only to end up in a pitiful clump on the stamped concrete floor.

"Duke, you're pitiful, ol' boy." I patted his head but refused to pat his boo-boo. "So what did y'all do all afternoon?"

Thomas curled his feet up under him as if he were ten and turned his ball cap around backward. His green eyes became expressive with his recounting of their "picnic on the grounds."

"We ate and told old stories. Mother told me things about her life when she was growing up, stories I don't think I've ever heard."

I tried not to act all that interested and turned around to fix myself a Coke. "Like what?"

"Like about how she would go out behind her house and smoke when she was little."

I turned back around in amazement. "No way! Victoria Phillips never smoked."

"Oh, yes she did! But if you told anyone, she would deny it."

I sat down beside him on the table. The coffeepot began spattering and sputtering, and the fresh aroma of coffee began to take over the aroma of yesterdays.

"There is no way our mother, Miss No-Cigarettes-No-Alcohol-No-Nothing-but-Coffee, would ever have smoked."

Dad poured his cup of coffee while looking amused at our exchange.

Thomas added. "She did, I swear! She said she could have even been addicted."

Dad laughed out loud.

"She could not!" I slapped Thomas on the arm and went back to my Coke. Duke looked up once again just to make sure we hadn't changed our minds about inviting him to join us on the table. Dad poured his coffee and leaned against the side of the counter by my Coke machine.

Thomas took my Coke from my hands and took a sip big enough to force me to have to get more. "Yes, she could have. She said it herself. You'll have to get her to tell you all about it. It is hysterical." He jumped down off of the table.

"What else did she tell you?"

"Oh, lots of stuff. About her parents. About how her mother started going to church when they moved next door to one. How their lives changed. How she felt when they died. All those kinds of things."

"Well, sounds like a nostalgic afternoon. Mine was pretty interesting too."

"That's nice, Savannah. Okay, Dad, let's go back. Mother's going to be singing a special."

"Heaven help us all."

"Plus the judge is working around the clock to make sure this monument stays. And I wouldn't mind catching another glimpse of that Ms. Austin lady. That woman is—" Dad gave him a playful slap on the back of the head.

I tried to hide my hurt at their lack of interest by pouring myself some more Coke.

Thomas turned around to look at me. Hiding my feelings from him seemed a wasted effort. He took no notice of them anyway. "Are you coming with us, Vanni, or heading back to your hole?"

I raised my right eyebrow at him in total disgust at his disregard for my choice to have a life. "No thanks. I really need to get home and start putting together my story."

"Whatever you say."

Dad locked the door behind us and put his arm around me to walk down the alley and back to the square. "Did you have a good afternoon?"

I stopped to ponder my tea-stealing stranger. The thought of her made me smile. "I had an interesting one, to say the least."

"Good, I'm glad. We missed you though. Your mother was disappointed."

I knew what her disappointment was: extreme sighing, dramatic chest clasping, pouty red lips.

I gave in. After all, this square was my story. "Well, let's go see what the crowd out there is up to, shall we?"

"Yeah, let's do."

The size of the crowd seemed double that of yesterday. Apparently most people had Sunday off. Except for the lawn boy, the schoolteachers who weren't even going to let their minds rest today, and Mr. Fisher. But a large portion of Savannah's workforce seemed to be standing shoulder to shoulder, making clear their passion toward a monument of ancient truths.

Judge Hoddicks came out of the courthouse about the time

we made it to the end of the square. Even the newsmen who sat through the hymn rose to take note of Judge Hoddicks's arrival.

The judge cleared his throat as he stood behind the makeshift podium. Beside him stood a distinguished-looking gentleman with smooth, dark skin and hair sprinkled with gray, suggesting wisdom. His tiny gold-framed glasses and steady eyes solidified his importance. I paused and tried to determine who he was and why he was here. Then I saw the familiar figure beside him. He saw me at the same time and tried to hide his white smile beneath his chocolate skin while acting dignified and important.

So it was clear now: Judge Tucker from Mississippi had indeed come to support his old friend. I was certain Gregory had come along for the sheer entertainment value of it all.

Judge Hoddicks introduced Judge Tucker to the captive audience. Well, at least one was truly captive. After giving an uninformative "update," he motioned to someone in the crowd. For a brief moment I expected my mother to heave that monument atop her back and follow. But instead I watched as Ms. Austin headed his direction. She had traded her cascading ponytail for cascading curls that reached midway down the back of her brown sleeveless top. Her lean legs covered in matching slacks followed the judges and my partner in legal battles, Gregory, up the stairs.

"That's her," I mouthed. "ACLU lady."

His face made it clear he didn't mind following her at all. And I suspected that every man within a two-block radius—maybe except for Jake—wished at that moment they were an old judge or a young law clerk from Mississippi.

My mother looked as if her mind was processing a thousand things. Which wasn't any great phenomenon because she did usually have trouble focusing on one thing at a time. Her appearance, in contrast to the raven-haired beauty, had never before looked quite so unkempt. Granted, her level of unkemptness would pale in comparison to most people's, because on a good day she was

Queen-of-England caliber. In other words, she looked like a normal woman on a Saturday. The rushed makeup job. The not-going-
to-iron-because-it's-Saturday wrinkled clothes that had been lying
in the floor, but looked remotely clean. The hair-will-do syndrome.

But on Vicky, well, let's just say it wasn't pretty.

Her blue suit was extremely wrinkled. And the two stains from
yesterday had apparently been poorly attacked with some Shout
wipes, only to leave water marks and were now joined by three new
stains. Her makeup looked reapplied and was nearing the "hard"
arena. Her hair had lost its "edge" and was now teetering on the
squashed, might-need-a-wash brink. And this was my mother.
Sitting in front of that monument, with as much pride as a mother
watching her child graduate from college after three previously
failed attempts, was my mother.

It was obvious she hadn't seen herself in a mirror in two days.
Because if she had, she would be like any common criminal who
holds up their handcuffed arms to shield their face from the cameras. The wide-brimmed hat, in a complementary shade of blue,
had replaced the umbrella and averted a few prying eyes.

"Does she know how horrible she looks?"

"Savannah, your mother doesn't look horrible. She looks, well,
she looks alive."

"Oh, that's a new line. Try that one on her and then hand her
a mirror and see whose going to need the new apartment. And
another delicate matter I've been pondering . . ."

"And what would that be?"

"How does the woman go to the bathroom?"

"Very well actually."

I punched his arm. "You know what I mean."

"Ever heard of a Porta Potti?"

"There is no way."

"Trust me, there is a way."

"Victoria Phillips would not use a Porta Potti in the middle of
a Savannah square."

"You don't know your mother like you think."

"Please tell me I was adopted."

"It's never too late." Dad began to head in her direction. "Now come tell your mother hello."

"I will later. I'm not into crowds."

"You mean you're not into uncomfortable," he said, leaving me to myself. My rather uncomfortable self.

CHAPTER SIXTEEN

Elderly tourists are easy to spot. They have a walk. A slow, stop-and-look-at-things-that-don't-even-matter walk. The elderly tourists that had been at Paige's yesterday were coming down the street away from the square I had yet to vacate. No sign of their son, Prince Charming. Paige hadn't mentioned him at church earlier today, though she did enter smiling and depart quickly. Nor did she answer her cell phone when I called to invite her over for my "picnic on the stoop." Who knew? But this twosome could be perfectly captured in a comic strip with their attire teetering on ghastly and plunging over the wall of tacky.

Then I watched as he patted her tushie. It was a soft pat, a love pat. A pat that happens between two people who have loved each other way past the point of teenage desire. Or at least one should hope. But it was the familiarity that caught me. She slapped him teasingly, and by the up-and-down movement of her shoulders it was evident she still got a kick out of him.

He wrapped his arm around her and tugged her toward him. It wasn't a smooth movement, the way Dad took Vicky in his arms the other night. No, this was an eighty-year-old's tug. A shaky tug, because of the old-people tremors. A cushioned tug, padded by years of good eating. But it was real. It was engaging. It was as it should be.

An ache formed in my gut. The ache of longing for that kind of familiarity. For someone who knows how you like your steak cooked and what makes you scared. For someone who knows even the things about you that you are too proud to admit.

It was a Grant ache. I flipped open my cell phone and speed-dialed Paige.

"Where have you been?"

"At the mall."

"I've tried you for *two days*."

Paige sounded perturbed. "My phone hasn't worked."

"Why?"

"Why? Well, that would be because I flushed it down the toilet."

"Ooh, nice."

"Yep, real nice. Happened on my date."

"Ooh, tell me all about it."

"He went to one bathroom. I went to another. Leaned over to flush with my bag strapped over my arm, and out went the phone. It's somewhere in the Atlantic now, or lower Savannah. Who can be certain?"

I was laughing hysterically. "Why didn't you reach in and get it?"

"So funny, aren't we? All I could do was let out a scream. My date was waiting at the door with a rather perplexed look on his face."

"He heard you, huh?"

"The whole thing, I'm certain. Got home from Tybee Island quicker than if I'd have driven myself."

"Scared him, huh?"

"I think it was when I yelled, 'Don't make me come in there after you!'"

"Well, no need in both of us losing our men. We've got to develop a plan."

"Hello to you too."

"I can't just let him get away, walk into the arms of a stranger without a fight. What am I thinking, sitting around here like a doormat? I'm smart and talented and sometimes funny. Don't you think?"

"I think you are all of those things, dear one, but don't leave out 'borderline insane.' He is only weeks away from getting married."

"So? I know people who stole fiancés only a week before the wedding. Even left notes on church doors saying, 'Due to circumstances beyond our control there will be no wedding here tonight,' when they couldn't contact all the guests. Why should this be any different?"

"That's a good point."

"I thought so too. I mean, he is my soul mate. We have loved each other our entire pubescent lives and then some. So, what's your idea?"

"What's my idea?"

"Yes. *What. Is. Your. Idea?* You always have great ideas. You know men. You love men. Not so good with phones, but I don't need an idea for a phone. I need an idea for a man. I've got to win back his heart and get rid of that redheaded annoyance."

"Ooh, catty. I like it. Okay, let me think. I'll get back to you."

"Don't take long. Time's a-wastin'."

"Time's a-wastin'?"

"Just get to work or I'm liable to have to go home and clean something. By the way, have any suggestions on a cleaning lady who cooks and isn't named Mrs. Gonzalez?"

"You sure are needy today."

"Not as needy as you'll be if that pastel-plaid-arrayed duo become your in-laws."

"You don't have to worry about that. I wasn't crazy about him anyway. Poor fella was cute, but still lived at home with Mommy and Daddy. At thirty-five-years old—"

"*Thirty-five?!* My word, that man is old."

"Ancient, I know. But anyway, forget about me and let's stay focused. We've got to get your man back. Stay close to your phone and I'm going to the drawing board."

"You're going to go paint?"

"I always think better when I paint."

"Well, whatever works. Call me soon."

"Bye." And she hung up to rescue me one more time.

Needing a bite of something sweet, I walked down York Street to get a key lime square from Wright Square Café. Opening the door, I was shocked to see Ms. Austin standing at the counter. She turned around holding a key lime square and bottled water.

She looked at me and smiled a beautiful smile. Her lips were covered in a rich red that accentuated her perfect smile and rich complexion. "Savannah, right?" Her soft Southern accent kept the words lingering for a moment.

"Yes, Savannah," I said, pointing to myself as if discovering who I was for the first time. "And you're Ms. Austin."

"Oh, please call me Faith."

"Okay. Well, I see you've found one of the best things in town." I winked at Eric, the college student who worked here during the summer. He stood behind the counter, unable to take his eyes off of our new guest.

"What is that?"

"That square of sheer delight you hold in your hands."

She studied the key lime square between her fingers. "Oh, is it good?"

"It's beyond good; it's divine. I came in for one myself." I thought that might be Eric's cue to get me one too, but I had to actually ask before he turned his attention back to me.

"I'm sorry about my mother," I said, paying for my dessert.

"I deal with people that fana—that dedicated all the time." She took a seat by the window. "Would you like to sit down?"

"Sure. So, how long have you been a crusader?"

She laughed and opened her bottled water with her perfectly

manicured left hand. "Well, I've never thought of it that way." Faith twirled her single strand of pearls as she looked out of the large, paned window. "A crusader, huh? Well, ever since I graduated college almost, oh Lord, well, almost ten years ago now."

"You've been out of school for ten years? You look great."

She raised both eyebrows. "Well, I'm not that old."

I felt my face flush. "Oh, I'm sorry, I didn't mean it that way."

"It's okay. Thirty-two sounded ancient to me when I was your age. How old are you? About twenty-two?"

"Twenty-four actually."

I watched her take a bite of her square. "Oh my goodness. This thing is delicious." Eric leaned over the counter as if he would have wiped her mouth himself. I squelched my intense desire to roll my eyes.

"So, will you be here long?" I asked.

"Until this is over. Probably only about a week. I figure the courts will remove the monument soon and life will be back to normal."

"Normal. Now, that's a concept."

"You have a rather adventurous mother, I take it."

"Oh, let's just say she is involved."

"Well, it seems like you have a great head on your shoulders." She finished up her square and wiped her mouth. "You were right, Miss Savannah. That was one of the best key lime squares I've ever eaten. I think I'm going to take another for the road."

"You're going to eat two?" I asked, amazed that she could maintain such a figure while eating sugar slathered across some graham cracker crumbs. Might as well just slather it on my thighs.

"I do most anything I want, Savannah." She gave Eric a wink as he failed miserably in catching his drool. "I have to get back to work now. I hope I'll see you soon." I scratched my left hand. "You okay?" she asked.

"Yeah. My hand's just itching. But it's a good thing. It means you're going to get some money."

"Ooh, well, call me when you do." She eyed me suspiciously.

"Yeah, I'll do that." I laughed a dorky laugh. Fortunately she was already answering her ringing cell phone and was oblivious to my world of dork.

"Take care."

She offered me a wink and a mouthed, "You too."

I walked back to the cooler, debating another Coke. I consumed excessive portions of the sugar-laden caffeine drink each day. Here at the café, it looked beautiful sitting in that cooler all chilled and inviting. I had never debated such a concept before. And Ms. Austin had just given me permission. So, I didn't tarry long. As I handed it to Eric, he looked rather perturbed.

Once he slammed the cash register shut, he and three vibrant young men came running out from the back and watched Ms. Austin all the way up the street. I looked at them with nausea, threw my napkin away, and had to part them to make my way to the door.

"You do that every time I leave too, don't you?" I quipped. They never responded. The dark-headed siren, sauntering up the street, rendered them deaf. And the tired, old, worn-out-looking twenty-four-year-old slipped out utterly undetected.

CHAPTER SEVENTEEN

The familiar face came around the corner with a smile. He nodded at Ms. Austin as he passed her while he headed in my direction. I gave Gregory a hug. "Okay. Now tell me what happened in that meeting and how quick this is going to be over."

He turned around to walk with me up the street. "I'm not supposed to talk about what goes on inside a meeting like that."

"Why? We're friends."

That caused Gregory to chuckle. "We're friends? Wouldn't that be a good ploy to suck information from lawyers. 'Oh, but sir'"— he made a pathetic attempt to mimic my voice—"'we're friends.'"

"Okay, smart aleck. I don't want to know anyway."

"Well, just be careful."

"Be careful with what."

"That woman there." He pointed to Ms. Austin's disappearing back. "She's got no shortage of venom underneath that sweetness."

"Oh please. She's obviously very talented. She wouldn't be here representing an entire organization and body of people without being good at what she does."

"She's good all right. Which is why I'm just warning you."

"Whatever. How long are you here?"

"We're heading back now."

"Now? I thought we could grab dinner and talk."

"Sorry, no time. The judge needs to make it back for a Sunday-afternoon nap."

"You won't get back before evening."

"So he'll have to forgo the nap and just go to bed early. I'll talk to you this week."

"Okay. But if I need you, I'm going to be calling you."

"I don't doubt it." He started to walk off and I grabbed his arm. "Ooh, don't turn around. I don't want him to see us."

He turned around of course. "You don't want who to see us?"

I jerked him back. "That curly-headed guy, Joshua."

He turned around again.

I slapped him. "Would you stop that?"

"The guy with the golden retriever?"

"Yes," I said, pulling him back up the street toward where we had just been. "He works with me, and he is rude and annoying."

"Oh, he is?"

"Yes. He's condescending and has a dog who can do tricks."

"Oh my word," he said, stopping dead in his tracks. "Savannah Phillips. You're crazy about him."

I stared at him in wide-eyed wonder. "I'm what?!"

His white smile beneath his chocolate skin was just too pleased, as if his ridiculous revelation was some kind of epiphany for the world. "You're crazy about him."

"I am in love"—I straightened my chest—"with a man I have loved since I was a child. And I will get him back. Don't you have to leave?"

He laughed a caustic laugh. "Yeah, I've got to go. And you, my friend, need to come to grips with reality. Fantasy only exists in beauty pageants." He winked and sauntered away. "Just remember to send me an invitation."

"I'll send you an invitation all right, mister!" I yelled at the back of his head. "An invitation to . . . to a therapist who helps the delusional!!"

He raised his hand but never turned around.

I gave him a good hand raise myself.

As I sat in the house alone, again, going another night without food, again, I knew I had to move. I mean, it was coming eventually, so why not this week? I had to take charge of my world. Construct my chaos. Tailor my tune. Okay, that was stretching it, but one would rather starve and be alone in her own place than die a slow, drawn-out death in a home where a family *should* be. And because I had a pretty good week in which Victoria would be preoccupied with other matters, it might be wise to make the most of it. I was fortunate enough that my soon-to-be-home was already vacated and waiting. And my anonymous landlord had made it so affordable that as few as three paychecks would at least get me moved in.

One week. One good week to move out while my mother was, shall we say, tied up and unlikely to come up with any campaigns to keep me at her home.

Only one problem: I had only one paycheck. So two more long pay periods stood between me and my first month of freedom. But I knew someone who had money. And she must have known I was thinking about her. Because after waiting on her all day, she finally called.

"Okay, I've got it. It's perfect." Paige's excited voice came on the other end.

"Tell me; I need to know."

"I can't. I'm still working out details. I'll tell you at lunch tomorrow."

Monday was our standing lunch-date day. "Oh, my Lord! Tomorrow is Monday!"

"Yes, Savannah. It's Sunday . . . then Monday . . . then Tuesday."

"Paige, please. I have a story due by Tuesday and I don't have a clue what I'm going to say."

"Nothing odd about that. But I would think you'll be writing on what is happening down there at the square. My word, you can't get any more human interest than that."

"Well, yes, but I haven't even formulated my thoughts, interviewed anyone. Well, basically I haven't done a thing."

"Just voice both opinions. Make clear the controversy. Let the people decide. Just make the humans interested, and the rest will take care of itself."

"Hmm . . . I'll think on that. Anyway, are you crazy? I can't wait until tomorrow."

"Well, you'll have to. Just trust me, it will be perfect. Now sleep tight, precious."

"I'll have to take something."

"No, you just rest knowing that your man's coming home to mama."

"You think?"

"I know. Now, good night."

"Good night. Oh, wait, one more thing. How is your bank account looking these days?"

"Why, Savannah? Has my mother been asking you questions?"

"No, I just want to try to get out of here before Mother gets unshackled. It will make for a much more peaceful transition. Except I don't have a pot to pee in."

"Ooh, I don't need to be informed of all your issues. Plus, I hear you could borrow your mother's."

"Nor do I need to be informed of all *her* issues."

"How much?"

"A month's rent and enough to turn on my utilities and the chance to pay you back in installments, no interest. About twelve hundred dollars."

"Sounds good."

"You'll do it?"

"Of course. I'll even help you move."

"I love you."

"I know."

"I owe you."

"That you do. Tomorrow."

"Tomorrow."

As soon as I hung up, the phone rang again. Thank the Lord for caller ID. Mother obviously needed to say good night before she spent another evening under Moon River. Her message thanked me for coming by yesterday and delivering such wonderful news. She added how she loved her picture in the paper, except for her eye makeup. She left me suggestions on my article for Wednesday's edition and offered to do an exclusive interview with me if necessary. After all, she had just spent another evening with Rita Cosby and was all warmed up. She felt most people would be interested in her as a human, and as I was a human-interest writer, well, it might look good on my résumé.

I deleted her ideas from my voice mail and ordered my dreams to be sweet. They were. Grant was in them, walking with me through Forsythe Park. Then we were holding hands and kissing on a bench. It was like old times. Except that when he left, he rode his bicycle home.

CHAPTER EIGHTEEN

You need to go to the dentist," I informed the stank-breath mutt who was perched atop my bed, staring at me. "I hate Mondays." He sat up, making it clear he agreed. He hobbled off the bed.

"Moving a little slow, are we?"

He cocked his head. The poor soul looked weary. He was used to sleeping on a down pillow in the air-conditioning. The concrete didn't agree with him. Okay, I wouldn't make him learn a new trick today. The poor soul just looked too beat-up.

Making my way to the bottom of the stairs to head out for some tilling time, I picked his leash up off the Asian altar table that takes up a large portion of the main foyer wall. Duke sat at the top of the stairs, simply staring at me.

"Don't you want to go walk?"

He didn't budge.

"Just a short jog?"

Was he glaring at me? This animal had never refused a stroll. For him to refuse the opportunity to sniff schnauzers and fire hydrants could only mean he had suffered severe psychological damage in just a few short days. I climbed the stairs to try to coax him. I attached the leash to his collar.

"Come on, we haven't been together in days." I headed down the stairs. That dog would have none of it. He planted his feet, and by the time I got to stair number twelve, his leash fully extended, his stationary weight forced me back to stair eight via my haunches. I looked back at him from my now-seated position. All four of his paws had scooted up to the front of his body. I was surprised he hadn't wrapped himself around the iron railing to hold on for dear life.

I crawled up the stairs so I could stare at him directly in his deep dark eyes. "You really don't want to go outside?"

I heard a brief whimper and then he dropped to the floor with a sigh as only his eyes looked up at me.

I rubbed his head. "She's not out there."

He raised his head slightly.

"I promise. I will not take you to the courthouse, or even make you walk on the sidewalk. We can trot in the grass if you want to."

He sat up on that one.

"I will protect you from the crazy lady."

It took some more coaxing, but he did walk slowly to the door. But as I opened it, the poor soul just couldn't bring himself to walk through it. And I would not be remembered in his beautiful strawberry blond head as the woman who led him to undue anguish. No, Vicky would keep that title.

I walked out the door not knowing if Duke would ever till with me again. It was a sad day. Until I remembered my conversation with Paige. Then, the hope of redemption swept over me in my prison of unrequited love with the calming effect of a southern siesta. Well, if you're from southern Mexico.

The sounds of Josh Groban filled my iPod. In the middle of his and Charlotte Church's rendition of "The Prayer," I began to say some of my own. But tilling today felt exceptionally challenging. Somewhere between naming and claiming my destiny with Grant, and binding my mother's reckless foolishness, the receiving end of my tilling felt rather . . . empty. I pressed on anyway. Today was Monday. Not that I thought heaven had Mondays. But just in case it did, I would give it the benefit of the doubt.

Classy and elegant hangs in the closet across the hall.

Classy and elegant has not been seen in my closet since I purged it of such nonsense after a quarrel over my refusal to wear a suit to a two-year-old's birthday party.

As I scanned my closet for something to wear I longed for classy and elegant. Who knows why. I just felt the need to get away from anything in the dark and dreary family. I had been shopping last week at Banana Republic on Broughton, so I sifted through the new assortment, longing for something a little un-Savannah.

Tucked in the back behind my new acquisitions was a straight-lined khaki skirt of brushed cotton. It had been a gift from Paige, who once ate one too many bags of Doritos and couldn't get into it the next morning. In her fit of frustration, I gained some rather cute separates. It was a fitting compliment to my calves, falling just below the knees. I matched it with a baby blue cotton button-down with three-quarter sleeves.

As I slipped on my flip-flops and studied myself in the mirror, the word *dowdy* came to mind. The look was sleek, but the shoes didn't fit. But the khaki opened-toed Coach-emblemed slip-ons with a small heel, purchased by my mother, were a perfect complement. As I tucked my standard flip-flops back into the closet, I resolved not to tell anyone what I discovered today.

Feeling a little flirty, I pulled out a strand of pearls worn only on Sundays or to the occasional Saturday wedding. Today they seemed fitting. Finishing it off with dainty pearl-stud earrings, I studied myself one more time. Sleek ponytail: classic. Pearls: elegant. The entire look was, dare I say, perfection. I could compete with the best of them. This look could turn heads in windows. And I'm not talking pet-store windows either.

"Well, Savannah Phillips, you look like you stepped out of some kind of fashion magazine," Louise said, stopping her dish-washing midstroke as I entered the back door of Jake's.

I looked down, running my hands over my skirt, trying unsuc-cessfully to smooth out the two wrinkles that the trip over here had created. "It's not all that."

Then Dad walked through the doors and stopped midstride as well. "Well, what do we have here? I thought you already got a job."

"So are you saying I only dress up for job interviews?" I refused to look at him and focused on my morning breakfast out of a fountain.

"I'm just saying it's either an interview or church, and it's not Sunday. Or it could be a funeral, but unless it's slipped by the pry-ing eyes and listening ears around here, no one's died lately."

"Somebody's about to die." I thought I heard Louise mumble as she returned to her dish washing.

I took a long sip of my Coke. "You're crazy. I'm a working woman. There is nothing unusual about me looking nice to go to work."

"Whatever you say. Well, have a good day." He kissed me on the head and started back to the front.

"Still washing dishes?" I asked.

Louise mumbled again. This time I was pretty certain a death threat was involved. Even Mervine wasn't smiling today. And that is enough to cause anyone to ruminate over the current state of affairs. I scurried to the front, before Louise was finished mumbling and Mervine took to imitating a scene from *Psycho* with that knife she was washing.

"Anyone willing to listen to correction that can lead them to life can consider themselves in company with the wise." Jake's thought for the day. Dad watched me as I read. "How do you know everything?"

"Savannah, you're the crazy one. I don't know half of anything."

"Yes, you do. You know all of most, and the rest of all."

"I just want to be prepared."

"Prepared for what?"

"Prepared for living."

"You're prepared, for everything from skinned knees to natural disasters."

He laughed. "I've had a lot of practice."

"Am I prepared?"

"Only you can answer that. Are you? Are you prepared for your article tomorrow?"

I rested my chin in my hands and looked up at him. "I know the topic. But not the details. How is that for prepared?"

"Shaky, but at least you have a topic. Anyway, if you can't think of anything, at least you'll look like a professional."

"Well, I'm so glad I've given all of you something to talk about today." I said with a smirk.

The chime on the door announced the entrance of the cappuccino-loving television personality. Every head turned in tandem.

"Told you she'd be back," I stated with shameless pleasure. Dad's face filled with regret. "Ooh, look. Maybe I'm smarter than I thought." Our raised right eyebrows mirrored each other's, and I headed to a place that would respect my newfound discernment and my professional attire.

Old Betsy hiccupped when I turned her off. The Saab still looked good (on the outside at least) for its eight years of age and close to 150,000 miles. Reaching across the seat, I grabbed my taupe Coach handbag that matched my shoes. I laughed at my mother's diligence in making sure I possessed some sense of style. With her out of sight for a while, I could enjoy carrying it without her taking credit for instilling me with good, albeit expensive, taste. I opened the car door and practically collided with the last face I needed or wanted to see, standing there grinning at me.

"Why are you in the parking lot when you ride a bike?"

"I don't want it to get scratched." His grin absolutely grated. "And how was your evening?"

"It was fine." I would try to ignore him. Taking a step forward, my perfect grace and elegance was held back by the fact that I had shut my skirt in the car door. My attempt to walk jerked the ensnared skirt so hard that the force pulled my feet out from under me and flung them underneath the car. My purse flew out of my arms, and all of its contents ended up at Joshua's feet. And there I was, held in place by the fabric of my skirt, elbows digging into pavement and sleek ponytail covering my face.

"Oh, Savannah!" He tried to catch me, yet unsuccessfully thwarted my fall. "Here, let me help you." He opened the door and my knees came down to the concrete with undue pain and suffering.

"Ow!" I declared of both my pride and my body. He helped me squirm out from underneath the car and lifted me to my feet. He was about to brush the gravel from my now miserably stained skirt and shirt. I slapped his hand. "Well, pardon me, but I am more than capable of wiping myself off."

He tried to hide his intense delight but proved totally incapable. I brushed the residue of embedded gravel from my unfortunate apparel and looked in horror at the contents of my purse, displayed across two parking places. We both saw them at the same time. The feminine items. Everyone knows a woman has feminine issues that require feminine products, but no one wants them exhibited across a parking lot and stared at by their latest affliction.

But he never made a remark as he picked up every item, including those "products," and placed them back inside my purse. I snatched it from him and straightened, refusing to give him any glory in my plight. Then I tucked the dangling hair back behind my ears and made a mental note to fix that as soon as I could get to a bathroom.

He opened the back door for me without saying a word and let me go to my desk without further comment or insult. As soon as his back was turned, I made my way to the ladies' room. Long gone was the classic and elegant look of the morning. Here in the mirror stood a pavement-stained skirt, gravel-pitted blouse, scuffed-up sandals, ratted hair, and bleeding knee. The trashed pride wasn't even worth mentioning.

Halfway into trying to salvage any semblance of being well-groomed, Jessica—my boss's abrasive secretary—walked in. *Just what I need to top off my morning.*

"I'll come back when you're through," said the snippy petite blonde.

"I'm through. Trust me." I made my way to the door.

"You might want to rethink that." She said in a perfectly pain-in-the-behind tone while backing away from me.

"What? Are you afraid I'm going to kiss you?" I referred to my kissing her on the cheek last week, assuring her I would make her like me. Looking back now, I wasn't sure of that small fact at all.

"No!" But she backed up even farther. "You better not anyway."

"Well, as I said, I'm through." And with that I walked around her to head out the bathroom door that she was holding open. I lunged for her as I walked through. Poor child about crashed into the paper-towel dispenser. I didn't even feel like laughing. So I just walked slowly to my cardboard world that needed walls and a door and an intercom system so I didn't have to come out until all the world had fallen into the ocean.

CHAPTER NINETEEN

My Styrofoam world had only been mine for one week today. I had tried to make it home the best I could. It wasn't great. How could any office without a door be considered great? But at least there wasn't quite so much gray.

I was going to be a writer. A writer of books. Actually, I did write a book. *The Road to Anywhere* it was called, about four girls on a road trip. Won a huge competition. A competition that would have made me a published author. A competition I was certain my mother had rigged. She hadn't. Didn't find that out quick enough. So, here I sit. A journalist for the *Savannah Chronicle*. A new destiny. But today it felt rather daunting. I was filling the shoes of an icon. A lady named Gloria Anderson, who had written stories that were life changing and thought provoking.

My most recent article took two long weeks to produce, and I do mean long, so long an entire book could be written about them. Come to think of it, I might just do that someday. But first I have to figure out what to say in the article for this week.

What part of the story shaping up on Wright Square would challenge a person, truly change a person? The events represented so many opinions and passions that it wasn't clear to me how to effectively portray their real breadth to my readers. And, after only one week on the job, I still worked in prove-yourself territory.

Even though this city has known about me and my achievements for years because of Vicky's incessant need to recognize me publicly—mostly in this very newspaper through, shall we say, rather large announcements—this effort of mine was different. And the world seemed to be watching. Every network-news team and several cable stations had collided in the heart of Savannah, giving me unprecedented opportunity to prove to the world my rational side, to be an effective and unbiased journalist. To portray the facts. Let the readers form their opinion. Let all humans reading this newspaper garner their own perspective by the views that had made us a city in the spotlight.

"That's it," I said to the ashen wall staring back. "I'll just state the views, the perspectives. Let the readers form their own opinions."

I got to work, trying to succinctly base the foundation of my story on the manifold conversations I heard around that square over the last three very long days. It was a human-interest story based on multiple humans.

By noon my computer screen was full but my stomach was empty. The cold Pop-Tart that I found stuck inside one of Dad's desk drawers in his study hadn't proven to be a substantial breakfast. The Coke had helped. But to be honest, I considered it an extraordinary achievement that I had been able to concentrate on anything other than how to bring my love home.

Paige and her plan awaited.

As I packed up my bag, the chatter of two girls a couple of shelters up strayed over the top of my own.

"You are so paranoid," one announced. "Who in the world will care if you take an hour or an hour and a half lunch break? No one will even notice you're still gone."

"I'm not sure I should appreciate that observation."

"Oh, you know what I mean. We work hard; we deserve to

take however long we want to for lunch. Now go and have fun. You can show an hour on your time card and no one will know the difference."

"Well, I'll think about it."

I headed out the door, certain that after only a week, I wasn't going to be pressing any luck with that one. At least not yet.

Clary's was our constant. Our North Star. Well, it wasn't all that, but their BLTs were the bomb. Helen had our drinks waiting. A Coke for me and a fake Coke for Paige, who pranced in late as always.

"Don't drink. Just talk," I told her.

She took the straw that was touching her lips and sucked on it long and hard and bugged her eyes out at me. "You're just nasty lately. Are you PMSing it?"

"Permanently! But enough about me. Let's talk about your plan for me."

"Well, at least you give me credit for the plan."

"I'm feeling generous." I smiled.

Helen sat our plates down in front of us. Her eyes darted between Paige and me. "Savannah, child, you look too thin. I'm getting you a milk shake." With that she darted back behind the bar to prepare me extra caffeine.

"Am I Two-Ton Tilda or what?" Paige asked loud enough for Helen to hear. Helen chose not to.

"Don't worry about her, I'll share. Now go on."

As she began her strategy for our conquest, the young man at the table next to us began to raise his voice at the other two elderly men sitting with him. "Do you have a medical degree?" he challenged. He expressed little regard for the fact that either of the two were old enough to have been his father. "No, you don't. You don't take people's hearts out of their chests and hold them in your hand and then put new ones back inside and save their lives. Do you do that?"

"You can lower your voice, Peter," one of the gentlemen encouraged.

"I'm not going to lower my voice," he assured us all. Apparently he was clueless that I had a plan to hear and he was getting in the way of it. "You two come in here trying to tell me what procedures I can and can't do in my operating room, while you push bureaucratic papers through, trying to keep Joe Public happy."

"Paige, just talk a little louder."

"Huh?"

"TALK A LITTLE LOUDER!"

"I CAN'T TALK OVER THAT!"

The snot-nosed surgeon continued to attract the attention of the entire restaurant and even got a few *shh*'s from different directions. Had Helen not been in the back kicking up a milk shake for me, she would have come out here and thrown him out on his keister.

Looking down at my watch, I realized my lunch hour was evaporating. And unlike some people, I didn't have the luxury of being tardy. Finally, with no relief in sight, I took relief into my own hands.

"Excuse me, Paige."

"HUH?"

"EXCUSE ME!" I got up. Placed my napkin back on the table, pried the backs of my legs off of the plastic-encased seat cushion and entered the firing zone.

"Sir?"

He didn't look up.

"Um, sir." I cleared my throat. He wouldn't even look in my direction.

"SIR!" That one got him and just about everybody else. About near startled myself.

"What do you want?" he snapped.

"I, no, we"—I motioned to the now totally engrossed audience—"we want you to either pipe down or leave."

"I beg your pardon?" He rose from his seat. He was a pretty big fella.

"Please don't get up unless you're going to leave."

"I don't know who you think you are—"

"I'll tell you who I am. I am a patron of this restaurant, and I have thirty minutes to eat, hear a story that I have been waiting all day to hear, and get back to work before my lunch time expires. You have just wasted ten minutes of my time. And unless you hold the ability to heal *broken* hearts, then your discourse on all your other skills won't do me a lick of good. So, if you will please keep it down, the rest of us could get back to our nice lunch and not have to endure your insufferable, self-righteousness, and obnoxious behavior."

I got quite a few "amens" on that one from the other parties in the dining facility.

"George, let's go," the elderly gentleman said to his quiet friend.

They both rose, and the gentleman who had yet to add anything to this basically one-sided conversation stood. He looked at the yapper and said, "Peter, you may be a wonderful doctor. You may even be a gifted surgeon. You may have the knowledge of the latest innovations in the medical field. But you have not been nor will you ever be a 'savior' to anyone. That is one thing you should never forget."

The two left, and the irate man in front of me could have procured the role of Michael Douglas's character in *Falling Down II.* But I didn't wait to watch. I went back to my table and made Paige pick up where she left off, at the beginning.

"That was good," she said, finishing off the last of my milk shake. Even Helen hadn't noticed that Paige had consumed my shake, until she turned around, because she, too, had been frozen beside our table during the exchange. When she did realize Paige's ungrateful behavior, she slapped her on the back of the head with her dirty towel.

"Gross."

"You deserved that." And away Helen went to prepare another.

"Okay. I'm a desperate woman; now talk."

For the next twenty minutes we ate, and Paige laid out one of the best plans I had heard in a while. Well, actually the only plan. It was subtle but effective, and it would take place tomorrow night. As we walked up the street to our cars, we finalized the details. "So can you get all of that done before seven o'clock tomorrow night?"

"I think. Dad closes the store down at five and he'll be with Mom by six, so that should give me plenty of time. But let's do seven thirty to play it safe."

She scanned my attire and her eyes rested on my skirt. "Okay, seven thirty it is. But you need to come without grease stains."

"You're funny. Seven thirty, and I'll look fabulous."

She headed back to her studio, and I longed for five minutes to run into my house and change, but I was still behaving like a good little new employee. Set a good example. Get there on time. Don't overdo lunch. And avoid the boss at all cost.

"Mr. Hicks wants to see you in his office." The grating voice of his assistant came over my phone no sooner than my purse hit my desk.

"Okay. I'll be right there." My first attempts to learn my way around the building were met with a few detours through broom closets and men's lavatories, but my confidence was building. This trip was successful. Unfortunately, the welcoming committee wasn't all too welcoming. In fact, all Jessica did was snarl and remind me of a four-legged hairy creature that had taken to sleeping on sidewalks.

She hated me all because I was the daughter of Victoria Phillips, who also happened to be the woman trying to force Jessica's family into getting rid of the enormous satellite that resides in their backyard and can be seen from three different streets. Or so Vicky says.

"Savannah, come in and have a seat," Mr. Hicks's gruff voice summoned me from the other side of his glass window. "Close the door."

He seemed exceedingly irritated. The fact that I was on a four-week probation period meant it wasn't in my best interest to attract attention. But as he held up a stack of papers and flopped them back down on his desk, I was overcome by the sense that his irritation was all about me. "Savannah . . ." He paused, eying my tainted appearance. He simply shook his head and made his way to the edge of his desk. As he sat, the desk moaned and his tummy came to rest, albeit after a few bounces, over his belt. His suspenders did the rest of the work. "Savannah, papers on the whole try to remain fair and impartial."

I eyed him carefully, thinking few newspapers I had ever read in this world were capable of such a feat. "We do have columns, however, that reflect definite opinion. But for a human-interest writer, it's best to capture the sides of human interest without defining your own personal parameters quite so clearly."

"I'm not sure what you're talking about sir."

He held up the cover of yesterday's paper. "This is what I'm talking about."

"But you wouldn't have known it was me, if someone hadn't put my name in there."

"Well, Miss Victoria Phillips's daughter"—he waved the stack of papers in front of my face—"these are e-mails incensed about your presence there."

"Well, who approved my name in the caption?" I asked. "Apparently someone wants me to fail, wouldn't you think? Or at least portray this as something it's not. You are the editor, are you not?" I tried to remain as respectful as possible even though my face was flushed with anger.

"Yes, I did approve it. Because it happens to be one of the biggest news stories we've had in a while." He also tried to stay calm. "So you don't adamantly support your mother's position?"

"My mother's position is that of a woman standing on a side-walk chained to a slab of concrete. Would you support that position? No, I support the position of feather beds and duvets."

He crossed his arms and stared at me. "Savannah, you know what I'm talking about."

"Yes, sir, I do. But my mother was hugging me because I told her President Bush was coming to town. The people who wrote those e-mails have done nothing more than derive opinions from false assumptions. But frankly, I've had to deal with that since I got here."

"Well, I just felt you needed to know what was going on." He moved back to his squeaky leather chair, which immediately propelled him backward.

"I'm doing the best I can. I don't know why people care what I do anyway."

"Savannah, people need a winner and loser; they don't like draws. And if they don't agree with the outcome, they need someone to blame. If you don't want to be blamed, don't put yourself in a place of opinion."

"That's kind of hard with what I do."

"But not impossible. You tell the story. Let others form the opinion. And believe it or not, it is possible to do that while having a clearly defined opinion yourself." He winked. "You're a writer, Savannah. Tell the people a story. Make the moment real. Make the people real. And then make the revelation real. You'll have an opinion. And it will be clear. But what matters is the journey people take in order to get to theirs."

I'm not sure I had one clue this side of Saluda what he was talking about. But at the rapid rate things were declining around me, it came as no real surprise. I stood up to leave. "Am I getting fired?"

His belly bounced with his chuckle. "No, Miss Savannah, you are getting educated."

His secretary had disappeared. I wasn't surprised. Truth be known, she had taken my picture and turned it in herself. Truth be known. I didn't care. Truth be known. That was a lie.

CHAPTER TWENTY

If that had been the e-mail, Lord be with the mailman. I tried to keep my mind busy. I ordered my notes and decided to focus on the great debate and clearly portray both sides. Fairness and balance would hopefully silence my critics.

Curly Locks left me alone. Either he was too busy to bother me, or he didn't want to associate with Savannah's newest source of disheveled contention.

I picked up on one of Vicky's calls by mistake. She had resorted to calling from someone else's phone. She was good.

"Honey, do you want to have dinner with us tonight? It's like having a dinner party with strangers. You'll love it. This has been the most fun I've had in years. And if it weren't for the noise of the protesters it'd actually be peaceful."

"Well, I'm glad you're enjoying yourself. But actually, well, I, I really have to work on my story. It's due tomorrow at two and I'm still putting it together."

"Are you sure you don't need to interview me?"

I had to be quick with this one. "Well, no, not for Wednesday. Maybe I'll need some comments for Friday's story."

"Well, you know your mother always wants to see you. And I think there are a couple new people coming to spend the night tonight. So, it could be fun. At least come by and see me if you don't stay."

"Well, I'll have to see. I've got a lot of work to do."

"You can't work all the time, Savannah," she said in a Southern drawl that was drawn-out even for her. Miss Working Twenty-Four/Seven.

"Who is taking care of your job?" I asked, trying not to sound catty.

"Honey, I'm in control of my job. Ran me an extension cord into the courthouse and plugged in my cell-phone charger. Your father brought my laptop, and I'm a working machine. If that little diva from Atlanta would leave me alone, I might get more work done."

"You've talked with her today?"

"Oh, she has something to say to me every day. Most of the time she does it all nice and syrupy." The mere mention of syrup caused me to lick my lips. "She tries to act like Ms. Perfect. But she's perfectly evil I tell ya."

I couldn't picture such a refined woman speaking evil things to a woman attached to a monument in the middle of a city. The heat was getting to her. "Well, I've got to run. I'm getting buzzed by Marla."

She ended her performance in a perfect pout. "I love you, darling. Come see Mother soon, okay?"

"Bye, mother." I clicked over right before Marla gave up. Her own Southern drawl came over the phone. "Savannah, I have some messages up here for you."

I wasn't sure why we didn't have voice mail around here, but with Styrofoam walls, who was surprised? "Be there in a minute."

Upon arrival she handed me a stack of pink slips.

"All of these in a half an hour? Please tell me they're from the beauty queen."

"Wish I could, but most are from not-too-happy Savannians. But don't worry, honey. They'll get over it. They always do."

As I started to the back, I noticed a little odd-looking doll-like creature Marla had sitting on her desk. "What's that?"

"Oh, this?" She picked up the odd-looking creature. "This is my good-luck charm. I got it on my thirteenth birthday and have had good luck ever since. It helped me win ten thousand dollars on *The Pyramid*; then I won the showcase showdown on *The Price Is Right*, and the biggest thing it has done is got me in the audience at Oprah's 'Favorite Things' Christmas show."

"No way! That show is like the bomb! People try anything to get in the audience of that show. How in the world did you accomplish that?"

"Saved up for a whole year to go see Tom Cruise on her show, and then she surprised us when we got there. And I wasn't even disappointed."

"I'd say not. Sounds like you need to hang on to that little thing."

"If it weren't for this thing, I wouldn't have had any of that happen."

"Well, I don't know about that, but you at least have some great stories to tell. Did you meet Donny Osmond?" I asked, trying to hide my secret attraction.

"Yes, honey, I did, and that man is"—she leaned across her desk and whispered—"well, he's just plumb perfect."

"He is kind of cute, huh?"

"Ooh, honey, and when he hugged me after I won that ten thousand dollars, I just held on as long as I could without looking suspicious."

I couldn't help but giggle. Her innocence and Southern charm were so refreshing. "Have a great night. Thanks for the notes."

"It'll die down. There'll be something more interesting tomorrow."

"Hope so."

I stopped off at Jake's on the way home. Louise and Mervine were already gone for the day. At seventy-five they deserved to leave whenever they wanted to. Richard was heading out to his car when I pulled up behind the store.

"Your dad's already gone, Savannah."

"I figured. Just wanted to grab a Coke before I went home."

"You don't have any Cokes at your house?"

"We don't have much of anything left at the house. The milk's sour, I ate all the leftovers, and we've been out of Cokes since Saturday."

He paused as his dark brown hand grabbed the doorhandle of his new Ford Taurus. He said the dealership gave him an incredible deal, but he really thinks Dad had something to do with it all. "You don't know how to go to the grocery store, Savannah Phillips?"

"Okay, Richard, that's enough. Don't you start in on me too. Yes, I know how to go to the grocery store. It's the cooking part that has me stumped. Know of any good cleaning ladies that can cook? I'm desperate."

"Savannah Phillips, your mother would have your hide if you brought someone into her house, let them into her kitchen, and had them changin' her sheets. Now, you know that would be the undoin' of all undoin'."

"They would just be, shall we say, filling in."

"Child, you ain't like no other child I've ever seen. But there ain't no way I'm recommendin' anyone to step into your mama's kitchen. She ain't gonna be handcuffed to that thing forever. She will come home one day."

I laughed. "You're a chicken."

He chuckled. "Call me what you will. But stupid I ain't." He gave me a wink and climbed in his car.

I walked over to a park bench across from the court-house to eye the day's activities from a distance and took a long, burning swig of my Coke. The sound of it fizzing inside the cup was like a childhood comfort. And the burning was like a purging of the yuck of the day. I watched as two women came out of the legislative building with their sleeping bags rolled up under their arms. They sat down quietly about a yard in front of my bench and proceeded to establish their accommodations for the evening.

Listening to the low sounds of continuing conversation, it wasn't hard to gather this city's opinions, because few people talked about anything else. For all intents and purposes, the world of Savannah had stopped except for right here, on this square. And on the front pages of the *Savannah Chronicle*, of course.

I peered into the store next to Dad's shop. Through the window I noticed two kids fighting over what seemed to be a sucker. Their mother leaned down to take it from them. Her again. Emma. Savannah's rumor mill said that Emma hadn't been seen on the streets in years without a cigarette hanging out of her mouth or hair that needed scrubbing. But I could see that sister had obviously found the ashtray and the shampoo. Her blond tresses were pulled back into a neat ponytail, and her lips were painted the same soft pink shade as her floral Lilly Pulitzer sundress. I needed to talk with her. I couldn't avoid her forever. I decided to wait until they came out of the store.

A hand on my shoulder about caused me to jump out of my skin. It was none other than my new park-bench partner in her customary floral attire. "Well, hello, baby. That's a lot of commotion going on over there, isn't it?"

"Sure is, Joy." I so longed to blurt out, *Why in the world are you still wearing that same dress?* But fear that it may be the only one she owned caused me to refrain. "What have you been doing all day?"

She paused and turned to look at the ceaseless activity by the courthouse sidewalk. "Observing. What about yourself?" She eyed my stained outfit.

I tried to ignore her stares. "Pretty much the same thing. Except I was writing down my observations."

"You're a writer, Savannah?"

The mere word *writer* pricked me. After leaving college and letting go of my dream to become a novelist, the thought of what I had let go of was a tad overwhelming some days. "Well, I guess so. I write for the paper."

"What kind of writing?"

"Human-interest stories."

She chuckled, and the flowers across her belly shook. She nodded to the events across the street. "Well, you've got your work cut out for you, don't you, sweet girl?"

"You would think so, wouldn't you?"

Joy's attention was diverted for a brief moment to Miss Sally. Miss Sally is a peculiar creature. She pushes her Yorkie in a baby carriage and walks her canary. I lie not. Would I lie with a monument sitting across the street declaring, "Thou shall not lie"? She actually carries the canary in its cage in one hand and walks it around as if it needs fresh air. I can't help but be thankful she doesn't have a cat. Poor thing would have declawed *itself* by now.

"What is that?" Joy asked, wide-eyed.

"Crazy in the flesh. Ever seen it?"

"Just did." Then she was back to the things that really mattered. "So, what are you having for dinner tonight?" I wasn't sure if she thought we would be having dinner together every night, or if this was just the next step in our conversation.

I looked toward the monument, growing increasingly irritated. "I have no idea. I've had to eat out a lot lately."

"Ooh, food issue has Savannah a little testy."

"Yeah, sorry. It's just a sore spot with me."

"Why so, baby?"

"Well, you see that big mass of people over there?" I nodded to the clump surrounding the monument. She turned to look. "Well, hidden behind all those people is a petite fireball who happens to be my mother. And as long as she is strapped to that monument, I'm eating out."

Joy squinted, trying to find my mother among the masses. "Your mother is strapped to that monument?"

"Chained, is more like it."

Her expression changed to grave concern. "Oh my. What did she do? Commit a crime?"

I patted her hand and giggled, trying to relieve her of her worry. "No. Sister Vicky committed no crime except that of abandoning her family."

"She abandoned your entire family?"

"Well, actually, the rest of my family is probably out there right now gathering dinner to take to *her*. I think they're just creating a bigger monster."

"Don't you call your mother a monster, Savannah. I don't care what she's done."

"I'm just frustrated."

She turned to look at me with her deep brown eyes. I had no question a theological revelation was on the horizon. But she paused extra long. Her eyes looked past me, through me, as if she was remembering something. Her own experience. Her own moment.

"Miss Joy, you okay?"

Her eyes registered with mine once again. "Oh yeah, baby, just thinking."

"Thinking what?"

She stood up and tugged at her skirt to try to get it to come down from where it had bunched around her waist. Then she tugged at her stockings uselessly. "Thinking I probably need to go."

"Oh, well, okay. I guess I'll just see you later."

She stopped. Her gaze went up the street and stuck on something that was probably invisible to those of us in this world. "Parents, Savannah, don't always make the right decisions. But they make the best decisions they know. And at the end of the day, the choice is yours to honor them or not. But don't forget that every choice has a consequence, be it good or bad."

As if her other realm dissipated, she turned her gaze back to me. "A lot of people waste time being angry when anger affords no results. Your mother's not trying to hurt you, Savannah. She's trying to rescue you. That's what good parents do; they rescue. They rescue their children's futures. They rescue their children's heritage. They rescue their children's hopes. They don't always do it in the way you think is best. But they do it the best they know."

She left me there on that park bench as confused as I was when I left Mr. Hicks's office. She waddled through the square, humming that familiar tune, the one that was now officially driving me crazy because I couldn't place it. She patted people's heads as she went, each person lighting up when they saw her. By the time she disappeared up the street, she had been given a 16-ounce Coca-Cola, what appeared to be a sandwich, and an entire bag of Doritos. If Paige spotted her, Joy would be the one having to share *her* dinner this evening.

Sometime during my conversation with Joy, Emma had slipped away. Not that it mattered; I had already forgotten her.

CHAPTER TWENTY-ONE

The sea parted long enough for me to catch a glimpse of my mother. Poor thing was looking downright pitiful. Surely if she had any real idea of her present state of disgrace, she would be hiding *behind* the boulder instead of displaying herself in front of it. She stood there with her hair having been haphazardly brushed out and standing on end. Even from this far away I could see her mascara.

Her blue suit would probably have to be burned after this incident. Miss Savannah United States of America, one Amber Topaz, was at her side, posing for the cameras. She was looking exceptionally fabulous in a black strapless sundress with a white ribbon around the waist. Her golden tresses cascaded down her shoulders from a matching ribbon headband. As I stared at the two of them, it was hard not to wonder if maybe they should have been mother and daughter. After all, they both loved pageants, accessories, and high heels.

Clearly, that didn't work for me. In fact, pageants had never worked for me. Amazing enough since they had once been the core of my mother's world. I boycotted pageants effectively for over ten years until last week, when Amber invited me to one. I was working on a story that made the pageant a mandatory affliction. Had it not been for that, I would still be on a pageant "fast" as I called it.

The fast began at the age of fourteen, after my mother's attempt to get me to be a part of the "pageant system" as it is identified by anyone who knows a thing about them at all. The mere shock of it forged in me a fear of anything that sparkles, a fear that still pretty much exists to this day.

It was a Victoria and Savannah "date week." I should have boycotted. I should have feigned a seizure right there in the middle of the marble-covered foyer. But Vicky would have called a paramedic and delivered me to the pageant à la ambulance, via stretcher. She'd have propped me up with a drip if necessary. But either I was going to a weeklong pageant, or I was going to be grounded from Coca-Cola for the week. I figured, how long could a week be? Had I known, I would have sacrificed Cokes for a month.

She sat me on the front row and she wore her tiara. I won't even tell you the battle that precipitated that final outcome. But the curtain opened that first night with the "Salute to Broadway" serenade, and the reigning queen belted out the song "One" from *A Chorus Line* while somebody's fishnet-stocking-covered leg kept kicking out from the side curtain. Well, a person would rather have her toenails pulled out with pliers.

"How long does this last?"

She elbowed me. "Sit back and enjoy, Savannah." Then she sang along and beamed from ear to ear.

"What is that?" I asked in horror as the two grown men came out from each side of the stage and sang Don Quixote's "Man from La Mancha." Just imagine Rick and Bubba doing such, and you pretty well get the picture. Except one poor soul had a hairpiece that he should have sued over. They were joined by two old women. Well, at fourteen, forty is old. And they all sang in unison until the final note. When they gave a downright unfortunate attempt at four-part harmony, I decided they should have just kept that puppy unison the whole way through.

"You should ask for your money back," I told my mother.

"You should act like a duchess and keep your mouth closed if you can't be nice."

I thought that was nice. Far nicer than what I had been thinking anyway.

Each contestant began to introduce herself. One child seemed to crack herself up just by saying her own name.

"Do they think we're deaf?" I asked as each passing participant screamed into the microphone above their head. "Look like a bunch of strained-neck whooping cranes, if you ask me."

"I didn't."

For an entire week I endured swimsuit competition, talent presentation, and evening gown. Some women with thighs the size of Georgia pranced around as if they were Tinkerbell. I was certain the stage was shaking.

Talent presentation took the cake.

"Does she know she's tone-deaf?" I asked the pageant professional seated next to me.

"It's the monitors," she assured me.

"Ooh, whoa, girl," I almost hollered as a tap dancer turned one time too many and about ended up tapping via her backside.

The operatic aria, in Italian I presumed, offered more fodder. "You do realize she could be singing pig latin for all we know."

Mother looked at me incredulously. "No, she couldn't, Savannah. Because I *know* pig latin."

When the violinist took the stage and played a number that I'm sure the original composer never intended to be interpreted in such a way, I couldn't help but ask, "Can you hear her?"

"Oh, yes. Isn't it amazing? She just started two weeks ago."

"Ya think?"

The poor emcee, a local news personality, introduced each contestant like a Southern gospel preacher. "And-a ladies and gentlemen-a, please welcome-a, The Very Golden-a, Miss Golden Highway-a!"

But when Miss Upper Georgia took the microphone and tried to sing like Whitney Houston, I had to squint from the pain. About downright scraped the leather off the armrests of my chair. "Please tell me it will be over soon."

"Not soon enough." Even Vicky had had enough by evening three, for a totally different reason, I assure you.

I watched, drugged, the final night. And I do mean drugged. I laid in bed all day, moaning in agony, sheer agony. Agony from the knowledge that I had to endure yet another evening. Mother gave me half a Valium. That and the revelation that this would be *it* gave me the fortitude to endure.

After the top ten were announced, I was certain that beauty contestants and flight attendants went to the same school.

"Where do you learn that?" I quizzed.

She wouldn't even respond to me. But when it came to the final onstage question, Sister Savannah came to her apex. Even though I was half-comatose, I was aware that Miss Merry Christmas had taken the stage in a rather bright red and green ensemble.

"Miss Merry Christmas-a," the evangelist asked, "do you-a think-a women who have been abused-a are better suited to speak out about domestic-a violence-a than women who haven't-a?"

Well, nothing could hold me back. From my front-row seat, I jumped to my feet, and you would have thought I was in the parade of contestants myself as loud as I got.

"You have got to be kidding me!" I screamed, throwing my hands up to slap my own head.

Vicky reacted immediately. She threw her hand across my mouth, but I was ready for a fight, and this one she would not win. "Yes, genius! I want a woman to be beaten, just so she can be better qualified to speak out against domestic violence! And that's what it's called—'domestic violence,' not 'domestic-a, violenc-a!'"

I left freely and waited in the foyer. I do believe Mother

crawled out underneath the chairs during the final song, when the Rick (or was it Bubba?) impersonator came out donned in a multilayered crinoline evening gown and blond curly wig as Glenda the Good Witch from *The Wizard of Oz*. It was the beard that gave him away. We didn't speak for a week. But I was eternally relieved of all pageant-going responsibilities.

The chamber of commerce is the sponsor of the Miss Savannah United States of America Pageant. This could be the very reason Vicky wanted to be the head of the chamber. Even now she attends every summer with the reigning queen for two solid weeks.

She always invites us to join her. But who would forfeit two weeks of sheer pleasure? Junk food! Unmade beds! Late-night movies! Duke sleeps on Victoria's side of the bed. I even try to get Dad to put Duke in Vicky's Jacuzzi tub. Give the dog some real enjoyment. But Dad didn't want dog hair to come flying out of the jets during Mother's next soak, so he refused. Duke abhors Vicky's return. She even has to fight him a couple good evenings to rescue her pillow from him. Usually, after she threatens to buy a cat, the poor thing takes a dump in her slippers and gives her her bed back.

Secretly though, I know she pines for someone who would enjoy her world of whipping with her. *Whipping* is the coined phrase for what those girls do when they turn themselves around so the judges can catch them from all sides. Now, staring at her and Amber Topaz Childers, the reigning Miss Savannah United States of America, I was certain that Amber would have made a much more suitable daughter.

"Vanni, looks like you're thinking too hard," Thomas said as he kissed me on the cheek.

He was the lucky one. The one who escaped being named George. Mother wanted to introduce him as "My son George from Georgia," but Dad saved him from such a fate by naming him after himself, Thomas Jake Phillips II. So, he failed to deliver me from my curse, but going through life as a girl named Tommy probably wouldn't have made my life much better anyway.

"No, just remembering." I said wiping off the perspiration the mere memory had caused. "I didn't even see you."

"I could tell. Ooh, you look like you've been trampled." He ran his hand through his lengthening hair. Every summer away from the hallowed halls of the Citadel, Thomas would grow out his hair and refuse to cut it all summer. Then football camp came, and bye-bye went the mop.

"Thank you. You look nice yourself." I stared at his frayed khaki cut-offs and his wrinkled T-shirt bearing the face of one Mr. Rogers asking, 'Won't you be my neighbor?'

He motioned to the rowdy protestors and asked, "Did they do this to you?"

"No. They are not to blame for these smudges. So where are you sleeping tonight? On the left or the right?"

He sat down on the stool beside me. "Oh, I'm sleeping at home tonight. That concrete is killing me." He rubbed his pained areas. "And I hear Amber's sleeping out there, and the last thing I want is a slumber party with that girl."

I laughed. "Well, you haven't totally gone mad then, have you?"

"So how about I have dinner with my sister tonight?"

I stood up to head back to my car. "I would like that."

He got up to follow me. "Would you mind changing first? You might embarrass me."

"Oh, I'm sure that would happen." I laughed. He wrapped his arm around me and walked with me to my car. "Oh, did I mention I'm moving this week?"

He laughed. "You are either extremely brave or extremely crazy."

"Do I get to choose which?"

"What bank did you rob?"

"I didn't rob a bank, just borrowed from one."

"Dad?"

"Now who's crazy?"

"Paige?"

"It's none of your business. But I figure if I'm going to starve, I may as well starve in my own house."

He opened my door for me and headed around to the other side of the car. "You could learn how to cook yourself."

"Yes, I could." And that was the end of that conversation.

CHAPTER TWENTY-TWO

Bistro Savannah would feed me tonight. I was thankful. We walked into the quaint atmosphere of the bistro on West Congress Street. Thomas wanted to come here because he had just gotten paid. And every good-ol' American boy wants a steak on payday. So where else would we go but the restaurant that was voted "Georgia's #1 seafood restaurant" by the Zagat Survey. Rest assured, they do steaks as well as they do seafood.

Thomas gave me a chance to change. And dinner gave us a chance to talk. We walked into the bistro, located in the historic market area, and ordered dinner. Now, staring across the table at him over a fabulous plate of potato-crusted salmon with chive butter sauce, it was hard not to notice how he had grown. Not necessarily matured, but definitely grown. Our years together had afforded us each other's confidence. Even though we easily irritated each other, we trusted each other. When we first moved to Savannah, we were pretty much each other's only friend. He found new ones quickly. I found Paige. Thomas loved her. First, because she got me away from hanging out with him and his friends. Second, because she got me away from hanging out with him and his friends.

He is the lover of the family. He's always kissing and hugging on people. He is also the schmoozer of the group. He can schmooze you out of something—usually money—before you know you've even been schmoozed. Dad is onto him. Vicky's a sucker. Me? Well, he learned most of his tricks from me, so I'm totally not snared in his tangled web.

He looks a great deal like our dad. And it seems that people have the same attraction to him as they do toward our father. Thomas has won the hearts of most of the older assistants at the courthouse—all women. Broken the hearts of quite a few of the interns—all women. And most of the judges assure him he needs to be a lawyer and needs to attend their alma mater—all ego. I've always thought he would be a great lawyer, because he will argue his point until you give in, give up, or slap him. The trait of debate he got from the one who birthed him. That even he cannot deny.

"I got some great songs off of the Internet today free. It's like Napster used to be."

"Are you hanging out with a rapper?"

"Do you live in this century?"

"Last I checked."

"Honestly, sometimes it's like a ninety-year-old woman crawls out of your body and lands into my conversations."

I placed the fork back on my salad plate. "Is there something in the water about relating me to old people?"

"Napster was a Web site where you could download free music until some law got rid of that as an option. But people still find a way to do it."

"Sounds illegal."

"No more illegal than what record companies are charging for CDs."

"So, what songs can you get?" I asked, taking a bite of the salmon that sat before me and letting it melt in my mouth.

He didn't bother to stop chewing the steak that he had just put in his mouth. "Any song. Just click and it's yours."

"Can you get Donny Osmond songs on there?"

"See, I knew it! You really are ninety. There is no way you, a twenty-four-year-old woman, should even know Donny Osmond songs. You should be singing Bon Jovi songs, or I'll even give you Boyz II Men or that Jonathan Pierce guy, who's not half-bad. But my Lord, woman, not Donny Osmond. Next thing you know you'll be talking about Barry Manilow tunes."

"I actually love—"

"Don't say it, Savannah. I swear, I'll dig you a hole in the ground when we leave here."

"*I'll dig you a hole in the ground when we leave here.*" I mimicked. "I am not old. And you shouldn't swear."

"See, you sound just like our mother. And to top it off you're wearing pearls on a Monday." He swung his fork at me, causing a piece of his potato to swat me in the face.

"Would you put that down before you gesture, please?" I wiped my face with my napkin. I had forgotten to take my pearls off when I changed clothes. They didn't really match my jeans and T-shirt. "I'm trying to look more professional."

"You're trying to look like that Ms. Austin lady. And you will never look that good," he said, not looking up from his plate.

"I am not. And I will too."

He looked up at me with a totally annoying-brother kind of look. "You want to refuse who you are, to become something you're not. And you don't even know if what's on the cover is an accurate representation of what's on the pages. Are you getting me here? Because I'm trying to relate to your world."

"Whatever."

"You like what you see, but you don't know that what you see is all you will get. And once you get all that you see, you might not like it."

"You have just crossed over to loo-loo land."

This dinner wasn't enjoyable anymore. I got up to go to the restroom. My cell phone rang on the way.

"Hello?"

"Where are you? You sound like you're in a well," Paige's voice declared.

"I'm in the restroom."

"Gross! You're not using the restroom and talking to me at the same time, are you?"

"Like you haven't done that to me a thousand times. And no, I'm standing here at the sink. And you better not be calling to tell me our plans have fallen through."

"Actually, my darling, I'm calling to tell you that I have successfully contacted Grant. And I will have him at the door of Jake's promptly at seven thirty."

"You are fabulous."

"Yes, sweet girl, I am. You owe me big."

"He'll owe you bigger," I assured her.

"Now go get on with your business."

"I'm going back to get dessert."

"Ooh, have some for me."

"Sure. My pleasure. Thank you, my friend. Love ya."

"You too. Tomorrow."

"Tomorrow!" I declared in sheer delight as an elderly lady walked through the bathroom door, only to back herself right back through it upon my outburst.

Back at the table, Thomas appeared in no way disturbed at our conversation. He was just stating the facts as he saw them. He was like Vicky in that way. Neither realized or even concerned themselves with the immediate effects of their words. They just simply stated how they felt, what they observed, and that was that.

"I'm not in denial, and I know who I am. And I'm not old. So I would advise a man who desires to live eternally with his mother to quit dissecting my personality and talk about other things. Like this free-music stuff."

"Oh, it really is amazing. Just pick a song. Download it. And bam! You've got new music."

"Could I just download them to my iPod?"

"Anything you want."

"Anything?"

"Even Donny Osmond." We shared our desserts and speculated how Amber and Mother would spend their evening under the stars. We came up with many options and expressed thanks that we would be present for none of them.

CHAPTER TWENTY-THREE

elevision at ten, featuring Mother and Greta Van
Susteren, was a bad idea. I tried to turn it. But like a train
wreck, it held my attention. Old Vicky did pretty good until the
end, when she didn't know the microphone was on and she asked
Greta who had done her fabulous eye job. Then she offered poor
Greta the number of her hairstylist so she could get some help on
that end while she was in town. But since I didn't hear my name
surface one time during the interview, I didn't even care that Ms.
Susteren had been insulted.

As I sat on the sofa, curiosity got the best of me. I'd witnessed
Mother sleeping outside, but Miss Amber Topaz sleeping on a sidewalk was something that needed to be seen. Thomas refused to
accompany me. He said it would take weeks before his body
recovered as it was. Mother had called us during dinner, but I made
Thomas talk to her while I ran to the bathroom again. That way
he could honestly say I wasn't available.

The commotion around the square had died down. Propped
up against the monument this evening were Victoria and Miss
Gemstone. Dad was across the square, talking to a couple men who

looked like journalists packing up for the night. Mother and Miss Gemstone had their silk eye masks propped on the tops of their heads, obviously confident their assignments for the evening had concluded. Mother was looking ever the worse for wear, and they were gabbing it up at ninety miles an hour. It wasn't clear to me how at the end of the day there was still so much left to be discussed. My vocabulary ceased after dinner and abandoned me until after my first morning Coke. But these two, these two incessant chatty Cathys, seemed to find conversation in mere conversation.

"Does this concrete not leave marks?" Amber asked, rubbing her backside.

Mother giggled. "Honey, my poor body will never be the same after this. I'm glad I'm so physically fit."

I tried to stifle my laughter. That woman had only used her in-home gym once. Once. Hadn't even gone down there since to see if anything was even still there. And here she was declaring that her physically fit body was helping her. The only thing that kept her fit were the countless miles she logged from walking all around these squares, making sure things ran the way she deemed they should run.

Amber looked up at her. "Well, I'm thankful I started those Pilates videos last week. Ooh, that's what I should do. I should show you some of those moves that I've learned."

I thought for sure mother would protest. It would have seemed appropriate. But she didn't. And the next thing I knew, two grown women perched themselves atop their sleeping bags and began doing Pilates. It was ugly. If that was Pilates, someone should be charged. Amber had my chained mother doing things in public that should be downright illegal. Cirque du Soleil wouldn't be auditioning them anytime soon. Eventually, Dad finally noticed them and made them stop. They were flabbergasted at his request, but he didn't leave it up for discussion. He simply told them to get back in their sleeping bags and get to sleeping. At least all of his good sense didn't leave with this new way of life that had overtaken our world, our Savannah. Duke growled at Amber when she tried to get him to lie on the end of her sleeping bag. Instead, he walked all the way over to the other side of Dad and plopped himself down with an extended sigh. If he knew Thomas was at home in a warm cozy bed, Thomas would suffer the ill effects of chewed-up underwear for no less than a year.

"I wish Savannah were here," I heard my mother whisper.

"I do too." Amber pouted.

Those women were certifiable. I sat down to make sure I wasn't spotted and leaned back against one of the stately live oaks. It was kind of nice out here. Neither the death-grip of summer nor the "love bug" infestation had yet to truly seize us. And the evenings of quickly dissipating spring still held gentle breezes and sometimes a need for a lightweight jacket.

"May I join you?" came the voice of Faith Austin.

"Sure, it's a big tree." I scooted over. "So, where do you rest your head at night?"

"Well, not out here, that's for sure." Her dark tresses seemed to reflect the light of the moon. "I'm staying over at the Westin Resort. It has computer access, which helps. Why aren't you up there with your mother, supporting her cause?"

I chuckled at the thought. "Well, my mother and I aren't much alike. She likes the spotlight; I prefer lowlight. My mother has a way of continually moving toward the press, wherever it might be at the moment."

"So you think that's the only reason she's up there?"

"No, couldn't be."

"Why?"

"'Cause she wouldn't sleep outside four nights in a row if it was just about media exposure. No, she adamantly believes in what she is doing."

"So you don't support your mother's views?" she asked, digging a Snickers out of her purse.

"There are a lot of views my mother has that I don't support. Then, there are some I simply don't understand. In this case, I simply fail to see the necessity of chaining oneself to a statement."

"Want a bite?" she asked. It was nice for someone to offer *me* food for a change.

"Sure." I took a bite out of my portion of the Snickers. "How do you eat all of this stuff and look like you do?"

"Who knows. Good metabolism. Always working. Never enough sleep. All of those good things." She took another large bite.

"Do you work like this all the time?"

"You have to in this world, Savannah. But I love work. Even thrive on it. It defines me. Plus, you have to work hard if you want to stand out among the rest."

"You don't have much trouble standing out among anyone."

She laughed softly. "You're kind."

"Why are you really here, though?"

"I told you. Because this is my job." She gazed at the silk-masked ladies who were still chatting.

"I don't mean here in Savannah; I mean here, in the middle of this controversy at all."

"Savannah, one day you'll realize that life isn't black and white. Absolutes are relative. Most only restrain you. Kind of like your mother is over there."

"She would be restrained all right." I watched as Vicky tried to find a comfortable position beneath her down sleeping bag and her chains.

"Well, I was restrained long enough. Don't have any desire to do that again." Her gaze wandered off for a moment. But she was back as quickly as she had gone. "And the church doesn't belong in the states' business. They're clearly separated by the Constitution. I mean, nowhere is God mentioned in the Constitution. Church people need to keep their stuff inside their churches and out of schools and city squares."

"So that's why you're here, to make sure church and state don't mingle?"

"Pretty much, Savannah. Just trying to keep those lines clear, you know."

"But if there are no real absolutes, then how can the separation of church and state be so cut-and-dry?"

"Touché, Savannah. It basically comes down to this: The courts need to effectively be able to do their job without a conservative few dictating a nation's way of life."

"Sounds diplomatic enough." I finished off my half of the Snickers. "I had to learn diplomacy in college. I was the president of the student body my senior year in undergrad. So I can relate to the need of taking an important issue with two clearly defined opinions and trying to make the best of it."

"So you understand what I'm saying."

"Yes, in part." I let my mind wander off to those beautiful days of college. I returned. "But I never negated what was true to appease either side. That's because I believe in absolute truth."

"I guess that's where we're different." She picked up her thousand-dollar handbag that sat next to her.

"Yeah, I guess that's where we're different. But so long as everyone can respect each other in spite of their differences, I guess we're really not that different at all."

We were interrupted by Mr. Shelton from the market up the street. "Oh, Ms. Austin, I didn't think you would be out here so late."

"Yes, Mr. Shelton, just enjoying that Snickers I got at your store, with my new friend." She gave me a wink. It was clear Mr. Shelton was entirely smitten.

"I've got more if you'd like me to go open up the store for you." He grabbed a key ring the size of a horseshoe from his belt loop.

She held her hand up in protest. "Oh, no sir. That's all right. I think we've had enough for the evening. I have to go get some sleep anyway, before another busy day tomorrow." She turned her attention to me, apparently having forgotten what I just said to her. "Well, if you ever want to come see what we're all about, you can always come to Atlanta."

"I used to live there actually."

"I know. Your father told me. A nice man. A little over-the-top with the board and all, but a really nice man. Cute too."

"Whatever." I laughed.

"Well, when you come, you'll have a new friend to visit." She wiped off her brown-and-khaki-striped linen pants.

"We'll see you tomorrow?"

"I'm sure." And with that her perfectly manicured hand slid into Mr. Shelton's arm as they strode up the street together. She was stopped no fewer than six times by people who obviously wanted to talk to her. Eventually, Mr. Shelton bid her good night. I watched as she disappeared toward the Riverfront and one of the last evening ferries that would carry her across the river to the Westin. Mr. Shelton watched too.

The beaming floodlights of the eleven o'clock news finally all shut off, and the steady music of the crickets lured me to sleep.

I woke up in the dead of the night, covered in dew and hurting from the top of my head to well below the caboose area. I leaned against the rock to help me stand and tried to wipe off the dampness and bark. Then I caught sight of it: I had been leaning against Tomochichi's rock. I tried to stifle my screams. But the jig I did around that rock, beating my backside from any remnant of dead people, didn't go unnoticed. I shivered no less than twenty times and looked like a bad Jim Carrey impersonator. Those around me stared in their own postures of terror.

I tried to compose myself to make it home. I looked back once more at the concrete monument that had stolen my family. There lay two women with an umbrella perched over their heads to capture the dew (a concept lost on me), silk eye masks over their faces, (another concept that would forever be lost on me), and my dad curled up by my mother with his arms wrapped around her.

Looking at this scene, hearing the sounds of people snoring

and seeing sleeping bags strewn from one entrance of the court-house all the way to the other, and hearing the low murmuring of those who were praying through the midnight watch, I was struck by the lengths people would go to express their beliefs.

Ms. Austin had made it clear why she was here. At least I think she had. These people were making their reasoning clear as well. They were standing for principles others had given their lives for. They were fighting for what judges only a couple years before had been fired for. They were doing that which America so beautifully allowed people to do. They were standing up for what they believed in.

I had yet to understand the breadth of it all. The extremity of it was beyond me to begin with. But I knew that in the end, all would reveal itself. Life always does that. In my case, many of those revelations came through my mother. No matter how crazy she drove me, or how different she was from me, she deserved admiration. And the man lying beside her admired her the most. He didn't always agree with her, but he completely admired her.

As for me, well, I went home dancing a few more involuntary jigs along the way.

CHAPTER TWENTY-FOUR

Forsythe Park is the essence of our city to me. It seems to embody the heart of Savannah. Every element of our character seems to merge here and is represented somewhere in this two-block area. Tilling here with Duke—this morning he was desperate enough for sanity that he agreed to accompany me—was such a perfect way to start a day. The manicured shrubs lined the perimeter, the branches of towering trees cascaded over the sidewalk, the soothing sound of the fountain bubbled out of the center. The kaleidoscope required one to focus on something central.

Every morning it brought me to focus on communing with my Creator. Not some life force that gave us morning beauty and evening splendor. Not someone who only mattered when recognized, but who recognized us even when we treated Him as if He didn't matter. It was our time. His time to remind me of eternal things. My time to remind Him of my much-needed graces.

Somewhere between my attempts to make more headway than I had the day before, a redheaded flame passed me. She was wearing short shorts and had legs up to heaven. Her curly mane was pulled back in a ponytail. She had her earphones on but was singing. It was clear she wasn't tilling, because she obviously didn't realize how loud she was.

She didn't recognize me, or at least didn't let on if she did. I'm sure Grant had a picture of me somewhere. As many memories as we had made on film, it wasn't possible he had removed every trace of me from his existence. After she passed me I slowed up, forcing Duke to retreat with a gagging sound, as I hadn't forewarned him.

You have no idea your world's about to be rocked, do you, sister? Well, I don't want to have to hurt you, but love is difficult.

"Isn't it, Duke?" He looked at me, seeming a tad irritated and confused. "Love is difficult. Don't you know?"

Of course he knew. His gaze wandered to a poodle coming up the sidewalk. But he couldn't fool me. I knew every dog made him dream of Lucy. He had pined for that dog since she got antique-store broken. But Mr. Newman knew Duke's reputation. Duke has a wandering eye, that must be admitted, which is why Dad has to keep such a close eye on him. And why Miss Alberta carries her Chihuahua in her purse. Rumors of his philandering float the streets of Savannah. As do a few suspicious-looking mixed-breeds.

This distraction from my tilling was rather frustrating. But it did affirm that my evening plans would be worth all the heartache I'd endured.

We entered Jake's through the back door. Duke began growling at the swinging doors immediately. I peeked out to see none other than Miss Television Time perched at the counter, talking to my father.

"She must really like it here." I patted Duke on the head. He growled again. "What's into you, anyway?"

"He doesn't like that little lady," Richard said as he came out of the stockroom with more napkins.

"Growls at her every time she comes in," Louise said, looking up from the dishes she was washing.

"How often does she come in?" I asked.

"Oh, three, maybe four times a day. Only wants your father helping her. She likes him."

Their drama cracked me up. "She's a silly lady. She knows my father is married."

"Savannah, child. Some women don't care 'bout that kind of stuff," Richard said, putting away some cups that Mervine had just dried.

"Please, what would that woman want with my dad? He's old enough to be her father." I took a quick peek out through the slats of the door. I patted Duke on the head. "Come on, boy, let's try to get ice out of the ice dispenser again." He wasn't interested. I sighed and turned my attention back to the manual dishwashers. "Anyway, when is that dishwasher getting here, ladies?"

"I called that little twit again this morning. He said he would have it here this afternoon," Louise said, becoming slightly more aggressive with the cup she was washing. "I told him if he didn't he would have me to contend with when I showed up on his front porch."

"Ooh, call me before you go. I'm needing a good human-interest story." I headed to the door.

"Better not have to go. And you could do an interest story on all these demanding people that keep coming in here, wanting stuff we don't have. If one more young'un asks me for a Frappuccino, I'm going to beat his big old—" Mervine slapped her wet hand over Louise's mouth, leaving Louise to spit out soap suds.

"Well, you two just keep that woman away from my dad," I shouted as I went to close the door.

"Hard to keep women away from a good-looking man, Savannah." Mervine spoke with a sly smile.

"Oh, that's disgusting."

I heard Mervine laugh. That was about all she offered. Probably wouldn't hear from her for another week.

As I walked out to my car, I could hear my mother's voice talking lively and loudly. Turning slowly so as not to attract attention, I saw the top of her red mane shooting out above possibly ten microphones. It was when I heard my name mentioned that red blood cells in me began to swim upstream and land inside my face. I was tired of being her topic of discussion. She wanted me to interview her for my article. There was no need to. She had given me everything I needed to know in her sound bites.

"Gave up on the heels today, huh?" my office partner asked as he stared at my brown leather flip-flops. "And the pearls? Where are the pearls?"

"Do you monitor everyone's clothes, or do you just need someone to irritate at the crack of dawn?"

He couldn't hide his perfectly white smile, even though he tried to feign disinterest. "Well, only the attire of those who like to dangle beneath cars, and it is nowhere near the crack of dawn."

I sat my Coke down on my strip of desk that ran from one end of my Styrofoam heaven to the other. The metamorphosis of my cardboard world to some semblance of an office was slow, menial, and probably impossible.

"You are such the comedian. Do you work or just walk around?" I turned my back on him and sat down to cut on my computer.

He produced a pathetic mimic. "*Do you work or just walk around?* Actually, I work while I walk around, and bike and sit and all kinds of things. So what are you going to write about?" He pulled up a chair.

I turned to look at his black curls, which were drooping into his eyes. His tanned and masculine hand pushed them away, leaving his black eyes to stare at me. The richness of them caught me off guard and I looked away. "Did I invite you here this morning? Because trust me, I've met my irritation quota for the day."

"No, but I'm not invited to most of the places I end up. Anyway, you're too young to be irritated so early in the morning. So quit avoiding the subject. What are you going to write about?"

I began to check my e-mail so I wouldn't have to look at him. "I'm going to write about what everyone is talking about. It would be rather odd for me to act as if nothing is happening around here, wouldn't it? Especially after I was highlighted in the *paper!*"

"Well, I'm sure there is plenty to say. So are you going to talk about your mother?"

I finally turned to him. He sat there with his elbow leaning on my desk and his face resting in his hand, like a two-year-old just needing to talk. "You can read it with the rest of the city. Now, would you please go away?"

"You don't look like you want me to go."

His words startled me. I stopped, not knowing where he was getting his imaginary information. "You . . . you are beside yourself this morning, mister. Trust me, I want you to *go!*" I said, adding a little push to his arrogant arm that rested underneath his chin.

His face fell but he lifted it with an evil smile and got up, returning his chair beside the door. "I gotta get to a meeting anyway. I'm going to cover the chamber of commerce."

"I thought you couldn't cover them anymore since you referred to my mother as Vicky in your first coverage."

He peeked back around my opening. "She won't be there now, will she?"

"Touché."

"Adios, Ms. Phillips. Adios."

Adios, Ms. Phillips. Adios. I don't want you to go? You must be out of your mind. I am a woman in love with a wonderful man who is going to be thrilled that I have finally come to my senses. You need to get over yourself and join up with the woman who loves you. Miss Amber Topaz. You wll be perfect for each other. Then she can finally be Mrs. United States of America.

The pace of a newspaper seems consistently frantic. There is always the sound of a printer echoing in the hall. There is the sound of the pecking of computer keys. The smell of coffee. The fizzing of Coke. And the chatter of televisions. I wasn't used to this pace. I was a person who stole away and wrote in parks. Who sat in cafés and sipped Coca-Cola and snacked on chips. Most deadlines I created for myself. But now things were different. Life was different.

I stared at the computer screen in front of me and could make out my own image in its black reflection. Even though I had just written a story one week before, the simple task of turning yesterday's stream-of-consciousness efforts into an article suffocated me. I turned my hands over and watched as the dampness seeped its way into the lines on the palm of my hands. I had expected different things in my life.

I had expected Grant to marry me. I had expected to be a novelist. I had expected the circle of life to end up, well, in a circle. But somewhere Savannah's train had missed the junction, and I was heading into a land of uncharted territory and frightening change.

My fingers crawled gingerly up to the keyboard. And with the steady well of irritation that had been pent up for the last five days, the dam burst. What I had feared, flowed. I typed like a crazy woman. I typed and laughed and grimaced and typed. It was downright cathartic. I didn't need to make a revelation of ideals. I just needed to talk about the human factor. After all, I was a writer of human interest. And nothing was more of human interest than interesting humans. And my word, there was a human factor on that square bigger than all get-out.

By my two p.m. deadline, my third human-interest article was printed and tucked neatly away in a folder and placed on Mr. Hicks's desk. The truth about this city would be revealed by one of its very own, Ms. "Savannah from Savannah."

CHAPTER TWENTY-FIVE

My stomach was calling for lunch. A Greek salad sounded good today, so I walked across to River Street and headed to Olympia Café. The lunch rush was gone. But tourists lined River Street at any time of the day in the summer. Passing by Savannah's Candy Kitchen, one of my childhood staples, I saw the floral-clad Ms. Joy staring into the window.

"What do you see?" I asked.

She turned to look at me and her face lit up. "Oh, I was just admiring those caramel-covered apples." She turned back to stare into the window. "I used to eat those all the time when I was a little girl."

"Well, go get you one," I encouraged her, not wanting to tell her I was headed to get lunch, lest she want to make it a family affair.

"Yeah . . . yeah, I'll do that." But she didn't move.

I felt such sympathy for this woman. I wasn't sure why. Maybe it was the same dress, or the old straw bag. Maybe it was the direct words encompassed by the compassionate tone. But I was certain why she wasn't moving. It was the same reason she wanted to know what I was having to eat every evening for dinner. "You know,

Ms. Joy. I was thinking how good a caramel apple would be too. Why don't you come in and let me get us both one."

She let her head dip low and said, "Oh, baby, no, that's okay. I can get one later."

"No, you won't," I said, putting my arm through hers. "This is my treat to you today."

"Well, if you really want to." She giggled and we walked inside.

Savannah's Candy Kitchen is two storesful of any kind of candy you could want or remember. We filled up two large bags for her of all different kinds of gumdrops and jawbreakers and caramels from the huge barrels that sit on one side of the store. As we walked to the middle of the store, we got her a small, ice-cold, glass-bottled Coke from the large barrel that held the pieces of heaven amid the cold ice cubes. Then we got her some homemade fudge and topped it off with a caramel-covered apple.

She stared in amazement at the taffy conveyer belt, which made taffy on one side of the room and wrapped it and sent it across a conveyer belt that runs across the ceiling and deposited it in another barrel.

Then she and I strolled to the other side of the store and took in the wonderful ice creams and watched for a few moments through the paned glass that allows curious eyes to survey the culinary masters at work on indescribable fudge. She missed nothing. She was like a child having her senses filled with every pleasant part of childhood. When I left her at the small iron table that sits outside in front of the window, she had her two bags of candy, a small Coke, and was chowing down on a caramel apple, with her fudge tucked safely in her straw bag. She would save that for later. She never even noticed me leave.

The smell of Greece was so inviting that the Greek salad I chose required accompaniment. I added some gyro meat, pita bread, onions, and sauce to my salad. I didn't care who I had to talk to the rest of the day. This child was hungry.

Mr. Euzinidas came over to say hello.

"This protest thing driving you crazy?" I asked.

"Honey, I've made more money these past few days than we make most of the summer. Your mother can keep this up until January for all I care."

He could tell by my dejected expression that didn't interest me in the least. He left me to look out the window at the waterfront and enjoy my lunch. Until I saw the curly head flash by the window. He saw me too.

"Savannah!" he panted, doubling over at the entrance of the door. "Come on! I've got to take your car."

I sat my fork down and looked at him. "I just stopped to eat. Can't people leave me alone for two seconds and just let me have lunch?"

He came over to my table and grabbed my plates with one hand and my arm with the other. "You can eat in the car." He informed me. He asked Mr. Euzinidas to wrap up my lunch quickly so I could take it with me.

I jerked my arm from his grasp. "Joshua North. I'm not going anywhere. I'm going to sit down here and finish my lunch." I tried to get my plates back from Mr. Euzinidas.

"No!" Joshua took them away from me and gave them back to the poor man behind the counter who was ready to go sit down and eat my lunch himself. "I have to borrow your car."

"Why in the world do you need to borrow my car?" I asked, reaching one last time for my plates.

"Savannah, please." He calmed down yet kept pulling my hand away. "Trust me, please. I need you to just take me up the street. It will only take a minute. I just need your help, Savannah!" he finally said, exasperated.

I could tell he was serious. We grabbed my lunch and headed to the car. I handed him the keys, then snatched them back. "Do you even have a license?"

He reached for them. "Yes, Savannah. I ride a bike because I want to."

I offered them back hesitantly. "Where are we going?" He came around to open my car door.

"There's apparently been a shooting," he said as he climbed into the driver's seat.

"Joshua." I unbuckled my seat belt. "I am not going to any shooting."

He pulled the seat belt from my hand and buckled it back in, but I held on. "I've got to go. If I ever want to cover anything other than meetings with people who are half-dead or half-crazy, I've got to prove I can do something more."

I noticed something in his face that I had yet to see. A vulnerability. Mr. Curly Locks had passion. "Okay," I said, taking my hand off of the seat belt. "Go wherever it is you feel you need to go."

"Thank you." He started the car.

We drove about five minutes outside of the Historical District. And I turned to look at his face. His complexion was olive and baby smooth. His dark eyebrows framed his black eyes as if they were made for his face. Well, you know what I mean. And his eyes were focused today, not dancing like they normally do. He was thinking about something other than his bicycle or my issues.

I broke the odd silence. "Do you have any idea who got shot?"

"Not sure of his name, but apparently it is the boyfriend of whoever is Miss Chatham County United States of America."

"You're kidding. Wonder if she knows?"

"I'm almost certain. If my sources are right, she's the one who pulled the trigger."

"Oh my Lord, have mercy." I stared straight ahead. We drove for what felt like another long, awkward silence. "So what are you trying to accomplish with this?"

"I'm trying to get this story first." He glanced over at me to see if I had a response. I didn't. "I want to get it written and on

Mr. Hicks's desk before anyone else, so he'll take me as a serious journalist." He stared straight ahead now.

I turned in my seat to see him more clearly. "You don't think he takes you seriously?"

He paused for a long moment. "Honestly, no, I don't. I don't think many people around there take me seriously. They see me as a guy who can't afford a car and who wears flip-flops. Mr. Hicks has even said as much, so I've heard." I could see a glint of something in his eyes. Some remnant of frustration.

"Don't believe everything you hear. Lord knows I don't."

He laughed. "I bet you hear all kinds of things. Like how you only got your job because your mother agreed to buy lifetime advertising."

I raised my right eyebrow. "Actually, no, I haven't heard that one."

He looked at me and winked. "Well, don't believe everything you hear, right?"

I changed the subject. "How long have you been at the paper?"

"Almost two years. I started after I graduated from the University of Florida."

"Oh, is Florida where you're from?"

"Yeah, my family's from Jacksonville. Lived there my entire life."

"How in the world did you get to Savannah?"

"Insanity, I have come to believe."

"Me too," I said under my breath.

"Needed to get away from home. Find my own space. I'd driven through here quite a few times and just thought I'd try it. Got a job pretty quick. Liked the people and haven't left. But Mr. Hicks told me he would let me start doing hard news stories last year, and I'm still covering school-board meetings."

"Shoot, I hear those can be hard news themselves anymore," I offered.

"Mr. Hicks doesn't give me the time of day. So I figure the only way to make him notice my work is to give him some work to notice."

He pulled the car over to the curb on a narrow side street and cut the engine. "Okay, let's go see what we can find out."

Before I knew it he had grabbed his satchel and was around to my side of the car with the door open. I got out and looked at him. "Thank you," I said, trying to avoid the awkward moment.

"Let's go." He turned to walk up the alley, making it clear it wasn't any big deal.

We came out directly opposite a house that had more activity going on around it than any square in downtown Savannah. Except the one my mother occupied, of course.

Two police cars sat in front of the house. And people strained to catch a glimpse at the activity. About the time we emerged, a van passed us with "City Morgue" written across the side.

I felt every part of my body go weak. "Uh-uh, no, brother, this sister don't do dead people." I turned on my heels and headed in the direction of the car. I wasn't even sure if my legs would get me there.

He grabbed me and swung me around. "It's okay. We won't be here long." I wasn't reassured.

"Serious." I tried not to sound as afraid as I really was. "Dead people scare me. Like that movie when the little boy said, 'I see dead people.' Just the preview made me drive home with my interior car lights on. I had to call my dad to meet me at the curb and walk me to the house." I bounced up and down trying to stay as calm as possible. Failing miserably.

"Are you seriously that afraid?" Glints of compassion and laughter passed through his eyes at the same time.

"Yes, I'm serious." I tried not to look at the morgue van and tried to hide the burning tears that were rising to the surface of my eyes.

"Okay." He placed his hands on my shoulders. "It's okay. I'm sorry I brought you out here. I had no idea. Really. Just go sit in the car. You won't be able to see anything, and I'll be back in just a few minutes to take you back to the office."

"Promise?" I said, looking at him for a moment as if he would really protect me.

"I promise." And I believed him. "I'll be back in one minute."

I tried to gather my composure and turned around to head back to the car. But as much horror faced me in that direction. Because I spied, with my little eye, something coming up the street fast and fabulous. Miss Amber Ruby Diamonique, driving up the street in her Mercedes coupe, and I was with her man. "This can't be happening!" I said loud enough for Joshua to hear.

"What? What's wrong now?" he asked, coming back to me. I think the poor man was afraid I was about to hurl.

"It's Amber. She's coming up the street!" I said, doing one of those yelling whispers as if she could hear me inside of her car.

"So? Don't worry about her. Just go on to the car."

"Don't *worry* about her?" I yellspered. "She is in love with you and she thinks I'm her new best friend. If she sees me with you, she will think we . . . we . . ." I said, moving my index finger back and forth between us frantically.

"Think what? That we like each other?" he asked incredulously.

"Yes, Mr. Ambulance Chaser! That we like each other!"

"You worry way too much." He turned his attention back to the scene in front of him. "Now, either go back to the car or stand here while I go get the information that I need for this story."

I jerked his tablet from his hand and threw it up in front of my face. Amber had just gotten out of her car and was headed in our direction. I could only pray her two-and-a-half-inch heels would get stuck in a crack in the concrete and contain her until I could get to the car. No such luck. She spotted Joshua. Then she spotted me. Only after Joshua jerked his notebook from my hand and proceeded to leave me. She gasped. I did too. Both for entirely different reasons.

CHAPTER TWENTY-SIX

O ne man exited each side of the city morgue van. They opened the back and pulled out a gurney with a wadded black mass laying on top. I looked over at Amber, who was looking in horror at the scene. Maybe she would forget all about the fact that Joshua and I had been standing there together.

I watched her eyes get wider and reluctantly turned my attention back to the door of the house. I resisted the urge to watch the events play out through cracks in my fingers. A petite, disheveled blonde young woman in jeans and a T-shirt was being led from the house by two police officers. Her hands were behind her back as they walked to the back of a patrol car.

"That's her, Savannah. That's Courtney White," Amber said in total disbelief. I had never seen her so subdued.

"Miss Chatham County United States of America?"

"Yes, Miss Chatham County United States of America," she murmured.

As soon as the police car pulled away with Courtney in the back, the two men from the van exited the house with their gurney and what was undeniably a body underneath the black bag.

"Oh my Lord, Savannah! He's dead!"

I couldn't move. The insides of my stomach begin to churn. I instinctively turned my head away. "Are you sure it's her boyfriend under there?" I asked over my shoulder.

She didn't move either. We carried on our conversation staring straight ahead. "I'm absolutely certain. You know my friends Tina, Miss Swainsboro United States of America, and Trina, Miss Sandersville United States of America. The twins." I knew them. Sad but true. "Tina said he was cheating on Courtney; that's why she shot him."

The twilight zone that surrounded me had begun to play music in my head. Things were coming in and out of focus. Before my rationale returned to extricate me from this entire experience, Amber interrupted the Muzak.

"Oh, Savannah," she said, a moment of genuineness transforming her. "She was such a nice girl."

"Amber, do you even know for sure if it's her boyfriend?"

She looked at me as if I were absurd. "Savannah, Tina and Trina live with police scanners attached to the sides of their heads. Trust me, if they say it is Miss Chatham County United States of America's boyfriend, it's Miss Chatham County United States of America's boyfriend.

"Let's get closer." She jerked at my sleeve. I jerked it back.

"No way, sister. I was just about to leave."

"Well, I can't go over there by myself; it would look too inconspicuous."

I patted down my sleeve and kept my face turned from the scene playing out in front of me. "I think you mean *suspicious*. And why do you want to get closer anyway?"

She came around to look at my face. "Just because," she said, trying to tell me something with her tilted head, pursed lips, and wide eyes framed with fake eyelashes.

"Because *why?*" I pressed. But I knew. Her eyes darted over my shoulder. I turned slightly to see the man eagerly scribbling down information on his stolen legal pad.

But there was no need for us to go to him; he was now coming to us.

"Hello, Amber." He nodded politely.

"Joshua." She was unable—or maybe simply unwilling—to hide her attraction.

"Savannah, you ready? I think I have everything I need."

"Oh?" Her eyes became wider. "You two came together?"

"Well . . . we . . . actually . . ." I started.

Joshua finished. "Yes. I needed to get here to cover this story, and Savannah was the first person I spotted with a car."

Truthfully, coming from his lips, it was clear how totally uninteresting her discovery actually was. And it seemed to be enough for her.

"Well, I'm glad you are getting to know my new best friend. Isn't she the greatest?" She grinned from ear to ear so we could both enjoy the glow of her Crest Whitestrip–bleached ensemble.

"The greatest. Okay, Miss Wonderful, I really need to get this story back before I'm too late."

Before I could help myself, I blurted out, "Oh, just go ahead and take my car. I'll catch a ride with Amber."

He looked at me as if my personality number two had just effectively risen to the surface. But this would rest better with Amber. And it would prove to anyone in doubt that I had no interest in Joshua North whatsoever.

"That would be just fabulous," Amber offered.

"Whatever." And with that he was gone with no hesitation.

As the people began to clear, I saw Miss Tina and Miss Trina themselves walk down the street and hop into matching yellow VW bugs. Amber and I proceeded to her luxury vehicle, a perfect replica of my mother's except for the color.

Amber turned the car in the direction of the paper. We were

both peculiarly quiet. As we pulled up to the sidewalk, I opened the door and turned back to notice a tear had formed in the corner of her eye.

"What's wrong, Amber?"

"A man just died. And a girl I know killed him."

"I'm really sorry."

She never looked at me, just stared straight ahead. "I know we seem catty and petty. But we're like family, really. Even though you want to win and think you hate the person who does, you still want the best for them."

I couldn't help but smile at her simple view of life. "But you never wish this on anyone," she continued. "I mean, you wish ripped seams, or broken straps, or even dresses put on backward, but nothing like this. I'll have to go see her. Yeah, that's what I'll do; I'll go see her."

"I think that would be nice." I said as I held the car door in my hand.

Crocodile tears began to fall down her face. She looked at me. "You think so?"

"Yeah, I do."

"And I'll encourage her, Savannah. I'll encourage her like you encourage me."

"Well . . . I . . . I don't quite know what to say, Amber. Thanks."

"Do you want to come with me?" she said, begging with her deeply set aqua-colored eyes. "You could encourage her so much better than me."

"No, Amber, I think this might be something you need to do yourself."

"Should I take Tina and Trina?"

"Probably not."

"Okay. I'll just go by myself. I'm glad you were there, Savannah. It just made the whole thing easier."

"I'm glad I could be there too," I blatantly lied. Well, it was almost a lie. "I'll talk to you soon."

She pulled a tissue out of her purse, dabbed her eyes, and then blew her nose like a foghorn. "Thanks for being my friend."

"Thanks for letting me. Call me if you need me." I knew she would.

Making my way up the stairs to get a Coke, I knew what the headlines would read in the morning: "Beauty Queen Kills Boy-friend." And yet the world wouldn't stop. Even now, as a family was about to hear tragic news, the world would keep moving. People would keep laughing. Men would keep telling coarse jokes. Children would keep learning lessons in schoolhouses. Businessmen and women all around this city would keep on working. Vicky would stay chained to a monument.

And me, well I'd keep on climbing stairs, going to vending machines, and drinking Cokes.

But one family's world would be changed forever. Dinners would never be the same. Holidays would miss a person to open presents. Grandchildren would never have their son's eyes. As brutal as the reality was, it was still reality. The world stops for no one. Even on days like September 11, when the majority of people were paralyzed in front of their television sets, mothers were still in hospitals, giving birth, and doctors were still on call to make sure that life entered the world.

It felt downright wrong to continue living. I'd never seen a body bag. I'd never been that close to death. Burying a pet gerbil named Dufus just doesn't count. The guy in that bag was somebody like me. The girl who shot him was somebody like me. As real as the death was, so for a brief moment was the murderer. A girl for a moment gone crazy. Her life would never be the same either.

My phone rang.

"Are you getting excited?"

"Excited? About what?"

Paige reacted in complete horror. "Savannah? You have got to be kidding me."

"Oh my gosh, yes, I almost completely forgot. This has been a . . . well, shall we say, rather eventful day."

"Well, I don't know how something could be more eventful than what you are about to embark on tonight. Do you have everything ready?"

"Yes, everything is ordered, outfit is pressed and lying on my bed, and every womanly weapon I own, checked."

"You have womanly weapons?"

"I thought I did. Do I not?"

"I haven't seen or heard from them in a while."

"Me either. But they're ready. Maybe a little rusty, but they're ready."

"Well, I'll be there on time, so you just make sure you're ready."

"I'll be more than ready, honey."

"Okay, call me if you have any questions."

"I will. Bye."

Five o'clock found me walking to my car in attack mode. But the smell of my forgotten lunch had turned into a disastrous stench. Driving down Bull Street, however, my mind was so focused on my evening of resurrected love that I forgot the smell and nearly hit the flowery mass that walked right out into the street. Slamming on the brakes, I was propelled with such force that my lip hit the steering column and started bleeding. I looked up to see my bumper only inches away from Joy. Déjà vu.

I jumped out of the car and ran to her, instinctively throwing my arms around her. "Joy, are you okay?! I could have killed you!" Stepping back to survey her, she seemed fine as a Georgia peach. "What in the world were you doing just walking out in the street?! Did you not see me coming?!" I reprimanded her like a child.

She smiled her silly grin. "Oh, Savannah, I'm sorry, baby. I didn't mean to frighten you. I just wasn't paying attention, I guess. But I'm okay." She giggled at my arms, which were still holding on to her.

"Well, I'm glad. But you have got to be more careful." I released her from my grip. "Now, why don't you just get in the car and let me take you home?"

"No, baby. I'm fine. I've got a few places left to go today, and a few people I need to see. You just get back in your car and head on home. I promise I'll be more careful."

"You'd better. You scared the heebie-jeebies out of me."

She reached her hand up to my face. "Your lip's bleeding, baby. Are you okay?"

I touched my lip, which felt like it had swelled to half the size of my head. "Yes. It won't make for an attractive evening, but I'm okay."

About that time a car honked having obviously discovered we were both okay. I looked back and gave them a raised right eyebrow and walked Joy over to the sidewalk.

"Now, Savannah, you need to be careful too. You seemed rather preoccupied. And preoccupation is often a sign of misplaced priorities."

"Okay, Joy, thank you. But I've got to go now. You be more careful." I walked back to my car and opened the door, then glared at the obnoxious car behind me.

"I will, Miss Savannah. But remember, nothing's worth consuming yourself over. Everything has its place. And when everything is in the right place, nothing is out of place."

"That's real good. Now, stay on the sidewalk."

I watched her climb onto the sidewalk and begin to sing quietly. I drove home trying to figure out how much makeup it would take to disguise my ever-growing lower lip.

Life was going on.

CHAPTER TWENTY-SEVEN

The lip protruded like a bad collagen job. But by six o'clock I was cascading down the front staircase and back to my car looking, shall we say, like "a Southern lady fit for dining." Which was pretty much exactly what I was about to be.

"Well, what do we have here?"

I stared straight into the face of my father and tried to regain any amount of composure I might have possessed. I had taken great lengths to avoid anyone who knew me, because such attire at six o'clock on a Tuesday evening would pose questions for which there were no appropriate answers.

"Oh, I juth haf a meething thif evenith."

That wouldn't do. He took a stance like he had nowhere to go fast. "What kind of meeting?" He scanned my pale blue stretch-cotton skirt with white embroidery and white capped-sleeve v-neck sweater.

"Oh, jthuth a thinner meefing. Buf ith's nofing importhanth." I gave him a quick kiss on the cheek, causing a searing pain to shoot through my lip. "Ow."

"What did you do?"

"Jthusth a booboo." I answered, dodging eye contact and starting in the direction of my car, trying to walk gracefully in white two-inch heels with only two thin straps holding them into place. "I'll thee you lafer. Mayfee I'll come fee you and Muffer," I added shamelessly.

"Savannah Phillips."

I hated it when he did that. I turned around, reminding myself to look nonchalant. The shoes prevented it. "Yef?"

"I hope you aren't up to something you shouldn't be. And I *will* expect to see you this evening." With that, his suspicious stare disappeared with him into the house.

How in the world do they always know? It's downright sick, I tell ya. And why in the world would he think the worst of me? I'm a grown woman just going to a meeting. What would he want me to wear, blue jeans and flip-flops? Heaven forbid I would actually take pride in my appearance. The monologue continued down six alleys, past three squares, and into a safe parking place an entire street removed from Jake's coffee shop.

I made sure the coast was clear and entered the coffee shop with a wonderful story about why I was there, should anyone need to hear it. I was thankful that all parties had departed. All the front blinds were closed, which was a blessed sight. It would prevent Jake from passing by and seeing anything out of the ordinary going on inside his little retirement office.

I opened my bag of goodies and sat them on the counter, releasing a sigh of relief at the fact that I had carried these to the car earlier. The questioning with my dad would have resulted in downright accusation had he seen me bearing picnic gear. The back table that sat against the far wall would be the safest. It would prevent anyone on the street from seeing the flickering of the candlelight through the closed blinds.

I shook out the white linen tablecloth and smoothed it with my hands. I retrieved two beautiful yellow bamboo candles, borrowed from Mother's stash, and placed them in two silver candlesticks. I placed Mom and Dad's white china trimmed with silver neatly at each place and finished it off with Baccarat stemware.

"Wellf fath looths faubulus." But my lip did not. A quick glance in the mirror made it clear the swelling wasn't going down. Cramming a piece of ice into a paper towel, I placed it gingerly on my lip and headed to Bistro Savannah to pick up the dinner order I had inconspicuously placed last night on a trip to the bathroom. While picking up two seared beef tenderloins with shiitakes, scallions, and crisp corn pancakes topped off with horseradish sauce, I tried to avoid as much conversation as possible. By my return it was already seven fifteen.

"Are you ready?" Paige's voice came over my phone.

"Yesf."

"Why are you talking like that?"

"Don'th askf."

"You've hurt yourself, haven't you? Miss Grace, you might need to get checked. Do you at least look okay?"

"I lookth butiful."

"Well, do you have it on ice?"

"Yesf."

"Good. Well, don't worry; it will be okay. We'll be there at exactly seven thirty. Have the door unlocked. Your life's about to change, sweetheart."

Bathroom to window, window to bathroom, I paced, trying about fifteen different locations in the store for ideal placement upon Grant's entrance: leaning against the counter looked too desperate; sitting daintily at the table looked too not-me. I even tried a striking pose across the bar. That just plain hurt too bad. Anyway, all would have proven fruitless anyway, because I had to go to the bathroom. Thus, I was officially indisposed when I heard the bells on the door.

As I came from the back room, I could hear Grant's shock. "Why did you bring me *here,* Paige?"

Then his eyes caught a glimpse of me. From the neck down I

looked pretty good. From the neck up, well, let's just say I could have done a commercial for an ambulance-chasing attorney suing over a plastic surgery catastrophe.

Paige's eyes caught a glimpse of the same and rolled.

His poor green eyes protruded frighteningly and made their way from me to Paige, eventually returning back to me. "Savannah, what are you doing here?" Then his eyes caught a glimpse of the table and the candlelight and the dinner. The expression that began in the eyes and worked its way down to his beautiful mouth made it altogether clear: Grant knew he had been set up.

"Well, my job is done. You two have a wonderful evening," Paige said, patting Grant on the back. She left with a wink and a thumbs-up. He protested. She wouldn't hear of it. And she left us there all alone.

There we stood. Two familiar strangers. I decided to break the awkward silence. "Wouf you wife thoo thith thown?" I asked, motioning to the two chairs that flanked the cozy table, arranged in such a way that two old loves could rediscover one another.

Grant stared at me and walked slowly to the table and sat down. "What did you do to your lip?"

Well, at least we could get that out of the way early. "I hadth a liffle affithenth. Wuff you life sofing thoo thrink?"

"That would be nice." Then, as if he had come to his senses, he stood. "No, Savannah, I don't want something to drink. I don't want anything but to know what this is all about."

I looked at him in disbelief. This wasn't part of the script for the evening. I had gone over it a thousand times, and this wasn't in it. "I thjuth wanfed thoo thalk wif you."

"Savannah, this isn't about talking." He motioned to the room, then picked up one of the silver forks at the table. "This, Savannah, is about far more than talking. And this isn't part of what we do anymore. Now, either you can tell me what this is about, or I'm going to have to leave."

For a moment I felt a sting rise up in my throat. But I pushed it back down. "Thith ith abouth uth." I tried to keep my composure. "Thith ith abouth you mafing a therrible misthake. Thith ith abouth uth noth ruining our wifes."

"What? Our wives?"

"No, I said, our wifesth!"

"Savannah, I haven't ruined my life. I haven't made a mistake either. I just went *on* with my life. And I only made that decision the day you sat at that table right there"—he pointed to the table for two at the front window—"and let me know that school was your priority. Do you think I would marry someone while I had unresolved feelings for another woman? If you think that, then you never really knew me at all, Savannah." The expression in his eyes was one of hurt, which I had only seen from him on a couple of occasions. But there was something even different in them tonight. A resolve. He had thought this one through, and long before he walked in a few minutes ago, hoodooed by Paige.

"Buff thif wafn't how if waf thuppothe thoo be. We were thuppose thoo be thogether forefer."

"What?"

He was making this painful. "You're killingth me here. *I saith . . . we were thuppose thoo be thogether forefer!*"

"Supposed to be together forever? So, I was just supposed to wait until you got through doing everything else you wanted to do and then, when you were ready for me, I was supposed to be right there waiting for you?"

I looked at him with a look Duke has used on me many times. A look that said, "Well, when you put it that way, it has a slightly different ring to it."

"Don't cock your head at me. That is exactly what you thought. And I knew you thought that. And the mere fact that you thought that proved you didn't love me the way I loved you."

As he said that, his expression softened. And he walked over to me and put his hands on my bare arms. But he hadn't even noticed my lovely spring attire. No, he was looking straight into my eyes.

"I loved you from the time we got caught in Wesley Monumental Church at midnight with Pastor Mason. I loved your quirkiness and your clumsiness." He pointed to my lip. "I loved everything about you. But that day, sitting in this very place, I realized you didn't love me that way."

"Buff I—"

He placed his finger in front of my face. "Don't talk anymore. It is painful for you, obviously, and painful for me to decipher." That made us both smile. "It's okay, Savannah. It's okay that you had dreams and visions and plans. And it's okay that you weren't ready. But I've changed. I'm not the kid you caught fireflies with or skipped school with or got your first kiss from. I'm a man. A man in love with a wonderful woman. A man fortunate enough to have loved two amazing women in his lifetime. But our chapter is over."

I studied his gaze to see if there was any hint of doubt in his own words. One glimmer of apprehension was all I would have needed to grab him and hold him and share the gentleness of a kiss we had once known. But there was none. No doubt. No hesitation. No second thoughts. I suppose I had known that already. "Now you go out there. Change the world. Love will find you. When you're ready, it will find you." He laughed. "I'm not sure it can handle you, but it will find you."

He kissed me gently on the cheek. And a small tear fell from the corner of my eye that surprised even me. He took his thumb and gently wiped it away. As he held my hand and led me to the front door, my mind raced with what this man had been to me. He would never know he held my greatest secrets and my *only* kisses. He would never know that years down the road, stories would be written about him. He would just never know.

He opened the front door, let go of my hand, and turned back to me. "This is over, Savannah. It's time for you to start writing the next chapter of your life." With that I watched him slowly disappear up the street and take his place in a world of past conversations and onetime loves.

"I wuff you," I said quietly.

Unfortunately it was loud enough for the harassing curly-headed pedaler to have heard. He had apparently witnessed the entire part-ing episode. He and his dog. He pulled his ringlets right up next to me and stopped. Peeking his head inside the coffee shop, he leaned back and shook his head.

"Shuffup!!!" I declared straight into his smirking face. I might have even sprayed him with a little spit, but who cared? My soul was broken, floating on the barren sea of heartbreak. I slammed the door closed and locked it before he could dare to enter.

Jake's had lost its sparkle. Jake's felt cold and lonely. Jake's had apparently held Grant's heartbreak years before, and mine today. What a wretched place. Once my place of joy and laughter, now my home of bitterness and woe. Packing up two cold steaks, I put them in the refrigerator so Duke could at least experience some pleasure in what had come to be his concrete world. Duke and I were more alike than woman and beast ought to be. Our worlds were colorless and our meals takeout. After folding the white linen tablecloth and placing it neatly atop the other items of lost hope, my picnic basket felt like a heavy pack of burden. This wasn't the way moments like these were supposed to end. It wasn't the way my practiced ending had transpired. I had us slow dancing to the music we would hum together. Our new song, "Ready to Take a Chance Again" by Barry Manilow. What I like is none of Thomas's business.

I pushed the table back to its place and walked through the swinging doors that led to the back room. I turned off the lights, and with them the light of my heart. As I closed the door behind me, I knew it would be years before I could ever enter Jake's again. Well, okay. I'd show up tomorrow morning for a Coke. But only because it was utterly necessary.

CHAPTER TWENTY-EIGHT

Talking was too painful. Both physically and emotionally. Paige let me sleep on her sofa. She consoled me and helped me wipe away my tears. Well, there weren't any more tears, but there was a lot of slurred whining. However, our top ten list of "Why Savannah was a better catch than Miss Redhead"—made in conjunction with the viewing of David Letterman—was rather cathartic.

Morning came crashing in hard and furious. My head was killing me from a caffeine overdose. The only highlight was that my lip had retreated to a somewhat normal level. And the lowlight was my mother's message regarding my depiction of her in today's column.

I stared at Paige's check in my hand. Two thousand dollars. Liberation.

Ms. Austin was on the morning news. The local news-caster found it hard to believe that she was born and raised in the South.

"Why? Southerners aren't all big hats and afternoon tea. Some of us like our coffee as espressos and some of us favor black to pastels. There is a progressive voice of the South that is unmistakably being voiced and heard."

The recent journalism-school grad responded, "I can see where that would be true."

"I'm just trying to help people from my part of the world realize that the conservative mind-set of the old South isn't what this new generation needs or truly desires."

"What *do* you feel this generation desires?"

"Someone who listens. And actually hears. Then fights to help implement their concerns and ideals. And who helps their voice to be heard."

"Well, we're glad you had a few moments to spend with us this morning. Ladies and gentlemen, Ms. Faith Austin."

Faith smiled that perfect smile. She had it. Whatever *it* was. She had it.

I tilled alone. It was best. God and I had a lot of talking to do. He seemed quiet. Again. So I just kept the conversation going. Reminding Him how miserably last night had transpired. Nothing to my liking. And nothing to His, I was certain. Reminding Him that if He was passing out more *it,* I would like some of my own. By the time I was through, the only consolation I could imagine was Coke. Coke and flip-flops. No pearls today. *It* hadn't rained down. No use in trying to pretend. At least for now.

The question slammed into me as soon as I entered the back door. "I expected you last night. You said you would be there."

"No sir, I said I would try."

He leaned against the steel counter that held my liquid delight and extended a cup.

I took the cup from his hand, filled it full of ice, and watched the dark, powerful fluid flow. "My meeting took a detour and I had to regroup." I leaned against the counter while the events of last night came back like a stampede. I took a long swig of my Coke, which burned all the way down. Nothing was so good. "Whoo! That's good stuff."

"So, your dinner with Grant didn't go as you expected?" he asked with a perfectly stoic expression.

Had I possessed any remaining liquid in my mouth, it would have surely escaped through every cavity in my head. "I'm not sure I know what you're talking about."

"Savannah, did you know that not telling the entire truth is really not truth at all?"

I pursed my lips and wrinkled my brow and turned to stare at him. "How do you know everything?" He started to give a quick response. "No, seriously, Dad. How do parents know everything? Is there not one thing I can do that you wouldn't know of?"

"You know how we know, Savannah? Because there is part of us inside of you. And we know ourselves very well." He tapped me on my nose, then proceeded to head back into the front of the shop. "By the way, your article was . . . interesting."

I headed straight to the paper and snatched a copy of the morning news from Marla's desk. I greeted her quickly but friendly and headed to my hallowed haven. But I wasn't to sit. No, Jessica buzzed me as soon as I entered my hole; Mr. Hicks wanted to see me.

I would be fired. I was certain. Who wouldn't be certain? I couldn't do anything right. Except create a blaring headline. Oh, yes, I had mastered that one. I walked slowly. Even wanted to scream, "Dead woman walking!" But who would care? Most would be glad. I would give Paige her money back. I would live with my mother and die old and wretched.

Jessica had disappeared into obnoxious oblivion. I was grateful. She made me weary. Mr. Hicks was snacking on a country ham biscuit and had more crumbs on his tie than around his mouth.

"Oh, Savannah. Come in, come in." He tried to brush away the remnants of breakfast from his face unsuccessfully. "I wanted you to know you did a great job with your story. You gave me a kick," he said, chuckling. "I wish I could have seen your mother in a silk eye mask. I didn't even know all the activity that was happening around there."

I sat down across from him more confident. "Well, thank you, sir. I'm glad you liked it."

"Yeah." He placed the other half of his biscuit aside and brushed the crumbs from his desk. "I thought you would give us some 'sidewalk sermons' like your mother has been giving on the evening news. But you branched out, young lady. Gave us a laugh and kept self-righteous opinions to yourself. Couldn't have written it better myself. Now, go get ready for tomorrow's deadline."

"Well, thank you, sir. Really, thank you so much." As I started out the door, I noticed a yellow file on his desk bearing Joshua's name and a "Dated Material" stamp. Joshua's story. Unopened. I couldn't help it. "Did you not read Joshua's story?"

"What?" He looked down, confused. "Oh, this?" He picked up the file. "No, I haven't gotten to it yet."

"But it's dated. It was for today's paper!"

"Oh, I didn't notice."

"How could you not notice?" I asked, incredulous.

"Because I *didn't,* Savannah," he snapped.

"Well, you should have. You really should have."

I left, my cadence not as enthusiastic as Mr. Hicks's compliments of my work warranted. And the nuisance coming up the aisle conjured the usual dread. Jessica turned the corner and headed in my direction, with none other than Faith Austin at her side. The city's new darling looked exceptionally fabulous today. Her long dark hair spread symmetrically across her shoulders, and her camel-color pants and matching lace top looked almost tie-dyed.

I hesitated for a moment. I felt too casual next to this woman in my flip-flops and white capris. Jessica didn't even notice me until we were practically flip-flop to Ferragamo.

"Hello, Ms. Austin," I said with a nod. "Jessica."

"Savannah," Jessica snipped.

"Hello, Savannah. How are you this morning?"

"Doing great, thank you very much. Just heading back to work. What are you ladies up to this morning?"

"We were trying to have a conversation," Jessica snapped. "And I believe this conversation was between *A* and *B*"—she pointed to her and Ms. Austin—"so why don't you *C* your way out of it?"

I raised my right eyebrow and fought desperately not to laugh in her face.

Ms. Austin had trouble hiding her smirk as well and spoke to me anyway. "I liked your article today. I expected a downright assault. But you were rather refreshing. The Pilates episode got me good."

"Well, I'm glad you enjoyed it. I'm still trying to wrap my mind around the whole thing though."

"That shouldn't take too long." Peanut gallery.

The two mature ones tried to ignore the child.

"Ms. Austin!" came Mr. Hicks's voice. He was smiling like a child with a crush on the teacher. "Come on in here and let's get this interview going." He ignored both Jessica and me as he took Ms. Austin by the hand and began to lead her to his office.

She looked back with a smile. "Maybe we can have dinner soon." Her cell phone rang as she turned around. She answered it with a rather perturbed, "Hello?"

Mr. Hicks closed the door behind them and left Jessica staring at the veneer.

"I guess you'll have to *C* your way out," I said with a shameless giggle. I deserved to laugh.

"Be careful with those two," came the voice over my shoulder as I descended the stairs. The same voice that had snickered over my shoulder yesterday as Grant walked out of my life and into the land of regrettable remembrances.

"Well, I would think you would find both of them stunningly

beautiful," I said, ignoring the bounce of his curls that I was certain were following me.

"You clearly have no idea what I find beautiful. I can see right through women like them." He kept his steps on my heels.

"Oh you can, can you?"

"Yes, and I can see through women like you too."

I opened the door to the first floor and turned to stare him down. I expected a smirk. Even a wide-eyed smile. But he just stared back. It was a look I'd never seen on his face in the less than two weeks we'd known each other. It forced a nervous laugh. Odd for me, with this annoyance. "See through me? What are you talking about? Everyone else seems to like my article, Mr. North."

"I'm not talking about your article. That is an issue in and of itself. I'm talking about yesterday at the coffee shop. You acted pathetic, Ms. Phillips."

"How dare you talk to me like that? I don't have to listen to this, coming from a man who doesn't even have a car." I turned on my heels, or not, to my pitiful world. My word. I had just defended this man to my boss. I knew he would follow. I knew he would reply. But he didn't. He left me there. With *pathetic* and *Ms. Phillips* dangling like piercing participles in the air.

CHAPTER TWENTY-NINE

A person should be allowed to enjoy lunch. It should be an unstated law: Lunch hour is to be enjoyed. Add that as commandment eleven, and Vicky would willingly stay chained the rest of the year. Despite Joshua, this was a good day. And I was going to enjoy the rest.

Coke from Jake's for lunch was the only thought on my brain. Until I got the Coke. Then the thought of food began to cross my mind. I opened up the refrigerator to see if Richard or the twins had brought anything desirable from home. Only the aluminum wrapper of two cold-hearted steaks caught my eye.

I closed the refrigerator and stared at my hand that held the handle. Then I opened it again. Snatched the steaks out of the refrigerator, laid one in Duke's bowl, and took the other one along with the morning paper and my Coke to the park bench directly across from the coffee shop. A raised hand was all I offered those who greeted me as I passed.

As I sat down, a tune caught my ear, and my new bench buddy caught the corner of my eye. I hid my steak beneath my paper.

"Savannah, I had no idea I had met a star."

"Good morning, Joy. You haven't been walking into any more streets, have you?"

Her floral belly shook. But her hair looked neatly combed. She sat down on the bench, oblivious to the fact that I was about to have a moment to myself.

"You wrote a nice piece, Savannah."

"Actually I was just about—"

"But it wasn't clear what you really think about what is happening." She pulled an orange out of her purse and began to peel it.

"It's not really about what I feel. It's more about what I observe through the lives of others."

"Is it?"

"Yes, stories are about what interests people. I try to tell others' stories."

She continued to peel and never looked up. "Well, you told other people's stories all right. Your poor mother hasn't smiled all morning. And that tall, beautiful, but extremely loquacious girl that follows her around carrying a tiara didn't fare too well either. And pity the people who were in their company this morning."

I stopped and looked at her. She apparently needed me to help educate her on what newspaper reporters actually do. "I just tell it like life lives it."

"But isn't life really about how events affect us and change us?"

"Yes, life is, but not necessarily human-interest stories."

"So, you don't want your stories to change people?"

"Well, yes, that is the intent of all my stories. That was why I wanted this job. Because the lady who did this before me . . ." I paused for a moment and thought of Gloria Richardson, who had held this position prior to my arrival. The brief time that had transpired since Gloria's death and my first day on the job blew by me and came to rest inside my thoughts. I looked down at the paper lying on my lap and my picture staring back at me in the same place Gloria's had through my six years of college and graduate school. "Yeah, my stories should change people," I muttered.

Joy put a piece of orange in her mouth and chewed slowly. She wouldn't speak until every morsel was dissolved. She was a lady that way. Forcing me to wait.

"Well, if you want your stories to change people, then they first have to change you. Your story was witty and charming. But it didn't say anything. You just told me what I can come down here and see for myself. See, I need you to tell me the things I don't notice. I need you to reveal to me what I've missed myself." She stopped for a moment and that distant look took over her face again as she stared at the large group of people that still surrounded the monument and my mother.

"All this, Savannah"—she motioned across the street—"This hasn't changed you, Savannah; it's just annoyed you." Well, I would beg to differ; she was the one to annoy me. She must have read it in my face. "Now, don't get mad at me, baby. I've grown fond of you. But take it from an old lady: Living should change you. It shouldn't leave you apathetic or annoyed, or dare I say, cynical." Apparently she dared. "It should leave you changed. I'm not even sure this event has changed this city yet either. So far it's just transpired in the middle of it. But everyone will be changed before it's over. I guarantee you that."

"Changed, huh?"

She wrapped up her peeling inside a napkin and stuffed it in her purse. Then her black eyes looked up at me to make sure I was listening. "Yes, but you can't be changed until you know what you believe, Savannah." She knew I was listening.

She bent over and tugged at her drooping stockings before she stood. She pulled her dress down as she rose and took her tired straw bag in her hand. Those eyes looked straight into my soul and refused to look away without one final parting Joy thought. "Yeah, you need to figure out what you believe, Savannah. But it's even more important to know why you believe it." With that she left to greet a news reporter camped out underneath a nearby tree. Wonder what he needed to change.

I stood up and threw the steak away, because I had lost my appetite. I tucked the paper underneath my arm. I had no need to read it. Joy had just made it clear what it said. A bunch of nothing.

I would have returned to Jake's, but the memories were simply too painful at this time. I had no desire to enter the newspaper either. Entering meant interacting, and I was downright tired of interacting. Didn't care if I saw another woman carrying snacks in her purse or another curly-headed coworker.

I flung the newspaper onto the passenger's seat. The front page unfolded, and staring back at me was a beautiful young woman with long flaxen hair and breathtaking green eyes. Next to her, the picture of a nice-looking boy with hair close to the same color. Both looked to be in their late teens, early twenties. The headline declared, "Local Beauty Queen Arrested for Alleged Murder of Boyfriend."

I had forgotten. Over a nonexistent dinner with a hopelessly former love, and then a morning of enjoying my own weak press, I had forgotten. Life was supposed to have been altered forever by yesterday's events. I had declared it myself. But life happened, just like always. I had dressed myself up, bought dinner, gotten dumped and then humiliated, and spent the evening mentally trashing a woman I didn't even know. And this morning I had debated over heels or flip-flops, bought a Coke, got puffed up, and then had my balloon popped by a practical stranger, all while worlds just around the corner had stopped.

My selfishness and shallowness slammed into me and stuck like a stretched flower around Ms. Joy's upper thigh. It was what it was. Not one for avoiding confrontation, confronting myself seemed far less desirable.

So much for avoiding interaction. Because interaction didn't care a thing about avoiding me. It greeted me at the front desk. It greeted me rounding the first corner. It greeted me even in my little Styrofoam world.

"Oh, Savannah. I'm so glad you finally got here. I just need you. I'm having nightmares. I can't eat. I can't sleep." Miss Amber Topaz was pacing. And if she wasn't careful, she would run right into my Styrofoam wall.

I knew why she was really here. I was certain that this whole thing was nothing more than a brouhaha to see Joshua. She was in love with him. I still wasn't quite sure if that was because she really liked him or because she saw him as the shortest distance between her and the title of *Mrs.* United States of America. And since her discovery that his desk was perched directly across from my own, I could never assume her visits were simply to see me. No, her dropping by would be for one reason alone: to run into Mr. Bike Boy. I was no fool. Maybe a witless wonder, but not a fool.

Then she started to cry. *Well, maybe she is here to see me.*

"Oh my, I think I'm going to hyperventilate." She collapsed into the chair by my small orifice that would have been a door had a person been privileged enough to have an office *with* a door. "I might need mouth to mouth." I was certain she peeked across the corridor.

I grabbed my chair, pulled it up next to her, and sat down. "Amber, get a grip or I'm going to have to slap you."

That got her attention. "Why would you slap me?" She sniffled.

"Because that's what people do to people who act hysterical. Now, what in the world is going on?"

"It's just yesterday, Savannah. The whole thing. The body, the police, Miss Chatham County United States of America in handcuffs. I even went to see her!" she wailed.

That one got me. "You did? What did she say?"

"Oh," she said, blowing her nose and trying to gain her composure. "I couldn't go in. A guard wanted to search me. Well, my Lord have mercy, Savannah." She sat upright in her chair and straightened the skirt of her teal sundress. "I've never had a man touch me in such places in my life, and I wasn't about to have the first time happen by a complete stranger in a jail, now, was I? No, I'm waiting for Mr. North when he makes me Mrs. North and, well, let the party be—"

"Please!" This child was crazier than I. "You and Joshua getting married isn't even a present reality. Stick to the facts. So, you didn't go see her?"

"No, I just couldn't." She started tearing up again. "But I'm going to. I just want you to go with me. I *neeeeeeeed yooooooou*, Savannah." She wrapped her arms around my neck and threw her head down in sobs.

Her head was bobbing from her heaves. I removed her arms from my neck. "How is it you are so hysterical today, when I heard you were back outside with my mother last night trying to do Pilates again?"

She cocked her head at me as if that was the dumbest question she had heard since the mayor emceed the Miss Georgia United States of America and asked her to tell why she should be the next Miss Georgia United States of America. Shouldn't the answer be piercingly obvious? "Savannah, I called your mother last night because I was in such a mess. She asked me to come spend the night with her, and she spent our entire dinner encouraging me and giving me advice, and then she held me while I *criiiiiiiied*." She started blubbering again.

"My mother did all that?"

"Yes. Then she had me laughing, telling me crazy stories about when she was young, and before I knew it I was showing her more Pilates moves. It's not like I just walked up and said, 'Okay sunshine, let me teach you some Pilates.' I mean, please, Savannah, I'm not totally callous."

Ooh, right word. Right way. "Well, I'm sorry. I shouldn't have just assumed."

"It's okay." She grabbed a tissue and snorted loud enough to alert the Atlantic's ships of fog. "Your mother's really special, Savannah. I'm not even her daughter and she makes me feel like I am. You should be nicer to her."

But before I could respond, the sound of a familiar voice came up the hall. I stood up and peeked around the corner. Ms. Faith Austin was walking down the hall, accompanied by Mr. Hicks's "charming" secretary once again. Looking down at Amber's lovely dress in teal, it became clear to me that she was too . . . well, too teal. But I didn't want to miss the opportunity to speak.

"Hello Faith. What has you at the paper so long today?" I asked as they walked past my door, clearly on their way to the elevator.

Jessica would not let the poor woman speak. "Savannah, Ms. Austin and I are in an extended meeting with Mr. Hicks, and we don't have time for chatting."

Faith stopped anyway. "Oh, Mr. Hicks and I are just going to wrap up our interview from this morning."

"Well, I hope it has gone well."

Amber blew once more. "Oh, excuse me. This is Amber. Uh, my friend." I tried not to wince from the pain of the proclamation.

"Nice to meet you, uh, Amber," Ms. Austin offered.

"We really need to be going," Jessica snipped.

Amber ignored her. "Well, hello. I'm Amber Topaz Childers. I've seen you, haven't I? Down there at the monument."

"Yes, I have work I'm doing down there."

"Well, I hope it goes well. You just let Ms. Victoria know if you need a thing. That lady would do anything for anyone. Well, ladies, I need to skedaddle. Have to sort out some things down at the visitors center. We have some issues with this group out of Atlanta, AFUCLA or something. Probably a bunch of sorority girls trying to stir up the dickens. Well, gotta run. Nice to meet you. And you too, little one. Whatever your name is." I thought for a moment the six-foot Amazon Amber might actually pat Jessica on the head.

"Bye, Amber. I'll talk to you soon. We'll figure something out."

"I know. You always do." And with that her teal skirt reflected fluorescently off of the drab gray carpet and white walls until she safely turned the corner.

Jessica chimed in first. "What an idiot." She flung her hair around.

"She's not an idiot, Jessica."

"Sounded like you thought she was even in your own column today," she sneered.

"You missed the point."

"No you missed *a* point." She took Ms. Austin's arm and they continued to the elevator. Ms. Austin turned back with a wink. I had nothing to offer in return. Therein lay the whole problem.

CHAPTER THIRTY

T hese are for you." I turned to see Mr. Hicks standing in the doorway of my cubby. He laid a thick legal-size envelope on my desk and then looked casually around my partition-style walls. "Well, you've made this rather homey, Savannah."

"Remember that probation period we talked about when I first started last week?"

"Yes, I do." He placed his arms atop the set of twins he was packing above his belt.

"Are these"—I pointed toward the folder he had laid down in front of me—"Are these going to cause me to hasten my departure from these homey quarters, or could I dare bring in a few more items of hominess?"

"Well, ignoring the fact that *hominess* isn't a word, you should know not all the correspondence in that folder there is negative. And today's story partially redeemed you. And controversy sells newspapers, Savannah." He headed back up the hall toward the elevator that would lead him to his real door and his beautiful view of Bay Street.

He didn't answer my question. But I had a lot of questions that needed answers. And obviously to him and the little bundle of sheer delight that answered his phones, being hated one day and liked the next was no big deal as long as people bought newspapers.

Perusing the stack of letters, I was shocked by how much people actually cared about what happened on the cover of a newspaper. The opinions were straightforward and strong. People cared one way or the other about what was happening on Wright Square. People had opinions that I had ignored for one reason alone: evasion. I was a chicken.

Gloria Richardson had never been a chicken. She talked about things that were uncomfortable. Told stories that ignited passion and compassion. And I wanted to be well liked at other people's expense.

You have to know why you believe what you believe. Joy's words wouldn't leave me. So I would confront them. I would make a business trip this afternoon. I might come out with stink all over me, but it was a trip that must be traveled.

"Savannah Phillips, you haven't been to my house since the day you picked up that last pot of butter beans I made you."

Granny Daniels never changed. She had always looked old. But not old in a bad way. Just old in an old way. Some people just always look old. You didn't age with them. You didn't enjoy their early years. You just know them old. Well, that is how Granny Daniels has always been to me.

I also never quite remembered what she wore, except that there was always a hat, a black hat. But I couldn't recall the style of hat, or what was under the black. At that age, most of the people she knew were dying left and right. I imagine she decided to simply stay dressed for the occasion.

But today I noticed. Today I wanted to notice. I wanted to notice detail. Not my own, but someone else's. She didn't have a hat on today, and her gray curls were neatly pressed, tight up around her head like a knit cap. She wore a simple coat-style dress in a pretty bright shade of pink. No belt, no buttons, just a zipper up the front, and short sleeves cuffed at the bottom.

The shoes were similar to Joy's. In the sandal family, black, and with pantyhose sticking out from the toes. She was thicker than I had ever realized. But she was wearing fewer clothes than I had ever seen her wear before, either. Her toy poodle yapped at me as soon as I entered and sniffed my legs for the first thirty minutes of our conversation.

"Do you mind if I come in for a few minutes?" I asked, standing at the red front door of her modest white-siding home.

"No, honey. You come in here and sit your little self down and let Granny Daniels fix you some good eatin'."

I couldn't do it. I could sit here and smell mothballs, but I couldn't put them in my mouth. "Oh, that's okay. I'm not hungry."

I sat down at her small kitchen table while she fixed her a plate and I tried to disguise the noises coming from my stomach area.

"Well, what brings you here, sweet girl?" she asked, sitting down next to me at the table. Her plate looked so good. Fresh biscuits, fried pork chops, cabbage, and some kind of potato casserole. This meal and her age were proof: Lard doesn't necessarily kill you young. It could have been one fine meal. But I was certain it looked far better than it would taste. Of course, with the smell so thick inside the house, I might not even be able to smell it in the food. But it just wasn't worth the risk.

"I don't know. Just had some questions."

"What kind of questions, honey?" Butter dripped down her fingers as she lifted that steaming biscuit toward her mouth.

I tried not to lick my lips. My eyes glazed over, and for a moment I lost my train of thought. "Uh, well . . . I was . . . I was just curious what you thought about everything that's been happening around here?"

"Well, it has been rather eventful lately, hasn't it?"

"Yes, ma'am, it sure has."

She leaned back in her chair and took a long sip of her sweet tea. "I've got a lot of thoughts, Savannah. You don't live this long and not have a lot of thoughts on a lot of things. I mean, let's face it: I'm old. Pretty much have always felt old." She chuckled, and I kept my thoughts to myself. "But we're facing times, Savannah, that will probably determine the future for you and your children."

"What do you mean?"

"I mean your mother and hundreds others like her are out there trying to preserve a defining line for you and your children."

"Chaining herself to a monument is defining me all right."

"Is that all you see, Savannah?"

"Is what all I see?"

"Is all you see that your mother is chained to something? Do you not see the bigger picture?"

"There's always a bigger picture for my mother. But the manner in which she chooses to state her cases is usually all I can focus on."

"Then you've probably been robbed of a lot of powerful revelations."

She noticed my pause and she continued. "You are so focused on your fear that your mother will damage your life or reputation that you forget she's her own person. Do you know what's really happening around that square?"

I was certain this was a trick question. "Let's hear your thoughts."

"Life, Savannah. People are declaring life as they have chosen to live it. Some are saying they have chosen to follow the principles carved in that piece of stone. Others are saying anything of a 'Christian viewpoint' has no place on public property. But do you know where the Ten Commandments reside as we speak?"

"No, ma'am, I can't say that I do."

"They rest on the floor of the National Archives Building. And a picture of Moses holding the Ten Commandments—or 'the tablets of the law,' some say—is on the outside of the building that houses the U.S. Supreme Court. Do you think when 'In the Year of Our Lord' was written into the Constitution that some hidden meaning, some hidden god, was being referred to?"

I wasn't sure if this needed an answer.

"No, it was the one true God." See, it didn't. "People can argue all they want that God isn't mentioned in the Constitution. But He is the basis for the Constitution, Savannah. It was written because of who He is."

"But what about the separation of church and state? Isn't that also part of the core of who we are?"

"Well, that's nowhere in the Constitution."

"Yes it is!"

"Where?"

She had me there. "I have no idea."

"Because it's not. That phrase was originally taken from a statement in a letter by Thomas Jefferson that said there should be a 'wall of separation between church and state.' So in a move totally separate of Congress, the courts took what had originally been a prohibition against the Congress establishing a national church and changed it into a prohibition against any acts of religion by the state government—or anyone affiliated with it."

This woman was good. "But in spite of all of that, how is anyone really listening, when everyone is screaming their positions?"

"Some people will never listen, Savannah. Some people will set their course and die for what they believe in."

"My mother would."

"Yes, she would. But she listens too. She may not always act like she's listening," she said with a slight laugh. "The question is, what are you listening to? Truth, or your own set of ideals?"

"It depends who you ask."

"But the answer doesn't change what is true. A person's opinion, even perception, doesn't change truth."

"I know, you're right. Truth is the one constant, isn't it?"

"It is."

"And you might just find it on a slab of concrete strapped to my mama."

That made her chuckle, causing her thickness to shake. "Yes, Savannah, you just might."

On my walk back to the office, I noticed Vicky's countless touches in the streets of Savannah. The landscaping in the squares reflected her taste. The tongues of the passersby often held her name. The Pumpkin House that faced me as I turned the corner held her animosity.

Four years ago, a man from Atlanta purchased the stately home, which required substantial renovation. He began by painting it a lovely shade of Halloween pumpkin orange. Once the update began, Mr. Atlanta ran into some financial troubles. Thus the renovations were completely halted for two years and have run at a virtual snail's pace since then.

Had he known my mother, he would have known that getting approval for the color on the streets of her city would prove rather difficult. About as difficult as his money woes. As a member of the Historic Review Board, Vicky was certain pumpkin orange was not a period color. So, in a rather precise letter, the board informed him that he must repaint his house in a color that was truly representative of the historic period.

They didn't know who they were dealing with either. Mr. Atlanta had done research of his own and proved that his "Pumpkin House" was indeed a period color. Well, Vicky is still confident he fabricated the whole thing, even forged history books, but don't be fooled by her frustration. His house is still orange.

So, seeing her touch everywhere reiterated to me her passion. The same passion that was denying her of down feathers and hot showers was the same passion that propelled her to aid underprivileged families to tidy up their neighborhoods and preserve their dignity. The same woman that was out there praying, singing, and having evening dinner parties was the same woman who had taken this city to new heights in, dare I say, the eyes of the world.

Though *ordinary* on any scale cannot be found within sight of her, extraordinary shows up quite often. The world may laugh. People may ridicule. But in the end, for those who know her, all eventually conclude she's an all right kind of lady.

"Okay, Mr. Attorney, I have a few questions."

I could hear Gregory's heavy sigh on the other end. "What now, Queen of Denial?"

"I've never been the queen of anything, except the okra-seed-spitting contest, and Vicky refuses to allow me to mention it."

We both laughed.

"Seriously, I have a few questions. Sergeant Millings has issued my mother something called an Order to Disperse. He said if she doesn't hightail it home by Friday afternoon at five, he will put her in jail. Can he really do that?"

"Is he a federal officer?"

"No, he's a Savannah officer who should have retired years ago. But after all this attention, he will probably stay around for the next ten years."

"I would think this would be a federal issue, with her being in front of a Federal Courthouse."

"They're still wrangling over that one. Sergeant Millings is fighting them tooth and nail to be the one who gets to handcuff Victoria Phillips right back up. Of course, if she got too close to him, poor soul would have a coronary. But could my mother really go to jail? I mean, the woman's good, but Martha Stewart she ain't. My mother would crumble at a strip search."

"Well, if he gave her an Order to Disperse, our Criminal Code Section 39-17-305 says she could get arrested for disorderly conduct if she doesn't comply. I'm not sure if it's the same for Georgia."

"So you're saying she very well could."

"Yes, my friend, she very well could. I'm surprised they haven't gotten her for Section 39-17-307, obstructing a highway or other passageway."

"She's on a sidewalk, Gregory."

"Yes, a passageway to the courthouse."

"I couldn't stand to see her get thrown in jail. That just wouldn't be right. Plus, the local police shouldn't be forced to endure her for thirty days. Maybe we should break into Sergeant Millings's office and find that order and throw it away."

"That—"

"That would *not* be stealing; that would be misplacing."

"You need help."

"I know. I need yours. Will you come defend my mother?"

"She'll have to pay me more than you."

"She has more money than me, genius."

"Sure. If it gets that far, call me. Now, have you dealt with your other issue?"

"I don't have any other issues. Ooh, I think my phone's beeping. Check your calendar. We'll need you by Friday."

"Savann—"

"Ooh, gotta run! Beep, beep, beep! Bye."

"Yeah, Mr. Hicks received almost a hundred letters about her picture in the paper." That little snide secretary made sure I could hear her.

"Hello, Savannah." Ms. Austin was apparently leaving and looked rather startled as I rounded the corner.

"Hello," I responded to her and the tormented one. The little tick turned up her already upturned nose and asked. "Ooh, what's that smell?"

"It smells like mothballs," Ms. Austin said.

"Yeah, I smell that in the foyer every now and then too," I assured them.

"Well, I've never smelled it before," Jessica said.

Joshua came around the corner right behind me and about knocked us all down. I was actually glad to see him. He bumped into Faith and gave a quick "Excuse me" but offered nothing else to any of us.

Ms. Austin scanned him up and down, and her eyes followed him down the hall. I found it rather uncomfortable. "Who is that good-looking man?"

"Oh, that's Joshua North," Jessica responded. "He is one of the cutest things around here. Doesn't pay much attention to anyone though. Trust me, I've tried for years . . ." she recalled the two of us were present. "Oh," she said, semiembarrassed.

Ms. Austin's cell phone rang. "Ms. Austin . . . Yes . . . I know. Would you lay off? I told you I'd call you when I got through." She slammed the phone shut.

Jessica jumped. "Well then, if you'll excuse me, I need to get back to Mr. Hicks. The paper never slows down for anyone."

"Sure. Thank you, Jessica, for your hospitality today." As soon as Jessica was out of earshot, Ms. Austin unleashed. "My God, that woman is simply insufferable. She's been breathing down my neck all day long. Well, Savannah. Always good to see you. Let me know if we can get together soon."

Her outburst startled me. I watched her as she walked away. Granted, Jessica was condescending, downright annoying and, well, a pain to be certain, but hearing someone else say it felt a little awkward. The woman in the thousand-dollar outfit and bust-the-bank cosmetic line left. I watched her leave. After all, that's what people did.

CHAPTER THIRTY-ONE

Do you want me to come help you pack?" Paige asked over the phone.

I looked out my car window and stared up at my house. I'd spent a long afternoon staring at a blank computer screen. Tomorrow, my friend and real-estate agent, Claire, would bring me keys for my new place. Yet the whole moment felt slightly overwhelming. "No, I think this is something I need to do myself."

"You sure?"

"Yeah, I'm sure."

"Are we still moving you out tomorrow night, though?"

"Yeah, Thomas has agreed to help. Not much to move though."

"We'll have to move your whole bedroom suite."

"Yeah, but that's about it. I don't have anything else. And with what I have to pay you back, I'll be eating sitting on my bed for the next year."

"You'll be surprised how quickly things will change."

Thinking back to all the happenings of this week, I knew things had already changed. "I'm already surprised."

"Well, have fun. It's a new day."

"Yes, it's a new day. I'll call you later."

"What are you going to do? Plop you a monument in your front yard?" The younger man asked the elderly gentleman as they walked past my house.

"If I need to, I will. Wouldn't hurt you anyway, young man."

"You are so totally out of touch with this generation, Grandpa."

Their conversation rounded the corner as they did. But the pitch of the grandfather's voice made it clear who was in touch with whom.

I stood at the bottom of the steps to my house for what seemed like forever. I looked around at the ivy. It was so perfect. It ran neatly up the brick wall that surrounded the Abercorn side of our house. Each shrub had been maintained by Jake and his good friend Wayne, who had helped him for years. Every detail was attended to. Everything had its order. Its place. Just like my father. A man of order and detail. He commanded the whole while paying attention to the one. Looking at his handiwork, I was confronted with how much I'd yet to learn about life, about love, about work, about this family. Lord have mercy—about pretty much everything. I couldn't handle one thing, let alone one thousand things. My stars, I couldn't handle myself half the time. I heard a hum.

"You going in, or just going to watch the ivy grow?"

Poor sister always gave herself away before she even said a word. "I'm going in eventually."

"Things have changed, little one." I could feel Joy staring at me.

"How can you tell?"

"See it in your face."

"Look older, huh?"

"You're an old soul, Savannah; a person can't help that."

"Could we talk about something else?"

"Want to talk about dinner?"

I turned and looked at her wide black eyes. Then I cracked up. I laughed until I was doubled over. I even had to hold on to Joy so I wouldn't fall down on the pavement. People were watching, but I didn't care. I deserved to laugh. Somebody needed to laugh. Things had gotten way too serious around here. Before I knew it, Joy was laughing too. We were both trying to hold each other up, but we couldn't, so we finally surrendered and plopped ourselves down on the bottom step. And by the time we were through, neither of us could even remember what had been so funny.

I leaned back on the stoop. "Joy, ahh, you make me laugh. How do you do it?"

"Do what?" She used one of her plump arms to try to lower herself down onto the step beside me. I reached out and helped steady her down.

"Stay so happy. I mean, you're always singing or smiling. Every now and then you get a faraway look, but you're just full of . . ."

"Full of what, baby? Joy?"

I laughed. "Yeah, crazy, isn't it? You are your name. You're just a joy."

She looked at me as if this was no revelation to her at all. "Well, what else would I be, Savannah?"

"Well, I know, but what if your name was Suzy? You'd still be full of joy."

"Ever the clever one, aren't you? Destiny's in a name, Savannah."

Here we went again. "You think?"

"I know. Ever met a child whose parents called him *stupid* all of his life? Stupid is what he turns out to be. Ever met a kid whose parents told him he wouldn't amount to anything? I bet if you looked him up now, you'll find he hasn't amounted to anything. But tell a child he can do anything, and he won't know any better but to believe you. Call a child a champion, or a hero, or a young girl a lady, or a woman of grace, and see what she grows up to be."

She turned and looked at me with that look. That Joy look. That "I'm about to say something you should write down" look.

"Or name a girl Savannah, and she will forever have a destiny for that city. You were meant to be here, baby. You were meant to affect this city. Just like your name says, that is what you were created to do."

"You think?" I asked again, except this time with a totally different attitude.

"I know," she answered, still as confident as she was the last time. "Just like Victoria is meant to bring people to victory. Your mother knew what she was doing when she named you, Miss Savannah from Savannah."

I stared across the street into the window of Clary's. To think my name had a purpose. To think what I called people had an effect on them. Well, that just created a whole other set of issues for me and my life.

"What about Jake?" I asked looking at her.

"Now, that's a man's kind of name."

"That pretty much defines my father, a real man. What about the name Mr. Hicks?"

She snickered. "I'll have to look that one up, Savannah. But today, why don't you just think about who *you* are. What you're here for. And why you were given such a substantial name. Maybe because you have a substantial purpose."

With that she got up and hummed her way down the street. I went inside to close a chapter of my life. And contemplate this new challenge.

As a writer, it is interesting to write the end of a chapter. You want things to be neat and tidy. You want dilemmas to be solved and your characters to be okay. You want your reader to end satisfied. As if the last drink offers the most satisfaction. But unfortunately, that kind of ending creates little anticipation. So you create drama, conflict, questions.

That was what this was for me. As much as I wanted to leave home, create my own life, have my own space, I was scared. I was torn. I was homesick. I was hungry. And I knew a few of those things would only get worse. But it was a necessary closing. It was a necessary journey. I couldn't stay here forever. Victoria and Jake were where Savannah had come from. But it was time for Savannah to clearly define where she was going. I had to fly, grow, change, somehow. And this was the next step in all of those things.

As I walked up each step leading to the front door I decided to make this moment different. I would memorize and remember. And that is what I did. I knew I would be alone to accomplish it. The rest of my family was having supper on a sidewalk. So I took my time. For an hour I did nothing but walk around my house and remember.

Our parlor (or living room, if you're normal) beckoned me. In truth, the monstrosity of a picture over the fireplace—my mother in her tiara, draped in her Miss Georgia United States of America sash, and rather expansive hair—forces one to look. It caused me to smile. It used to cause me to pity her. But tonight was different. Tonight was not about just her. It was about us.

I remembered birthdays and arguments. I remembered sneaking out of windows with Paige and sneaking Grant in for midnight conversations. I remembered countless dinners around the table that had seen far less action than this week and remembered Jake and Victoria and Thomas and Duke and how life had been made better because they were in it. Not perfect. Nothing can reach such standards. But Savannah perfect. Perfectly fit for me. Perfectly created for me.

I walked to Dad's study at the back of the house, across from the kitchen, tucked beside the powder room on the other side of the stairs. I sat down on his leather sofa and looked at the perfect door that only years before had to be entirely replaced. It was the day of Victoria's garden tea. Who knows what for. And who knows who was there. But one person, or canine rather, had been banned and sequestered in Dad's office. Vicky thought that would work. Mistaken child. Duke could see them from Dad's window. First he barked at them. Vicky shut the blinds. Then he howled at them. Vicky turned on Harry Connick Jr. Then he flat decided to come through the door. She hadn't prepared for that one.

And a grand entrance he made with half of Dad's study door wrapped around his neck like a rather large flea collar. She tried to pull him inside. He pulled the other way. It was a tug-of-wills. Duke lost, but only after he had successfully knocked over two tables, feasted on overpriced caviar, and peed on an elderly lady's leg that looked amazingly like a tree stump. I can't help it; the woman had substantial calves. Then he was taken away by Thomas to Dad's store, where he spent the next week in "time-out." Truth be known, Duke probably didn't lose after all.

I walked up the stairs and noticed the gash in step number six. That took place during a rather lively discussion I was having with Thomas that prompted the throwing of a stapler. It had been unsuccessfully patched. I had been successfully disciplined.

I climbed into the attic and retrieved the necessary boxes to pack up my room. Scanning my wall of bookshelves behind my bed, I took each book down carefully and laid it in a box, remembering something about each one. The sight that followed was really not surprising. Hillary Clinton's book *Living History* lay hidden behind all of my other books. No need to ask who put it there. No need to ask why. Because standing upright next to it was Dick Morris's book, *Rewriting History*.

"Sad lady. Sad lady." I laughed.

My eyes were drawn to one of the eye-level shelves and the works of C. S. Lewis. Of all the authors I have read, few have captured the essence of the soul like Lewis. I looked at each of his books stacked neatly in a row in alphabetical order by title.

I picked up *Mere Christianity* and leafed through its pages, chuckling at the oxymoron of the title, pondering the thoughts of Lewis as he decided to place that label on the weight and depth of those pages, making it clear in such relevant terms that Christianity is anything but *mere*. I recalled his statement in *The Weight of Glory*, where he said, "If you have not chosen the Kingdom of God, it will make in the end no difference what you have chosen instead."

I read over and over the underlined text and my own thoughts, written in the margins. Each of them trying to understand what I was reading, even while experiencing revelation. I thumbed through *The Screwtape Letters*, *The Problem with Pain*, and *The Great Divorce*. And by the time I was through, it was evident why my tilling time had been so nonproductive over the last week. Because tilling had been all about Savannah.

Not about a bigger plan, not about a greater purpose, not about a discovered destiny, but about me, my wants, whims, and selfishness. Joshua was right; that's why he drove me mad. He saw through me. I knew it, and he surely knew it. And the whole thing drove me crazy.

I wasn't an evening tiller. But tonight I didn't have a choice. I had some core issues to settle. I had some demons of my own to purge. I had some monuments of my own that I needed to chain myself to for a while.

As I ran through Forsythe Park, the tears flowed freely. The comprehension of my own lies and idols and pride were almost more than I could handle. But I didn't care. He who handles tilling time could handle this. And He did. He stopped the world for me. He spoke and I listened. He challenged, and I was willing. He rebuked, and I knew it was all true. He reminded me of my limits, and I agreed. He offered His strength, and I gladly accepted.

And then I noticed, for the first time since I had returned to Savannah almost three weeks ago, the most beautiful rose garden I had ever seen, right in the middle of the park I ran through every morning.

I approached the white-columned enclosure with reverence. The iron gate that surrounded it was willing to let me enter. The two iron benches that sat on either side of the garden were available. But

the stone bench that sat in underneath the concrete arbor was inviting. Next to the bench was a small plaque declaring, "Everyone
needs to stop and smell the roses."

I remembered Joy's words of wisdom. "You need to stop,
smell a flower . . ." I hadn't smelled a flower in years. I hadn't
stopped in years. I probably hadn't listened much in years either.

I leaned over one of the most beautiful yellow roses I had ever
seen, suddenly understanding why an entire song was written
about them. It was stunning. Perfectly opened. Smelled like, well,
like a rose, and before I knew it I was dancing around that garden
like Julie Andrews in *The Sound of Music.* I smelled the white ones,
the red ones, the pink ones, the pink with white ones. And then I
sat down on the bench and just smelled them all. For the first time
in years, Savannah smelled a rose. And for the first time in weeks,
Savannah was listening. Really listening. And amazingly enough,
when I fell quiet, a wealth of wisdom waited.

CHAPTER THIRTY-TWO

Hey, child, smelling flowers?"

She always found me. Every time I stepped outside, she found me. "Yeah, I am, Joy. I'm smelling flowers." I turned to look at her. Yet her expression seemed lost. She looked at me like a stranger. "Joy, you okay? It's me, Savannah."

"Yeah, yeah, Savannah. Hey, baby." Her eyes sparkled with the recollection of me. "I see you found my secret place." She sat down on the bench. Her side squeaked under her weight.

"It's beautiful. Can you believe I never noticed it?"

"You wouldn't be the first. Most people around here haven't noticed it. No one has time. Too much craziness going on." She patted her fading floral. I watched her drift off in thought. "Emily Dickinson, though, once wrote a friend that 'consider the lilies of the field' is the only commandment she never broke."

I chuckled. "I'd just have to add it to my list."

"Mine too, baby." She laughed. "Mine too."

Finally, it was too much. It had to be asked. "Joy, why do you wear that dress every day?"

She looked at me, puzzled. "This?" she paused. "Oh, well, I don't really know. I guess I just have a couple of the same kind. Just comfortable, you know. So, what's your favorite one?"

She was back to flowers by choice. I would respect that. "Couldn't pick if I tried."

She stood up to leave. "Well, enjoy my secret garden."

"Where are you going?"

"Oh, got a lot of work to do. A lot of people left to see this evening. You take care of my special place, now."

"I will." I assured her. She wandered away. Looking lost. And without commenting on food or facial defects. And no humming. Something was amiss. But she wasn't ready. I would know when she was.

Paige was sitting on the steps of my house as I cleared the side of Clary's. "Why in the world are you running in the evening? Are you still dealing with deeply rooted issues?"

I proceeded up the stairs past her, into the foyer. "I am a deeply rooted issue."

"Well, how much have you packed?" She followed me up the stairs and into my room. "Oh, you've packed five entire books. Don't really want to go, do you?"

I turned to look at her; then I looked into my bathroom and spotted some toothpaste splatters on my mirror. "My bathroom looks filthy."

She grabbed my arm and jerked me back. "Oh, no you don't, Miss Hygiene Freak. You will not avoid the question."

"What question?"

"You know what question."

I sat down on the bed and looked out of my window and stared up Abercorn Street. "It's not about wanting to go; it's about having to go."

"Is this going to get real deep, because I might need some Doritos and a Diet Coke."

She made me laugh. I couldn't help it. Looking at her cute

little button nose and perfectly messy bleached-blonde short tresses, she cracked me up. "No, not deep tonight. Come on, help me pack. Grab a book." I tossed her one from the bookcase. "So, what are your parents doing tonight?"

"Oh, I think my dad went to hang out with your dad at the coffee shop and play some cards, while Mom is at a Mary Kay party with your mother."

"Oh, that's right. I forgot about that," I said laughing. "I should have known Mother would have it no matter what. I bet that's a sight—a group of women painting themselves up while one poor soul is in shackles."

As soon as it came out of my mouth, we both stared at each other. And without a word we threw the books in the boxes and took off down the stairs and across the black marble floor of the foyer and slammed the door behind us. We didn't stop running until we hit "Monument" Square.

"Do not let them see us," I said, panting and squatting behind a tree. It was close to seven o'clock and the sun had a good thirty more minutes, but they didn't care; there were enough television crew lights for the seven o'clock news that a 747 could have landed on the sidewalk.

"Lord, if they see us, we'll be their guinea pigs."

"They'd take us on as their goodwill project."

We leaned against the tree, Paige on one side, me on the other, but each of us with a good enough view to enjoy the production. And a production it was.

Each woman had donned a lovely white terry-cloth headband. Except Miss Amber Topaz; she had chosen a pale pink one. The Mary Kay representative had them eating out of the palm of her hand.

"Now, ladies. This is the latest in skin care. This mask will continue to purge your skin of its deepest blackheads long after you've gone to sleep."

"Now, that's a visual," Paige added.

And before we knew it, each of the nine women was covered in white cream, looking like a white version of the Blue Man Group. And there they sat, for the next ten minutes, while tiny blackheads screamed for refuge across all nine of their little faces.

"I want them to get to the makeup," Paige said.

"Be patient. Good skin care is essential to your daily skin regimen."

She looked at me as if a poltergeist was about to come out of my body. "What do you know? You use Noxema."

"Do you forget that is *my* mother up there?"

"Oh, right."

The Mary Kay consultant continued. "Now, ladies, apply your foundation smoothly, and make sure it matches your skin tone."

"I don't wear foundation," I offered.

"What's to cover up?" Paige asked.

"My ever-increasing age, I hear."

"Let me look." Paige came rather close to my face. "Nah, you look great. Need some waxing done, there on your lip"—she rubbed the top of my lip, and I slapped her hand—"but besides that you don't look a day over twenty."

"You think?" I asked, patting my face.

"Absolutely. Oh, *don't do it!*" she yellspered in terror toward the entertainment. But Amber wasn't listening and with the speed of an expert had applied bright blue eye shadow to her lids.

"Looks like my grandmother," I said.

"Not as bad as I thought. Kind of a retro-nouveau look. Everything comes back, you know." She squinted to get a better look.

"Some things shouldn't," I assured her. But it did look good on Amber. Of course, that girl would look good in a floral print muumuu.

"Ooh, look at that lipstick," Paige said, eying the pale pink color that Amber was applying to her lips.

"Ooh, that's nice. I could wear that."

"Oh, yeah, that would look great on you, with that pink toe nail polish you always wear."

"Oh, and look at that blush."

"Maybe *we* should have gone to this thing," Paige said, then looked at me. We both busted out laughing.

As the women finished, applause rose from those pilgrims who had gathered around to watch. Amber struck a pose or two, and mother tugged on a chain. But she did look the best she had looked in weeks. If the poor soul could get her hair washed and that outfit changed, she'd look downright clean.

"Let's go finish packing."

Paige stood up to follow me as we headed back to the house. "I could sneak my mother's Mary Kay book out of the house or get one from that Mary Kay lady and we could order some of that stuff."

"I don't think they have books. That's Avon."

"Oh, well, I like Avon too."

"And they're called consultants, not 'Mary Kay ladies.'"

"Well, I still want some of her stuff, whatever I need to call her."

"You just like to spend money."

"Other people's, preferably."

"Me too!"

"Yeah, I know."

CHAPTER THIRTY-THREE

The mind is a frustrating instrument. If not for the necessity of it, I'd have banished it long ago. But then I would have become the witless wonder Thomas has declared me to be for two decades. See, the mind never stops. It harasses you. Take the simple task of getting up and trying to brush your teeth: it forces you to stare at the toothpaste splatters on the mirror and quizzes you over when you're going to clean them.

Or the simple task of driving to work: Which of the three routes there will you choose? And once you choose, it questions whether you've chosen well. It teases you with the possibility that another option would have had less traffic or fewer red lights. And when you pass the window of Katherine's Corner Bookstore, the mind sends you down a memory lane of your own vanished opportunities for literary fame and store-window showcases.

The mind never leaves you alone. When you're trying to read, it barges in with to-do lists. When you're trying to listen, it barges in with your next question. And when you're trying to let go of love, it barges in with every reason to keep fighting.

But when I need a Coke—well, in large part my mind and I

are usually in agreement. Until lately. Lately it has been making an issue of Coke. Coke! As if it were an addiction. As if it mattered. As if I would care. As if everybody didn't deserve one. I mean, compared to the addictions I could have chosen, my mind shouldn't be harassing me. Trust me. I would be a witless wonder before I would be a former Coke consumer.

"Where is our dishwasher?!" I heard Louise asking rather clearly and with an extra dose of volume. The man staring back at her just tried to smile, looking as if he couldn't determine exactly what the problem was. When she flung her hand out of the soapy dishwater and splattered suds across the front of his shirt, she didn't apologize, and I think he determined the problem.

Jake rounded the corner from his office. "Louise, I'll handle it from here." And Louise let out a rather loud *humph* and returned to her dishes. I thought about staying hidden, but I didn't want to miss anything. So I proceeded to stand by the Coke machine.

"Mr. Phillips, the dishwasher will be here this afternoon, I assure you." He gave my dad a slap on the arm. "Doesn't hurt a woman to wash a few dishes."

I leaned back against the counter and took a long swig of my Coke and flung my eyes toward Louise. She and Mervine both turned around on that one, and the little man seemed to shift closer to my father.

"Ron, you have told me that every day for a week." Dad calmly wiped his hands on the towel draped over the tie of his apron. He was smooth.

"I know, sir. But I promise it will be today!"

"Well, you know what? That's not good enough."

"What do you mean?"

"I mean exactly what I said, Ron. That's not good enough."

"Well, I don't know what else to do."

"I'll tell you what you can do: you can write me a check for the deposit I paid you and consider our business finished."

"Well, that isn't possible. I've already paid for the deposit on your dishwasher."

"Then you should get your money back from them, after they've given you the runaround." Jake paused. "Unless, of course, they never told you they could have it here the next day. If that's the case, then this is apparently your problem and your problem alone."

"Well, I think you're being hasty." The little man began to twitch nervously.

"I don't think I'm being hasty, Ron." Dad sure liked to say his name. "I'm just making you keep your word."

"I'm getting you your dishwasher, Mr. Phillips! That *was* my word!" the man said rather rudely.

"No, your word was you would get me my dishwasher by last Saturday. Today is Thursday. On Saturday you said it would be here Monday. On Monday and Tuesday and Wednesday you simply decided not to return our calls. And you are only in here today because I dragged you in here after I saw you in the market. In fact, I haven't seen hide nor hair of you since I wrote you a check. A substantial check." By this time Jake was leaning against the counter himself.

Mervine and Louise and I were just enjoying the whole scene. The little fella was becoming progressively smaller and increasingly more fidgety. "Well, I think you just have unrealistic expectations."

"Well, if expecting someone to do what they *say* they're going to do is unrealistic, then yes sir, Ron, I guess I do." Poor soul would know his name by the time Jake was through with him. "But if you had told me it would have taken a week, then we wouldn't even be having this discussion today. You should have just been honest with me from the beginning."

I was about to feel sorry for the meager man when his lower lip began to twitch. "I just haven't been able to help it, Mr. Phillips. See, my wife and my kids—"

"Stop it right there. Don't you try to exploit your family. Your wife and kids are fine. I have seen them out at the square almost every day. But haven't caught a glimpse of you, come to think of it. So this is where this conversation needs to end. I want my check, and I want it now."

Dad never raised his voice. Never really even changed his tone. But you would have thought he had stood over that man and berated him like a schoolboy, the way ol' Ron shook when he reached for his checkbook. As he ripped out the check and laid it on the counter, he turned to leave. But before he did he tapped my Coke machine and said, "If you ever need a new one of these, I know where to get you a good one at cost."

"Ahh!" I said, pulling my Coke from my mouth and slapping his hand. He jerked away quickly. Wise move. "Don't you even think about it." I glared at him.

He walked to the door. But Dad wasn't quite through.

"One more thought, Ron. You might want to remove the fish emblem from your invoices. There's something downright distasteful about using a symbol of integrity to manipulate people into thinking it represents your character as well. I would think about that, sir. Because I've learned something in the business world." Well, I guess Dad had two more thoughts. "All your giftings might get you to the front of the line, but if your character's not in order when you get there, it can destroy you."

The little man morphed into a wee little man as he left with his tail between his legs.

"Louise, Mervine, I'm sorry. I'll have a dishwasher in here by tomorrow morning," my dad said. Then he kissed me and headed back to the front of the store.

His heart was heavy, I could tell. Jake didn't like hurting anyone. He was a tender spirit. But he was the real thing too, a man. So to receive any less from someone else wasn't acceptable to him.

"Are your hands shriveled prunes?" I asked as I gave them both a sideways hug.

"No, we've just been mumbling. Truth be told, your father and

Richard have washed as many of these dishes as we have. We're just spoiled," Louise said with a chuckle.

"Me too," I mused. "Me too. But had that man touched my machine again, I would have kicked his heinie."

"Savannah Phillips! Watch your mouth," Louise snapped.

"What? I said I would have had Duke lick him shiny!"

Mervine tried to stifle her grin. I didn't. "Child, don't you have a job?" Louise laughed.

I headed to the door to go check on my dad. "So they tell me. So they tell me."

As I opened the door, I noticed Dad and Duke sitting together at the front table. Dad was in a chair; Duke was at his feet. Although no one would have been surprised had Duke been sitting in the chair opposite him. He really was an immensely talented dog. These two had an unusual bond. You could tell just by observing them. Dad sat there rubbing Duke's head while they both stared out the window. Who knows what they were thinking. But by their identical expressions, it was probably about the same thing: spending another night on concrete.

I'm sure their perspectives of it were very different. But Duke would do anything for my father. And my father would do anything for Duke. He had been purchased for Thomas, but he had been treasured by my father. They go everywhere together. And when Duke must make way for Vicky, he ain't at all happy about it. And when Vicky has to deal with red dog hair, she ain't too happy about that one either.

But there Jake is. Loving the dog. Loving the woman. And adored by both while the two drive each other ferociously insane.

As I rounded the corner to head to the office, I noticed a slight commotion in front of Walgreen's. A short, fair-haired maiden was letting loose on one Sergeant Millings. Poor thing shouldn't have stood a chance with that man. But from the looks of it, the poor man didn't stand a chance with Paige. I drove by with a beep and a smile.

"I heard they stole her purse. Poor kid probably needed it. That girl has enough of her own. She should have just given it to him," Jessica said into her cell phone as she made her way in front of me through the front door.

"Don't feel bad, Savannah," Marla said as she saw me come through the door behind Jessica. "She never speaks to me either."

I made my way to my cubicle to work on my story. All newspaper systems were go. Feet were scurrying. Fingers were pecking on keyboards. The sounds of a soda can being opened and a tug-of-war with a bag of chips was coming from the cubicle in front of me. I sat down at my computer to lend my talents to this pressured world. After my talk with Granny Daniels, the issues were coming into focus. I would dive in and see what I came up with.

By the time I came up for air, she was my human-interest story, and her knowledge of history, happenings, and life would surely be as interesting to the readers as they had been to me. I printed it out around eleven and set it on my desk. But I wasn't going to deliver it until I got back from lunch. I had only been here for two hours, but it felt like a full day. I made a motion for an early lunch. There were no objections.

"My, my, child. I thought you just left here," Richard said as I entered the back door of Jake's.

"It's been a long morning already, and I needed a Coke. Thought I'd take an early lunch." I was distracted by a growling noise staring at the doorway into the shop. "Is she back, Duke?" I asked, walking to pat his ornery head.

Much to my surprise, Jake's was empty, except for Dad's persistent admirer. I guess everyone had paused to check out whatever was going on across the street, and few people partook of lunch at eleven. So, that left Jake and his new friend alone. She looked

rather striking today, her brown hair coiffed in an updo, her microphone still attached to her flowing blouse, waiting for the noon
report, I figured. She was sitting at the bar and was rubbing the side
of her cup, in what was a rather flirtatious, dare I say provocative,
move. Dad stood behind the counter refilling the coffeepots for the
lunchtime crowd. His business had grown along with the group
outside.

"So, how long have you been married, Jake?"

"Twenty-five years, Susan. Can you believe that?"

"Oh, they've gone to first names," I told Duke, patting his
head. He was stiff as a board.

"Are you happy?" She rubbed the side of her coffee cup again
and tilted her head.

"She's downright shameless!" I said. Duke looked up at me
with a "Where in the world have you been?" kind of look. By this
time an old African American and two ancient twins were peering
over our shoulders.

"As happy as one can be in this life. I have more than I could
ask for."

"Haven't you been lonely this past week, with your wife out
there strapped to a pillar of concrete?" She batted her false eyelashes, over what I was now certain were eyes of equally false green.

"Actually, I've been out there with Victoria every night.
Almost feels like camping."

She gave a vain attempt at laughter. "You are a remarkable
man, Jake Phillips, a remarkable man." She stood up and patted his
hand softly where he had laid it on the counter. I'm almost certain
I was growling at that point.

"Well, have a great afternoon," Dad offered as he removed his
hand and headed around the counter to wipe off a table by the far
wall. The next action happened so quickly that about all five of us
fell out of the doorway. As Dad made his way to the table, she cut
him off at the edge of the counter, grabbed him by the edge of his
apron, and laid one on him as if she were Angelina Jolie. Well, poor

Duke had absorbed all a canine could take. That gentle golden retriever took off before any of us could stop him. In the meantime Dad had grabbed a hold of Susan's arms and pushed her away. Duke finished her off. He pounced between them and had that Mary Kay reject flat on her back in two seconds flat. He hovered over her like a scene from *Scooby Doo*.

"Way to go, boy!" I screamed, dancing a jig to meet them. "Tripping?! What is *that*?! *My* boy can lay a woman flat on her back!" Then I stopped, the shock of it all setting in. My father had just kissed another woman. Well, maybe not technically. After all, she did grab him, by the apron no less. We were throwing that thing in the trash before day's end.

"Duke, get off of her!" Dad shouted.

Duke didn't pay him a lick of attention. He stood atop her, growling from ear to ear. Every time she tried to squirm, he would flinch in that direction. That poor woman whimpered like a trapped puppy.

"Duke! I said get down, now!" Dad demanded. This time Duke obeyed, but he still hovered right beside my father, snarling and growling all the way. Richard, Louise, and Mervine had indeed fallen through the swinging doors at my departure and were standing exposed by the counter, staring at the raucous affair. I'm sure we all looked like a *Girls Behaving Badly* episode. We stood, mouths agape, and eyes wider than a hoot owl's.

Dad graciously lifted up the wanton woman. "I'm sorry, Susan," Dad said, trying to stifle a laugh. She wasn't laughing.

"You need to get that dog under control." She wiped off her skirt as best her trembling hands could manage.

"I think *you* need to get *yourself* under control," Dad said to her.

"Well, it's about time!" I offered rather loudly. Dad looked at me as well.

"Savannah, stay out of this."

She gave us both a glare that would have made mouths drop open and eyes bug out, had that not been a preexisting condition.

She snatched up her purse and headed for the door. Dad gently took hold of her arm and made her turn around. "Susan, you are a beautiful woman. But when someone has given not just a pledge but a commitment to someone else, you need to respect that."

"You need to come into the real world, Jake Phillips. My Lord, man, you don't even sell iced coffee, Frappuccino, or cappuccino. Do you know it is the twenty-first century?"

"Yes, I do. I also know that just because years pass and trends come and go, some things aren't up for modification. There are some absolutes. Coffee being one of them." My word, don't insult the man's coffee! "Whether you like it or not, they still exist. And the covenant I made to that 'concrete hugger' across the street is one of them."

"Well, then you deserve her."

"No, I don't deserve her, Susan. But I am thankful she's mine."

She didn't stick around for any more of his discourse. Duke followed her to the door.

"Okay, show's over," Dad said as he passed the four of us and went into his office. The man had had a rough day. Duke stared at Susan from the window. She looked back only once. Duke snarled. She winced. Dog, one. Naughty newscaster, zero.

CHAPTER THIRTY-FOUR

The park bench gave a little as I sat down. The scene had expanded immensely over these full six days. Each side had grown larger and louder. Each sign had grown bigger and bolder. Each prayer was offered with greater passion and fervor. And each opposition to each prayer was offered with greater passion and fervor.

I heard the slow shuffle of black sandals and the swooshing sound larger thighs make when the nylons they are wearing brush together as one is walking. And I knew my lunch partner had arrived.

"You need to go talk to her, Savannah. At the end of the day, she's your mother."

I knew Joy was right. I needed to deal with my mother. She was out there fighting as hard as she could for what she believed in, while her daughter ignored her and other women kissed her husband. She deserved my respect. She had gone to great lengths this week, in large part for me alone. Well, for me and Thomas.

I didn't respond to Joy verbally, but actively. Walking toward my mother, I noticed the raven-haired beauty was rather close to her. I might have recommended she rethink this, as Mother had spent a week's worth of evenings in the humid outdoors, in the same attire. Granted, her makeup was fresh from the Mary Kay adventure, but the rest of her was disintegrating rapidly.

I approached unnoticed. That wasn't hard anymore. Things around here had grown to such a chaotic level that no one noticed much except what was blasted from a bullhorn. I slipped in under the volume of the other conversations, the protests, and the prayers. But in spite of the noise, I did hear Faith. I heard words that I'm sure were meant for my mother alone. But I heard each one of them. And let's just say, what followed wasn't pretty.

"You're nothing but a self-righteous, self-promoting little woman who has made herself a laughingstock in front of the entire nation. You should be more like your daughter and try to see at least some of the humor in this situation." As she backed her charcoal tresses up, her thousand-dollar designer pantsuit didn't look so attractive anymore. But the expression on my mother's face locked itself in my memory for what I knew would be forever. After all, who could ever forget the look of a shocked pig as it discovers that it is, well, a pig.

That raven lady could talk about this city. She could talk about my writing. She could talk about me, for crying out loud (which she had, and rather nicely). But now she had talked about my mama. If Faith were a Savannian, she'd know better than to talk about my mama, or to label my mother's actions as self-serving. Only I can do that. Plus, "self-serving" may have gotten Vicky here, but if I knew anything, I knew "self-serving" wouldn't have kept her here.

I stepped forward and startled the two beauties. "You need to step back, Ms. Austin."

"Savannah, this doesn't concern you. You've proven you're nothing like your mother," she quipped, no longer trying to hide her blatant disdain for Vicky. And she turned to go.

"So, is that what you do?" I asked. "Explode all over people and then walk away without giving them the opportunity to respond?"

She turned back around. The friendly look that she once

bestowed upon me had gone bye-bye. "You had an entire news-paper article to respond, Savannah, and you couldn't even come up with any passion of your own. Granted, it had humor, but there wasn't any substance in it."

"Don't bring me into this," I said getting rather uncomfortable with where this was going.

"Yeah, this is between me and you, sunshine!" my mother yelled, tugging at her chains.

"Mother, please." I motioned for her to move back.

"Well, isn't that what you and your mother do? Seek attention from the city? Use it to promote yourself?" She crossed her arms. I liked her better from the back.

"We don't use this city, *Ms.* Austin." I made sure the *Ms.* came out with a hissing noise. "We love this city. And no one loves it more than my mother. And she's not self-righteous. She lives what she believes."

"Give me a break. You're both hypocrites. You want to point out everyone else's sin and not admit to your own."

Well, if I had thought about confessing any sin, I wouldn't begin here on a sidewalk in the middle of a Savannah square. Because if I wasn't mistaken, every journalist in the place had just moved in about ten feet closer.

"That's what you people do, isn't it, Savannah?" she said, hiss-ing to herself. "You sit your self-righteous bodies in position of power and try to determine the standards by which the world should live, while hiding the ghosts in your own closets." She began moving in closer. I wasn't sure whose closets she had been snoop-ing in, but me and sister Vicky don't do ghosts. Or dead people. I began looking for Duke. He had already about eaten one woman for lunch today; he could go two for two. He wasn't anywhere to be found. Why would he be? I was standing next to my mother.

She moved in even closer. We were about to touch noses. And hers was a perfectly proportioned nose, I might add. But her eyes weren't quite as inviting as they had been in the past. "So why don't you quit hiding behind your little monument"—she turned to look at my mother—"and quit trying to make me look like the bad guy, and let the world know what you're really like, Savannah Phillips"—she turned back to me—"because this Miss Perfect performance has gone on long enough."

It was more than I could bear. It was as if a dam burst, and before I knew it, I threw both hands in the air, lifted my face to the sky, and screamed, "Okay, I STOLE A CAR DADDY!" Some gasped. Others cheered. Some laughed. My mother grabbed her chest, did a Fred Sanford move backward, and Ms. Austin didn't try to disguise her smirk. Every camera within the square started rolling, and pictures were snapped like I was Anna Kournikova.

"Yes, I stole a Sugar Daddy!" I confirmed to the listening world. "I saw a little girl licking it. It looked good. I begged for a lick, and when she finally held it out in her little hand, I snatched it and took off like a streak. Are you happy now?"

"Grow up, Savannah." She started walking off again. The crowd roared. But I wouldn't let her off so easy. Cheers or no cheers. I would follow.

"I have grown up, Ms. Austin. And I grew up in a whole new way this week alone."

She turned around one more time, not happy that we were having this song and dance. "Savannah, let's drop it. This will be over by the weekend anyway. The courts will get this monstrosity out of here, and you children can all go home to your million-dollar mansions and million-mile denials."

"You're the one in denial. And I'm not dropping it, because you started it." Another group cheered on that one. "I may have stolen a Sugar Daddy when I was seven, but you try to steal a person's good name and reputation, something it takes a lifetime to create. You destroy it with a sentence. I may have my own demons to deal with, but I would say you do too."

"I do not. And I don't steal Sugar Daddys *or* reputations."

"You just tried to no more than five minutes ago! You just

stood in front of a thousand television cameras and declared to the viewing public that my mother was here for no other reason than to get exposure. Well, that right there was breaking Number Nine, sister. And I've seen every other commandment broken this week too, in this very town."

"You need a life, Savannah."

"No, I've just learned to observe, Ms. Austin. In less than a week this city has lied about one another and stolen dreams, purses, and employers' time. I've listened to people who think they're God and then heard God's name used in more horrible ways than should be legal. I've watched women worship "lucky" dolls and Coca-Cola. I've even watched children shamelessly disobey their parents." Mother glared. I traveled to more comfortable ground. "I've even seen a woman try to commit adultery with—" I stopped. Well, maybe that ground wasn't too comfortable either.

"What?! What did you see?!" Vicky asked with eyes still in animated horror over the Sugar Daddy revelation.

"Well, that one doesn't need to be delved into right now. But my Lord, have mercy, someone was even killed this week. All of that, right here in the heart of this city. In the heart of *my* city," I declared, with a finger that tapped my own chest. Then I opened my arms to encompass the entire span of nuts. "This entire city has fallen apart in less than a week."

"Then you've said it yourself, Savannah. You can't, and these people can't." She motioned to those who had closed in around us. "None of you can even live by the very principles you're fighting over. Stealing a Sugar Daddy." Her laugh was only half-mocking. "I still say you're nothing but a bunch of hypocrites."

At those words, my mother tugged at her chains just far enough to grab the back of my shirt. She snatched me away and looked me square in the face and said, "Sit down, and sit down now. I will handle this from here. And when I'm through, I'll handle you and whoever this Sugar Daddy fella is that you've stolen."

I was about certain at that moment that the entire square gasped. The woman in chains had taken a deep breath and morphed into a woman that few had caught a glimpse of this week. Everyone stepped back and the path between her and Ms. Austin cleared.

"Ms. Austin, come here," Vicky summoned.

For a brief moment, Ms. Austin looked downright terrified. "I'm really through here."

"No, you're not through. Now, please, please come here, Faith." With those words mother's voice softened to that of just a mom. Not a monument percher, not a chamber of commerce president, not a city of Savannah commander and chief, just Victoria Phillips, a mother.

Ms. Austin inched closer, still uncertain whether the woman would leap. "You know what, Faith, you'd be right." That one made her stop. It made about everyone else stop too.

Ms. Austin coughed out her question. "About what?"

"You're right about the hypocrite part." Most everyone on the square gasped again, then leaned in closer. This was going to be good. "We do have things to learn. I learn ways I've screwed up every day. Well, almost every day." She was at least trying to be diplomatic. "But we all have things to learn. And right now *you* need to learn that I'm not self-righteous or self-serving. I'm out here for this little girl behind me." She pointed in my direction.

At times a mother's reference to you as her "little girl" fills you with warm, childlike euphoria. Standing in front of Ms. Austin, camera bulbs flashing and television cameras rolling, was not one of them.

"She's old enough to take care of herself." I wanted to agree with Ms. Austin there, but now didn't quite feel like the right time.

"Yes, she is," Mother said, looking back at me with a goofy smile. "But life is different now, Faith. You and my daughter belong to a generation that believes truth is a relative mind-set. It isn't."

"You and I have different opinions on that."

"Then we have fundamental differences, Faith."

"And, I've never stolen a Sugar Daddy," she spat like a two-year-old.

"Neither have I." Mother glared at me. "But trust me, that will be dealt with. And trust me on this, Faith: just because life changes, truth doesn't. Paint it black and call it brown and it's still black. Paint it mauve and call it aubergine and it's still mauve." I rolled my eyes. "That's what this means to me." She walked over to the monument and placed her hand atop it, never minding her chipped manicure. "But even if this monument crumbled into the sidewalk, the truth it holds at this moment would still be the truth."

Ms. Austin's phone broke the silence. "Ms. Austin." I was grateful for the reprieve. "What?!" she screamed into the phone. "I don't care! I don't give a flying flip what you want or what you think! I told you I would let you know. That means when I know something, you will know something! And right now I know I'm sick of answering this stupid phone!" And with that Ms. Austin's phone took a flying flip of its own, right across about six heads, skimmed a rather large swooped updo, and crashed into the wall of the Federal Building.

Ooh, sister's got a few issues with her cellular. Sergeant Millings woke up from his horse nap and grabbed his gun. That could have proven dreadful, had I not screamed out at him, "Whoa, doggies. Whoa. It was just a cell phone."

He looked around as if he was going to rid this city of all cellular activity, but he calmed down after a moment.

Ms. Austin's face began to grow redder than it had when she was screaming in the phone. Even strands of her hair had shaken loose from her ponytail during her breakdown. When she regained her composure, her mortification was apparent to all. I didn't mind. I needed the company.

She didn't ask again if Mother was through. She just turned quickly and walked away quickly. I watched her go. I liked her. I could have been her friend. Shoot, I could have been her. I didn't know what circumstances had brought her to the choices that framed her perspective. But I knew her decisions had determined her future.

Mother was still leaning against the monument. I realized now that she had been here for me, and for Thomas. All her efforts this week had been about preserving something of value for us to be able to preserve for our children. How strange. That was the same thing this monument was offering.

The treasures of what we have and have become can be found in the faces of those who raised us. Yet some never find a treasure there. So they fight forever to escape the faces of abuse. Others fight forever to run from faces of addiction. Some of us will even fight against faces that are just plain extraordinary. But looking at my mother, I realized ordinary would be boring. Who would want that?

I sneaked off before she remembered me. It would take her two hours to realize that Sugar Daddy was a candy and not a strange man I had stashed under my bed since I was a child. And I didn't need any other misunderstandings in the paper. So, I left her to return to work. But I would be back. I would be back to check on her soon.

"You left out something," Joshua's voice came as I rounded the corner to the back alley to head to my car. He was leaning up against it.

I was too tired to brush him off. "Did you hear all of that?" I asked, half-embarrassed, half too stressed to care.

"Every word. But you missed one."

I leaned up against the car and stared back. "And what *one* would that be?"

"The last one. The one about wanting what isn't yours."

"Joshua, just drop it." I opened my car door.

He shut it promptly. "No, Savannah. If you're going to deal with your 'demons,' as you call them, deal with all of them. And a perfect place to begin would be with this incessant desire of wanting something that isn't yours. You don't want Grant for any reason other than the fact that he belongs to someone else."

"You don't know what you're talking about!" I snapped.

"Yes, I do. You don't even look at him the way a woman looks at a man she loves."

"You don't know how I look at him."

"Yes, I do." He was as perfectly sickening as a half-rotten cucumber. "I saw you. You looked at him like a woman who was sad she had lost."

I abandoned all calm. "I love him, Joshua North! And how dare you try to make six years of commitment so . . . so meaningless and petty!"

"I didn't. You did."

"Leave me alone!" I said, trying to pull the handle to my car door, but he wouldn't move his arm to allow me to retreat. I wanted to cry. I wanted to scream. I wanted to slap him. I wanted to kiss him. I wanted to wrap my arms around his neck and lay one on him. And he knew I did. And that made it all the worse.

"You don't love him, Savannah," he said as he inched closer to my face. I could feel his arm behind my back as it held the door firmly closed. I refused to let any part of him affect me. I returned his cool demeanor with a cold stare. "He doesn't make your eyes dance. I've seen them dance. And it wasn't when you were looking at him." I felt his breath across my face. He let those words settle in the air between the two of us. We both knew what he meant. "Let him go. Let your pride go. Let this so-called hurt go. Let the desire to have what isn't yours go, just because it isn't yours. You're passionate Savannah. You deserve passion in return." He removed his arm from my car door. The very presence of it as it brushed my shirt created a feeling I refused to allow to surface.

"Are you finished?"

He got on his bike and headed down the alley. "I'm finished," he called back.

He and I both knew things had only begun.

CHAPTER THIRTY-FIVE

I collected myself in Katherine's Corner Bookstore before heading back to the office. Few places brought such comfort. Few things as well. But books, well, books were living entities to me. They triggered as many memories as poorly chosen love songs or badly splintered park benches. They brought to mind vacations and good years, and I enjoyed just looking at them. And if I could get a few undistracted minutes, maybe I could actually finish the one I've been reading.

"Savannah, I haven't seen you since lunch Friday."

"A lot has changed since Friday, Katherine." I smiled at the striking, petite, middle-aged storeowner approaching me with her undeniable freshness.

"I hear your mother has been at the monument since then."

I tried to focus on the new-books section. "What you hear is true."

She walked over and replaced a misplaced book on the shelf in front of me. I watched her graceful olive hand with short red-painted fingernails. Katherine was a former beauty queen herself. But she defied every stereotype known to the common population of man. Victoria was the personification of rhinestone tiaras, mascara cries, ridiculous talent costumes, and post-traumatic stress disorder. She is what every good novel or bad press coverage would define as the typical beauty pageant contestant. But Katherine, she was different. She was elegant and calm. Self-assured yet humble. Stunningly beautiful yet perfectly unassuming. We had met two weeks ago, when I discovered this world of hers for the first time. She had given me some of her secrets. But best of all, she had given me her friendship.

"How are you doing with that?" she asked me. "With everything that is going on at the courthouse?"

"I don't know."

"You mean you don't have an opinion?"

"Oh, no, I have a multitude of opinions. I'm just not sure what I know about all the opinions that I have. Couldn't you tell by my article?"

She laughed. "Savannah, you are too young to be so complex."

"And I hear I look the worse for wear because of it."

"Who told you that?"

"A stranger in a floral dress. She said I looked old, or maybe she called me tired. No, actually I think *worn out* were her exact words."

She giggled at my pouty lips and droopy demeanor. "Savannah, you look beautiful. Are you talking about the elderly African American lady with the straw bag?"

"That's her! Has she been in here too?"

"No, but I've seen her on the street a couple times. The dress caught my attention."

I sat down on the steps that led to the fiction section of the bookstore. "What do you think is up with her?"

"Probably lonely. Maybe retired, or her spouse has died."

"But don't you think her children would tell her, 'Mother, let's please don some different attire'?"

She laughed. "You crack me up, Savannah." She sat down beside me, and her pressed khaki pants slid up at the ankles, fully exposing her cute little black slip-on sandals.

"And she follows me."

"She follows you?"

"Yeah, and she wants my food."

"What?"

"Serious. I had to share my lunch with her on Sunday. I mean, I didn't mind, but with Mother up there strapped to cement, I've been a little sensitive about the whole food issue."

"Well, who knows? Maybe she's sent to teach you something. Get yourself a good book and put your mind at ease."

"I've got one I can't find time to finish. Besides, everything in life shouldn't be a lesson." I stood and scanned the books. The title *Ten Minutes from Normal* jumped out at me. "I'm glad Karen Hughes knows where Normal is. I couldn't find it with a wall map and a day to waste."

"Well, you could ask her where it is. I hear she'll be with the president tomorrow."

"Oh, my word, I forgot the president was coming tomorrow. He's one president I won't have to read about. I already know his life story."

"You do, huh?"

"Oh, yeah, Vicky has the hots for him."

"Savannah," she said, giggling, "you shouldn't talk that way about your mother. She is in love with your father."

"She may be in love with my father, but I shall not tell a lie after the kind of day I've witnessed: the woman would love to be Laura Bush for a day."

"She would whip your heinie for that."

"I wish she was home to whip my heinie; that would mean she was cooking too."

"You could cook for yourself."

"Tried it. Didn't work."

"Some things have to be tried more than once."

"And some things are better left to the experts." I gave her a good-natured wave, and the bell gave its *ding-a-ling-a-ling* at my departure.

"You sure can find a way to get into the middle of things," said a strange voice as I closed the door.

"Emma!" I was unable to hide my shock. "What happened to you? I mean, you're clean . . . I mean . . . you're . . . well, you're just clean."

"You made your point." She tried to stifle a laugh. "Are you always so honest?"

I felt my face flush. "I'm sorry. It's a curse. Man . . . you just look . . . you look fabulous. I thought I'd seen you around town a couple times. I just wasn't quite sure it was you."

"Well, it's me." She ran her hands along the seams of her tailored khaki sundress. The black piping lay strikingly upon her golden skin. The sallow tone present just last week was gone.

"What happened?"

"Uh, humiliation maybe?" She looked straight at me.

I tried not to flinch. "Are you going to yell at me again?"

She smiled. "No. I was harsh. But you deserved it."

"I deserved worse, actually."

"I probably did too." She lowered her head and fingered the bow at her delicate waist. I tried to change the subject.

"You been eating?"

"What?"

"You just look a little healthier."

"Yes, I've been eating."

"Do you want to go eat with me sometime? Maybe talk, like normal people?"

"No," she said flatly.

"No?"

"No. I'm not really ready to be your friend."

"Eating lunch together would make us friends?"

"Yes." She turned to go. "Well, try not to add to anyone else's troubles."

"I'm really sorry for hurting you, Emma." I hoped she knew I meant it.

She turned around to look at me with the beauty I remembered from her high-school days. "It didn't turn out all bad, Savannah. Look at me." She held her arms out at her sides.

I nodded. "Yeah. Look at you."

She left, but I would see her again. And one day I'd buy her lunch.

Peggy Noonan's book was lying on the corner of my desk. I lifted it up in my hands, and it opened to page 65. The red underlines from my own pen caught my eye. They marked her reflection on Reagan's character as it related to his stance on communism.

"It was in this drama that Reagan's character was fully revealed," she wrote. "In a time of malice he was not malicious; in a time of lies he did not falsify; in a time of great pressure he didn't bend or break; in a time of disingenuousness he was clear and candid about where he stood and why. And in a time when people just gave up after a while and changed the subject, he remained on the field through all the long haul."

I laid the book down and saw my article still resting on the corner of my desk. After the events of my lunch hour, it didn't feel like the right story to tell. No, as backward as it sounded, the human-interest story I really needed to explore was mine: the story of the bystander, the uninvolved, the ill-equipped, the student, the one who hadn't broken under the pressure but avoided it altogether. Maybe exploring this story would help to establish the depths of a relationship, the trust that comes with a writer and her audience. Maybe it would help them to understand me. Maybe it would help me to understand me. The city and I had both suffered our share of upheavals this week. Maybe in a few paragraphs I could help us both discover what we'd learned.

I worked hard until two o'clock. And at the last moment, with no time to spare, the pages slipped out of the printer, and I headed to Mr. Hicks to meet my deadline.

Jessica all but ducked under her desk when she saw me come around the corner.

"Hello, Jessica." I peered over the corner of the low-walled cubicle that surrounded her desk.

She didn't respond.

"You can't stay under there forever."

She didn't respond again.

"I'll catch you when I come back." I proceeded to Mr. Hicks's open door and knocked lightly.

A loud thump came from behind me. "Ow!" And the blonde carpet inspector came up rubbing her head.

"Come in," Mr. Hicks offered. "What's so funny, Savannah?"

"Oh, nothing much," I said, trying to control myself.

"Is this your article?"

"Yes, sir. All finished."

"Are you pleased?"

"Pleased? Let's just say I've come to terms with myself."

"Well, let's hope that's a good thing."

"It is." I turned back to the door and paused to ask a final question. "Am I going to be on the cover of the paper tomorrow?"

He looked up from his desk with a slight smirk. "From the reports from the field I have received, yes ma'am, I believe you are."

"Arms spread-eagle."

"That's the one."

"Declaring I'm a thief?"

"Very probable."

"I figured."

"You did?"

"Yes, sir, I'm pretty good at figuring nowadays."

I sneaked into the ladies' room before I went back to my cubicle. Three Cokes and no lunch made for an uncomfortable situation. I peered underneath the stalls just to make sure I didn't walk in on any unsuspecting soul. There were feet in two but none in one, three, four or five. I settled for three. As I locked the door, another pair of feet came to occupy four.

I like to look at feet underneath stalls. Even wrote an entire short story on them for my junior year creative writing course. "The Stories of Shoes in a Stall," I called it. Today's feet both wore flip-flops. Stall number two's flip-flops were black, and the toes were short and plump. They housed their small, unpainted toenails with great padding and protection. As if they just plumped right up around them. Stall number four housed white flip-flops.

I love this place. The owner of the white flip-flops had long toenails painted a deep metallic rust. The nails hung slightly over the toes and were long and narrow. Downright weird. Toenails tend to be a reflection of the individual. Vicky wears red. Always red. Paige wears clear. Always clear. I wear pink. Always pink. In-your-face Victoria. Always-brutally-honest Paige. Always trying to be not quite in your face and hopefully honest, at least when possible, me.

As we each arrived to wash our hands at the same time, I had known before I saw them what they would look like. Their feet had given them away.

"Knock, knock," came the voice on the other side of my nonexistent door.

"Hey, Claire. Welcome to my office. Come in and have a seat." This friend of mine was solely responsible for acquiring my apartment with her fabulous real-estate skills.

"I don't have much time. I've got to go show a house in a few minutes. I just wanted to drop off your new keys so you could get your stuff moved in." She held out the two keys that hung from a long metal loop with a Cora Betts Realty marketing tool at the end.

"This is it, huh?" I asked, holding out my hand cautiously.

She dropped them into my hand. "Yes, my sweet friend. These are the keys to a new way of living." I looked at them as if they were some medieval torture device. "I'm not sensing an overwhelming rush of excitement."

I looked up at her pretty yet uniquely proportioned face. "It's just all happened a little quick."

"This has been years in the making, Savannah."

"Yeah, I guess." I glanced down at my toes, then returned to her pleasant smile. "Where do I drop off my rent again?"

"Here," she said, handing me a sheet of paper with a ten-digit number on it. "Go to Bank of America and make a deposit into this account. That's all you have to do."

"You still won't tell me who it is?"

"He doesn't feel it's necessary. Makes his life less complicated if everything goes through me. Now, enough worrying. I'll stop by later, when I get off work. I'll help you move if you need me."

"Oh, no. I think I'll be fine. I don't have a lot of stuff. Thomas and Paige are helping me."

"Well, call me if you need me." She lifted my chin and put her other hand on my shoulder. "This will be one of the most exciting things you have ever done."

"Do I have the look of someone who needs added excitement?"

"This move is about you, Savannah. Not your father, not your mother, just you. This is a grown-up thing."

"I need to be grown up?"

"Yes, you do. Now I've got to go." And she gave me a hug and walked off.

"I'll miss my mommy," I whispered. But she was safely out of earshot. I was glad. I was wishing I hadn't heard it either.

CHAPTER THIRTY-SIX

Police dogs were sniffing a Shih Tzu. And she wasn't any too happy about it. The entire strip of Bull Street was blocked off by the secret service and local police squads conducting a sweep of the Historical District in preparation for the president's appearance here tomorrow. Their presence forced me to go on down a block farther to Lincoln Street and cross back down East State Street to get to Jake's. In the hubbub of the last week, I had failed to ask why in the world the president was actually coming here. Victoria probably knew every last detail of his schedule. She did have Internet access, remember.

I pulled into my covered parking place. The Culpepper's Buick no longer resided here. That had left almost a month ago now. And it was no longer the *future* home of Old Betsy, but the present home of one Savannah Phillips and Old Betsy. Old Betsy had never seen shelter a day in her life. If no one else appreciated this new stage of our journey, she would.

I didn't even go into Jake's. Everyone had left already anyway. I slowly climbed the stairs up to the back entrance of my new residence. There is a front entrance as well, a door to the side of

Jake's. But this one closest to the carport would be the one I'd use most.

I put the key into the door and for a brief moment hoped it wouldn't fit. Then I could regretfully delay this transition of life. But it turned with ease. And as the door opened, so the next page of my life's book turned. I had no clue what it would tell.

I walked slowly through the halls and through each room. I opened cabinets and turned on lights. I tried to imagine how life would play out here. But some moments in life aren't even imaginable. Some you can only experience. This would be one.

I sat down in the middle of the bedroom floor, and the enormity of this moment slammed into me like a lovebug on the windshield of a semi. I cried. I'm not sure why. It just felt like what I needed to do. So it is what I did. And I continued until I lifted my head and caught sight of the green tennis ball lying in the far back corner of the closet, whose door was opened. Then I began to laugh. That ball reminded me that I wasn't really leaving home. That ball confirmed that my "anonymous" landlord and his "golden" companion would always be just one floor below. And inside my heart after hours.

"When did you get here?" I asked Paige as I got out of the car. She was sitting on the bottom step of my parents' house.

"Oh, about thirty minutes ago."

"Do you keep office hours?"

She scrunched her lips and crinkled her nose as if this question required deep thought. "No."

She followed me into the house, and we heard Thomas pull up as we headed inside. You couldn't help but hear him. His Jeep was rather loud. Vicky lost her battle for an LTD the same way she lost the one to get me in a Lincoln Town Car: vanquished by Jake. Her argument for me was safety. Her argument for Thomas was if he was going to a military school, he should have an American-made car. She made this point one afternoon as she climbed into her powder-blue Mercedes two-seater convertible. And Jake went and bought Thomas a Jeep and let her know that it *was* made in America.

Thomas bounded up the stairs and came into the room. "You two ready to get moving?"

"Why are you in such a hurry for me to leave?"

"Because he wants your bathroom," Paige said.

"You better stay out of my bathroom with your filth," I warned him clearly.

"I have my own bathroom, in case you two forgot. And truth be told, yours isn't my shade of yellow. Now, grab a box and let's get this party moving."

"What's this?" Paige asked as she picked up the tiny tan box with orange stripes and white lettering.

"Give that to me!" I snatched it from her hand.

"It's empty, Savannah."

"No! It's not empty." I looked at it, trying to stifle the lump in my throat. "It's full! It's full of memories. Memories I'm not ready to get rid of!"

Thomas walked over and stared at it, squinting. "It looks like the box to a tiny halogen light bulb."

"That's exactly what it is." I jerked it out of his sight and turned my back.

Paige jerked me back around. "Who gave you that?"

I refused to answer.

"Savannah Phillips, who gave you that little box?"

"Grant! Okay, Grant gave me this box."

"Well, no wonder you dumped him, if that's his idea of romance." Thomas sat down on the floor, realizing we weren't going anywhere fast.

I sat beside him. "It was romantic, Thomas. It went to a lamp we had found in an alley on our first date."

Paige surrendered to the moment and collapsed on the floor as well. "Wait. You were walking in an alley on your first date?"

I looked at her with disdain. "Yes! He was walking me to my

car that I had left behind Dad's store. And the Culpeppers had left this great lamp by their trash. He picked it up and said we should restore it. That we'd have a memento from our first date."

"A lamp from a trash can was your memento?"

"We were sixteen, Paige. For crying out loud, we didn't have a pot to pee in."

Thomas quipped, "You would have if you'd gotten a job."

"My occupational past has nothing to do with this conversation."

"So why in the world do we have to keep this box?" Paige mused.

"Because for four years we never could find a lightbulb. We had repaired the lamp, made it absolutely beautiful, but it never worked, because it needed this specific kind of bulb that we couldn't find."

Thomas fell back on the floor and closed his eyes. "My Lord, this is a long story."

"It's a story of love, Thomas. They don't occur in ten-second sound bites."

"They should."

"Well, one day, during my sophomore year, I'm in my bed-room studying, and I hear this knock on my door. When I opened it, Grant was standing there. He holds up this little box and says, 'I found it!' 'Found what?' I asked him. 'I found the bulb. I finally found us a bulb.'"

Thomas let out a moan. I kicked him.

I held the box up and felt the tears return to the brim of my rather long eyelashes. "Grant drove all the way from Clemson just to tell me he had found us a bulb. So, now you know why there is no way in the world that I can ever throw this box away."

"Oh, baby!" Paige said, wrapping her arm around me. "You keep that as long as you want to. That's a precious story."

"It's a stupid story! And you're both pathetic," Thomas said as rose to his feet and slapped us both on the tops of our heads. "The boy is getting married, Savannah. Give it up!" He was starting to sound annoyingly like Joshua.

"It ain't over till he's walked down the aisle," I informed him.

"Whatever you say, little dreamer. Now, grab a box." He tossed one to each of us. I tucked my little memory inside my purse and shoved Joshua's ridiculous accusations to the back of my mind. I would find a safe place in my new home for one. And a trash can for the other.

For the next two hours we loaded up every last piece of my furniture and made trips to my new apartment. The one that required us holding the mattresses on top of Thomas's Jeep was a rather interesting haul. Paige refused to sit on top after Thomas declared her behind too big. That caused a few moments of tension. But we just hung out of the windows and rested our elbows on top, while Thomas meandered through a maze of roadblocks and men in black.

By eight o'clock we all collapsed on the floor of the living room. And when I entered the kitchen to drink out of the faucet— since I had no cups or anything else to put in a kitchen for that matter—I was welcomed by a sight of a stack of plastic cups, plastic flatware, paper plates, a bag of ice, Cokes, and a large cheese pizza. Oh, and there was a note. A note from my new landlord, welcoming me to my new home. Signed, well, "Landlord." A trip he must have made in between our final loads. And a pizza just like I would like it. A pizza that only a father would know.

"Dinner is served." I distributed pizza to my hungry helpers.

"Ooh, let's sit on the balcony and eat. That way we can see what's going on across the street," Paige said as she flung open the French doors to the balcony. We had a perfect view of the square. And a perfect view of my mother.

"This is like dinner and a movie," Paige said, ripping into her pizza. "It would be perfect with Doritos."

The child was ill. "Mom looks kind of nice," Thomas said, guzzling down some Coke.

I patted him on the back as our feet dangled over the balcony.

"You are a sweet son, you know. To find 'nice' in that is optimism in it's finest form."

"Well, she did freshen up her makeup," Paige added. "Maybe that's what he's noticing."

I looked hard. I wanted to see it. But the harsh floodlights on the sidewalk that saturated her with unflattering shades of white made her look, dare I say, plumb nasty. "She needs a bath. I mean, this woman might see the president tomorrow, and she looks like Homeless Hannah."

Paige nodded. "But in very expensive shoes."

"Yes, and matching handbag. Don't forget the handbag," I said.

"Oh, yes. Of course."

"She needs a mint, too." Thomas responded. "She's battling Duke for just plain stank! Shoot, I bet that's what the people on *Survivor* smell like."

"*Survivor*! Oh my gosh, she missed *Survivor* tonight!" I said in total shock.

"No, she didn't. She's got a TV out there. Look, she's watching it right now." And she was. Battery-operated TV. Headset. And she was talking to the TV. She was watching *Survivor* all right. "And it will be over in perfect time for her interview on *Hannity & Colmes*."

No one was surprised.

"Oh, I think that Sean Hannity is a fine specimen of a man," Paige offered, drifting away.

"He is cute," I offered. "I think he should have won sexiest newscaster."

"He would have if that MSNBC man hadn't shamelessly promoted himself," Paige retorted.

Thomas threw his two cents in. And trust me, that was a high estimate. "You think anything that walks and breathes is fine."

Paige retorted. "I do not. You aren't all that."

"*You aren't all that*," he mimicked.

"Just tell me she's not going to have another *Survivor* party this year," Paige said.

"Not if I can help it," I assured her.

"Well, it's your fault, Savannah," Thomas added. "If you hadn't told her to watch that very first season finale, none of us would have to endure it at all."

"It's not my fault," I protested. "I was just trying to help her branch out."

"Well, you better hope this season isn't in Africa, because I'm not giving Jeep rides to a soul," Thomas assured us both. Like we were the ones who would ask him.

"Well, I'm not wearing a colorful sarong that calls my tribe *Victoriajumanji* either."

"I guess we should just be grateful that she's never tried to enter herself. Watching her audition tape would make safari tours in my Jeep feel like a bearable punishment."

I comforted him. "She couldn't audition. Contestants are allowed only one luxury item. That woman would vote herself off by day two if she couldn't wax, pluck, and inject."

He nodded across the square. "I would have agreed with you there last week. But not anymore. She has effectively brought to ruin any notion of what I thought she would and would not do in this life."

The mere observation caused each of us to groan.

Paige interjected. "Neither of you should complain. At least you get pizza every Thursday night."

"On china plates," I informed her. "And I did not say *Chinette*."

"And I didn't say your mother wasn't half-crazy. I just said you got one night to eat something that came out of a box."

"But it is made from scratch," I assured her.

"Whatever."

"I think I'm going to buy me a sundress."

Paige's face contorted. "To wear to your mother's *Survivor* party?"

"I'm not talking about *Survivor* anymore, Paige."

"There are drugs for that."

"So, should I?"

"Should you what?"

Thomas broke in. "Should she buy a dress, Paige. My word, even I know what she's talking about."

"That's because your illness runs in the family."

He flicked her. She flicked back.

"Why do you want a sundress?" she asked me. "You hate dresses."

"I don't know. I just think they're . . . well . . . kind of pretty. Maybe it's stupid."

"Yes, it's stupid," Thomas said.

Paige glared at him. "It's not stupid. It would be lovely on you. Okay, enough fun," she said as she began to rise. "Ow, ooh, oh, that hurts." She moved slow for a vibrant woman of twenty-four.

Thomas showed no mercy as he stood up. "You're pathetic."

"She's an old soul, Thomas."

"With old parts, obviously."

Paige reprimanded us both. "Would you two quit talking about me like I'm not here?"

"You need to work out," I told her, setting our plates on the counter. I'd need to get a trash can.

"I don't work out. I'll mess up my sleek lines." She ran her hands across her stomach and the little pouch that had formed after her four pieces of pizza. "And I wouldn't have this pouch had your landlord brought Diet Coke."

"You're sad," I said, giving her a hug.

"Well, you're a homeowner." She hugged me back.

"Renter," I corrected.

"Whatever. You don't live with your mama anymore. What are you doing? Is your foot itching again?"

"Yes. It means—"

Thomas answered for me. "It mean's she's going to walk on new ground. And if her hand itches, one means she's going to get pleased; the other means she's going to get money. And if her nose itches, someone's coming to see her. And if her head itches, it means . . . that she's realized it's empty."

I slapped him.

"I know what it means," Paige said. "She was doing it the other night at my house. Sister might need a new pair of sneakers with all the walking she's going to be doing."

"Well, you two girls have fun. I'm going to check on Duke."

"Yeah, I've got to go back to the house for a few last items."

"Toilet paper?" Paige asked.

Toilet paper hadn't crossed my mind. They could tell. "Are you sure you'll survive?" Thomas asked.

"She has to. She owes me money," Paige said. And we laughed our way to the sidewalk.

"Oh," I said, bounding back up the stairs. "I forgot to lock the door."

I heard Thomas in the distance. "I'll give her a week."

Paige's faith in two weeks wasn't any more affirming. I shut the door and searched for the keys. They were sitting by the still-open balcony doors.

"I've got to do better than this," I muttered. I looked out over the packed square, and the sight of my mother reached my eyes like a lighthouse beam through a settled fog. The very woman I was trying to escape was as close to me now as she had been on most evenings. Yet seeing her here felt reassuring, dare I say comforting. No, I wasn't moving from her—I was moving toward me. But truth be told, I would sleep better tonight knowing she was right outside.

CHAPTER THIRTY-SEVEN

My bedroom looked different. The shelves were empty, save the dust that had collected from the lack of attention since Sister Victoria had become Savannah's patron saint. I walked around the hardwood floors that echoed with the flipping of my flops. I peered out my window at the familiar scene of Clary's and the cracks in the sidewalk and the street I had awakened to every morning.

I left the drapes up. I didn't know how to hang them anyway. And I had to leave Vicky something to do for me when she was released. I wandered over to my bathroom and stared into the completely clean space. There wasn't even dirt to imagine. It was spotless. And my galoshes and knee pads were packed up.

I sat down in the middle of my floor. I peered at the perfectly round smudges on my yellow walls from countless games of fetch-the-slobber-ball. There was the small dent in the door frame that I made with Thomas's head after a mean battle of wills over who was going to get to the first pool party of the summer. I lost by default. There were the notches I had made in the windowsill, recording the times I had sneaked out through the years. Vicky thought I was keeping track of most-outstanding-student accolades. Jake knew and eventually put an alarm chime on my window. I disconnected it right after installation.

The thought of that made me laugh. The memories were really priceless to me. And no matter how many times one dreams of spreading her wings and flying away, or up the street, the actual event means one has officially grown up. College isn't growing up. College is a supervised transition. You still live off of Mom and Dad's money. Well, some of us do; there are always exceptions. And you live with a bunch of other mindless, overexalted youth like yourself.

But moving out. Paying rent. Sleeping alone. Those are grownup things. Waking yourself up for work. That is downright elderly. But necessary. And my growing up was happening today.

The distant sound of thunder caused the hardwood to vibrate underneath me. It brought me out of my soap-opera moment. I stood up and walked over to the windowsill and flaked off a small wood splinter sticking out from one of my last notches, brought on by a need to have ice cream with Paige and Grant at a godforsaken hour of the morning.

The sky over Savannah had turned pitch black. It was already almost ten, but there had been stars out on my last trip home. Looking up, I was met with another clap of thunder that felt as if it had just landed on top of my house. My entire body shook. And before I knew it, rain was pouring from the sky like Savannah hadn't seen in over a week.

The rain felt poignant for the moment, a washing of the old to begin the new. Then the reality of what was happening struck me about the same time the lightning hit the tree across the street.

"Oh my stars, my mother!" I screamed as I looked out of the window.

The next few minutes were a flurry of activity. I ran around that house like Robin Williams with his fake boobs on fire in *Mrs. Doubtfire*. In less than five minutes I was flying up the street only to be blocked by yellow barricades. I swallowed the desire to curse and instead drove around the block and parked on the curb behind the courthouse. If they wanted to come out in this mess and tow my car, have at it.

People were scampering under makeshift shelters, running for cover under local shop awnings, and scurrying up the street, racing the cockroaches. I reached Mother only to find her resembling a wet rat. It wasn't pretty. It was downright grisly. Her umbrella offered no escape from the blowing rain. And the tent the local funeral home had loaned was being chased across the square by a couple men. Vicky's Mary Kay had slid to her chin. Her hair was plastered to her scalp, goo stung her eyes from the way she was batting them, and her clothes were waterlogged. And the poor thing had taken to crying. Well, more like blubbering, but I wasn't about to throw stones. I hadn't been outside for almost an entire week and had still done substantial blubbering today myself.

"Hurry, help me set this up," I commanded my father, who was running up the sidewalk. In a few minutes we were all soaked but sheltered by Thomas's camping tent, with only the end of a chain sticking out on the other side.

"Thank you," my mother cried and gasped at the same time. "Thank you, darling, for saving your *mooootheeeer . . .*" She wailed and threw her head in my lap.

"It's okay, Mother," I said, patting her head. I picked up my hand and tried to sling off the product that she had apparently thought should be added each day. "This is disgusting." I mouthed to my father, who rested on the other side of her in our tent.

"Be nice," he mouthed back with a smile.

"Don't leave me, Savannah. Please don't leave me," she cried, never looking up. It was a most heart-wrenching moment.

"I won't, Mother. I won't." I rubbed her rain-drenched arm and watched as the water dripped from her elbow onto her pants.

"I'll leave you two girls for a while."

"You sure you want to do that?" I asked, my eyes making clear what I desired him to do. Stay.

"Yes, I'm sure. I better check on Duke anyway. He's probably floating up Abercorn somewhere. I'll be back later." And my only remnant of sanity walked out into the deep, dark, night.

"Okay, you need to get up now," I said, trying to pull her by the elbow.

"I don't wanna," she moaned.

"Mother, seriously, who's the parent here?"

"It should probably be you at this point." Her sounds were muffled as they tunneled from the side of my leg.

"Really, get control. We need to make you beautiful." I tried to tug her again.

"That's impossible. Have you seen me?"

So she had seen herself. This was worse than I thought. The woman had seen herself and still stayed out in public. "Yes, I've seen you. And you look . . . well, you look worn."

She wailed louder. "I've paid a heavy price for freedom."

"People have paid heavier, I assure you."

"I *know!*" and she wailed one more time. This made me laugh. "Don't laugh at me. I'm bruised."

"I'm not laughing at you, I'm laughing . . . well, with you."

"That's impossible! Because I'm not laughing."

She had a point. Who was to know what was water running down my leg and what was snot at this point. "Please, Mother, seriously. Get up." I tugged with great effort, and the battered and tattered former Miss Georgia United States of America rose with her own hair looking as if it had formed itself into a matted tiara of its own.

"Ooh, nice."

"Savannah Phillips. Do not laugh at me. I'm not in the mood. I'm sore and I'm wet. And I haven't had my own cooking in a week."

"Well, let's not even go there. This could ruin a perfectly good evening."

"Do you know what I would fix for dinner if I were home?" she asked, eyes glazing over, tongue fluttering across her lips. "I'd fix a chuck roast, slice some potatoes and carrots in there. Cover it with a little flour, salt and pepper, add some onion gravy and mushroom gravy. Bake it at 350 for three hours." She was hallucinating. "Fix some butter beans, corn, macaroni and cheese, get out some hot peppers and make homemade biscuits."

I was hallucinating. "Stop it! Stop it!" I snapped my fingers in front of her face. She came back to our world. "I will not talk with you about food one more moment. If you do, I will leave."

She grabbed hold of me in a death grip and started to wail again. "Please don't leave me, darling! Please! Please!"

I jerked her up again. "Now, get a grip! I am here for one reason and one reason alone. I am here to make you beautiful."

"Look at me, Savannah. Are you blind, child? I am permanently maimed. My beauty is a forgotten treasure. My song a forgotten cadence in the Savannah atmosphere."

"Okay, drama queen, enough." I squared her at the shoulders and faced her head-on. "I have starved this week. I have had to turn my underwear on inside out. And I have had to sleep in a house by myself. So, we have no place for drama this evening."

"Why are you here?" she asked, brown eyes looking like the local lush's after a ten-day drinking binge.

"I'm here because my mother is not going to meet the president of the United States looking, well, looking like . . ."

"Go ahead, you can say it. Like a former beauty queen."

"Actually no, I was going to say, like a streetwalk—"

"Savannah!"

"But, if former beauty queen makes you feel better, then that's what you can have."

"You better have magic in that bag with that kind of talk."

"Sister, I've got anything your heart desires. But we are starting from the top down. We begin with the hair," I said, pulling some shampoo and conditioner out of my huge duffel bag. "The rest of you is wet, so let's get this hair cleaned up."

"How will I rinse it?"

"You will stick your head outside this tent in that downpour and let nature have its way."

"Ooh, good idea."

She about drowned on the final rinse. But I told her if she put herself facedown instead of nose up, she might be able to breathe without water going up her nose. I scrubbed that head like one would scrub Duke after a mud bath. We wrapped a clean towel around her saturated head, and then we got to work on that face. We cleaned it from top to bottom, and then we dealt with the breath issue. I treaded sensitively and did not subject her to any comparisons to Duke before he got his two rotted teeth pulled.

"Now, how are we going to change your clothes?" I asked, studying the once pale baby blue pantsuit that had turned a lovely shade of burnt teal.

"Oh, that's an easy one," she responded nonchalantly.

"Oh it is?"

"Oh sure. I've got the keys to the handcuffs right here in my purse. I can just take them off and change real quick and then put them back on."

"You mean for six days you have worn the same outfit every day when you could have changed clothes?"

"Duh, Savannah. Do you think I would let someone else keep the key to these chains?"

"Please don't say *duh*."

"Okay. Uh, Savannah"—she could be a total smart aleck—"I couldn't very well change clothes every day. Wouldn't that have made a real statement. This process has meant something to me, and I wanted to make sure people realized that."

"Well, nothing could have said that more than Victoria Phillips in the same outfit for one week straight."

"My sentiments exactly," she said, nodding and thankful I had finally discovered her obvious intentions.

"Well, you can't wear that tomorrow to see the president."

"You don't think?" she asked, looking down. It was kind of like the look a person gives you when you question whether they have gained weight. Because it came upon them gradually, they don't quite see the degree to which they really need intervention. And the hand passes over the body as if feeling for themselves to make sure the other's assessment is accurate.

"No, that outfit, my sweet child, will have to be burned."

"Burned?!"

"Yes, burned."

"Do you know how much this cost?"

"I have a good idea, but this outfit is ruined. And this is not Burger King, so, you can forget about having it your way today."

"Blah, blah, blah." She could be so childish for a forty-five-year-old. "Well, I don't have to decide that today." And she didn't. I would decide it for her. Because it was going in the bag I had, and she would never see it again.

"I brought you some pajamas." I pulled some beautiful pale pink cotton pajamas out of my "magic" bag.

"Ooh, I didn't know I had those." She eyed them like a bowl of Ben and Jerry's chocolate-brownie-chunk ice cream after a four-month chocolate fast. Then her delight turned to puzzlement. "Why didn't you bring me a nightgown?"

"Because you are sleeping on the s-t-r-e-e-t."

"Oh."

She had her a nice sponge bath and put on her warm pajamas, and because of the safety of her makeshift home, no one was the wiser that for the first time in a week, Victoria Phillips was free from chains. I looked down at her once beautifully jewelry-adorned right wrist, which had been handcuffed to her chain, and noticed it was now adorned with a huge red strip of swollen skin where the hand-cuff had rubbed her for the last six days. But as soon as she slipped into her pink pajamas, she handcuffed herself once again.

"Mother, no one will know you don't have those on. You could sleep without them for one night."

"I would know. That would be enough." She pulled her arms

up around her, enjoying the feeling of being clean. "My pillows are soaked." She pointed to the pillows that sat next to her rolled-up sleeping bag that we had pulled from the rain.

I gave her a wink. "I've got extra." I pulled two perfectly fabulous down-feather pillows from my bag.

"You got drugs in there too. 'Cause I think you're high as a kite." Her brow crinkled.

"Would you hush and let me dry your hair?" I jerked the towel on her head. We decided instead to let her hair dry naturally to avoid electrocution from the downpour. Then we would use the battery-operated curling iron that I had brought before she went to sleep. We could fluff it up again in the morning. But at least she was clean.

We dried off her sleeping bag, tossed her foul clothes in the bag, and sealed them up. When those were safely tucked away, I laid out a beautiful pink suit that I had brought, with cream pumps, for her viewing of the president of the United States tomorrow.

I pulled us out two bottled waters, but she declined hers. "I try not to drink much. You know. The bathroom thing and all," she whispered. She hurt my heart. Until tonight I hadn't thought about all she had been going through.

We fluffed out our fresh pillows and laid down on the sleeping bag. "This was fun, Savannah. Thank you. Ooh, my right hand's itching. That means I'm going to get pleased. But I couldn't be any more pleased than I am right now." She looked up at me, smiling.

"You know, I think we're going to have to deal with that."

She gave me a look of an exasperated child. "Now what?"

"That old wives' tale stuff. It's either number one or two on here," I said, tapping the concrete monument behind us. "I'm not sure which. But we shouldn't be believing in it."

"You don't think?"

"No, I really don't."

"Well, my Lord have mercy, I'm sitting here chained to this monument, and I'm breaking these commandments even as I breathe."

"It's okay. We're going to do better." We nestled down into our sleeping bags, and I stared up at the ceiling of the red nylon tent. "Tell me a story, Mother."

"What kind of story?"

"You know, like the stories you told Thomas on Sunday."

She giggled. "Oh, about my antics as a little girl?"

"Yeah, those kind of stories."

"Well, after that we need to talk about your little-girl antics."

"Oh, the whole city will be talking about that tomorrow; let's save something to talk about for then."

"But, Savannah, who is this 'Sugar Daddy?' Did you have a crush on Virginia Cooper's daddy, Sug?"

I belly laughed. "Are you for real?"

"Are you depraved? My stars, child, you were just a baby."

"For your information, crazy woman, a Sugar Daddy is a piece of candy, and Sug was Virginia's mother's pet name for her husband, Larry. I stole candy, Mother. Now, get over it. No more talk about it. Please."

"Well, thank the Lord and call off the cavalry, because I was about to search your room from stem to stern, and see where Sug was hiding." She giggled after that. She may play stupid, but we both knew she was smart as a tack.

For the next two hours my mother shared some of the funniest, silliest, and greatest stories I have ever heard. And for the first time in a week, I slept like a baby. Who cared that the newspaper would declare I was a thief tomorrow. Who cared that I was sleeping on the sidewalk, in a tent, in front of the courthouse, with a crazy mama. She was *my* crazy mama. And I was immensely proud of her.

CHAPTER THIRTY-EIGHT

O w, pain." I tried to stretch my body out.

Mother pulled her earplugs from her ears. "What?"

"I'm battered and bruised," I said, rubbing my backside.

"I know. I'm permanently debilitated," Mother said, rubbing her eyes. "But you get used to it." This from a woman who takes her own sheets to hotels.

"There ain't no way."

"Don't say ain't."

"Don't boss me around at the crack of dawn."

She laughed. "I am bossy, aren't I?"

"Totally," I said, leaning up on my elbow to look at her.

She rolled over on her side so we could talk face to tired face. "Your dad thinks I'm a control freak."

"You are."

Her eyes widened in complete shock.

"I'm certain of it."

"What makes you think that?"

"You are chained to a monument. What makes you ask?"

"But this isn't about being in control. This is about fighting for what I believe in."

"I'm sure it is. I'm sure it is. Now let's make you beautiful again." I sat up to help pick out her mushed do.

"It really is, Savannah. I know you don't believe me."

I started fluffing her hair. "No, actually, I don't."

"Why?"

"Because you are always in the middle of everything. And you couldn't be more in the middle of this unless you had been chiseled into that monument yourself."

"But this isn't about me," she said, trying to pout.

"I didn't say it was about you. I said it was a control issue. You don't think anyone could do it like you, so you think you have to do it yourself." I took her by the arm and unzipped the front of the tent. "Look out there, Mother."

"Ooh, pretty day."

"Not at the sky, at the people. These people slept out here last night too. Any one of them would have been just as capable as you of chaining themselves to this monument."

"But they wouldn't have—"

"There. See, you don't know what they would or wouldn't have accomplished. Because you didn't let them."

"You think they wanted to?"

"I'm not sure. But I know at least some of them would have."

"Well. Even so, I do believe in this." She ducked back inside the tent.

"I know you do. I do know it's not *just* about control. About controlling the city anyway. Part of it is about controlling me. My destiny. My decisions."

"You think I did all of this for you?"

"For me, for Thomas, for other people's children. You said exactly that to Ms. Austin."

"But I did it for me, too, Savannah. I did this because I believe in those words up there. I try to live them the best I know. I fail miserably and often. I do try to control too much. They should have made that commandment number eleven: Thou shalt not control. Then I would have successfully kept from breaking four."

Ooh, she had me wondering now. "Which three of the real ones have you not broken?"

"The ones about killing and the stealing. And the one about adultery. Who would want something else, when you already have the best?"

"You've used the Lord's name in vain?" I asked in complete shock.

"It slipped." She clearly felt shame over this.

A smile crept across my face as I looked at this naïve, bright, frighteningly pure woman. "I love you."

"You what?"

"I love you. You're completely strange, and completely abnormal, and completely perfect," I told her.

She started sniffling.

"Do not cry. We have to make you beautiful. You are going to see the president today."

Poor thing sucked up her tears and beamed in a most lamentable way for such a grown woman. But by the time we unzipped that tent and removed it from around her, she was beautiful. I mean, she was "local dignitary" quality. And she knew it. Those around her gasped. She beamed.

"Now, go get 'em."

"And where will I take 'em when I get 'em?"

"To the heart of who you are."

"You think they'll see it?"

"As long as you let them share it with you. They won't miss it."

I gave her a kiss. Packed up my tent. And left her there to think. And she was thinking. You could always tell. Thinking for Vicky required extreme quiet. A rarity. And extreme furrowed brow. A BOTOX miracle. Who knew what she would uncover in the process, but at least she would look good doing it.

I slipped away to till, making a stop at my old house for Duke and some clothes. Duke looked refreshed from his and Dad's evening indoors. About halfway around the corner I saw the long raven ponytail of one Ms. Austin flopping in front of me. I slowed my pace as she continued around the park. After yesterday's adventure I wasn't too sure that she would want to see me. Or I her, for that matter.

I eyed her as she headed around the corner of the back end of the park. When Duke and I turned the corner shortly thereafter, she had made her way to a park bench, facing the artsy-district side of the park. I would have to take either the mature route of pass and acknowledge, or the favored route of hightail it and run. With my very maturity questioned yesterday, I tiptoed onward.

"Hello, Ms. Austin," I said as I neared her bench.

"Savannah," she stated as if noting a minor detail in a mundane event. Just, "Savannah." Flat, dry, colorless. Not, "Hey Savannah!" with a singsong effect. Not, "Hey, Savannah!" with surprise. She wiped her face with a towel.

"May I sit down?"

"It's a public park. Public bench."

"Is that a yes?"

"That's an I-really-don't-give-a-flip." Well, at least she was offering some expression. "I'm leaving anyway." She stood.

"Please wait," I said, reaching out for her arm. I let go of her and sat down on the bench. She hesitantly followed. "This is Duke." Maybe his charm could ease the tension.

"I don't like dogs." So much for that. Duke heard her and turned his back on the both of us.

"I just wanted to talk about yesterday."

"Everyone will be talking about yesterday. Your picture is on the front page declaring you a thief, and your article pretty much identified everything you've discovered in this situation. And you made it clear what you thought of me too."

"I didn't even mention your name."

"No, you referred to me as a 'type.' Yes, I believe that was your word."

"No, I referred to your position as a 'belief,' Ms. Austin."

"My name is Faith," she said as if my calling her Ms. Austin was patronizing. She was right.

"I'm sorry. We all believe in something, Faith. And I said that in the course of this debate over whether this monument should stand or not, the core of people's beliefs are the issue."

"You know what I don't get, Savannah? This nice act of yours. You know, the one you like to play on people. As if you are so naïve and innocent."

"I think I made it clear in that article that I can manipulate with the best of them. Trust me, I learned a thing or two about myself this week." Then I noticed the look on her face. I could tell she thought I had tried to manipulate her. "I genuinely liked you. And you have the same 'nice act,' as you call it, need I remind you."

She glared back. "What are you talking about?"

"A few people warned me you could be vicious, but I didn't believe them. Then I caught a glimpse of it in your opinion of Jessica, and then with the cruel things you said to my mother."

"You never liked me, Savannah. You were looking for a story the entire time. I figured you out the first day I met you."

"Then you need to gear up on the discernment, sister. Because I not only liked you, I admired you. Your style. Your beauty. Your professionalism. My word, I even tried to dress like you."

"You did not." Surprise replaced her offense.

"Did too."

"You did?"

"Didn't work."

"Didn't?"

"Ended up under a car."

"What?"

"Long story," I assured her. "But you know what? I like you

now. I don't agree with you. I don't believe in your cause. And I sure don't like your technique. But I have to appreciate your passion. "

"You have a great deal of passion yourself, Miss Sugar Daddy Stealer." She laughed.

"I can't believe you got that out of me."

"I can't believe you shouted it in front of rolling television cameras."

"And snapping flashbulbs. Please don't forget the flashbulbs." We both laughed. "You know, it's funny. You resent in me the very things I resent in myself."

"What are you talking about?"

"Oh, the hypocrisy," I said, leaning back on the park bench. "The expectation that someone should be something that I have trouble being myself. Like the anger I felt when you talked about Jessica—I've called her worse in my head. The things you said to my mother's face that I've probably thought a thousand times. But I do try. I try hard to live the things I believe."

"I used to believe like you, Savannah. I used to have Sunday dinners with my family too, like you said in your article you have with your family. Back before Sunday ran like any other day of the week. We didn't work. We didn't fuss. We just were." She leaned back against the park bench herself, and you could see her mind drift back to those memories.

"Where were you raised?"

"The suburbs of Chicago."

"Cold?"

"Bitter. But home."

"You miss it?"

"I miss living. I'm tired of schmoozing and acting like I like people. And always being on call. And my cell phone always ringing."

"I think you already took care of that small matter."

She chuckled. "Yeah, I guess I did."

"I would think your life would be total excitement."

"Parts are. The travel. Many of the people. But some days I just want to live. Live for me."

"I read something one time."

"You do a lot of that, I notice."

"Can't help it. I'm addicted."

"Could have a worse one."

"I do. Coke."

"Savannah?! You?"

"Coca-cola."

"Oh, girl, you better be careful how you say that."

"I'd say you're right. But anyway, one of my favorite writers is a man named Frederick Buechner. Brutally honest novelist. Has scared his share of people in the evangelical world. But he's just real."

"I like real."

"Me too. He said in *Now and Then* in the last analysis all moments are key moments, and life itself is grace."

"You remembered that?"

"Couldn't help it. Changed me too much to forget it."

"You really believe it?"

"Have to. It's always been true."

"You mean every moment in your life has been a key moment?"

"Every one has led me to where I am now. Every moment of joy—like getting my job at the paper. Every moment of shame—like being exploited by that same paper," I said, trying to wipe the frustration from my face. "Every moment of pain—"

"You don't know pain, Savannah. Your life is too perfect."

"No life is perfect."

"My life was." She paused, eyes staring across the street at nothing. "Everything was perfect, until one day my perfect husband came home to tell me our perfect life was perfectly over."

"I'm so sorry, Faith."

"Oh, I don't care. He was a jerk who sat on the second pew of our local church and was remarried to the blonde choir member on the third row, fifth seat, in no less than three weeks, when she was three months pregnant. All that in a church."

"Could happen anywhere you find a human. Do you have any children?"

"Thank God, no." She turned her attention back to me.

"Be careful what you say. That stone monument might have influenced you more than you know." I smiled at her.

She chuckled. "Need to guard my figures of speech I guess."

"Not having a child sounds like a gift in a situation like that." She stared deep into me. "A key moment of grace." I studied her. "You know, we're not that different."

She turned and looked at me. "Yes, we are, Savannah. We're very different. You want a fairy-tale world to be a reality. I want a world that is progressive and moving forward, not trying to revert to stereotypes, slavery, and a takeover by a small fraction of society's extremists."

"Is that what you see?"

"From this side of the bench, that's what I see."

"That's funny. Because that's not what I see from *this* side of the bench. You know what I see?"

"I doubt that is a rhetorical question."

"I don't see fairy tales; I see a heritage. Ronald Reagan said Winston Churchill had the gift of vision, the willingness to see the future based on the experience of the past. I think if you throw away the past, Faith, you throw away the ability to rightly determine the future."

She considered this before standing up to leave. "Well, the court will make the final decision here, and they'll do it today."

"Maybe about the placement of a one-ton piece of stone, but not about the indelible imprint its engravings will leave on a heart."

She turned around. She had heard me. And I believe she knew they could strip every monument from here to Hawaii and not be able to erase the commandments from our hearts. "You're odd to me. You make me crazy, in fact. But you do have a sense of grace about you, Savannah. You really do."

Her words caused me to stop. More than being named Savannah, my name was Savannah Grace. I thought of Joy and smiled. "It's my name. I don't have a choice."

"What?"

"Savannah Grace Phillips. That's my name. So I don't have a choice."

"You need rest."

"My names declare me a woman with a calling for this city and hopefully the grace needed for the people here. Do you know what your name is?"

She refused to answer. I did it for her.

"When you were born, you were placed into your mother's arms and she looked at your face, and declared you to be Faith. The very thing you were destined to be is the very thing you have so much trouble with. The faith to believe in something."

"Oh, I believe in something, Savannah."

"Okay, then how about the faith to believe in *someone* again?"

She looked at me. And extended her hand. I responded in kind. This would stop here. I had made my point. She would make hers as well. Only time would tell whether she believed me, a woman who didn't share her views. I may never know for sure. But it didn't change what I saw in her.

"Do you respect me, Savannah?"

Odd coming from a woman whose mere presence seemed to demand it. "Does it matter?"

She paused. "Actually it does."

"I respect passion, Faith. I've just learned that passion and un-bridled anger aren't the same thing. My mother taught me that one. She is passionate. But not angry. That is one reason I can't help but admire her." I paused myself. "And learn from her, I must say. And trust me, I've learned much the hard way this week."

She stared into me. Not with a question. Not with a thought. Just with a stare. "It was a pleasure to meet you, Savannah Phillips."

"And you as well, Faith Austin." I took Duke's leash, but he still wouldn't look at either of us. I hadn't defended him. He was none too happy about it either. I looked up at her as she turned to go. "I hope you find what you're really looking for. And I think when you do, you're going to be shocked that it was really seeking you."

She didn't respond. She just walked down the sidewalk of Forsythe Park and out of sight.

CHAPTER THIRTY-NINE

It was buried in the back. Buried behind the red ruffled blouse and the canary yellow lace pants. I don't know when she bought it for me. Obviously, I had refused to wear it. But today I was surprised that I had hidden it. It was exactly what I would have bought myself. Wearing it could prove dangerous. Mother might think we should start shopping together. Worse yet, she might tell people she was dressing me. But if she could just keep it coming and keep her mouth closed about it, we might form a rather nice relationship.

I slipped it on. The neckline was curved, causing the straps to look as if they laid across my shoulders. The black fabric was complimentary of the rest of my wardrobe. And the dainty white polka dots that covered the entire dress gave it a feminine effect. But it was the pink flower that resided on the left side that down right took it over the edge. This dress was no where near the "tad" category. It took me to the land of down right daring. I looked almost as good as Miss Amber Topaz herself. The flowing skirt fell just below my knees.

"I can't go out in this. It will ruin me. Amber will want to buy a matching outfit." I turned in front of the mirror. I simply looked too good not to risk it. For a moment I wondered if Joshua would laugh. Then I decided I didn't care what he thought. I was free to wear those canary yellow pants *with* the red ruffled blouse if I wanted to, though if I wanted to, I would need to be committed. I was free to do anything, no matter what Joshua North thought. But he would think something. Of that I was sure.

The black, small-heeled flip-flops—or maybe you would call them thongs, who can be sure these days?—with the faux silver buckle at least gave me some semblance of familiarity. I gave myself one last gaze, running my hand over the front of my waist and down the sides of my skirt. Then I remembered. The president was coming. Who in the world would care what I was wearing?

"Nice dress." Mervine spoke.

"Did you know the president's coming today, Mervine?" The humming dishwasher caught my attention. "Duke, I do believe these people have been liberated."

It was the busiest time of the day at Dad's shop, people clamoring for their morning coffee. I filled up Duke's water bowl and checked to see if he had eaten the steak. He had. Only the bone remained. And that was being generous. Apparently he felt life had returned to normal. If normal is eating steak out of a dog trough at eight in the morning.

I reached for a Coke. A ritual of mine for the last 365 days of each of the past nineteen years of my life, and a few more if you count leap years. But today as I looked at the fountain, I wondered who controlled whom. Faith ate and drank anything she wanted simply because she wanted. Until this exact moment I had done the same. But for some reason, today, I felt I needed to make a statement to myself. To my own personal "demons," as Joshua tried to remind me. And as much as I loved that Coke in the morning and, granted, the afternoon, and as an end to a perfectly good day, well . . . if it controlled me, then I had to change.

No one wants such change. To stare a new revelation in the face and deny it is for some an everyday occurrence. But with what I now knew, especially what I had realized over this past week, that would not be possible for me. I took my shaking hand and got some ice. A magnetic force tried to pull me to the Coke. It was a war like few others my mind had ever waged. But it was one I would win. I wasn't giving up Coke. I was just letting it know who was boss. I drank water.

For the first morning in nineteen years, I drank water. Had anyone seen me, they would have had me committed. Had I not just lived through this entire week, I would have committed myself. The only thing I knew was that Savannah Phillips had learned something: any priority above the ultimate priority is out of priority. Well, Joy had said something to that effect. Maybe I would have her just write it all down.

Dad's eyes scanned me. "Nice dress, Savannah."

"Did you know the president's coming today?"

He laughed. "Yes I did, actually. So, did you have a nice evening?"

I tried to sit down at the counter. "A painful one."

"Painful how?"

"There are two kinds? Oh, yes, we are speaking of Vicky now, aren't we?"

"Savannah, it is *Mother* to you, not Vicky."

"Oh yes, I believe you're right. Actually, Mom was tolerable. It was the sidewalk that was painful." I took a long swallow of my water. It didn't burn, but it was appropriately pleasurable. "Ahhh. I see your dishwashers have retired."

"Thank the Lord. We got it in yesterday."

"You gave that poor man Ron a fright."

He motioned in the direction of the twins. "Honey, I paled in comparison to what he endured from those two creatures."

"I can only imagine."

"Hey, you! You're that girl from the park. The one that listened to my conversation and sat on my bench." A finger-pointing little twit headed toward the counter. I recognized him as the one who made the berating phone call in Forsythe Park.

"Excuse me?"

"Yeah, it is you. And then you wrote about me today in your little article."

He had me on that one. I just couldn't believe he remembered me. Or that he knew I was talking about him. Well, what do they say, admission is the first step to change. Or change is the first step to admission. Or something like that.

"Yeah, what was it you said about me exactly?" He questioned snidely. "Oh, well, why don't we read it word for word." He snatched up Section B from the table where he had been sitting before he rose to annoy me. "Let's see here: 'I listened to a man as he berated an apparent employee on the phone in the middle of Forsythe Park. For him, life was about money and making it. It was about winning or losing. It was about being the "top dog." But my friend Joy reminded me it isn't about either; it's about just being. Just being kind. Just being faithful. Just being a friend. Just being available. Available for Sunday dinner and baseball games. Available for graduations and recitals. How can any man be those things when the very premise, the very foundation of his living, has been focused on the wrong hero?'"

"I think that's pretty good, don't you, Dad?" Surely Jake could shore me up in these here murky waters.

"If it's what you heard, it sounds good to me."

"Good?! You call that good! It wasn't even accurate."

"I just call it how I see it."

"I was talking to my father, you idiot. He's the owner of the company, not my employee."

"Then I would say your tone isn't the only issue you need to be dealing with, mister."

"I could sue you."

"Wouldn't do any good," Dad assured him. "Last I heard, she's in the hole as it is."

"He's right. I don't have a penny to my name. And no one will know it's you," I said, attempting to console him. "Unless *man* is your middle name." I turned around on my stool and left him to snarl at the back of my head.

"Jake, you better get control of this . . . this . . . this little Sugar Daddy Stealer," the man spat at the back of my head.

"Now you're getting personal," I said to the man behind me while looking at my father in front of me. "And those who live in glass houses shouldn't throw stones."

"Savannah, that's enough." I could tell my dad was trying not to smile. "Todd, I'll handle Savannah; you just try to have a good day at work."

He left. But he made a whole lot of ruckus in the process.

"You are an incorrigible child."

"You liked my article, and you know it. Or you would have told me first thing."

"You did a good job, baby girl," Dad said, sitting down beside me and picking up the paper. He began to read aloud.

I'm not here to write about choosing a religion. I'm here to share my experience that one can begin a journey unsure of the destination. But when the fork in the road comes and one path or another must be taken, a choice will have to be made. I had to choose. Not to choose would prove apathetic, a trait no one today can afford to have. And I could not choose a path that abandoned the beliefs I hold dear.

But the path I did choose led me to a very valuable revelation: Should every monument be hauled away, what I believe is etched in me. And I learned it this week by walking with three different women. One made me smile, taught me with her ever-present wisdom, and ate my food. The other caused me to think, challenged me with her divergent belief, and shared her Snickers. The third has offered me her food and her wisdom for the last twenty-four years. And each week I learn to respect her more as the woman she is, and not just because she's my mother. Each woman came to her own fork in the road. Each woman chose the path that reflected the core belief of who she is.

In the end, only one path will prove right. I chose the voice of experience on this one. And I followed the one of my heritage. The heritage of my family, and at the end of the day, the very heritage of my nation.

Until next week.

Savannah from Savannah

Dad put the paper down and stood up from his stool. He walked over and gave me a peck on the top of my forehead. "Good job, baby girl."

"Thanks. I'm listening."

"Would help if you showed it more often," he said, right eyebrow raised.

I met his challenge and then posed the ever-looming question. "Have you seen me on the front page of the newspaper?"

"Yep."

"Well, two stories about me in one day. I just might become my mother after all. Lord help us all." And with that I left him. Him and his little thought for the day in chalk above his head. *He who guards his way, guards his life.*

CHAPTER FORTY

I felt every stair. Yet I continued to climb to my new home. Opening the door, reality swept over me once again: life as I knew it was gone. Well, that had actually begun last Friday, so technically I was being prepared in advance.

Everything was as we left it. Sparse. I walked into my new bedroom, which felt nothing like home except for the fact that everything I owned in this world was in it. But then, 90 percent of what I owned, I had not actually purchased. Sad.

The small tan box with the orange stripe and white lettering rested safely on my nightstand. I picked it up and let it turn gently in my fingers. I knew I would come across pictures. I would find letters. I would battle memories. But I had to start somewhere. And as much as I detested the remote possibility that Joshua *might* be a smidgen accurate, I knew he was.

I had loved Grant. As much as I was capable of loving anyone up to this point in my life, I had loved him. But it wasn't the kind of love that included a lifetime of commitment. Grant had known it years ago. I wouldn't admit it until I knew he was gone. I could fight on. But what for? Pride? Jealousy? Resentment? The mere fact I didn't want to lose to a long-legged maiden? And I did love Grant enough not to cause him any more pain, or at least any more wasted evenings.

I walked over to the small stainless-steel trash can that I had brought up, with permission I might add, from Dad's shop. I stepped on the small black lever that opened the lid. To my chagrin the dumb thing worked. The lid opened. I dropped my small lightbulb box, and with it any chance of marrying the man who I had just assumed would wait for me forever.

He was just what I knew. Now I wasn't sure I knew anything. Well, I did know one thing: Joshua North would never be allowed the satisfaction he hoped to find in this moment. He may make me tingle. But I would die a thousand Vicky-induced deaths before he would ever have the satisfaction of knowing it.

Today's agenda: Avoid Joshua. Don't read the newspaper. Pretend that front page didn't even exist.

I set my goals too high. Joshua was on the receiving end of the door as it slammed into him when I opened it. And the newspaper was spread across my desk.

"Wouldn't have hit you if you had gotten out of the doorway." I passed by him and his conversation partner from the sports room and went straight to my four portable walls.

Then I picked up the paper. At least I looked good. Arms stretched out, head tipped back, not quite as tired as the day before. Outfit was a bit wrinkled, but besides that my hair was lying nicely around my face. It was the caption, however, that allowed me a moment of satisfaction: "Columnist Savannah Phillips, Researching the Very Heart of the Matter." He did like me. I knew it.

I was about to sit down when I caught a familiar face in the bottom right-hand corner of the paper. Right under the copy that read, "confessed to stealing a Sugar Daddy as a youth." I would come back to that later. The picture was Joy. Joy was in the paper. I sat down to scan the article, but the headline gave me a wealth of information: "Atlanta Family Widens Search for Missing Mother and Grandmother." My little Joy was a runaway.

"Wonder why?" I asked myself. Wouldn't have even had to ask myself had I read the article first. Seems that Joy was suffering from long-term memory loss, the result of a head injury she had sustained during a car accident a couple months ago. Her family feared that she had wandered off and forgotten her way home.

I ran to Mr. Hicks's office without stopping to get permission from Jessica. She didn't like it. I didn't care.

"Mr. Hicks," I panted. I hadn't waited for the elevator, painful thighs or not. "I know this woman," I said, laying the paper down in front of him.

"What?" His head was spinning from the flurry of activity that had just entered his office. Because Jessica was on my heels in adamant protest of my arrival.

"I know her. This lady. Joy. She ate my catfish!"

"Would you calm down?"

"I can't! I have to find her. And call her family! That's why she wears the same dress every day." I was talking to myself, but he didn't catch on.

"Savannah, if you will calm down one moment and speak sanely, we might get somewhere."

"Okay. Okay. I *knoooow* this lady. She's been wandering the streets around here for a week."

"This missing grandmother?"

I started pacing, and Jessica left. It was best for us both. "Yes. We talk every day. She's like, well, like my friend."

"Is she the lady you talked about eating your food?"

"Yes!" I collapsed into his leather chair, because that was all the energy I had left. "Yes, she's the one."

"Well, why are you sitting down?"

"What? Just because I'm a confessed candy stealer, now I can't even sit down? And I do owe you one for that headline." I smiled.

He winked but continued with his protest of my sitting position. "No, Miss Paranoia, you need to get up and go find this lady."

I jumped up, wondering why the thought hadn't crossed my mind. "Oh, right! Good idea."

"Now, listen. I'll call the number here in the paper. You bring this lady back here to my office, and I'll try to get her family to come here and pick her up."

"Her name is Joy. She has a name."

"*Okay,* Savannah, you . . . go . . . *find* . . . *Joy.*"

I put my hand on my hip and raised my right eyebrow at his drawn-out mockery. "I'm not a third grader."

"Would you listen? For one minute, just listen. Go find Joy. Bring her back here and quit making everything a discussion."

"Right. I'll get her. I'll bring her back. She'll have her family, and you can put a new picture of me on the front of your paper. 'Candy Stealer Redeems Self. Finds Missing Grandmother.'"

"Would you please go?"

I drove around like a crazy person. And when that was no longer possible because of the ridiculous number of roadblocks and police pandemonium due to the presidential visit, I simply got out and ran. Not easy in a sundress and wedged Stuart Weitzmans. I couldn't find her anywhere. She wasn't in the square across from the courthouse. She wasn't near Katherine's Corner Bookstore. She hadn't taken up outside of Savannah's Candy Kitchen. So, I headed back to our first encounter, Forsythe Park. There, lying on the bench amid "her" flowers, was one Joy Odom.

I knelt down by her bench. She was killing it. I hadn't heard snoring like that except from Duke. I wanted to see her as a helpless child, lost and alone. But with sounds coming out of a person that could raise the dead, well, let's just say I had to wake her up before she scared *me.*

"Hey, sunshine. Wake up." I tapped her arm. She startled with a snort and a jerk. "Whoa, missy. It's just me, Savannah."

"Savannah, my Lord, baby, you about scared the daylights out of an old woman."

She made me smile. Even when she lusted after my food, she made me smile. I just liked her. Everything about her. Even her old ugly floral dress.

"Ow," she said, rubbing her back. "That's a small bench for a big woman like me."

She moved over to the right side, and I was able to sit down. "Have you been sleeping out here every night?"

"No, a lot of nights I sleep out by the monument. But I was out here last night praying in this beautiful garden, and just got too tired to walk back." I realized at that point there was no telling how far Joy had walked this past week. Savannah may be built on twenty-two squares, but it is 2.2 square miles of squares, and nothing is as close as it seems. The poor thing should be skin and bones by now. Although, with all the dinners she'd been having, she was liable to have gained weight.

"Who do you sleep with out at the monument?"

"Some nice man with a golden retriever always has an extra sleeping bag. He lets me use it when I'm there. Gives me free coffee too. I really like him. He's pretty nice-looking too."

Ooh, this was odd. And after the kissing episode the other day, I was already dealing with undue trauma. I changed the subject. "How would you like to come hang out where I work today?"

Her face lit up. "At the paper?"

"Yeah. See what we do. How the paper is printed. Meet my boss. All those kind of neat things. Maybe even have lunch together, and maybe even buy a new dress. What do you think?"

"I think that is a glorious idea, baby." I helped her up off of the bench and took her arm to walk her to the car. "What are we having for lunch today, Savannah? Got some catfish?" Her eyes were like a two-year-old's.

I giggled at her innocence. "How 'bout we go get you a cup of coffee and a muffin at Jake's, and then I'll take you to Lady & Sons for some catfish or fried chicken for lunch."

"It's going to be a glorious day, Savannah. I feel it in my very bones. Just a glorious day." She had no idea.

Richard opened the door for us. "Ms. Joy, what are you up to today?"

"Oh, nothing, Richard. Just spending some time with this sweet girl."

"Who? Savannah?" he chided with a wink.

"Yes, this baby is taking me on a tour today," she said with genuine appreciation.

Dad walked from behind the counter and gave us both a peck on the cheek. "Just like you like it, Joy," he said, handing her a cup of coffee.

"This is a fine man," she said, poking me with her elbow. That was a rather disturbing glint in her eye.

"Joy, please, this is my father. I don't want to talk about him being fine, handsome, or kissable. I just want to think about him being a father."

"This is your father?"

Dad smirked.

"Yes, and he's not fine. No offense, Dad."

"None taken."

"He's just a dad. My dad. Who doesn't need women swooning over him all day."

"Well, my Lord have mercy. I should have known you come from such quality."

"Thank you, Joy." He gave her another peck. "And thank you for appreciating me too," he said, giving her a wink. He was becoming downright shameless.

The door opened, and Granny Daniels entered. "Savannah, what are you doing here this morning?"

"Just brought my friend in here for some of Jake's coffee."

The two women looked at each other. Granny Daniels's face lit up. "Joy! I missed you last night." And with that the two friends linked arms and walked to a corner table. Mervine and Louise took them a breakfast of muffins and coffee. Dad sat down beside me at the bar.

"They've both been sleeping out on the square?" I asked.

"Every night."

"That's amazing."

"Yes ma'am, it is."

"Did you get in touch with her family?" Dad asked quietly.

"How did you—" I whispered, getting successfully cut off by the rattling of the paper on the counter.

"I read the paper too, Savannah."

"Oh yeah, right. Yeah, Mr. Hicks is calling them. They should be here quickly. But she has no idea."

"Well, go show her a wonderful morning."

"I will."

"You like your new place?"

I couldn't help but smile. "Yeah, needs furniture. But it's going to be great. You can come see it after work."

"I'd like that."

"Me too." Even though we'd never let the other know, we already knew he had.

CHAPTER FORTY-ONE

I treated Joy like a princess. She toured every spot of that facility. Met Joshua. Liked him immensely. (She had been hit on the head, remember.) Didn't think Jessica had very good manners for a Southern young woman. (So maybe she wasn't hit real hard.) Loved to watch the printing press. Got her a snack in the break room. The woman couldn't pass up food if she was muzzled. She and Paige would have been soulmates.

We stole away to Jezebel's and got her a great yellow linen ensemble. Then I stole her away to my parents' house for thirty minutes to let her shower and to make her beautiful. If the newspaper thing failed, I definitely had a fallback career: personal stylist to street people. She was still beautiful but greasy by the time we finished lunch at Lady & Sons. But Miss Paula Dean made over her like she was royalty. Joy told her she had some recipes she would send, but she couldn't quite remember where they were right now. Miss Paula told her to mail them when she got the time.

By our return to the paper at noon, a page came over the

loudspeaker, asking me to come to Mr. Hicks's office. I knew what this meant. Joy was going home. I left her at my desk for a minute so I could make sure everything was okay upstairs. It was. And when I returned to fetch her, she had neatly folded up Section B with my article on top and laid it on my desk.

I touched her arm, and she looked up at me with a smile. "I'm proud of you, baby girl. Real proud."

I tried to fight the burning in my nose and the swell of tears in my eyes. "Come on, Joy. Let me take you to see my boss's office. He has the best view in the place."

"Oh, I'd like that, Savannah." She hooked her black arm around mine, giving them an Oreo effect. "I sure have enjoyed this day."

I smiled at her sincere black eyes. "Me too, me too." I put her black hand in mine and appreciated the nice way we had cleaned up her short nails. Her hair looked good too, for the rush job we did.

"Think we can do this again?"

I knew that after today I might never see my new friend again. "Sure, I would love that." And I meant every word.

I could hear voices coming from Mr. Hicks's office. And as soon as we rounded the corner, a fortyish man ran out of the room and down the hall. "Mama! Oh, Mama! We've looked and looked for you. Thank God you're safe."

When he reached her, he wrapped her in a death grip. And his arms made it all the way around her. I could see her eyes as her head rested on his broad shoulder. They were searching and almost frightened. For a moment I wanted to reach out and protect her; she thought he was a stranger. But this was his mama. He had lost her, and now he had found her. And he wasn't letting her go.

Finally she pushed him away and stared blankly into his matching dark eyes. He looked at her with such an ache. I couldn't imagine the pain of not being recognized by the one who took you to preschool and taught you to tie your shoes (or in my case, buckle your pumps). But then there was a flicker beneath the bewilderment. And her sweet and smooth hand went up to his face and touched it. "Baby boy," she said. "My baby boy."

And with that he fell back into her arms and began to cry. And she patted his head, just like a mama would. And he wept.

"Hush, baby. Mama's okay. Mama's just fine," she assured him as she stroked his head. By then her other children had surrounded us, and I stepped back to let them have this moment to themselves. I did notice there was no Mr. Joy. Just children. But no matter why Mr. Joy didn't exist, she still lived her name. Even *that* untold story refused to deter her from being Joy. Her children gushed over her and patted her and loved her and scolded her, and she just loved the whole thing. She laughed and talked and patted and told them stories. Oh, the stories she had to tell.

As they made their way to the elevator, I wiped my tears on the back of my hand. They thanked me and Mr. Hicks, even Jessica, because she had witnessed the whole thing. I didn't even care. Who would care about that at this point? I might care about it later, but right now it was all okay.

I listened to Joy's familiar swooshing sound and wished I had one more plate of catfish that we could share. I watched as the yellow ensemble made its way up the hall and planned to burn her old one with Mother's blue number upon my arrival home. I saw Joy reach her hand over to her oldest son and stop him. She turned around and looked at me.

She held out her arms. And I gladly accepted. I walked over to her and buried my head in her ample bosom, one I was certain had held many the head of a child through the years. My head fit perfectly. I tried to stifle my tears but couldn't. Again, I didn't care. I leaned up and whispered in her ear. "I'm going to miss you, Ms. Joy."

She whispered back. "I'm going to miss you too, Miss Savannah." She pulled me back and looked me square in the eye. Her eyes pierced me one last time. At least I hoped for a while. The woman had about worn me out.

"You see that man over there?" she asked me, pointing at Mr. Hicks.

"Yes, ma'am."

"His name's Samuel. I saw his placard on his door. Do you know what that means?"

"I have no idea."

"It means 'man who heard from God.' And men who hear, Savannah, teach. If they are any men at all," she said, peering up to give him a clear message.

He winked at her in response. She replied in kind. She looked back at me. "You're going to see a lot and do a lot, baby girl. You're going to touch people and tell people's stories and share more dinners with strangers." She was tickled with herself, and her belly bounced. "But you learned something this week. You're learning how to *be*. 'Cause you've *been* something to me."

I wanted to be stoic. I bit my lip in a vain attempt. But the tears fell freely. "And you've *been* to me, Ms. Joy. I've seen and heard every word. I'll never forget you."

"I wouldn't want you to. 'Cause we're going to do this again, remember?"

That made me laugh. She was telling me to remember. "I remember."

"And you chose the right road, baby," she said with a knowing smile. "You're right, every treasure you need for *being* is etched right here." She tapped her finger on my heart. "And no one can ever steal what is in your heart." She kissed me on my cheek and gave me one final penetrating look.

I stared into her beautiful dark eyes, which revealed her very soul. "You're an angel, aren't you?"

"No, baby girl. I'm a mother." She took the hand of her oldest son and turned to leave. She left humming.

That familiar tune rolled around in my head. Finally it hit me. "I know it!" I hollered loud enough to frighten us all. "I know what you're humming!"

"Took you long enough." She turned around with a sly smile.

"'Rock of Ages.' That's it, isn't it? It's 'Rock of Ages.'"

"You got it, baby girl. 'Rock of Ages.' And that won't change, no matter what happens up the street."

CHAPTER FORTY-TWO

Jessica was trying to hide a tear. Imagine that. My word, the child was actually human. I was beginning to think she was a short-circuited Stepford wife. "Gotcha, didn't it?" I said to her.

She flitted herself around to stare at her filing cabinet. "I don't know what you're talking about."

"Yes, you do, Jessica. See, you're not so mean after all."

She spun around. "I've never been mean."

"You don't call putting pictures of me in the paper in embarrassing and misunderstood situations mean?"

"I don't make the decision of what gets in the paper around here, Savannah. He does." She pointed to Mr. Hicks, who was still trying to recover from Joy's departure. She was right, of course. At the end of the day, Mr. Hicks made the decisions. I looked at him. He looked back. Joy had gotten him. I could tell. The grown man's eyes were sweating.

"Savannah, she's right. The buck stops with me. And about your picture. Well, I'll try to make sure that in the future your picture appears only above your article."

He nodded at me with a smile. Jessica wore no expression at all.

"One more thing, Savannah. Tell Joshua North I'll be talking with him shortly."

Joshua was at my desk when I went to grab my purse. He had, once again, invaded my personal space and was looking at the picture of me and Paige from a trip we took a year ago to Greece for part of the Olympic games.

"Did you knock?" I picked up my bag.

He set the picture back down and turned to face me. "Very funny."

He stopped and stared at me. The look in his eyes made me uncomfortable. "What?"

"You look . . . well, you look rather nice today." I knew he'd notice. He thought he had me pegged. I could tell.

"I've got to go," I said, heading back out.

He grabbed my elbow. "You can't ignore me forever," he said, trying to hide his smile.

"No, but I can ignore you for today. And I can deal with you tomorrow." I removed my elbow from his grip before offering him my hand upside his head as well.

He brushed past me on his way back to his own cubbyhole to answer his ringing phone. Mr. Hicks. "I'm not going anywhere."

"Well, I am."

"You're a mess." He laughed.

"I am not. I look much better today than the other day," I said, passing my hands over my skirt.

"I didn't mean the way you look; I mean you. But you're fig-uring it out. I can tell." Well, wasn't he just some master of life.

"Oh, well, I'm so glad you approve. Because at the end of the day, my greatest desire is for your approval." I tried to be as snide as possible. I exited with no further parting words. I didn't care to ever see him again. Not again today anyway.

"Ooh!" I let out my frustration as I straightened my cushion to sit down in Old Betsy. She let out a similar sound, and we were on our way.

Most every street from the newspaper to the court-house was blocked. It didn't matter. I would walk. It was hard to park nearby on a typical day anyway. The sidewalks were packed because the streets had been cordoned off with rope and police officers, so the presidential motorcade could drive directly up to the courthouse.

"Betty?!"

I turned to see Judge Hoddicks walking up the sidewalk with some men who were sweating underneath their black suits and death-grip neckties. He had called me Betty since I petitioned to change my name to Betty in the eighth grade. From that day forward, the name Savannah had never even crossed his lips.

"Judge! I haven't gotten to see you all week. Tied up, huh?"

He chuckled, wiping his sixty-five-year-old white eyebrows with his handkerchief and wrapping the other free hand around me as we walked. "I would say your mother has paid the tied-up price for me."

"You got me there."

"Are you heading over there to see her?"

"Yes, sir. Want to make sure she looks okay. You know, with the president coming and everything."

"She's proud of you, Betty."

"I know. And I'm proud of her."

"You should be. She's shown us what she's made of this week."

I looked at his tired eyes. Wonder what Joy would have said about him. "Looks like you have too."

"It's been worth it. We might not win here, but the message sent by the people who have flocked to this square is proof of what they're willing to fight for."

"You did good." I put my arm through his and rested my head on it as we walked.

"It's not hard when you love what you do."

The path cleared before us as Judge Hoddicks made his way to the courthouse. There were some pats, some cheers, and a few rather snippy remarks. Sergeant Millings raised his nightstick at the protestors, as if he would know what to do with it. I paused across the street from my mother while the judge went on inside the courthouse. Vicky was standing, talking animatedly with some women who were gathered around her. She looked beautiful, stunningly beautiful, considering the sweltering humidity of this first day of June. Of course, she was underneath her umbrella and holding a tiny motorized fan to her face, but in spite of that, she looked fabulous.

I didn't want to bother her. I just wanted to enjoy her. She loved these people. She loved this city. Her love showed in every gesture and every hug and every question about someone else's children. True, she wanted to control it, but at the core, she just wanted to see it succeed.

A lady on the roped-off sidewalk caught everyone's attention. "Watch it. Watch it. The president. That's his car. Look, look, the president's motorcade!"

All the action on the sidewalks and around the courthouse ceased. And in that moment in time, it seemed as if the entire light of the sun shone on one Victoria Phillips and the monument she protected. Everybody backed away from her, and she stood in front of the monument, waiting to meet the president. She looked regal. Almost queenlike. Handcuffed, perhaps, but queens had passed that way before as well.

I heard the sound before I realized what was happening. The roar of an engine. The squealing of brakes. I turned quickly from my position across the street from my mother. In one lightening-flash moment, the third car in the motorcade broke loose and headed directly for my mother and the monument.

The air was sucked out of the square. All I saw were the whites of Vicky's eyes, larger than life. They were like a Shih Tzu's with its ponytail too tight. In an instant, the car broke through the iron hitching posts and crashed into the monument. The sound of crunching metal, crumbling concrete, and piercing screams could be heard on Bay Street. Then silence. For an eternity no one moved. All that was heard was the hissing of the radiator of the engine and the clanging metal as the rest of the bumper detached itself and landed on the sidewalk.

"*Mother!*" I screamed as I ran across the square. Bile rose in my throat at the thought of what I would see. Before I knew it, two men who looked for all the world like morticians, grabbed me and pulled me away. The back door of the limousine flew open, and out climbed two secret-service men, followed by the president of the United States.

The president's car had killed my mother! The president scrambled out and ran toward the monument. The secret service men were in front of him and behind him. I broke free from the two men holding me and ran in terror to find my mother. As I rounded the side of the car, I noticed movement underneath some of the granite. My father rose from the mess, and underneath him lay my mother, virtually lifeless until she heard the president's voice. Then those Mary Kay mascara eyelashes batted open. The secret service men pulled my father up. He had a noticeable cut across his elbow and a small cut on his cheek. Other than that, he was mostly dusty.

The president then reached down to help up my mother. She wasn't quite the picture of perfection that she had been moments ago. Her hair was sitting predominately on the right side of her head, now a white ashen color. Her face was practically albino, and her pretty pink suit . . . well, let's just say it wasn't so pretty. She had a slight cut above her right eyebrow. She'd milk that one for a month. One heel was broken. She'd milk that for two. And her stockings were ripped to shreds, proving once again the ridiculous notion of wearing clean underwear during a wreck. Who's to say how the mess happens.

She tried to brush herself off. Make herself presentable for the leader of the free world. A vain attempt at uselessness.

And there in rubble, surrounding the woman that had protected it, lay the crumbled monument of the Ten Commandments. For the past week people had prayed by it, sung by it, slept by it, and fought over it. And today it was nothing more than a mass of chunks of marble and piles of dust. No court would decide its fate now. That had been decided by a crazed limousine driver.

Then I remembered Joy's tap on my heart. It was still intact in there, no matter what had happened to it out here. We would fight for the monument again. But no matter the outcome next time, it hadn't been shattered inside me.

CHAPTER FORTY-THREE

Are you all right, ma'am?" the Texas drawl of our forty-third president filled the air.

"Oh, yes, yes, I'm fine." Had she seen herself, she would have known better. Had she seen herself, she would have stayed under the rubble. Feigned death and sent a better picture of herself later. "I'm simply fine, Bushi . . . I mean, Mr. President." Poor soul was still dazed.

I made my way to Dad, who was being attended by a doctor. I would give her and her hero a moment alone. After her week, she deserved this. After her sacrifice, even the Lord had given her a treat.

"Are you okay?" I asked my father, throwing my arms around his neck.

"Yes, honey, I'm okay."

"Oh, thank goodness. How did you get to Mother so fast?"

He removed the ice pack from his lip. "I don't know. I just knew the car was coming and I had to get her out of the way. I grabbed the other side of that chain and just lifted it off of the monument and pulled her away."

"You saved her life, Dad."

"That's okay. She saved mine years ago." He looked at her with a love shared by people who knew what loving meant. We watched her gush over the president while a doctor attended her. The president and she talked and laughed. I couldn't help but notice the extreme sparkle behind the eyes in her dusty face.

"Is that lust?" I asked my father.

He laughed. "No, that's admiration."

"You sure?"

"After what I just did, it better be."

The doctors patched them up. The president gave a warm handshake to my father. "You're a fine man, Mr. Phillips, with a brave and honorable wife."

My father stood and returned his firm grip. "Thank you, Mr. President. I think so as well." Dad smiled at my mother, who seemed to notice him for the first time.

"I really wasn't trying to kill her." He laughed a nervous Texas laugh.

Dad laughed too, easing the tension. "It isn't anything I'm sure many people haven't thought about doing themselves a time or two." That caused both of them to laugh.

Mother didn't laugh a bit. "Jake Phillips!" she scolded.

"I just read a book about Ronald Reagan," I offered. They all stared at me. I was odd. Undeniably odd.

The president extended an invitation to the White House. One I'm sure he would keep after today. One I'm sure none of us would ever live through. With that the Texas gentleman gave a Southern kiss on the chalky cheek of my mother. "Thank you, Mrs. Phillips. What you did here will be remembered by some forever."

"Ooh, well it was the least I could do, Mr. President." She placed her hand against her chest. It was the most Southern of gestures, the lowered batting eyes, the dainty hand-to-chest scenario. Picture perfect. Perfectly Vicky.

Fortunately for the president, he had more than one car. He stopped as he passed me. "Nice dress, young lady." He was a charming man.

"Why, thank you, Mr. President. Thank you very much." With that he left, followed by the rest of his motorcade. Time would reveal the driver of his car had suffered a heart attack, so it really wasn't the "left-wing conspiracy" mother originally declared it to be.

When Thomas met me and Dad, we found Mother, who had slipped away, sitting atop a piece of stone that read, "Shalt Not Steal." She wanted to take it with her as a memento, but she couldn't carry it. She cried quite a few tears of desolation over those ruins.

We waited for her to speak first. "I can't believe it would end this way."

"It's not ever really over," Dad assured her as he gently wiped concrete dust from her face.

"You're right. We'll just go get us another one and start this whole thing over." Her voice grew louder with each word.

Dad took her hand and led her in the direction of home. "How about we just go rest for a little while first?"

Thomas and I sighed.

She let out a relieved sigh herself. "That would be nice."

We gathered Vicky and what was left of her belongings. Most were gathered as evidence. Or offered. She just wanted them to be *sure* it wasn't a left-wing conspiracy, so they took off with her sleeping bags and Thomas's tent. I was certain they would end up in some trash bin between here and the airport.

As we started our walk toward home, or our wobble, depending upon whom you were watching, others began to pack up their memories of the week as well. The cameras were packed away, and the trucks lowered their lights. Sleeping bags were rolled up, and coolers were hauled off. Hugs were given. Tears were shed. High-fives offered. But as we walked in the direction of home, the city of Savannah headed back in the direction of, well, Savannah. Still a little odd, no doubt. But our familiar kind of odd.

The first block, nobody said much. I broke the silence with my good news. "I moved out!" I declared. No better time than the present.

"You what?!" Vicky screeched. "Jake, you let our baby move out?"

"She was going now or in two weeks, Victoria. Why delay the inevitable?"

"It's an amazing place," Thomas offered.

"Really?" She was having trouble believing it. "Do you have furniture?"

"A bedroom suite."

"That's all?"

"Yes ma'am."

"What will you eat on?"

"I'll get a table eventually."

"Where will you sit and watch TV?"

"On my bed for now, I guess."

"Jake, my baby doesn't even have a sofa." She was truly horrified.

"Victoria, that's what happens when you move out on your own. You have to work your way up to those things."

"Darling, don't you worry. Your mama will take you shopping this weekend, and we'll get you set. If you are going to move out, then we're just going to make your new place beautiful." She hobbled along, broken heel in hand and a new mission in mind.

I wasn't sure that was best. It might result in free stuff, but it still required shopping. With my mother. Maybe she could just go by herself and surprise me.

"Maybe you should just get me a key," she said. "Then I could just come and do it whenever I was free." On the other hand, maybe one day of shopping would be better than a lifetime of drop-ins. "And your dress is fabulous, Savannah. Ooh, we could go get you some clothes this weekend." She had said *we*. Someone needed to rescue me.

"Anyone know what time it is?" Thomas asked, giving me a wink.

I looked at my watch. "Five o'clock. Well, Mother, I do believe you have just been saved from serving time."

She looked at us and rubbed her behind. "I did my time, I assure you." That made us all laugh. "But I would have stayed as long as necessary."

As well as I thought I had known my mother last week, I now knew her differently. I now believed that she meant what she had just said. I wrapped my arm around her. She would have reciprocated but her arms were a little tired. She just laid her ratty head on my shoulder. Truth be known, the whole thing had made me tired, as tired as Joy assured me I looked. And this after only three weeks back home. Two weeks at my new job. One day in an apartment I had yet to sleep in. I knew what I needed. I needed a vacation. Surely nothing could happen on vacation.

Reading Group Guide Available
at www.westbowpress.com

What could possibly
go wrong on vacation?

SAVANNAH BY THE SEA

Available in bookstores
everywhere

June 2006

WestBow
PRESS
A Division of Thomas Nelson Publishers
Since 1798

Discover More Great Novels at WestBowPress.com

A NOVEL

DENISE HILDRETH

I'm coming home to prove something . . . to my city, my mother, and myself.

It is a place known to most as Savannah. It is a place known to me as home. I wish I could tell you it was my love for this city that precipitated my return. But I did not return out of a mere longing for home. I returned because I have something to prove to home. I am Savannah . . . from Savannah.

WESTBOW
PRESS
A Division of Thomas Nelson Publishers
Since 1798

Discover More Great Novels at WestBowPress.com

CHAPTER ONE

Savannah is my name. It's also my world, my home. I didn't cherish it until I left. And when I returned, it was because I had something to prove.

My mother, Victoria, was born and reared in Savannah. My name is explained by her love for this city—that and my belief that she had a craving to spend the rest of her life announcing her daughter to every living creature as "Savannah from Savannah." For a time I thought she was just being cute. Then I realized that this was really how she intended to introduce me for the rest of my natural existence.

"Savannah," she said when I confronted her, "one day you will thank me. When you are famous and the whole world knows you as 'Savannah from Savannah,' children will envy you and long to be named after you. And me, well, I will be your mother."

By the age of thirteen, having no desire to be any child's envy, I went around my eighth-grade class and had all my friends sign a petition requesting my name be legally changed. Afterward, I walked straight up to the courthouse and into the office of Judge Hoddicks, one of my father's best friends. I withdrew my two sheets of moderately legible names from the pages of *The Hobbit,* where I'd stashed them for safety, spread them on Judge Hoddicks's desk, and informed him I would like to change my name to Betty.

"Why Betty?"

"Because my mom doesn't like any name that ends in a *y.* Just try calling her Vicky and see what happens to that southern charm of hers. It will fade like a vapor."

He directed me to a chair in his stunning office, with its rich mahogany bookcases and coffered ceiling. I passed the time reading my well-worn copy of Tolkien's classic until the glass-paned door opened and my mother made her entrance. I thought maybe he wanted to witness the meltdown of a southern woman in high heels and Mary Kay. But her arrival proved it was all about her ability to command any room as well as this city's inhabitants.

She looked fabulous—perturbed, but fabulous. Vicky always looks fabulous. She has never appeared in public in anything lower than a two-inch heel. She doesn't own a pair of jeans, and she wouldn't be caught dead with curlers in her hair, without makeup on her face, or without being fully accessorized by seven a.m.

Ten minutes later, as we left the office, I vowed that even if I called her Victoria to the world, she would always be Vicky in my mind. I took one last look back and asked Judge Hoddicks to give me a call if there was anything he could do. He assured me he would.

Today, eleven years later, my legal name is still Savannah Grace Phillips. To Judge Hoddicks, however, I will forever be Betty.

I have spent a considerable amount of my life trying to convince people that Vicky isn't my real mother. I mean how could I come from a woman I don't understand, a woman no one understands? Anyone with half a pea-pickin' ounce of perception can tell that Vicky and I are nothing alike. We don't talk alike, act alike, or do anything else alike.

And you wouldn't know I was hers by my looks, either. I have two inches on her five-foot-four frame. And I don't think our hair is the same color, although no one really knows what her original hair color was. My hair has always been golden brown and straight as a stick. Vicky has been blond, frosted, and redheaded. The best color of all was when she wanted to be platinum blonde, and woke up the morning of the annual Savannah Chamber of Commerce Ball with the majority of her hair lying broken off on her pillow. But we don't talk about that much.

The only remote proof that Vicky could actually be my mother is that I do, on rare, necessary occasions, feel the need to freely express myself in, shall we say, clear tones. My father, Jake Phillips, has the amazing ability to sit back and breathe before responding. I, however, like Vicky, tend to speak before thought has had a chance to register. This is a most exhilarating, dangerous trait that we share. Vicky has managed to envelop hers in charm. I have only managed to envelop mine in something begging to be refined.

I have tried to channel this intense need to freely express myself into the written word. Every Big Star notebook I've saved from school contains either words to songs, short stories, or entire movie scripts. In high school, I ran for student-body president just so I could write a speech. The speech was so good I didn't even have to campaign to win. I appealed to the students' deepest cravings: food, exemption from finals, and football. Tie those three things together and then close with a poem called "The Man Who Thinks He Can," and, well . . . my fellow students were mush. The poor girl who lost had her own campaign manager and spent so much money on pencils and posters that I almost felt bad for beating her.

That moment allowed me to catch a glimpse of how words can impact the human spirit. A few months later, a short story about an eighty-year-old named Lula who wore purple hats and sang show tunes at area nursing homes, à la a Victoria biography, secured me a scholarship to the School of Journalism at the

University of Georgia. College taught me how to craft my gift, a gift that would propel me into the highbrow world of publishing. I envisioned my books in the window of Barnes & Noble and day-dreamed of people rushing in to catch the latest novel by Savannah Phillips—or "Savannah from Savannah," as people back home would forever require me to be identified. And that probably would have been my life, had it not been for some intervening cir-cumstances and a newspaper.

For four years of college and two years of graduate school, Vicky sent me a subscription to our local paper, the *Savannah Chronicle*. She never acknowledged it, but when there is a half-page ad on page 3 that reads "To our Savannah from Savannah, wishing you all the best in your new passage, Love, Mom and Dad," you just kind of know. My first week of college, feeling somewhat liberated yet homesick, I picked up my mail and headed to a McDonald's right off-campus to grab a Coke. Then I would take my Coke over to a small café across from my apartment and get a chef's salad with Thousand Island and blue-cheese dressing on the side. There, along with caffeine and fat grams, I consumed every article and ad in the paper.

For years, I considered Savannah a town of the near-dead and dying, a place frequented by people who'd come to pick out retire-ment facilities. I had never realized that it was so vibrant, alive. The main reason for this newfound impression appeared every Wednesday and Friday at the bottom of the front page of section B. Beside her column in the local section was a picture of a distinguished-looking lady with frosted hair, probably in her mid-fifties. Gloria Richardson. Her smile looked genuine, and her human-interest stories made me believe that unexpected kindness and prevailing strength just might exist in Savannah after all. So twice a week for six years, I spent lunchtime rediscovering the place I thought I knew and had longed to leave.

One Wednesday in the last weeks of the final semester of my master's work, I picked up my mail and my *Chronicle* and headed to McDonald's, and then the café. With Coke and salad at the ready, I flipped through the envelopes first and paused at a return address labeled "Fiction Achievement Award." I couldn't believe the results were already in.

Over the past six years, I had dedicated myself to consuming other writers' work and sharpening my own. For my thesis, I turned in a 450-page novel about four female college dropouts who left home to discover the world. It was a delightful tale of searching and survival, crafted over an agonizing two years. My dean entered the novel in a fiction contest for unpublished writers. A portion of the winning story would be published in a leading literary magazine, and leading fiction houses would consider the manuscript for publication.

Surely I held in my hands a rejection letter, sent out first to the really bad entries. Not only was I not picked to win, but my book was so bad they wanted me to know two weeks early how truly pathetic I am!

I sat up straighter in my booth and tore the letter open. "Let the guillotine fall quickly," I said.

Dear Ms. Phillips,

After careful consideration, we are pleased to inform you that your novel, *Road to Anywhere*, has been selected for the Fiction Achievement Award. An excerpt from your novel will appear in a future edition of the *National Literary Review*. We look forward to meeting you in person on May 15 with Taylor House Publishing in New York. All pertinent information has been sent to Dean Hillwood at the University of Georgia. The awards ceremony will be held on May 16 at the Waldorf Astoria. We have reserved a table for you and nine of your guests.

Congratulations. We are pleased to help you pursue
your dreams of becoming a successful author.

Sincerely,
Jeff Peterson
Chairman, Awards Committee

"Oh my stars! Oh my stars!" I said, throwing the letter into the
air and jumping out of my booth. I caught my Coke before it traveled south and smiled at a surprised couple at the closest table. This
was a moment to savor. I had finally achieved what I'd spent years
working for.

I have no idea who I passed or who passed me on the dance
back to my apartment. I'm not even sure what route I took, but I
made it back, walked upstairs to my room, and sat down on the
edge of my bed. I opened the letter and read the words again and
again. I walked over to the phone and laid the envelope and letter
down on the desk. For the first time, the addressee information on
the envelope registered with me. Though the letter itself was
addressed to me, the envelope read, "Victoria Phillips."

At first I laughed, thinking how funny that they had mistak-
enly used my mother's name instead of mine. Then reality surfaced.
There was no way in the world they would know my mother's
name unless they knew my mother. A weight drove me into my
chair. I couldn't move. I couldn't breathe.

What had she done? Why in the world would she get involved?
I had worked so hard, trying to make this novel good enough to
win on its own merits. Two hours passed, as did two classes. Around
three that afternoon my eyes turned from the window to the
phone. I picked it up and dialed.

A thick New York accent greeted me. "Taylor House Publishing."

"Jeff Peterson, please."

"May I tell him who's calling?"

"Yes, yes you can. Would you tell him it is Victoria Phillips from Savannah, Georgia," I spread the southern belle accent so thick the receptionist would be talking about it for the rest of the day.

"One moment, Ms. Phillips," and with the press of a button, I was dumped into the land of Muzak.

"Well, Mrs. Phillips. So, good to hear from you," said a lackey's voice. Disgusting. "So your daughter has received the results of the contest. I trust she's happy."

After all the years of mimicking Vicky, I could have auditioned for *Saturday Night Live*. "Oh, she is, Jeff, she is. She got the letter today, as a matter of fact, and she was thrilled."

"It turned out to be a really fabulous piece of work." Was that a smirk in his voice?

"Well, I just wanted to thank you again for your help and discretion in this matter."

"Don't mention it. I look forward to meeting you and your daughter next month."

"Oh, you don't know how much I look forward to meeting you. Good-bye."

"Good-bye, Mrs. Phillips."

And with that, my dream ended and my mission began.